Hens Reunited

Lucy Diamond lives in Bath with her husband and their three children. *Hens Reunited* is her third novel.

Hens Reunited

Lucy

DIAMOND

PAN BOOKS

First published 2009 by Pan Books
an imprint of Pan Macmillan Ltd
Pan Macmillan, 20 New Wharf Road, London N1 9RR
Basingstoke and Oxford
Associated companies throughout the world
www.panmacmillan.com

ISBN 978-0-330-46447-5

1 3 5 7 9 8 6 4 2

A CIP catalogue record for this book is available from
the British Library.

Typeset by Set Systems Ltd, Saffron Walden, Essex
Printed and bound in the UK by CPI Mackays, Chatham ME5 8TD

Visit www.panmacmillan.com to read more about all our books
and to buy them. You will also find features, author interviews and
news of any author events, and you can sign up for e-newsletters
so that you're always first to hear about our new releases.

For all my hens: Ellie, Hayley, Jo, Jude, Marns and Rachel, as well as Fiona, Kate, Fran, Saba and Nicky. Cheers, girls!

Acknowledgements

2008 was the year I (finally!) got married and had my own hen night, so it was a very fitting year in which to write this novel. I'd like to thank the following people who all helped in various ways:

Imogen Taylor, Jenny Geras, Trisha Jackson and everyone at Pan Macmillan for their editorial input and all-round loveliness, plus Simon Trewin, Ariella Feiner and all at United Agents, for sound advice and support. Victoria Walker, Kate Harrison and Milly Johnson for feedback and encouragement during writing. The witty and talented members of BWBD and the Novel Racers who keep me writing week in, week out. My parents, Kate and Adrian Mongredien, for their love and support, and my children, Hannah, Tom and Holly Powell, who are just fabulous in every way. Huge thanks also to everyone who's taken the time to write or email to say they enjoyed my first two novels — I really appreciate it (and you!). As for you, Martin, husband extraordinaire . . . you're the best.

Katie's Hen Night

February 1994

'Cheers to the hens!'

Katie Taylor picked up her champagne flute and thrust it into the air. Seven flushed faces beamed back at her along the length of the restaurant table. Her best friends, Alice and Georgia; her younger sisters, Charlotte and Laura; two friends from work, and, down at the far end of the table, her future sister-in-law, Nicki.

'Cheers!' the chorus came back as they all lifted their glasses and clinked them against each other. 'Yay!' added Alice, her apple cheeks shining in the candlelight. 'Cheers to the blushing bride, too!'

Katie adjusted the plastic silvery tiara on her head – it had slipped over one ear again – and slugged back a large mouthful of bubbly. 'Well, I don't know about *blushing*,' she said, cocking an eyebrow saucily, and everyone laughed. 'Seriously, though,' she said, suddenly feeling a lump in her throat, 'it's so great that you're all here for my hen night.' Tears pricked her eyes as she gazed at them, friends and family out together in the new T.G.I. Friday's off the ring road. She thought for a moment she was going to start blubbing all over her chicken-in-a-basket, and dabbed at her eyes with the paper serviette. 'Thanks, Alice and Georgia, for organizing everything,' she went on, her voice wobbling slightly as she raised her glass to each of them in turn. 'You're the best hens and bridesmaids a girl could ask for.'

'You haven't seen the strippergram yet,' Georgia teased, tossing her dark hair over one shoulder so that it fell down her back in a sleek, shining mass. She arched a perfectly plucked eyebrow. 'You might not be saying that later . . .'

Alice grinned. 'She's only winding you up,' she told Katie, dipping one of her fries in ketchup and swallowing it whole.

'Yeah, I'm only joking,' Georgia said, and winked. 'It's a gorillagram really. Big, butch and hairy, just the way you like them, Katie.'

Everyone giggled. '*Really*, Georgia?' asked Charlotte, Katie's youngest sister, who was only fifteen and thought Georgia the most glamorous creature ever to be seen in Wiltshire. 'Is there *really* going to be a gorillagram?' She stared around eagerly, eyes wide, hoping for a glimpse of some male dangly bits to brag about to her friends at school. What with the alcopop she'd tried for the first time in her life AND the electric-blue mascara that Laura had let her borrow, this was turning out to be the most exciting night she'd ever had.

Georgia pursed her blood-red lips. 'You never know,' she said, tapping her nose confidingly.

'Big butch hairy men aside,' Alice said, raising her glass in Katie's direction, 'here's to you, Mrs Watkinson.'

'Oi, not yet,' Katie retorted, laughing. 'I've got one week left of being Katie Taylor before I'm a Mrs anything.' She allowed herself a secret shiver of excitement at the thought of the wedding next Saturday. Mrs Watkinson. Mrs Neil Watkinson! It sounded so married. So grown up! She glanced down at her engagement ring, the gold glinting under the bright restaurant spotlights, and felt goosebumps breaking out along her arms. 'I mean it, though. I'm having a fab night tonight. And I just know the wedding is going to be the best one ever!'

Two hours later, Katie was feeling decidedly ratted as she swung around the dance floor to Chaka Demus and Pliers. Georgia was shaking it up nearby with a bloke wearing stupid rapper trousers, and Alice was making Charlotte drink pints of water at the side, after some Pernod-and-black-related vomiting incident in the loos. Oh, it was so brilliant having Alice and Georgia here, Katie was really chuffed they'd come all the way from London for tonight. She'd missed them, more than she'd expected to. It had all been a whirlwind, meeting Neil, leaving London, making plans for the wedding and a whole new future...

The song changed and suddenly Georgia was at her side. 'You're Lulu, I'm Robbie,' she said, spinning around on the spot. 'Alice! Over here! You're Gary Barlow!'

Alice left her Charlotte-tending duties at once and ran onto the dance floor. 'I'm Mark Owen,' she bellowed over the pounding music, wiggling her hips. She wasn't really a confident dancer, Alice, always too self-conscious about how her body looked (unlike Georgia, who was going for it big-style with her routine, punching the air and singing into a pretend microphone), but the first time the three of them had ever been out together to the Friday club night at the student union, they'd all had such a laugh dancing to 'Could It Be Magic' that, since then, hitting the dance floor for Take That had become something of a ritual.

'Cos I neeeeeeeed your love!' Georgia screamed, grabbing Katie's hand and spinning her round.

Katie laughed uncontrollably as she saw the looks her workmates, Beth and Andrea, were giving her. They both knew Katie as the rather quiet, sensible new girl in the office, helping with the accounts, mucking in with the tea- and coffee-making. They probably hadn't realized they worked with a disco diva who had such mad Robbie

Williams-impersonating friends. Oh, who cared what they thought anyway? It was only a stop-gap job until she sorted out another college course. And she hadn't had a proper dance for ages – too long.

She made a hand into a pretend microphone of her own and went for it.

By two o'clock the next morning when the music stopped and the club lights suddenly went horribly bright, Charlotte was asleep on a velour banquette with Laura trying to shake her awake, Beth and Andrea had long gone, and Nicki had been picked up by her fella for a lift home. 'See you at the wedding,' she'd said, kissing Katie goodbye.

'That was an ace hen night,' Alice said, as the cab dropped them back at Katie's mum's house. Her fair hair was plastered to her head and someone had spilled a pint of lager down her side, but her eyes were sparkly with happiness.

'I loved it,' Georgia agreed, linking an arm through Katie's as they walked up the front path. 'What a laugh – my face aches from smiling all night. It's not been the same without you, Kate, our Friday nights. Are you sure you can't persuade Neil to move to London?'

Katie wrinkled her nose. 'I doubt it,' she said, unlocking the front door. 'And now that I've got this job in his dad's firm, I—'

Lucy Diamond

Everyone jumped as a large figure loomed in the doorway. Alice gave a scream before clapping a hand to her mouth and giggling nervously. 'Back so soon?' slurred Mrs Taylor, leaning against the door jamb. Her skin was mottled and puffy, her eyes glazed. She was slaughtered, as usual. 'Thought you might have pulled and gone off to some bloke's house.'

'We're not all like you,' Katie said tartly, elbowing her aside. 'Come on in. Laura, are you all right with Charlotte?' She could feel her skin prickling. Mum had to spoil everything. 'Go up to my room,' she hissed to Alice and Georgia. 'I'll be there in two minutes.'

'I've told her, she's making a mistake,' Mrs Taylor said, her eyes small and mean. 'But does she listen to her old mum? No. She'll learn. She'll soon—'

'Oh, shut up, Mum,' Laura snapped. 'Or I'll get Charlotte to puke on you.'

Mercifully – and surprisingly – Mrs Taylor sloped off to bed herself without another word.

Alice and Georgia were squeezing into Katie's old bedroom for the night, and when they'd all whispered and giggled their way through make-up removal and teeth brushing, the three of them lay in their sleeping bags in the darkness.

'Sorry about my mum,' Katie said, still mortified at what had happened. 'She's such a nightmare.'

6

Alice reached out and held her hand. 'Don't let it spoil tonight,' she said.

'Yeah, come on, Mrs Watkinson, think of happier things,' Georgia put in.

'Oi, don't start all that Mrs Watkinson stuff again!' Katie scolded, but Alice had already launched into song.

'And here's to you, Mrs Watkinson . . .' she warbled.

'Georgia-'n'-Alice love you more than you could know,' Georgia joined in, giggling. 'Whoa, whoa, whoa . . .'

Katie smiled in the darkness at her friends' tuneless singing. They were right – she wouldn't let her mum wreck her hen night. She was nearly Mrs Watkinson after all – and better times were just around the corner . . .

Chapter One

How Deep Is Your Love?

Friday, 13 June 2008

'So don't forget, this needs to be handed in to me on Monday, first thing, all right? Anyone giving in late coursework will—'

BRRRRRRINNNNNGGGGG!

The school bell interrupted Katie's words. Half the class had had an eye on the clock for the last ten minutes, of course – who didn't want to get away at breakneck speed on Friday afternoon? – and were up from their seats, bags packed and through the door before the bell had finished pealing without so much as a 'Bye, miss'.

'Coursework on Monday morning!' Katie bellowed after their departing backs. They were not supposed to leave the classroom until she'd given them permission to go – headmaster's rules – but it was the end of the week, and she decided she'd disregard it this once. Some battles just weren't worth fighting.

She turned back to face the remnants of the class who were busily stuffing their algebra textbooks into their bags. She could see it in their eyes, their hungry expressions, that they too were desperate to escape the classroom, but they at least were still obedient enough to wait for the official release. 'Okay, off you go, then,' she said. 'See you next week. Have a good weekend.'

Back scraped all the chairs from their desks as they got to their feet. A swell of chatter rose; you could feel the atmosphere change from that of endured confinement to sweet liberation. And off they went, iPods in, mobiles checked for new text messages (another blind eye turned – they were meant to wait until they were off school premises for that), talk of parties and shopping and sleepovers . . .

Their high, excited voices echoed for a while as they went down the corridors, then all was silent. Friday afternoon. Your weekend starts here.

She sat down at her desk, relishing the peace and quiet. It always seemed particularly dense, that silence, after thirty noisy teenagers had so recently vacated the space. She pulled over a pile of Year 8 homework books. Right, then. Now for an hour's marking before she went to the supermarket; the traditional start to the weekend. Not for her, talk of sleepovers and parties and shopping. Katie

Taylor liked a good solid structure at the centre of her life. It felt safe that way. There was no room for any silly fanciful notions when you had a watertight routine in place.

She pulled over the first book. Ella Townsend. With 'I ♥ Zack!!!!' in big letters on the front cover. Katie couldn't help but notice that 'I ♥ Danny!!!!' and 'I ♥ Miles!!!!' had been crossed out elsewhere on the cover. If Ella Townsend could just pay as much attention to her maths homework as she did to her love life, she'd be top of the class. As it was, with Zack Richards to moon over and write love notes to, her homework had taken a swerve for the worse this year. What was it with teenagers and their hopeless crushes?

Katie wrinkled her nose as she red-penned her way through Ella's equations. Cross, cross, cross, cross, tick, cross. Ella wasn't daft, either. Only a year ago, she'd been one of the most diligent students in the class. Now hormones had kicked in and schoolwork had gone out the window. The sad thing was, she didn't even seem to care.

Concentrate, Ella!, Katie wrote in red pen at the bottom of the page, having totted up the girl's score as four out of twenty. *I know you can do better than this!*

Still, they all had them, didn't they? Their silly romantic lapses of reason. Katie, too, had been like that, back when she was a teenager. But of course, she'd been even worse than Ella. She'd actually given up her degree to go and get married. To Neil Watkinson, of all people! So she was a fine one to talk.

Katie realized she was gazing out of the classroom window, almost as if she were expecting her ex-husband to gallop across the playground on a white charger or something. She stifled a giggle. Fat chance. Neil Watkinson probably drove a people-carrier these days, with a collection of kiddie seats in the back and his second wife in the passenger seat. Or third wife, even, knowing what he was like.

Neil bloody Watkinson, eh. It seemed almost unbelievable to her now, that she and Neil Watkinson had once spent all that money on the hired suit and dress, flowers, photos and a finger buffet, had pored over invitation lists, seating plans and honeymoon travel brochures. For what? A year of having to pick his dirty pants up off the floor every day, that's what. Cooking all those bloody Findus crispy pancakes, his favourite food. Ironing umpteen work shirts of his – how had that happened? How had they morphed into those husband/wife stereotypes so scarily quickly, when she was just as useless with an iron as him?

All that she had now to show she'd ever been married were a few faded photos, that nasty gold Ratners ring stashed in the depths of her knicker drawer and the cheeseboard her Aunty Wendy had bought them, gathering dust in the kitchen. She didn't even particularly like cheese; she was a Cheddar kind of girl, fine in a sandwich with a bit of tomato, but that was about it.

It seemed even more surreal to Katie that she'd ever taken her clothes off and lain there on the marital bed, letting Neil Watkinson clamber onto her and pump away, wearing his Bristol bloody Rovers top half the time (sartorial standards fell alarmingly, post-wedding). He was desperate for her to get pregnant as quick as possible. Not because he particularly liked children – he called the neighbours' kids all the names under the sun if they woke him up on a Sunday morning – but because he thought it would prove he was a Real Man. And that was really where their marriage started to go wrong, of course...

Katie shuddered at the fleeting flashback. She and Neil had got together during the long vacation after her first year of university. All her friends were heading off on adventures: Georgia had wangled herself an internship at the *Daily Mirror* as part of her journalism course. Alice was InterRailing with a few other mates. Katie had no such exciting plans – in fact, she was working as a barmaid in the White Horse, trying to pay off her debts. But then in walked Neil Watkinson and bought her a drink ... and suddenly life seemed to pick up.

She was smitten with him, instantly. His low voice, his crooked smile, the way his eyes sought out hers and lingered over her body. She'd never had a proper boyfriend before then, had never known what it felt like to be in love, but within minutes she felt as if she were drowning in the stuff. Two weeks later, she'd lost her virginity to him in one of the meadows by the towpath. And two months after that, he'd proposed.

Everyone had voiced their doubts when she said she was leaving uni to marry Neil. 'You must be barking,' Georgia had said with typical bluntness. 'Tie yourself down to one bloke? You're not even twenty yet – you've got years of shagging around ahead of you!'

'What about your degree?' Alice had added. 'You can't just drop out because you've fallen in love. Can't you wait a few years?'

But no. She didn't want to wait. She didn't want to 'shag around', as Georgia had so charmingly put it. Her mind was made up. Even her mum couldn't sway her. 'You're making a terrible mistake,' she'd said, shaking her head. 'Don't trust him. Lesson number one – men are all bastards.'

But that was like a red rag to a bull, of course. Katie was not going to take love-life advice from her mum of all people. She'd listened to her heart instead, she'd sorted out the white dress and tiara, and sent out the invitations. She'd been Mrs Neil Watkinson for a whole twelve months until the tension had begun to crackle between them, when she hadn't given him a baby, and he wouldn't give her any freedom, and ... well, you had to have your bottom line, didn't you? And stumbling upon your husband rogering Linda O'Connor from next door in the spare room was definitely what Katie called a bottom line.

What a relief it had been, walking out on him! She could see herself now, head high as she strode down that narrow front path, not looking back at the little two-up two-down terraced house, all her stuff wedged into sports bags (including the cheeseboard – God knows why she'd packed that, as a weapon perhaps, in case he tried to stop her going).

Neil, this isn't working any more, she'd written. *I've gone back to London. Sorry.*

It had been cowardly, sure, sneaking out of the relationship when he'd been at work, especially as he'd grovelled and begged over the shagging-Linda-O'Connor incident until he was blue in the face. He thought he was forgiven, but she'd just been biding her time, steeling herself until she had the guts to walk away. And the lightness that had filled her, the joy of liberation, she was almost giddy with it as she clicked the front gate behind her and left their home for good.

End of the marriage. Start of her new life. Easy as that. And no, she'd never truly trusted another man since.

She turned back to her desk and picked up the next

exercise book. Megan White. Who *also* loved Zack, by the looks of things.

Ten minutes later, Katie was interrupted by Miss Dickens, the school secretary, popping her head round the classroom door.

'Sorry to bother you, Katie dear, but there's a...' She looked flummoxed for a second, her nose twitching like a rabbit's. 'Well, there's a car waiting for you outside. A taxi.'

Katie frowned. 'A taxi? For me? But I haven't ordered—'

'Yes, for you, dear.' That faint look of consternation on her face as if she suspected a prank in the offing. Miss Dickens was very wary of pranks. 'Most insistent, the driver was. Said there'd been a change of plan and you needed to leave work now.'

'Change of plan?' Katie echoed. 'Leave now?'

Miss Dickens nodded and the silvery curls on top of her head bobbed back and forth. 'That's what he said. I hope nobody's mucking you about, what with it being Friday the thirteenth and all that, but ... well, if you wouldn't mind sorting him out, dear, only I'm right in the middle of the Year 10 class schedules for September and...'

'Yes, of course,' Katie said, cutting in. Given half a chance, Miss Dickens would be there until Sunday evening, sounding off about her class schedules. How irritating to be interrupted like this, though. Obviously, there was some misunderstanding, all this talk of a change of plan, and having to leave work. Friday the thirteenth indeed – Katie had no truck with fanciful superstitions. The driver was clearly confusing her with another person who didn't have twenty-five more homework books to mark and a Tesco trip to fit in by six o'clock, but all the same . . .

She grabbed her handbag and followed Miss Dickens down the corridor. It was still so warm – this June was turning out to be a scorcher – and she made a mental note to put some Pimm's in the trolley when she finally got to the supermarket. Pimm's, mint, lemonade, cucumber, maybe some strawberries. If a thing was worth doing, it was worth doing properly, Katie always thought.

She'd reached the front doors of the school that opened out onto the staff car park and drive. And there, engine purring, sat a large black cab, the sort you usually only saw in London. It looked swanky and decidedly out of place, waiting outside scruffy St Joseph's Comprehensive School in this particular Bristol suburb, which usually only saw Mondeos and Astras shambling around.

Definitely a case of mistaken identity. Oh well. At least this would only take two minutes to sort out.

She strode over to the car, an apologetic look on her face. 'I think you've got the wrong—'

'Katie Taylor?'

'Yes, that's me, but—'

'Birthday tenth March, lives on Warburton Road?'

She stared at the driver, momentarily taken aback. Had she met him before? She racked her brain but had no memory of his dark hair, thick eyebrows and greasy-looking skin. 'How did you know that?'

He consulted a piece of paper he had on a clipboard. 'Born in the General Hospital to Margery and Ian Taylor, two sisters?'

Katie could feel her cheeks flushing with heat. What was this? Some massive wind-up? 'Look, I don't know who sent you—' she began, trying to wrest back some control.

'Favourite colour blue, favourite smell lavender?' the driver went on, glancing up at her from his paper. He raised his eyebrows. 'Very nice,' he said to himself.

'Well yes, but—' She glanced around, wondering if some annoying teenage boys would be having a good laugh about this nearby. How did he know all this stuff? Had someone swiped a personal file from the office? It was probably Miss Dickens, befuddled by her class schedule, who'd given out a load of information about—

'Right, well, that must be you, then,' the driver said. 'He said I'd have to prove it before you'd believe me. Hop in, my lovely, and we'll get going.'

She put her hands on her hips. 'Go where? Who said that, anyway? Look, I really think this is a mistake. My own car is ...' She waved her hand at where her red Clio usually sat in the car park, waiting faithfully for her all day until it was time to go home. She prided herself on always parking it exactly between the white lines. You could have taken a ruler and measured each side, and it would be bang slap in the middle. Katie liked precision. But her eyebrows shot up now as she realized there was nothing in her parking space but shimmering heat. 'It's gone! My car's gone!'

The driver looked as if he was getting fed up. He turned the engine off and leaned against the wheel. 'Yeah, I know it's gone. Steve took it. That's why I'm here.'

'Steve?' Katie echoed, feeling more baffled by the second. What was Steve doing with her car?

'Yep, he picked up your car to be serviced. So I'm here to give you a lift. All right? Any more questions?'

Katie blinked. She felt as if someone had snatched her up from her ordinary everyday life where her car was precision parked and her day ran like well-oiled clockwork, and dumped her into a parallel universe where the mechanism of her routine had rusted over, and nothing made sense. So Steve had taken her car to the garage? But what was with the cloak-and-dagger Q-and-A session? Why all that favourite-colour stuff?

The driver was still staring at her, waiting for an answer.

One of his pink sausagey fingers scratched the salt-and-pepper stubble on his chin.

'Um ... no,' she said faintly in the end. 'No more questions.'

'Right. In you get then. Might even miss the rush hour if we go now.'

Katie thought briefly of the pile of homework books she'd left unfinished on her desk, then banished the image from her mind. She'd have to come in early on Monday and do them then. How incredibly annoying! She hated having work hanging over her for the whole weekend; she preferred to clear the decks first. Work first, fun later. She'd always been like that, even as a schoolgirl. *Conscientious*, her teachers had written in her school reports.

Still. She didn't want to start quibbling with this driver, not now he'd started the car again and was revving the engine so impatiently. Not now she'd discovered he was her only means of transport home. Bloody hell!

She pulled open the back door and sat down on the bouncy vinyl seat. She felt odd, disorientated, as if it wasn't really her, sitting there being driven along. She had work to do, and the supermarket shopping to get through! How was she supposed to do that without her own wheels?

Honestly! Steve didn't think things through sometimes. It was all very kind of him taking her car off like that, but he might have told her. Might have given her a bit of notice, rather than sending a cab round like this. But then, that was Steve for you. Him and his impetuousness...

She leaned back against the seat as the car rumbled through the estate. She and Steve had been together for just over two years and he was the first person she'd let herself get properly attached to since her disastrous marriage break-up all those years ago. She'd been so disillusioned after Neil that she'd sworn off men for a long time, only allowing herself brief flings and dalliances to keep from total Old Maid Meltdown. But no one had ever got close. She was just starting to think that her mum had actually been right all along about men, when she met Steve.

Steve was different. He made her laugh. He made her happy. And ooh, she really really fancied him, like she hadn't fancied anyone for years. He had sandy hair and brown eyes, a nice bum, and a wicked sense of humour. She'd kept him at arm's length for a long time, not quite able to let go and trust him. But he'd been persistent. Steady. He kept his promises just as consistently as he kept her warm in bed. And she hadn't intended to let him move in so quickly but ... it had just happened. It seemed easier that way. And it was surprisingly nice to live with a man again, curling up on the sofa together in front of *The Apprentice* and what-have-you, even if Steve did spend the whole programme doing his terrible Alan Sugar impressions. Throwing dinner parties together, and watching Steve across the candlelight as he made everyone laugh with his stories about work. Lying in bed on Sunday mornings, hearing his heart beat as she rested her head on his bare chest . . . yes, they were all good things. Very good.

Even *Georgia* approved. 'Well, he's a step up from Neil, I'll give him that,' she'd said when they'd met at a mutual friend's party. She'd exhaled a long plume of cigarette smoke as she and Katie watched Steve chat to everyone on his way to the bar. 'He's got social skills at least.'

'George! And the rest!' Katie had scolded. 'Come on, you can be a bit more generous than that.'

'All right, social skills and a sexy arse,' Georgia had conceded. 'And best of all, he's not Neil. Look, I'm complimenting the guy, all right?'

Katie jerked out of her thoughts now as she realized the driver was taking her the wrong way. She sighed crossly. For heaven's sake! What was he *doing*? She leaned forward. 'Excuse me – I live on *Warburton* Road,' she reminded him. 'You've gone past the turn-off, you know.'

The driver didn't seem to have heard. He was whistling along with Beyoncé on the radio and slapping the steering wheel to the beat.

Katie felt her hackles rising with annoyance. It was Friday, she was tired, she didn't like being messed around, she didn't like her plans being changed by *anyone*, and now she was going to spend half her precious evening being driven around Bristol by some moron cabbie ... 'I *said*, you've missed the turn-off!' she told him in her most teachery voice. 'You're going the wrong way!'

The driver still didn't answer. Katie was starting to feel disconcerted. What was going on here? Why wasn't the driver taking her home? Was this all part of Steve's plan, or was something more sinister going on? *It IS Friday the thirteenth, after all,* wittered Miss Dickens in her head.

Enough game-playing. She got her mobile phone out of her bag and brandished it so that he could see it in his rear-view mirror. 'If you don't pull over and let me get out *right now*, I'm calling the police,' she told him, her voice shaking.

To her consternation, he merely laughed. 'He said you might get cross with me,' the driver replied. 'He told me, just ignore her if she starts getting shirty. Sorry, sweetheart. But he's paying the bill, see, so...'

Katie's mouth dropped open in outrage. *Just ignore her if she starts getting shirty?* Had Steve actually said that about her? She glared as she imagined the words coming out of his mouth. She'd give him shirty! What *was* this wild goose chase he was sending her on, anyway?

'*I'll* pay the bill,' Katie said, fuming, as they turned into a leafy Georgian square. 'Just stop the car and I'll pay. I've had enough of this game now. I just want to——'

'No need for that, my darlin',' the driver said, indicating and pulling over. 'Because we're here. Allow me.'

He nipped out and held the back door open for her. She stared suspiciously at him, and then up at the hotel she was standing in front of. Berkeley Square Hotel? Why had he brought her here? 'And . . . dare I ask what happens now?' she said icily. 'All part of the joke, eh?'

His hands were up in a *Whoa!* gesture, and he was laughing. 'Calm down. He said to go and check in. You have a good weekend now.' And with that, he was back in the driver's seat, giving her a cheery wave and pulling off.

Katie watched him go, feeling bewildered. 'He said to go and check in?' she repeated to herself. 'What, in *there*?'

She eyed the hotel. She knew for sure that this was a wind-up now. Any second, Steve would pop out, laughing his head off, then take her to their favourite pub in town. *So where* are *you, then, Steve?*, she thought, looking around. *Very funny*, she'd say when she spotted him. *You had me going for a minute, then. I thought I was getting kidnapped!*

Steve didn't appear. She looked at the hotel again. It occupied several townhouses in the quiet Georgian square, and had a pleasingly symmetrical frontage, with its large sash windows and the olive trees in pots either side of the main door. It was meant to have an amazing restaurant, with luxurious double rooms. The sort of place she'd never go, unless someone was having a really special birthday do there. She'd read about it in the *Evening Post* when it had been revamped six months or so ago, had said, 'Ooh! That looks a bit flash for Brizzle', and then forgotten about it.

So deep down, she knew it was all a tease about her checking in there. It had to be, didn't it? Steve was probably taking a picture of her right now on his mobile phone from where he was hiding. He'd take the mickey out of her about it later. 'Did you really believe that cabbie?' he'd laugh. 'You dozy mare. What are you like?'

She was standing there like a lemon, not able to think straight. She might as well go inside the place, now that she was here, she supposed. She could always pretend she was checking out the facilities or something. And then, once she'd done that, she'd get the bus back home. Oh, and she'd send *Steve* out on the supermarket run. It was the least he could do after all this.

She stepped inside the hotel lobby. It felt cool and light, and practically smelled of money. Classical music was playing, and there was a small ornate fountain in the waiting area, water tumbling over slick white cobbles, which immediately made Katie need the loo. She felt sweaty and grubby in her Friday work clothes – whatever had possessed her to put on this skanky old vest top today, anyway? — and tried to smooth her hair behind her ears as she went up to reception.

The woman behind the desk smiled at her, foundation dewy on her skin, clothes immaculate, a subtle hint of sweet perfume lingering around her. *Maria Porter, Reception Manager*, it said on her name tag. 'Can I help you?' she asked in a pleasant voice.

Katie felt instantly ridiculous. What was she doing here? Why had she even come in? 'I . . .' she began uncertainly, her face flooding with colour.

Maria Porter sat there, looking composed as she waited for Katie to form a coherent sentence.

'I don't suppose . . .' Katie swallowed, '. . . you've got a reservation for Katie Taylor, have you?' Her heart thumped uncomfortably. 'Or Steven Patrick?' Her fingers squeezed together. She felt so embarrassed! Any second now, Maria Porter, Reception Manager was going to send her packing and she'd be back out through those fancy doors, with her tail between her legs.

'Let's see,' said the receptionist, turning to her computer monitor and pressing a couple of buttons with her highly polished fingernails. Click, click. 'Ahh yes, here we are,' she said after a moment. 'Mr Patrick is waiting for you upstairs. Your suite is on the top floor, the last door on your right as you come out of the lift. Enjoy your stay!'

This was a dream. This wasn't actually real. Things like

this didn't happen to her. Katie stared at Maria Porter for a full ten seconds, jaw hanging open so that all her fillings were on display, before remembering her manners. 'Thank you,' she managed to say, and she walked in a daze towards the lift. Her head was spinning. She had been so convinced that this was a wind-up, had been certain it was some elaborate trick. Apparently not.

Oh my God. This was so exciting. The sort of thing you saw in a film, and thought, Yeah *right*. Like any bloke in real life would ever do *that!*

But it seemed that Steve had. What was he up to? Had he been promoted, maybe, and was splashing the cash? He'd mentioned some big conference he was hoping to be asked along to, but there'd been no indication of a pay rise in the offing.

Up she went in the mirrored lift, horrified to see how pink her cheeks were and how scruffy her hair was. And was that really a splodge of yogurt on her top? She was half surprised she hadn't been frogmarched out of the building by now for being such a pleb.

The door slid open again at the top floor, and she stepped out onto carpet so thick and soft, her feet didn't make a sound as she walked along the corridor.

She knocked at the door at the end and turned the handle, her heart thumping as she went in.

There inside the room, sitting on an enormous double

bed, looking pleased with himself and nervous all at the same time, was Steve. Katie stared at him, taking in several things at once.

There was a bouquet of red roses on one of the bedside tables.

There was a bottle of Moët on ice on the other.

There was a neatly packed bag of Katie's clothes and make-up on a chair, with her best black dress already on a hanger.

Wow. Even better than a film. This was amazing! So romantic! So . . .

Her blood ran cold suddenly as she noticed that Steve had his hand outstretched. And there, on his upturned palm, was a turquoise satin jewellery box. He opened it up and she saw a silver ring inside.

Her eyes sought out his face, shocked. He was smiling. 'Katie,' he said, dropping to his knees and proffering the box. 'Will you marry me?'

Georgia's Hen Night

June 1998

Georgia Knight stared at her reflection in the mirror, patting more face powder onto her cheeks until beige clouds puffed up around her. God, she was trashed already, and it wasn't even midnight! They'd be peeling her off the floor when it came to kicking-out time at this rate.

She tried to look inconspicuous as one of the All Saints girls came in and started touching up her mascara just a metre or so away. Georgia wrestled with temptation for a split second then turned resolutely back to her own reflection. No. She wouldn't start getting into conversation with her, hoping to draw out some gossip. This was a night off. This was her hen night, for God's sake!

All the same, those Appleton sisters were hot tickets right now...

Katie came in just then, swaying as she walked, unsteady

on her high heels. 'George, hurry up! You've got six challenges left before the end of the night!'

Alice was there too — where had she sprung from? — looking distinctly overdressed in her lilac blouse and smart black trousers. She'd never been one for short skirts and thigh boots, Alice. Vicar's daughter, that was the look she went for, bless her. Pure as the driven snow. Not like Georgia. Ha!

'Not like me,' Georgia spluttered to herself, laughing at the thought. She had to cling to the side of the sink, it was so funny.

Alice and Katie exchanged glances. 'Come on, you,' Katie said. 'You're not getting out of it so easily. It took me and Alice ages to think of these.'

Katie and Alice seemed to have digested the encyclopaedia on hen-night duties, Georgia thought as she staggered out of the Ladies after them. They were certainly taking this very seriously. Challenges and drinking games, that ridiculous bridal headdress they'd produced for her to wear (she'd soon got rid of that, shoved into one of the sanitary bins in the restaurant) — and the L-plates she'd caught Katie fastening onto the back of her coat. Sweet, really. If kinda naff.

'Right,' Katie said, when they were back with the rest of the group. Georgia had invited twenty people to the hen do — loads of people from work, plus Katie and Alice, her best friends from uni. She'd lost track of some of the work lot – half of them seemed to have got left behind at the second club they'd been to. Only the hard core were still standing (albeit listing slightly, in some cases). Unfortunately, two of the hard core seemed determined to make her do all these ludicrous challenges. 'Are you listening, Georgia? Okay, your next challenge is to snog three random strangers.'

Ooh, risqué – *not*, thought Georgia. Did they not know that snogging random strangers was as easy as breathing for her? 'Male or female?' she countered.

'It's up to you,' Alice giggled. 'Just get some tongues down your throat.'

'No worries,' Georgia said, stumbling onto the dance floor. Tongues down your throat indeed! Sometimes Alice didn't seem to have changed at all from the shy eighteen-year-old who'd had the room next to Georgia in their first year at uni. Still, hey ho, there was work to be done. Now then. Who looked up for a bit of a smooch?

She tottered onto the dance floor, going over sideways on one ankle. Ouch. Bloody stilettos. She lurched into a guy with a naff Jamiroquai hat and sweaty Brazil football shirt – ahh, sod it, he'd do. 'C'mere gorgeous,' she said thickly, clutching the nylon folds of his top between her fingers. 'Come and give this virgin bride a big kiss . . .'

She stumbled as his lips closed around hers, only too

happy to oblige. And then, without warning, she was horribly sick down his throat.

'So here we all are again,' Georgia said some time later. It was three in the morning, and she, Katie and Alice were sprawled out on the huge squishy sofa, watching *Pretty Woman* on video, in Harry's flat. Or rather, hers and Harry's flat, as she had to get used to calling it. 'Hen night number two.' She grinned along the sofa at them. The flat felt much more like home now that she had her girls with her.

'And what a corker it was,' Katie said, crunching through a handful of popcorn. 'That club was fab, wasn't it? Bit classier than the student places I usually go to. I couldn't believe all the celebs we saw there.' She sighed dramatically. 'See, you two and your high-flying jobs, it's probably not that big a deal to you any more. Whereas for me . . .'

Alice gave her a nudge. 'High-flying? Are you joking?' She laughed. 'You've seen the tossers I have to put up with at the theatre, all the luvvie crap they dish out. I feel like Cinderella half the time, running about skivvying after them.'

'One day you'll get to the ball, Alice,' Georgia said, popping the cork on another bottle of champagne. She hoped it wasn't one of the really expensive ones Harry had forbidden her to open. 'In fact, we must sort another night out soon before Katie buggers off to Bristol, and I'm a respectable married woman.' She gave a little shiver. 'It's all happened so fast, I can't quite believe I'm getting married. It's going to be such a good party. Harry's guests are just A-list through and through ... There's even talk of a magazine deal, you know, his agent said one of the big glossies has been sniffing around, asking questions.'

'God,' Katie said, wide-eyed. 'What have the *Herald* said about that?'

'Well, nothing's definite. And they know they'll get some juicy stuff from me, whatever happens. Anyway, I'm their golden girl at the moment, Isabella can't get enough of me.' She handed out the champagne flutes feeling heady just thinking about it. Landing the showbiz-columnist job at the *Herald* had been so amazing, like the best dream come true, after plugging away as a freelance for so long. Sure, she had a feeling that being engaged to Harry Stone, mega-bucks playboy, had helped enormously, but hey, they wouldn't have given her the gig if she was completely talentless, would they?

'Well, cheers to you, Georgia,' Alice said, eyes shining as she held out her glass. 'We're dead proud of you, girl, you've done brilliantly.'

'Hear hear,' said Katie. 'Just make sure you remember your old mates when you're whizzing about in your limo and we're still in the gutter. Chuck a few crumbs our way now and again.'

Georgia laughed. 'Don't give me that!' she said. 'Nothing's going to change. And anyway, I'm dead proud of you two, too. The best friends a girl could ask for.' She clinked her glass against Alice's and then Katie's. 'Cheers to us!'

Chapter Two

Rule The World

Georgia barely thought about her failed marriage these days. It hadn't exactly been a big deal. Girl meets boy, girl and boy fancy each other's pants off, foolishly decide to declare their commitment in public at great expense involving all friends and family, then, six months later, decide they've made a terrible mistake, when boy's coke habit goes through the roof and he turns into a gibbering addict nutter. Still, at least you learned from your mistakes. She'd never be doing *that* again.

Luckily, Georgia was in the perfect line of work to bestow punishments on those who strayed from the path. She dealt out the public humiliations with an almost evangelical zeal. Film stars, TV presenters, sports heroes ... no man was too powerful to escape her wrath. If she found out a woman was being wronged by a bloke, Georgia would wreak vengeance in huge capital letters, with photos wherever possible. Bitchy anonymous quotes too, if need be. She loved making those up.

She gave a contemptuous little snort as she twizzled to and fro on her office chair, then began typing up her notes from last night. Oh yes. Call it her stand on behalf of womankind. Although not everyone appreciated the sentiments – but that was their problem, wasn't it?

It was 'Stenders super-stud Martin Browne's 21st birthday bash at the Bone Bar last night, and yours truly was invited, of course. All the soap stars were there, partying their Walford pants off – literally in some cases!

Georgia stopped typing for a moment, popped some nicotine gum into her mouth and chewed vigorously. God, this stuff was disgusting. Back when she'd got her first job in journalism, every self-respecting hack had a full ashtray on their desk and left silvery trails of ash in their wake, like Hansel and Gretel might have done if they'd had a forty-a-day habit. Nowadays all that had changed though, and the *Herald* ran a goody-goody no-smoking office, like every other place. It still drove Georgia nuts. How were you supposed to write scintillating copy without a ciggy between your lips? How were you meant to concentrate for five minutes straight?

She read through her piece critically, changing a few

words and adding the next tantalizing line. *You'll never GUESS who I saw Martin getting up close and personal with outside the Ladies,* she typed. *Only our favourite soap über-bitch, Tasha Woods. And him a newly married man, as well!*

She pursed her lips. Martin Browne would go tonto at that. She could almost hear his furious voice ranting at her down the phone when this hit the newsstands, calling her all the names under the sun. 'Should have kept your sweaty hands off Tasha's silicones, then, shouldn't you, darlin'?' she muttered under her breath, finishing the article.

Her phone was ringing, and she took one hand off the keyboard to grab it. 'Georgia Knight speaking.'

'All right, Georgy, my darlin', it's John here from the Cavalry.'

She rolled her eyes and chewed even harder. 'My darling' indeed. He was such a creep. 'What have you got for me today, John?' she asked, wedging the phone under one ear in order to grab a pen and Post-it note. As doorman at the prestigious Cavalry Hotel in Covent Garden, John Albright always had the dirt on some unsuspecting celeb or other. It was only the fact that he was such an excellent spy that stopped her from telling him to stick his 'Georgy' and his 'darling's right where the sun didn't shine.

He gave a low chuckle down the phone. 'Got a good 'un for you, Georgy,' he said. 'You're gonna love this.'

She waited, pen poised. 'Oh yeah?'

'It's a big 'un. Good and juicy.'

Is that what you say to all the girls, John, sweetie?, she felt like cooing. But she didn't, because knowing John Albright, he'd only go and believe her – and with an ego as massive as his, he'd take it as a come-on. Ugh. A girl like Georgia had her standards, and fat-necked doormen like John did not measure up, thank you very much.

She waited, tapping her pen against the fluorescent yellow. 'So . . . are you going to tell me then?' she asked.

'Well, you know we've got a certain girl group staying here at the moment?'

Georgia brought the phone a little closer to her ear. 'Yep – the Sistas,' she said. 'What have they been up to?' The Sistas were a sassy, streetwise girl band from New York who were touring with their new album.

'They were in the hotel bar last night, sinking the drinks like we were gonna run out of booze, and . . .'

'What were they drinking?' Georgia interrupted. She knew her readers loved this kind of detail.

John snorted. 'What *weren't* they drinking is the question. Tequila slammers, sea breezes, highballs . . . Anyway, so they have a bit of a party in their suite – a right racket, we've had to apologize to all the guests in neighbouring rooms – and they order up some room service in the middle of the night . . .'

'What did they order?' Georgia asked, scribbling *teq slam, sea b, hbls* on her paper. She was recording the conversation, naturally, but ever since the cock-up where her Dictaphone had packed up right in the middle of a deep and meaningful with one of the *Big Brother* girls, she took extra precautions just to be on the safe side.

'Five bottles of Cristal, twenty Mars Bars and Pringles. Salt and vinegar. Exact order, I checked it all out for you, Georgy. So Vicki – one of our waitresses – goes up to their suite to take them that little lot and Be-Be – she's the singer, in't she? – is passed out on the floor, naked apart from her knickers round her ankles—'

'Nice,' snorted Georgia, jotting all of this down.

'And they're ... how shall I say this? ... *entertaining* some of their backing singers.'

'Male or female?' Georgia interrupted.

'Male *and* female, sweetheart,' he replied. 'They're not fussy girls. And then...'

The call lasted another two minutes while John poured out details which might make less experienced showbiz reporters blanch. Not Georgia. She'd heard it all before, with bells on. And whipped cream and glacé cherries, in many cases. She doubted there was much of this she could print without the Sistas' management coming down on the *Herald* like a ton of bricks, but it was fun all the same. She thrashed out a few headlines in her head as he wound up his news and said goodbye.

SOZZLED SISTAS
ROOM SERVICING, SISTA-STYLE
SISTAS ON THE SAUCE
TOTALLY SISSED . . .

She turned back to her PC, about to start typing, and saw that a new email had arrived.

London Film Festival Awards Ceremony – details for after-show party . . . she read, and her eyes lit up. Fabulous. She'd been looking forward to that one, especially as rumours had been flying all week that Noel Bailey, the hottest Hollywood actor and most gorgeous creature on planet Earth, was going to be attending. She must get her nails done properly before the party next week – after all, a girl never could tell where she might be putting her hands at these kinds of events.

She began typing up her notes for the Sistas story with a smile on her face. God, she loved her job! How she loved her job!

Later that evening, Georgia was rolling on a bit of lippy in preparation for a party at a private club in Soho to celebrate the nineteenth birthday of Candi (no surname required), a precocious kid with a body like a Barbie doll and a brain to match. Nevertheless, with her current number one single, 'Hot 4 U', and her Chelsea striker boyfriend, she was the paparazzi darling *du jour*, and didn't she know it, the little brat.

Georgia was deep in thought about how she was going to muscle her way in to the inner sanctum of the after-show party. Sure, she had a legitimate invite to get in the place – a result achieved after mucho blagging to the lackey at the record company who'd been bought off with a few signed photos of soap stars Georgia had kicking around the office – but there was always a section cordoned off for super-celebs at these parties, to which Georgia was never permitted access. Not officially anyway. During her ten years as gossip columnist at the *Herald*, though, Georgia had become an expert at impersonating Natalie Imbruglia/Dannii Minogue/any other dark-haired celeb to whom she had a passing resemblance in order to get past bouncers and barriers, or she'd pretend to be a waitress, PA to someone famous, oh, anyone she could think of, basically. She was a mistress of disguise. Well, a bloody good liar, anyway.

Tonight, perhaps she could—

She turned from her lippy application as something edged into her field of vision. A bespectacled, nervous-looking spoddy type was standing by her desk, shuffling his feet as if he needed the toilet. For God's sake. There was nothing worse than an intimidated male. It made her want to start slapping somebody. 'Yes?' she said curtly.

He flinched as if she really had whacked him one. She might if he didn't pull himself together fast.

'I'm Benedict, a freelancer?' he said, or rather asked, as if he wasn't sure himself.

'And?' she barked, smacking her lips together and blotting them.

'There's a story in about Harry Stone — you know, the playboy loser, who——?'

The name was still enough to cut her to the quick. Even now, it brought a searing flush to her face, a stab in the guts. She unleashed a full glare on him and he backed away. She had to resist the urge to push him over, the flat of her hand on his cheap Primark shirt. One shove and he'd be on the floor, down on his back like a beetle scrabbling to get right way up.

'Sod off, Benedict,' she snarled instead. 'Don't you know *anything* about working here?'

She snatched up her handbag and stormed out of the office. She just had time to hear Juliet, one of the secretaries, tutting at the spod. 'Georgia never runs stories about Harry Stone,' Juliet said. 'Didn't you know? He's off-limits.'

Georgia slammed out of there before she heard the rest of the conversation. She could predict it, though. Had heard it before.

But why *is he off-limits?*

Because he's Georgia's ex-husband, that's why. Shat all over her. Not literally, but — well, you know. Done her up like a kipper.

So? Doesn't she want to print some dirt on him, get her revenge?

Ahh. Yes. Well, she did that. Quite a lot of that. In fact, she dug up such dirt, Harry Stone got mightily pissed off and threw a great big lawsuit in her face. She won't touch him with a bargepole now. Not even if he was caught giving Fergie one outside Buckingham Palace, snorting coke off her tits.

God.

Exactly.

Georgia's ears felt hot as she waited for the lift. She jabbed at the button. She hated people knowing her weak spot. Hated it.

The lift arrived and she flung herself into it. She was not what you'd call in a party mood now. The celebs behaving badly had better watch out.

Her mobile was ringing as she got into the cab. Georgia loved her phone. It brought her gossip, interviews, all sorts of interesting invitations. She fished it out of her bag and looked at the caller display. *Mum*, it said. She rolled her eyes and sent the call to her voicemail. Why oh why had she given her parents her mobile number? She should have known they'd be phoning her up every five bloody minutes. And what scintillating tale would it be this time?

Eh, George, you'll never guess, Mrs Bradstock has got new curtains.

Ever so nice they are, from that IKEA at Warrington. I must take you there next time you're home. When ARE you coming home, anyway?

All right, Georgie, you missed a cracker on Saturday at the footie. The lads played a blinder! I took our Ned and he loved it. Proper little fan he's getting nowadays, you should see him on the terraces!

Georgie, Nan wants to know if you're coming up for her birthday. Have you remembered it's her eightieth? She's hired the social club on the High Street and all her mates from bingo have clubbed together to put on a spread. Let us know, won't you? You're welcome any time . . .

Gaaahhh. Welcome any time. Right. Like she wanted to go all the way up the M6 to sit in Stockport Social Club with her nan and decrepit Aunty Ada and the rest of the cronies. Like she wanted to suffer the million disapproving looks from her sister Carol and her smug hubby David. Like she wanted to have Carol's tedious kids Ned and Elsie clambering all over her, leaking snot and other noxious substances on her designer clothes! Like she wanted to sit in Mum and Dad's brown woodchip kitchen, drinking tea out of Dad's Stockport County mug (Up the Hatters! 'You watch yourself with that, Georgie, a family heirloom that is'), listening to tales from their dull northern lives in the same house, in the same street, in the same grim part of the world.

Why – WHY – would she want to go there, when she lived and worked in London, had champagne-fuelled parties to go to every night of the week, had an address book stuffed with famous people's numbers, her very own flat in Clapham, a job that she adored?

Quite. No contest. So no, she wouldn't be going to Nan's party. And no, she didn't want to go and see the flaming Hatters with her dad, David and snot-dripping Ned. And no, not ever, would she go to Warrington IKEA with her mum. Not unless she was having some kind of mental breakdown.

Georgia had left The North behind her, thank you very much, escaping across the Pennines and down the motorway on a National Express coach, a letter from London University in her bag. And she'd never looked back, barely glanced in that direction again. She'd modulated her northern vowels, adopting an estuary London accent instead (although – annoyingly – every now and then, when pissed, she'd lapse into Lancashire far too easily). She never mentioned her family to anyone. It was easier that way. Travel light, was Georgia's motto. No family baggage slowing her down. No husband or boyfriend baggage holding her back. She was happy to go it alone. Happy to be here in a taxi speeding through London on her way to somewhere fabulous and glitzy.

So why didn't her parents get the message? Why couldn't she ram it into their thick skulls that she had shucked them off, like a coat that was too small for her?

Too small and too unfashionable. She'd never be wearing it again. Couldn't they see that?

''Ere you are, sweet'eart,' the cabbie said, pulling up on Greek Street.

'Cheers, mate,' Georgia said, signing the expense slip with a flourish. She slammed the taxi door shut, tossed her hair back and strode up to the entrance of the bar. With a polite smile at the bouncer on the door (you had to be nice to these people, you never knew when you might need them on your side) and a flash of her invite, she was in.

Straight to the bar as usual, a brief glance about her to see who she recognized on the way. There was her snapper, Alan, already taking photos of the guests, swift and sure, clocking everything of interest. There were a couple of young footballers, excellent, they were sure to get drunk and disgrace themselves. A girl band sipping cocktails and giggling. Hopefully up for some mutual disgracing with the sports studs. A couple of record-company nerds – she wouldn't waste time on them. Oh, and Candi's PR people of course, sucking up left, right and centre. Air-kiss, air-kiss, mwah, mwah, darling! No sign of Candi yet, though, but that wasn't a surprise. The birthday girl would have to make some kind of entrance.

Hmmm. There was an interestingly broody-looking guy further along the bar. Georgia's celeb radar was going overtime, but she couldn't place him. Sexy and chiselled, she wrote in her head, filing the details away in case she needed them later. Thirty-something. Battered brown leather jacket. Designer jeans. Dark brown hair artfully tousled with a sneaky slick of product. An actor, perhaps? Indie band member?

'Champagne, please,' she said with a big smile at the girl who was serving behind the bar. 'And . . .' She leaned over the bar — mercifully not sticky yet — 'do you know who that bloke is?'

The barmaid gave Sexy Chiselled man a glance. 'He's from that programme, isn't he?' she said, setting a champagne flute in front of Georgia. 'What's it, again? Me boyfriend likes it. That horrible one where they cut up bodies.'

Georgia didn't watch a lot of telly. Too busy out partying. But she tried to keep up with the big programmes, the ones everyone talked about, as best she could, with the help of her Sky Plus box. '*Silent Witness*?' she guessed. 'One of those forensic things?'

'Yeah, something like that,' the barmaid said, wrinkling her nose in distaste. 'Not my cup of tea, all those dead bodies, but . . .'

Georgia pressed a fiver into the barmaid's hand. 'Be a darling for me and find out his name, will you?'

The barmaid tucked the note into her jeans pocket. 'Give me two minutes,' she said with a wink.

Georgia sipped her champagne, checking out what was happening elsewhere while she waited. The footballers were getting rowdy already, bless their moronic little hearts. The girl band were becoming screechy and giggly, in a look-at-us-we're-famous sort of way. Très irritating. And ...

Her mobile was ringing again. Caller display: *Mum*.

For God's sake!!

Georgia put the call to voicemail again as the barmaid came back. 'Adam Tennant,' she said in a breathy whisper. 'Quite sexy, isn't he?'

'Thanks,' Georgia said, sliding off her bar stool. She took her champagne glass and walked purposefully over towards Chiselled Adam. 'Hi there, Adam,' she said. 'I love your work. I'm Georgia. How do you know Candi, then? Wouldn't have put you two together.'

Alan was there in an instant, with his camera. 'This way, Adam!' he called out, and Georgia slid her arm around the actor's back and batted her eyelashes for the shot.

Adam Tennant had been reading about England's disastrous batting collapse in the sports section of the *Standard* (not a promising start; who brought a newspaper along to a party, anyway?), but folded the pages at Georgia's introduction and laid the paper on the bar. 'Hi,' he said as she stepped away from him again, photo taken. 'Candi and I have the same agent. I can't stand these dos if you must know, but I promised Marcy I'd show my face, so ...'

He had a deep voice, a tinge of Scottish in his accent. Very nice. Shame he looked so bored and uninterested.

'So, what are you working on at the moment?' Georgia went on. 'More episodes of . . .' Should she say *Silent Witness*? What if the barmaid had got it wrong? '. . . of the show, or something new? I do love that programme, you know. I never miss it.'

He gave her a strange look. 'Never miss it, eh?' he said. 'Right. So you'll have seen that last season my character was murdered by a vengeance-seeking hitman?'

'Ahh,' said Georgia. She flashed him her best girlish smile. 'How could I have forgotten? So obviously you're *not* making any new episodes—'

He got to his feet. 'Nope,' he said. 'If you'll excuse me, I've just seen someone I need to speak to.'

And off he went. Rude Adam Tennant. She'd keep an eye on *him*, then. Try and work in a dig for her party write-up. Who did he think he was?

Her phone was ringing. Caller display: *Mum*. Again! She switched it to voicemail, jabbing at the button with a rising annoyance. For crying out loud! Mum might not have anything better to do than sit her big arse on the brown corduroy sofa and chit-chat on the blower all evening, but Georgia had to work!

She slipped her phone away again. The music from the

club seemed to have been turned up and was booming around her. Someone jostled her, spilling her drink.

'Are you Georgia? Knight On The Town?'

She turned at the voice, a shout above the thumping bass. There was a Page Three girl, huge creamy boobs jutting out of a ridiculously small white cropped top. SLUT was written across the straining material in bright pink letters. Classy.

Aimee Morello, Georgia reminded herself. Former girl-friend of Warren Blake, Arsenal's latest wunderkid.

'Yes?'

She had a fleck of coke dangling from one nostril, did Aimee. Chewing gum at the side of her mouth. Her eyes were glazed, and when she talked it was on super-speed. 'Well, don't say I told you this, right, but take it from me, Warren has got the tiniest dick I've ever seen. And I've seen a few, d'you know what I'm saying? But his is like a chipolata. And he don't even know what to do with it. Oh yeah, and get this, he's been paying all these call girls. Not for sex, right, he just wants them to spank him. Pervy like that, is Warren. Make sure you get it all in your column, yeah?'

Ahh, the woman scorned. Always wanting Georgia to run these 'crap-in-bed' snippets about their cheating exes. Sleazy as anything. Georgia felt jaded. She wasn't in the mood for this tonight.

'Sure,' she said, turning away. 'Leave it with me.'

She made a few cursory notes, eavesdropped on a couple of guys from a boy band slagging off their manager, and then a juicy confessional conversation in the ladies' toilets about a certain supermodel's latest tantrum, all the while noting the copy in her brain. The soundtrack, the outfits, the canapés, she was hot on the specifics, Georgia. It was what kept her readers hooked.

Her phone was ringing again. The caller display read: *Number withheld*. Ahh, the old number withheld. Usually an anonymous tip-off.

She pressed the button to accept the call. 'Could you hold the line, please? I'm just going outside where it's quieter,' she said into the mouthpiece, walking quickly out of the front doors. It was dark in the street now, and getting chilly. 'Sorry about that,' she said. 'Georgia Knight here. Can I help you?'

'It's Mum,' came the reply. 'I'm at the hospital. Bad news, love.' Her voice broke into a sob. 'It's your nan.'

Alice's Hen Weekend

November 2002

Alice Johnson lowered herself into the pool and leaned back against the tiled surface. Jets of water bubbled up beneath her Lycra-clad bottom, pummelling her thighs, making her insides feel as if they were vibrating. *Let's hope they break up the cellulite before the wedding*, Alice thought to herself, crossing her fingers under the water.

She closed her eyes and inhaled the warm, faintly perfumed air, trying not to think about how many bottoms had sat there before hers. Bubble, bubble, pummel, pummel. Quite uncomfortable after a while. Like having your legs in a washing machine on the tough-stains cycle, she imagined. Still, she was forking out enough cash for this place, she felt obliged to kid herself it was perfect.

'This is bliss,' she murmured dutifully, wondering how long she'd have to sit there before she could return to dry land.

'Mmmm, heavenly,' Katie said, from across the jacuzzi.

Alice wondered if there would be a jacuzzi at their honeymoon hotel. If there was, Jake was sure to want to have sex in it. He said all that spurting water turned him on. Mind you, anything turned him on. Just the word 'spurt' was probably enough to give him a semi.

Jake seemed to think about sex every other second. He was fond of telling Alice how often she gave him 'the horn', as he so charmingly phrased it. Bending over to put a video in the machine – that gave him the horn. Rolling over in bed at night – that gave him the horn. Whenever Alice was in the shower – oh yes, that really gave him the horn. She'd have only just squirted the shampoo onto her palm (squirt – another word that did it for him) and he'd be in there with her, cock at a right angle, telling her that God, he just couldn't resist joining her . . .

It was flattering that he wanted to get her knickers down constantly, really. A compliment that he was always attempting to feel her up when she was getting dressed, or making a cup of tea, or trying to watch *Coronation Street*.

All the same . . . it was exhausting. *Would marriage calm him down?* she wondered. *Would being a husband tame the rampant horn?* Somehow she doubted it.

'Where's Georgia, by the way?' Katie asked drowsily. 'I haven't seen her for a while.'

'She went off for her massage ages ago,' Alice said, opening her eyes and glancing around the room for a clock. No clock. Of course. People here were meant to be relaxing, not clock-watching. Georgia had been gone a long time, though, Alice was sure. Knowing Georgia, she was up to something. She'd probably lucked in with a fit male masseur who was giving her a very special rub-down. 'Any extras?' Alice could imagine Georgia asking in that throaty purr of hers. No doubt she herself would get a skinny bitch for *her* massage, who'd sneer disapprovingly at Alice's wobbly bits while Alice had her eyes shut. 'God, I had a dumpy one just now,' Alice could already imagine the woman saying to her colleagues afterwards. 'Legs like marshmallows, no muscle tone whatsoever!'

She tried not to dwell on that. Or on Georgia and her masseur, having a bunk-up in the towel cupboard.

Actually, now that she came to think about it, Georgia was probably on the phone to someone from the paper. Alice was amazed that Georgia had come all the way out of London, to the Cotswolds, for her hen weekend. Originally she'd said no, sorry, she was too busy with work and Alice had felt crestfallen because she'd only invited Katie and Georgia, and what good was a hen night with only one other hen?

Luckily, Georgia had called back to say that actually she

could come, but she could only stay the Saturday night and she'd have to get the train back early-ish on Sunday, okay?

Alice didn't mind the conditions. She was so grateful that Georgia was coming at all, she'd said yes, fine, thank you to everything. She couldn't help wondering if Katie had leaned on Georgia a bit, talked her into coming. Probably. Katie was nice like that. Or perhaps Georgia had had a tip-off that one of her celebs was checking in for a weekend too. She could never resist a sniff of gossip.

It still seemed something of a dream to Alice that she was having a hen night in the first place. A miracle that she, quiet Alice Johnson, was having a wedding, *getting married* to sexy, charismatic Jake Archer. A lot of the time, she found herself checking the ring on her finger, making sure she hadn't imagined the whole thing. But it was true. And he was so gorgeous. So funny. And such a good actor, even if Hollywood hadn't realized that yet. (Or Theatre-land in London, for that matter. But give it time. They were sure to realize he had talent with a capital T soon.) And oh yes, he loved her! He wanted to marry her! She could hardly believe her luck.

The bubbling and pummelling had turned her legs to jelly. She clambered out of the pool and wrapped a soft white towel around herself. 'I'm going for a swim,' she told Katie, who still had her eyes shut. 'See you in a bit.'

She was having a lovely time, she told herself as she wandered down to the main pool, cocooned in white fluffiness, hoping her legs weren't looking too much like gooseflesh. A hen weekend here in a spa, with a salt-scrub back massage to look forward to later this afternoon (she hoped it wouldn't be too painful) and an evening of good food and wine with her two best friends tonight. Best of all, she had a bed of her own upstairs – clean crisp sheets and duvet, and nobody pestering her for a shag in the middle of the night.

Not 'pestering'. No. That sounded as if she was moaning. And she wasn't, of course. Why would she moan about Jake? He was absolutely perfect. And, in just three weeks' time, he'd be her husband.

'So, not long to go, eh?' Georgia said that evening over dinner. 'Are you all sorted for the big day?'

Alice swallowed a mouthful of rocket salad (she'd barely eaten a single calorie for weeks) and smiled. 'Nearly,' she said. 'It's all just about coming together. I've finished the dress, pretty much—'

'Ooh, what's it like?' Katie put in, spooning more potatoes onto her plate and slipping a few onto Alice's.

'Well, the dress itself is quite ordinary – it's strapless and very tight on the waist, which is why I'm dieting like mad,' Alice replied, putting the potatoes straight back in the dish. 'But I've also made this gorgeous fluffy faux-fur muff and...' She bit her lip. 'I'm thinking about a cape as well. I've found this beautiful red velvet fabric, but I'm not sure if it's too much of a Superman vibe. Or Little Red Riding Hood.'

'Sounds fab to me,' Georgia said. 'I think winter weddings are lovely – really magical. How are you decorating the church?'

'Lots of holly and ivy garlands, big fat candles and fairy lights,' Alice said dreamily. 'And poinsettias too.' She giggled. 'Jake quite fancied some fake snow, but I drew the line at that. No sleigh bells either.'

'It's going to be brilliant,' Katie said. 'Go on, then, who have you put us on a table with? Has Jake got any sexy single mates you can seat us next to?'

Georgia glugged back her wine. 'Please tell me he's bezzy mates with Daniel Craig, Alice. Please!'

Alice shook her head. 'Sorry,' she said. 'Jake's mates are all scruffy indie-kid sorts. Anyway, what are you on about, I bet you're always bumping into Daniel Craig at your glam parties, Georgia. You don't need me and Jake to sort you out with some totty, surely!'

Georgia wrinkled her nose. 'Well, I wouldn't say no,' she replied. 'It's wall-to-wall WAGs and bimbos for me these days. I'm getting a bit fed up of it, to be honest. I reckon another year and I'll be done on the showbiz circuit.

Any longer and I'll be burned out, or an alcoholic. Or just a hard-hearted bitch, like some of the other gossip girls.' She poured everyone another glass of wine. 'It eats away at you after a while, this job. Sometimes I wonder about giving it all up to write my best-selling novel.'

'Oh yeah?' Katie looked up with interest. 'What best-selling novel is this, then?'

Georgia shrugged. 'Oh, you know, just a little pipe dream. Something I've been thinking about for a while. But I need to stockpile some savings first if I'm ever going to manage it, so I guess I'm stuck where I am for the time being.' She smiled. 'Anyway, enough about me. We're here for Alice after all. Lovely Alice and lovely Jake. Here's to years of happiness and hot sex.'

Alice blushed, but Katie was already raising her glass. 'Happiness and hot sex!'

Chapter Three

Everything Changes

Saturday, 14 June 2008

Alice turned the key in the lock and pushed the door. It didn't budge. Great. That was a good start.

She wiggled the key tentatively, twisting the door handle at the same time. Still nothing.

Behind her, on the front path to the cottage, Iris was crying in her car seat and kicking her bare feet. A bead of sweat trickled down Alice's back. Just her luck that she'd decided to move house on the hottest day of the year. Just her luck that she couldn't even get *in* her new house!

She yanked the door handle a degree more fiercely, turning the key so hard now she almost expected the top half to snap off in her fingers. 'All right, Iris, just a sec,' she murmured, trying to sound as soothing as she could, while her daughter ramped up the volume, veering danger-ously towards full-throttle sobs.

'You need to give it a shove, my love,' came an amused voice from further behind her. A rich country burr, strong enough to churn the butter, as her mum would say.

Alice turned and wiped her sweaty forehead with her bare arm. A man was leaning over the front gate, her dad's age, white curly hair, his face nut-brown, the colour and texture of shoe leather. 'Hello,' she said, feeling flustered as she joggled Iris's car seat with her foot. Still Iris wailed, becoming redder and redder in the face.

'Give the door a shove,' the man said again. 'It's swollen in the heat, is all. Always sticking, that door.'

Alice wasn't sure if she liked how familiar this complete stranger was with her new front door. But he was watch-ing her expectantly and Iris was still grizzling, hot tears spouting out of her grey eyes, fists banging up and down. So she put the key in again, twisted it (hard), turned the door handle (hard), and gave it a smart shove with her bottom.

The door swung open, and Alice went stumbling in after it.

The man hanging over the gate laughed. 'There she goes!' he said. He gave her a mock salute. 'Cheerio now!'

'Thanks,' Alice said, righting herself and standing on the threshold. But he was already off, whistling as he went down the road. 'Um ... cheerio!' she called after him, and he raised a weathered hand in the air in acknowledgement.

She bent down to Iris, who looked as if she were about to explode, and released her from the straps. 'Come on, tired girl,' Alice said, scooping her up. She could smell the lavender from the dusty flowerbed nearby now that she was crouching. Bees droned around the purple heads, dive-bombing through the leggy grey stems. Alice stood up and patted Iris's back. 'Let's go and see our new house.'

Iris sobbed into her shoulder, her tears wetting Alice's top, as they stepped over the threshold. Alice could see her daughter's point. It was dark and dingy in there after the glaring sun outside. Dark, dingy, cluttered with old furniture, and ripe with a choking musty smell. Oh God. It was so much smaller than she remembered it.

She walked across the room – which took all of three steps – and sank into an armchair that had stuffing leaking from its side like Father Christmas beards. It creaked under her weight and she leaned back gingerly, Iris still attached to her like a sniffling baby monkey. Oh no. What had she done, agreeing to this?

By rights, she should be with Jake, in their Chelsea flat, bought three years ago when his career went into orbit and he landed his first big Brit-flick deal. By rights, they'd be snuggled up on that ridiculously large bed he'd bought, all three of them, one big happy family on the Egyptian cotton sheets. By rights, Iris would be dressed top to toe in organic fleecy baby clothes, instead of charity-shop bargains, and . . .

The tears were leaking down her cheeks, dripping into Iris's tufty black hair like rain. Instead, here she was, making a so-called new start, in this grotty little cottage in the arse-end of Nowhere. How had things gone so spectacularly wrong?

'I never liked him,' her mum had said loyally. 'Never thought he was good enough for you. Nor did your dad.'

But that wasn't the point, was it? *Alice* had thought Jake was good enough for her (too good, actually, if truth be told). And once upon a time, Jake had seemed to think they were good enough for each other, too. He'd married her, hadn't he?

She looked down at her wedding ring, still on her finger. She couldn't bear to take it off. Her fingers had puffed up so much during the pregnancy that the ring had hurt her, cut into her, the metal leaving red tracks on her tender skin. But Alice — stupid, devoted Alice! — had ignored the pain and carried on wearing it. It was a symbol, wasn't it? A symbol of eternal love.

Ha. That was a laugh. Eternal disappointment, more like. The puffiness from her swollen fingers had long since gone; after Jake had unceremoniously ditched her ('In your condition, too! Has the man a heart of stone?' her mum had railed), she'd seemed to shrink with misery. The ring spun loosely on her finger now. One of these days it would drop off when she wasn't paying attention, and she'd lose it. Her mind, as well as the ring, that was.

Alice hoisted Iris higher on her shoulder and delved into her skirt pocket for a tissue. It hit her every now and then, the full sick horror of what had happened. She almost thought it would have been easier if Jake had died. At least then she could grieve his loss wholeheartedly, safe in the knowledge that a line had been drawn, a chapter closed. At least then nobody would say such bloody irritating things to her.

'Well, you've certainly seen his true colours now, Alice.' That had been Georgia, of course – before Alice had slammed the phone down on her. Like Alice gave two hoots for anything Georgia Knight had to say any more, after what she'd done. The bitch.

'You're well shot of the cheating pig.' Katie, trying to be supportive. But it was all right for Katie, wasn't it? She was super-confident and super-independent. She'd never bought into the 'til-death-do-us-part line in the first place – well, if you discounted that moment of matrimonial madness with Neil whatever-his-name-was.

'Plenty more fish in the sea!' And that tactless, completely unhelpful reminder had been from her mum. Fish – ha. Who wanted a fish? And why hadn't anyone thought to warn Alice about the sharks?

Alice got to her feet. She would *not* think about Jake anyway. The whole point about this wretched new start was that she was moving on from those miserable, exhausting months at her parents' house, where she'd stayed in the aftermath of the split. There she'd slept in her old bedroom, with the Eighties' grey-and-red zigzaggy wallpaper still miraculously intact, tossing and turning under her old Snoopy duvet on that single bed until her belly had been like a distended, vein-riddled space hopper.

Even then, she'd held out hope, through the last waddling days of pregnancy and right through the agonizing blur of labour. She kept expecting he'd stride into the delivery suite, clutching flowers, chocolates, helium balloons, soft velvety teddy bears. 'I'm her husband,' he'd announce to the midwives in his rich actor's voice, his eyes moist with emotion. 'I'm the father.'

But no. No such announcements. No plush teddies or balloons. It seemed as though being husband *and* father was too much for Jake to take on board. He hadn't shown. Not through the messy screams of the birth (and all that blood! Alice was quite glad he hadn't witnessed the full-blown gore of it. He'd never have wanted sex with her again). Not through the sweet moment of triumph when the midwife had placed Alice's warm wet baby into her arms and said, 'It's a girl!' And not for all those days and weeks after the birth, when Alice and her daughter had clung together, overwhelmed and bewildered, like sole survivors on a shipwreck.

She'd called him with the news, obviously. Well, tried to, anyway. She had left the news on his voicemail because he never took her calls. She'd sent him a card too, and some photos of her beautiful girl (*their* beautiful girl), face like a fuzzy peach, eyes tight shut, dreamy milky smile playing around her lips. Alice knew — absolutely knew — that once Jake saw just how gorgeous, how utterly enchanting their daughter was, he'd be back.

He wasn't.

She'd waited until the last possible day to register Iris's birth because she'd hoped Jake would sweep in at the final hour — his greatest romantic lead role yet — so that they could discuss baby names together. She felt unqualified to bestow a name on their daughter without his help. What if she chose a name and he didn't like it?

'Then it's his hard cheese, isn't it?' her mum had sniffed. 'He's had more than enough chances. How about Sophie?'

It had plunged Alice into despair, the naming business. It seemed such a huge responsibility to choose a name for another person. What if she got it wrong? 'Jake used to have a golden retriever called Sophie when he was growing up,' Alice had replied dolefully. 'I can't call her that.'

'Hmmph, and I bet he treated that dog a damn sight

better than he's treating his own daughter,' her mum had muttered. 'How about Rosie, then? That's pretty.'

Rosie *was* pretty, admittedly, but what if she went on to be a lawyer, a politician, an engineer? Was Rosie substantial enough a name? Besides, 'Rosie' always made her think of the Websters' daughter in *Coronation Street* and Alice found herself saying it 'Rurzeh' as Sally Webster did, to rhyme with 'jersey'.

The name Iris had come to her at the last. Yes, okay, if she was honest, it was partly because Jake had given her a bunch of irises on their first date. (Alice could still remember the way they'd dripped down her skirt through the soggy paper at the bottom of the bouquet. She'd pretended not to notice at the time.) It was partly the Jake connection, even though she doubted he'd get the link, doubted he even remembered where they'd *been* on their first date (a sweet little pub just round the corner from the National Theatre).

Flowers aside, there was also something wild and free and romantic about the name Iris. That was what Alice wanted for her daughter. Maybe not so much the wildness (she was already dreading the teenage years – Iris had a ferocious enough temper on her at the age of eight months). Freedom – that was what she hoped Iris would have. Freedom and romance. Two of life's most wonderful experiences. Until everything went pear-shaped, obviously.

The only thing she'd had from Jake since the split had been a cheque for a lot of money which his manager had forwarded. Jake had sold the Chelsea flat and had given her half the profit. Which was very handy and meant Alice wouldn't have to work for a while, but all the same ... There wasn't even a note from him, just a Post-it from his rotten manager explaining the sale. Big deal.

The last Alice knew of him — via a paragraph in *Heat* magazine — was that he was in LA auditioning for something with Orlando Bloom. No doubt her devoted husband would be knobbing every starlet he could get his hands on.

She sighed, ruffling the downy hairs on the back of her daughter's head. Iris reached out a pink fist and grabbed Alice's ponytail in return. Tug, tug.

Get over it, Alice. Move on. New start, remember?

She got to her feet. 'Let's look round our new start,' she murmured to Iris, who let go of her hair and began to make sucking motions on Alice's shoulder, nuzzling the fabric of her T-shirt to one side, in order to get a gummy suction seal on her bare skin. Alice kissed her daughter's head. It was nice, she reminded herself, having someone else crave her body, her bare skin, even if it wasn't her husband.

So this was the living room. Why did it look so titchy today, this gloomy little square of space? Cosy, the letting agent had called it, when he'd showed her the cottage the other week. Sweet, Alice had thought to herself back then, gazing around. The windows had been flung open, and there had been fresh white roses in an earthenware jug on the mantelpiece, scenting the room. The person who'd rented it before Alice had had colourful pictures on the walls, photos of grandchildren (she guessed) and bright drapes of material across the sofa. It had felt like a safe place. A place where good things happened.

'Of course, it'll be let fully furnished,' the letting agent had assured her with yet another smarmy smile. And Alice had gazed around at the small oak bookcase stuffed with paperbacks, the rich red rug in front of the fireplace, and the grandchildren beaming out from the photos with their brushed hair and spotless school uniforms, and said, 'I'll take it.'

Since then, Alice had stupidly remembered the cheerful accessories of her predecessor whenever she'd thought about moving in. She'd remembered the feel of the place, rather than what lay beneath the cushions and photos and roses.

Now the room seemed bare, with its rough-plastered walls, tiny window and manky greying net curtain blocking out the light with its dirt. There was a telly that looked as if it had been salvaged from the ark – she doubted she'd be able to get E4 on *that* – and dust on the old stone mantelpiece.

The front door, which she'd left open, cast a slant of

sunlight over the grubby carpet. The rug had gone, too, of course.

So, suicide-inducing living room aside, what other delights were in store for her here? She hardly dared look now. She'd probably discover there was no running water, or no electricity or something. Why hadn't she been more thorough about checking over her new home? Why had she been won over by someone's photos and flowers? What a sucker the letting agent must have thought her.

Into the tiny kitchen she went. It was clean, at least; she could see the faint smears of Flash or something similar on the hob where some well-meaning person had wiped around the gas rings. The bright blue teapot she'd seen on the previous visit had gone, along with the cluster of mugs. No checked tea towel lay drying on the radiator now. The dripping tap competed with a ticking clock as to who could mark time better.

Who lives in a house like this? Loyd Grossman said in Alice's head. *Let's consider the evidence. It's shabby and small. It's dingy and dusty. Of course! It's single-mum loser Alice and fatherless Iris!*

Upstairs wasn't a whole lot cheerier. One titchy bathroom with pink tiles and a smell of mould. (Why hadn't she noticed those pink tiles? Too busy looking at all the nice toiletries lined up on the shelves probably.) Two dinky bedrooms with ceilings that sloped so sharply Alice considered checking out bargain crash helmets on eBay. She sat on the bed in one of the rooms, the bare mattress prickling her legs, and joggled Iris on her knee, wishing that she'd taken her parents up on their offer to help her move in.

Right now, she wanted her mum to make her a cup of tea and produce a Tupperware box of butterfly cakes from her bag.

Right now, she wanted her dad to be checking the boiler wasn't about to blow up, and that there was a nice solid lock on the front door.

She wasn't going to cry. She was *not* going to cry. She was thirty-five, for heaven's sake, it wasn't like she'd never been away from home. It was just that after nine months in the safety of her parents' house, where the washing and ironing were always done, the fridge was always full, and the hot water was always piping, this felt like a serious crash back down to earth.

She'd been existing in some kind of safety chamber all the time she'd been staying there. A bubble of creature comforts – clean bedding, cups of tea every half an hour, the crossword to tackle with her dad every evening once Iris was asleep. A bubble where she was protected from all the horrors of the real world.

Alice Johnson has left the bubble, a deep Hollywood voice said in her mind, and she sighed. She just had to get used to normal life again, that was all. She was taking her first wobbling steps alone, after Mum and Dad had helped her along for so many months. She couldn't help wondering what they would be doing, now that she and Iris had finally moved out. When you spent a lot of time with people, you got to know their rhythms, you tuned into their daily routines. So let's see, Saturday afternoon. Mum would probably be out in the garden, watering her tomatoes or picking peapods to shell for tea. Dad would be listening to the cricket on the radio while he—

Alice froze. The front door had creaked downstairs. Was that the wind, or had someone just pushed their way past it?

She glanced out of the window. She could see fields and woodland — her brain dimly registered what an amazing view it was — but the trees were dead still. Not even a breeze to ruffle their shaggy green heads.

Her heart thumped as she heard footsteps. Someone was in the house. Someone was coming upstairs.

Now she wished more than ever that her parents were there. Her mum, with her scary line in questions and hard stares. Her dad, with a spanner snatched up from his toolkit.

'Hello?' A male voice floated up the stairs. 'Anybody in?'

She got to her feet, clutching Iris, her hands feeling clammy. 'Who's that?' she called as loudly as she could, trying to sound confident, as if strange men inviting

themselves into her house was an everyday occurrence. Well
– you know.

'Gah!' Iris pronounced, her fingers yanking at Alice's top
and pushing a fold of it into her mouth.

A man appeared in the doorway. 'Ahh – there you are,'
he said, ducking his head. He looked rather discomfited to
see Alice's bare shoulder and bra strap where Iris was
rearranging her T-shirt, and stepped back, whacking himself on the sloped ceiling.

Alice felt her heart slow. If he *was* a burglar, he was a
pretty inept one. She bit her lip, trying not to smile. It was
rude to laugh at someone when they'd just crocked themselves, wasn't it? 'You want to watch that ceiling,' she told
the man. 'It creeps up on you, you know.'

He was rubbing his head, smiling back at her. He was
quite nice-looking for a burglar, she thought, with his
untidy dark hair and open, friendly features. Tall, too – he
looked like a giant, hunched over in the small bedroom,
reminiscent of Alice in the White Rabbit's house. Suddenly
she felt conscious of the fact that they were both standing
here near the bed, two adults in a confined space. He was
blocking the doorway, the only exit other than the small
square window. She glanced back at it, just in case she
needed to escape.

'I'm Dom,' he said, holding out his hand. 'Your new
neighbour. Well, sort of. I'm down the road anyway. Maud

– the old lady who used to live here – she told me there was someone moving in today, so I thought I'd say hello.'

Very friendly. Suspiciously friendly? Alice had become wary of wolves in sheep's clothing. Particularly male wolves. She gave a polite smile and shook his hand. 'Hello. I'm Alice,' she said. She withdrew her hand quickly and returned it to the safety of Iris's warm body. It had been odd to see her fingers wrapped in another man's again. His palm felt rough and his skin was brown, unlike Jake's pristine white never-done-the-washing-up hands. He was probably a farm-hand or something, this Dom. She had a sudden image of him stripped to the waist, throwing hay bales onto a trailer, and felt her cheeks surge with colour.

'Well, nice to meet you,' she said briskly, hoping the room was gloomy enough for him not to have noticed her blush. 'I'd better start unpacking.'

Hint taken, he nodded and ducked carefully as he went out of the room. 'If there's anything you need, or anything I can help with . . .' he began saying.

Alice followed him down the stairs. 'I'm fine, thanks,' she interrupted.

He didn't seem to have heard. 'Shelves putting up, or a cot fitting together for the baby, or . . .'

'I can put up my own shelves, thanks,' Alice told him. She didn't mean to sound so curt, especially as it was a complete lie, but now she wanted him out. Friendly as he was, he felt like an intruder. She wanted to close the front door again and seal herself into the new house as quickly as she could. Just her and Iris, safe and locked in, where no one could get to them.

''Course you can,' he replied easily. 'You don't need some patronizing bloke coming round here with his drill and rawl plugs, do you? Sorry. I'll leave you to it, then. Bye!'

He raised a hand in farewell, and Alice felt wrong-footed. Had she offended him? 'Thanks,' she said, going along the path a few steps after him. 'Cheers, then. Bye!'

He was off, loping to the gate and dipping his head again as he went through the rambling-rose arch that adorned it. Suddenly Alice wished she hadn't been so hasty to get rid of him. She hadn't meant to sound rude, it was just that this was supposed to be her first stab at independence, wasn't it? It would have been a bit pathetic if she'd caved in and accepted help from the first random stranger.

All right, *second* random stranger, if you counted that old guy who'd advised her about shoving against the front door. All these men so keen to interfere and meddle with her new start! She felt like some prim Victorian governess repelling their advances, shooing them away.

Anyway, what did this Dom person expect, coming into her house – into her bedroom! – uninvited like that? There was friendly, sure, but there was in-your-face, too. She hoped the rest of the village weren't going to be so full on. They were probably all discussing her in the shop already. 'Seems a bit clueless to me. Couldn't even get into the house on her own!'

'Right bad-tempered she was to me. I was only trying to help!'

Alice stalked into the house, heaving up a suitcase as she did so. Dom would probably be back on his tractor or mucking out the pigs now, or whatever it was that he did. The old guy would be supping a pint of warm ale on a velour banquette in the Duke of York, the pub she'd seen on the main street. Meanwhile, she had stuff to do. She had to clean the floor before she dared put Iris down on it for starters. She had to tuck the stuffing back into the armchair too, before her eagle-eyed daughter spotted it and tugged out a handful to press into her little wet mouth.

Then she had to unpack her meagre possessions, get some shopping in for their tea tonight and ... Oh yeah. She still had Iris's cot, all in bits, in the boot of her car, to reassemble. Bugger. She wished more than ever that she'd taken Dom up on his offer now. She hadn't a clue how to fit the damn thing together.

She heaved a sigh and set to work.

Chapter Four

Love Ain't Here Anymore

Saturday, 14 June 2008

'I can't believe you said no. Are you completely insane?'

Katie could hear Georgia puffing smoke down the phone and found herself flinching away from the handset as if coils of the stuff might start filtering through the holes. 'I don't think so,' she replied, considering. 'Just ... freaked out. It was a bit of a shock.'

'God,' Georgia said. 'I can't believe it. You really said no?' She sounded incredulous. Appalled, even. Katie could imagine her dark eyebrows shooting into a ten-to-two position. 'Why? What's got into you?'

Katie snorted. 'What's got into me?' she echoed. 'Since when did you become Ms Happy-Ever-After? I thought you were on my side, that marriage was a waste of money and ... and a pointless charade, or whatever it was you said?'

'Oh yes, I agree with all that – for me, anyway,' Georgia said. 'But *you* – you're the marrying kind, Kate. In the nicest possible way, obviously . . .'

'You mean, I'm the sensible, traditional type while you're the bohemian free spirit,' Katie put in sarcastically.

'Well, no, but . . . Yes, kind of,' Georgia conceded. Georgia didn't just give you the truth, she beat you round the head with it sometimes. 'It's just . . . I don't know. I'd have thought you'd have said yes, that's all.'

'Well, I didn't. I said no. So there you go. Maybe I'm not as predictable and sensible as you think.'

'I never said—'

'How about you, anyway, how's work?' Katie asked, to change the subject. The disastrous proposal had thrummed around her head ever since Steve had asked That Question. It was like radio static, crackling away in the back of her mind, irritating, niggling.

Georgia sighed. 'Yeah, it's good, but . . . Hang on—' There was a muffled whooshing noise, like waves breaking on a beach, and Katie guessed she'd put her hand over the receiver. Then came the faint strains of Georgia snapping petulantly at some poor sod or other, 'Look, I'm on the phone! All right, keep your hair on!', then she came back on the line. 'Sorry about that. Aaaargh, the joys of nutters in Euston,' she said. 'I'm only off up north for my sins, aren't I? I'd better go. Train leaves in a few minutes and I'm still out here with my ciggy. Speak to you soon.'

Before Katie could even say goodbye, Georgia had hung up. *Strange*, Katie thought. Off up north? Surely Georgia wasn't actually going to visit her family for once, was she? As far as Georgia was concerned, family life was further down the relevance scale than the breeding habits of wood-lice, say. She'd had to be persuaded (by Katie) into inviting her family to her wedding, even! She'd said they would hate it, so what was the point?

'The point is that they're your family!' Katie had argued. 'You've *got* to invite them!'

Georgia had caved in eventually, but only two weeks before the wedding itself, in the hope that none of them would be able to make it. Obviously, they'd cancelled all their plans and come Down South for their Georgie's Big Day though.

It had, admittedly, been a mistake. The poor clan of Knights had been unilaterally shunned by the wild-eyed bride with the same kind of contempt reserved usually for a dog turd on the pavement. Katie had tried to make up for Georgia's shocking rudeness by over-compensating on the niceness front to them, to the point where they seemed to think she was rather odd, a stalker possibly. 'Who *is* that girl?' Georgia's nan had said in the end, in a too-loud whisper. 'Why does she keep talking to us?'

Katie sighed, and put the phone back on its base. She felt disconcerted by the call. Of all people, she'd have thought Georgia would be the one who'd understand best. 'Good for you!' she'd imagined Georgia hooting, with perhaps a punched fist in the air. 'Well said. Marriage, my arse!'

That was why Katie had phoned her in the first place, to get some support, some acknowledgement that yes, of course she'd done the right thing in turning Steve down. Accusations of insanity had *not* been what she'd expected.

She stared miserably out of the kitchen window at the back garden. The lawn looked parched and brown. Plants were wilting and drooping where they hadn't been watered during last week's shock heatwave.

Steve's face when she'd told him no … something in him had seemed to collapse and wilt, too. She'd tried to say it kindly, tried to explain how she felt, but he'd taken it so personally he hadn't seemed able to listen past that initial 'no'. A rejection of him, that was how he'd seen it. It wasn't, though! It wasn't at all.

'Being married to Neil … it was a mistake,' she'd told him, sitting on the bed, reaching for his hand. 'There was nothing good about it, nothing. As soon as we'd made our vows, it was over, practically. It was as if he enjoyed the chase, but once we were man and wife, the thrill evaporated for him. And for me too, if I'm honest. I felt trapped. And

I don't ever want to get in a situation like that again. End of story.' She'd stared at his fingers, unresponsive and stiff in hers. 'Sorry,' she added quietly.

His eyes were baffled; he looked like a child who'd had a toy snatched away from him. 'But it wouldn't be like that with us,' he'd said. 'Us being married would be different to when you married your ex. Completely different.'

Would it? She hadn't replied. Steve was in another league to Neil, sure. Steve wouldn't expect her to drop everything in order to produce his heir(s), cook his tea and go on pant-washing patrol. Steve had done his fair share of hoovering, toilet-cleaning and supermarket-shopping in the six months since he'd moved in, admittedly. He put his dirty clothes (and hers) in the washing machine. He straightened the duvet if he was the last one up. He cooked, too, if he was the first one home. Spag bol *à la* student was a particular speciality, with grated Cheddar on top, or sometimes a cheat takeaway from the Indian. Not that she was complaining. At all. But . . .

'Is that it, then?' he'd asked. 'All over?' A bitterness had crept into his voice.

She sat there feeling worse than ever as she saw the bag of her things that he'd packed and brought to the hotel – her make-up, her perfume, nice knickers, toothbrush . . . He was so kind. So thoughtful. Other women would be clambering over her to get that ring off him, wouldn't they?

Other women would drag him up the aisle in an iron grip. So what was *her* problem?

'Oh, Steve,' she'd said. A lump was in her throat. 'No! Of course it doesn't have to be all over. I mean, I still—'

'You still what? Like me?' He looked at her, his eyes hard. 'Is that what you were going to say?'

She put her head in her hands. 'I *really* like you,' she said into her fingers. 'I love you.' Christ, how had they reached crisis point so quickly? Two minutes ago, they'd been cruising along Romance Boulevard; now, they seemed to have taken a wrong turn and had ended up hurtling towards Dumpsville. 'I don't want us to split up over this. Can't we just carry on like we were before? I mean, what was so wrong with that?'

She looked up at him, tears in her eyes. His shoulders were slumped; he looked defeated. 'Nothing was *wrong* with it,' he replied. 'I'd just like things to move on, that's all. Show the world that we want to be together. Make some vows. Make a commitment.'

She couldn't speak. She couldn't explain why the word 'commitment' gave her the urge to run for the hills. It wasn't as if she wanted to be back in the singles scene or anything – God, no thanks! – but somehow, being an unmarried couple felt freer than being a married couple. Commitment brought to mind his and hers dressing gowns, monogrammed with their initials on the pocket, hanging together on the back of the bedroom door. She didn't want a uniform his and hers anything. She didn't want ''til death do us part'. She wanted to hold back, keep some independence.

'Steve, I . . .' The words failed her. 'You are so lovely, to have thought all this up, planned everything so brilliantly.'

He raised an eyebrow. 'I sense a but coming,' he said.

She managed a weak smile. '*And*,' she went on, 'I'm flattered that you feel that way — really, I am. But commitment doesn't have to be about spending thousands of pounds on penguin suits and a meringue dress, and a buffet for Great-Aunt Edna and all those weird relatives you never see, and . . .'

'No, I agree,' he interrupted. 'It doesn't have to be those things at all.'

'. . . and it doesn't even need to be official,' she went on, sensing that he was misreading her point on purpose. 'Commitment can be about us living together, owning a house together, sharing our lives, supporting and loving one another.'

He nodded. 'Sounds like a vow to me,' he said.

'Well . . . what I'm trying to say is . . .'

He put a hand on hers. 'I know what you're trying to say,' he put in. 'But it's not just about getting married or not. How do you feel about having kids, for instance? We've never really talked about that.'

Oh Christ, thought Katie. He was really wheeling out the big guns for this conversation. 'No, we haven't,' she replied cautiously, trying to buy herself some time. Damn right, they hadn't — and deliberately so, for her part. She swallowed. 'How ... how do *you* feel about having kids, then?'

'I'd love to have kids,' he said simply. 'Our kids. I'd love to be a dad. I've always assumed I would be.' He was smiling as he looked at her, but she couldn't smile back. 'And now that I'm with you and we've had two really great years together, well ... we should start thinking about it. It's not as if either of us is getting any younger.'

Katie felt as if she were falling down a deep, deep hole. She could no longer hear what he was saying. She'd always been one for making plans, sure — lesson plans for the term ahead, weekend plans with friends and family, Christmas plans — oh yes, she liked all of those, ticking off lists in her notebook, making spreadsheets on the computer. She was an organized person.

But *life* plans ... marriage and children ... these were not on the spreadsheet. Not in the notebook, waiting to be neatly ticked off. These were things she had purposely ignored for a long time.

Steve had stopped talking. This was obviously her cue. But what should she say?

'Wow,' she murmured. 'I . . . I don't know. This all feels a bit sudden.'

He put an arm around her back, shuffled along the bed so that he was closer to her. 'There's a lot to think about, I know. But the thing is, Kate, we have to make some decisions. Because, to be honest with you, I . . .' He broke off. 'This is going to sound really melodramatic, like some kind of ultimatum. It's not. I'm just laying my cards on the table. If you really really don't want the same kind of future as I do – I mean, the family life thing – then . . . I need to know. Because it's important to me.'

She felt as if her breath had been sucked out of her. Bloody hell. Not an ultimatum? It sure as hell sounded like one. His cards were on the table all right, facing up for the world to see: King, Queen and three baby Aces.

She stared straight ahead but she could feel her hands shaking in her lap. 'I appreciate your honesty,' she said. She felt very formal all of a sudden, as if she were speaking politely to a stranger. 'And . . .' She licked her lips. 'And I think I need a drink.'

What was it with blokes and their 'marriage and children'? That was what Neil had wanted too. He'd got progressively more and more pissed off when Katie's period arrived each month. Little did he know, though, that she'd been taking the pill non-stop, ever since she met him. She didn't want a baby – no chance. Hadn't she always had it drummed in to her from her mum what a burden children were, how they wrecked your life? She was only twenty, after all. She'd rather be back at college than pushing a pram.

It wasn't until Neil found the pill packets eleven months into their marriage that things got nasty. He was so angry that she'd deceived him. Furious. 'Why couldn't you just say in the first place, rather than lying about it?' he'd yelled. 'It's like there's a brick wall around you – you won't let me through.'

She'd congratulated herself on that brick wall in private later. Brick walls were good, weren't they? They stopped you getting hurt when your husband went off and had it away with Linda O'Connor.

'Told you so,' her mum had scoffed, when Katie had told her that she'd left Neil. 'Didn't I say he was no good?'

'Yes, Mum,' Katie had replied. 'And you were right. If I ever see him again, it'll be too soon.'

That Friday night, Katie and Steve had ended up getting royally smashed. Not in a joyous, celebratory kind of way, clinking glasses of bubbly and gazing lovingly into one another's eyes. It was more of a let's-get-through-this drinking session, where Katie found herself draining glass after glass of red wine as if it were some kind of medicinal broth that could take away the shock of Steve's words.

The subject of marriage and children hadn't been referred to again, although it hung between them like a toxic cloud, ever-present in the atmosphere. They'd made small talk about work stuff but she hadn't been able to concentrate on what he was saying. Then they'd had rather unsatisfactory sex in the enormous roll-top bath – not a fancying-each-other burst of passion, more a mercy shag where Katie felt she had to make things up to Steve and clambered on top of him, easing her wet body onto his. A guilt shag. A sorry-I-said-no shag. It was impossible to tell what he was thinking; the bathroom was dimly lit and his face gave nothing away.

'I do love you, you know,' she whispered when he'd come.

He wrapped his arms around her, but said nothing. No I-love-you-too. She felt as if they were in a perilous place for a moment, as if he were building up to another marriage-and-children ultimatum, and sighed, sending a small skiff of bubbles sailing onto the black marble floor.

Where to now? How did they navigate their way through these choppy waters? *Was* there a way back even, or was it straight on 'til Dumpsville?

Her thoughts drifted to the house – if he'd want to stay

there, or if he'd move out and demand some kind of recompense for all the mortgage contributions he'd made. Would she have to sell up to pay him off? God, she hated the upheaval, the sheer bloody hard work of it, the packing and unpacking, the . . .

She stopped, sickened by herself. Why was she being so bloody practical, at a time like this? Why was she hard-wired to analyse everything so cold-mindedly, as if emotionally detached from it all? Maybe Neil had been right – maybe she *was* cold. Lying bitch, he'd called her when he'd found the pills she'd kept secret for so long. He'd thrown it in her face, the foil packet had scraped her cheek. For a split second, she was afraid of him: she actually thought he might belt her one, he seemed so clenched with rage.

She sat up clumsily now, disentangling herself from Steve's embrace and sending a scented tidal wave sloshing over the curved edge of the bath. 'Just going to check out the minibar,' she mumbled, clambering out inelegantly. 'Want anything?'

Loaded question. He looked at her and, for a moment, the pair of them were frozen in this awful tableau while she waited for his reply. Then he spoke. 'Complete annihilation,' he said. 'Whatever they've got.'

Complete annihilation? God. That sounded pretty desperate. A broken man – and she'd done the breaking. Was it possible to mend the pieces of their relationship, glue them carefully back together, or were things shattered beyond repair?

It was Sunday now, and things still felt messy. Breakfast on Saturday had been a muted affair; a fry-up and coffee in the glitzy hotel restaurant, polite quiet conversation on neutral territory, flicking through the paper. Steve's eyes were the giveaway. He had sparkly eyes, Steve, blue-grey with rogue flecks of yellow, light and amused, the skin at the edges frayed with laughter lines. But his eyes were dull that morning, his face sagging slightly. He hadn't bothered to shave, and his iron-filing stubble seemed a reproach; a don't-kiss-me statement. Or was she being paranoid?

She'd sat there barely able to eat her egg on toast, feeling as if she were stewing inside with guilt. She was actually starting to wish she'd said yes now, if only to evaporate the choking melancholic haze that hung over them. If she'd said yes, it wasn't as if they'd necessarily have to *do* anything about getting married for years. People had long engagements, didn't they? Just saying yes didn't mean you actually had to go through with it. And as for the children bit ... Well. She'd have to work up to that one. Or not. Maybe she could put that conversation off for a while, too. Say a few years ...

Her heart thumped the more she thought about it. It

wasn't too late, was it? Could she backtrack, say that she'd reconsidered?

She sat forward in her chair. 'Steve,' she said suddenly. 'I've been thinking—'

'So have I,' he said, lifting his eyes to hers for what felt like the first time all morning. 'I think I'm going to move out for a bit.'

Crash. She felt faint, reeling from the slap of his words. She gripped the sides of the table as if the room were moving. 'No,' she said. 'I don't want you to.'

'I don't really want to either,' he admitted. His voice was dulled with sadness. 'But I need a bit of space. I need to think about . . . what we said last night. Or rather, what we didn't say.'

'No, wait,' she said feverishly. This was all wrong. She could see the whole chain of events playing out in her head – the proposal, the rejection, the difficult silence, the guilt shag . . . each knocking the next one along, like toppling dominoes. She hadn't expected the split. The last domino of all, falling flat on its face with a smack.

Cause and effect, her maths brain said. Question and answer. The *wrong* answer.

Her cutlery fell from her fingers onto the plate. Solid silver against china, clatter, clatter. 'Steve, listen, I—' She was trying to dredge up the right words, willing them to come to her tongue, but her brain felt overpowered by what he'd just said. 'I wish I'd said yes!' she burst out. Her throat constricted, tears dangerously close. 'Is it too late to say yes?'

He looked at her deadpan. 'Katie ... you said no,' he reminded her. 'You made it pretty clear last night.' He hesitated, looking wretched for a moment, then got to his feet. 'I'm going to pack my stuff. You stay as long as you like, I've paid for the room until eleven. And ... and I'll call you in a few days to talk.'

She got up too, and clutched at his hand. 'No, wait! You can't go yet! Can't we talk about it? You haven't even finished your breakfast!' It was so trivial. Why was she even looking at that lonely brown sausage on his plate, the triangle of toast?

He gently removed his hand from hers. 'I'm not hungry. Look – I just need to get my head round this, that's all. It's not a drama, okay?'

She looked away. Not a drama? A tear was rolling down her cheek. *Get a load of this, everyone!* she wanted to shout hysterically to the other hotel diners, some of whom were now looking up from their newspapers at them. *Check us out, we're splitting up! Right in front of you! No charge for the entertainment round here!*

'I'll see you soon,' he said, and left the room.

She stood there for a second, and more tears fell. She sat down heavily and saw them land plop, plop on the starched white linen tablecloth. 'They're all bastards,' she heard her mum's voice say in her head. 'Didn't I tell you? You're better off without him, girl. Let the sod walk away – and good riddance!'

Chapter Five

Never Forget

Saturday, 14 June 2008

The train seemed to be taking forever. Not that Georgia minded terribly. Part of her wished it *would* take forever, that she'd be stuck on it eternally, caught in its juddering limbo halfway through the Pennines. In many ways, thought Georgia, the journey was preferable to the arrival, particularly since she knew that her homecoming would mean the usual cocktail of recriminations and criticism that the Knight family excelled at.

So, what would it be this time? She'd forgotten to send a present for Ned's birthday the other week. And when she *had* remembered to get a card in the post, she'd bought one that said *Happy 5th Birthday!* on it. 'Only two years out,' Carol had snapped humourlessly. 'He's seven, Georgia, not five!'

Yep, she was due some grief for that little faux pas. Oh yeah. She could already see her sister's un-lipsticked mouth twisting with bitterness, could imagine her un-toned arms folding across that belly of hers, bingo-wings bulging at the sides. Just because she was a mum, just because she had given birth to two hulking infants, Carol thought she'd earned some kind of All-Woman badge of honour. It had always been like that with Carol, though. *I'm better than you!* All the way through their childhood like a broken record.

Ha. As if a boring husband like David and two gormless kids was something to aspire to, something for Georgia to feel jealous of. Dream on. *Don't flatter yourself, Cazza*, she muttered under her breath.

What else would she be in the doghouse for, then? She might as well prepare herself for the inevitable onslaught.

Not having phoned.

Not having visited.

Not having paid proper attention to the Hatters' performance last season.

Not having leapt at the chance to go to the Warrington IKEA.

STILL not having a steady boyfriend.

Having married the wrong man in the first place.

Getting so old and decrepit that her eggs would be shrivelling in her ovaries. Her mum was always clipping out articles from the *Sun* about women's fertility nosediving once they hit thirty-five. Big deal. Georgia would rather die in a car crash than ever wear maternity slacks like Carol.

Still, perhaps the black sheep of the family would be overlooked for once, with all the hoo-ha of Nan's stroke . . .

She wrinkled her nose as the train slowed to a halt in Stoke-on-Trent. *That was seriously bad taste*, she told herself. Naff of her to even veer in the direction of being grateful for Nan having had a stroke. Nan was the best member of Georgia's family by a mile. Statuesque, with hips like Blackpool Tower, and boobs like suet dumplings, Nan was a matriarch to be reckoned with.

Georgia shut her eyes, and a flood of images rushed into her head. Her nan wearing that big floral pinny to make jam tarts with Georgia and her sister when they were tots, the kitchen sweet and hot.

Her nan singing as she pegged out the washing in the back garden. (*My old man said follow the van, and don't dilly-dally on the way!*)

Her nan smacking ten bells out of the lad who'd tried to grab her fat black handbag one day at the shops. As a kid, Georgia had been thrilled and terrified all at once.

Her nan's mince and tatties, steaming gravy, the best Sunday roasts in the world, slabs of fruit cake on plates with doilies.

Oh, and of course her nan's cuddles, her great matronly bosoms squashing against you, the smell of ironing and clean laundry ... For a moment it was as if Georgia were eight years old again, awkward and scrawny with her dark plaits and scabby knees.

She hoped her nan didn't die. She hoped this stroke didn't wreck the end of her life. Somehow or other, she'd expected her nan to soldier on for ever, stumping back from the SPAR with her tinned peaches and evaporated milk, stirring stew at the stove and making that annoying high-pitched tuneless crooning noise, sinking a glass of bitter in the pub ...

She gave herself a shake. She was getting horribly sentimental. *Nan is not going to die*, she told herself firmly. People recovered from strokes, didn't they? And knowing Nan, she'd be up and about in no time. A trooper, that's what she was. A hardy lass, tough as old hobnails. She'd outlive the lot of them.

The more Georgia thought about it, the more reassured she felt. Her mum was a bit of a drama queen, all said and done. Georgia could already imagine her nan rolling her eyes about it. 'She never went and sent for you, did she?' Nan would exclaim indignantly to Georgia. 'By 'eck, she'll have me at death's door next! Well, I've got news for her ... I'm not going anywhere!'

Georgia opened her eyes with a start as someone sat down beside her. Typical! She'd managed to get a double seat the whole way from Euston and now, just one stop before she had to get off, some Stokey bugger had got on next to her. Well, he'd better not start doing that leg-spreading thing men always seemed to do on trains – oof, must just widen my legs to make room for my gigantic cock, darlin' – that type of nonsense.

She looked pointedly out of the window as he ferreted about in the bag by his feet, pulled out an iPod and book, stood up, dumped various bits and bobs on the seat, heaved his bag up to the luggage rack ... For heaven's sake! Could the man not keep still for two minutes?

She glanced over, her best withering expression on her face ready to stun the hell out of him, and then stared. Oh fuck. It wasn't, was it? Surely not.

It was. Andy Milton, from her class at school. Gob of the North, her dad had always called him. She shut her eyes and pretended to be asleep so that she wouldn't have to get into conversation with him. She wanted this trip home to be as swift and uncomplicated as possible. Straight there, spend a bit of time with Nan, and then back home to the real world, to her proper life. No getting bogged down with details of schoolmates from her past. No chit-chat with people she couldn't care less about.

She sat there as still as she could manage, hoping to remain unnoticed, while the train rumbled and shuddered along, rocking her on her seat as it thundered through the fields and villages, past houses and roads.

Andy Milton, eh. She hadn't thought about him for a while. Best friend of Carl Finchley, Georgia's first teenage love. Better not to think about Carl Finchley either though. He was water under the bridge. Best left there, too.

The train rattled to a stop. Here at last. She got to her feet, pulled her sunglasses on. All the better to fool you with, Andy. She really didn't want to get into a long-time-no-see chat with him. Not him, not now, not ever. 'Excuse me,' she said, squeezing past his knees. He was plugged into his music, tapping his feet, not paying any attention. She felt the warmth of his jeaned leg as her own bare calf brushed against it. It was a hot day, she had a short skirt on and flip-flops. She reached up for her bag, willing him not to look at her. Damn it, her bag was wedged right under his, which seemed to have a ton weight in it.

Crossly, she tugged at the handles. Bloody hell! The doors would close in a minute, and she'd be stuck on the train with Gob of the North right the way into Manchester if she didn't watch out.

'Hey! Are you ... Georgie, is that you?'

There. With a huge heave, her bag was free, and so was she. Ignoring the question, she turned on her heel and marched swiftly down the carriage, flip-flops slapping.

'Georgie! Hey, George!'

Her heart galloping, she stepped through the doors and onto the platform. She could hear a knocking – Christ, was that him, banging on the window at her? She wasn't going to turn around. She wouldn't! He'd give up in a minute, assume he'd made a mistake. She did not want the Gob of the North to know she was back. It would be all round town in five minutes; leopards didn't change their spots, did they? And then . . .

No. She wouldn't think about that.

In, then out, clean and swift as a needle, that's what she wanted. A kiss on Nan's cheek, a bedside chat, granddaughter duty completed, and then back on the train home basking in a glow of job-done relief – the last train tonight if she could possibly get away with it. No mess, no awkwardness, and definitely no harking back to the past.

I'm travelling light, she reminded herself, hoisting her overnight bag up onto her shoulder. No deadweights allowed.

The smell of her parents' home was one Georgia would have recognized anywhere. You could blindfold her and waft thousands of different scents under her nose; she'd know Eau de Knight from all of them every time. So when her mum opened the front door and flung her arms around her, Georgia felt (depressingly) as if she'd never been away when she first caught a whiff of that distinctive aroma: bangers and mash mixed with Poison perfume, with faint overtones of cat pee and a hint of coffee. Not a fragrance recommended by the home-makeover experts, but there you go. The Knights did things their way.

'Oh, Georgie! I'm so glad you're home!'

Home? This wasn't her home. Home, for Georgia, was premieres and nightclubs, black cabs, the office, feeling alive, in the thick of London life. Not this hallway, this house with its swirly brown carpet and woodchip wallpaper. Not for a long time, thank God.

Her mum's arms were clamped around Georgia's back; she hoped her top wasn't getting creased to death or marked by her mum's sweaty palms. 'Hiya,' she said faintly, turning her head so that her mum's springy aubergine-coloured curls didn't boing into her mouth. 'Nice to see you.'

'Is that our George?'

Ahh, and here came Tweedledum, lumbering through the narrow hallway, big soppy grin on his mush. Georgia felt herself melting just a little at her dad's face – his eyes moist at the sight of her, his nose a touch shinier and redder than last time, his hair so shockingly white now. 'Come on, Pat, let me have a turn,' he said to Georgia's mum, elbowing her aside. She obediently let go and stepped away, and he gathered Georgia up to him, just the same way he always had since she was a girl.

'Hi Dad,' she said, into his clean white shirt. He'd been retired for two years now, her dad, but still wore a shirt and trousers every day; no T-shirts or jeans unless he was on holiday. She could feel his vest through the starched cotton of his shirt, and found it both embarrassing and comforting at the same time.

'Good to see you, lass,' he said, clapping her on the back. 'A tonic for the eyes, that's what you are!'

'A tonic indeed,' Mrs Knight agreed, with a wan smile. It was only then that Georgia noticed how pale she was – blimey, no make-up on either. Georgia couldn't remember a time when her mum hadn't worn her mahogany No7 foundation and black kohl eyeliner like warpaint. There were wrinkles around her mouth that Georgia hadn't seen before too; dark creases underlining her eyes. 'Now, then. Cup of tea? Kettle's just boiled.'

Georgia hesitated. In all honesty, she'd rather have had a black coffee, or even a gin and tonic clinking with ice, its slice of lemon coated with clinging tonic bubbles. The big brown teapot her mum used had probably housed whole plantations' worth of stewing tea leaves over the years and was therefore something of a health hazard. But the worn expression on her mum's face curbed her tongue. 'Yes please,' she said meekly instead.

Over mugs of strong tea thick enough almost to be chewy and Rich Tea biscuits, they told her the worst. 'She'd popped in on her way back from the bakery, stopped for a brew,' Mrs Knight said. Her mouth seemed so soft and vulnerable without the usual slash of lippy, Georgia couldn't take her eyes off it. 'And thank God she did, because there I was mashing the tea when she just started saying all this weird stuff – I couldn't understand her. It was all like garbled. Nonsense words.' Her hands shook on the mug, her mouth quivered. 'And there's me, saying, Mum? Mum? What are you on about? And as I was asking her, one side of her face – the right – just sagged.' She demonstrated with a finger, dragging it down her cheek until her features distorted. Her eyes glistened with tears. 'It dropped – just like that. She was dribbling and everything, it was that sudden.'

Mr Knight patted his wife on the shoulder. 'Shocking, it was,' he said. 'We took her straight in to the hospital but she was all seized up on one side, we had to carry her to the car, didn't we, Pat?'

'You had to *carry* her?' Georgia couldn't imagine her capable, stout grandmother unable to walk on her own two feet.

Mrs Knight nodded. A tear brimmed in her lower lashes, bulged and spilled through them, rolling down her cheek. 'You could tell she was frightened,' she told Georgia. 'It was horrible. She was looking at me, all imploring and confused, and I . . .' She dashed away the tears with the back of one hand. 'I was trying to comfort her, but didn't know what was happening either, so . . .'

Georgia took her mum's hand and held it. Her own fingers — tanned and smooth with their buffed, French-manicured nails — seemed to mock her mum's pale doughy flesh. She could feel a lump rising in her throat. This hand of her mum's had peeled a million potatoes, ironed a million shirts, washed a million plates. No wonder it looked so tired and old. No wonder it trembled so.

Mr Knight took over the narrative. 'The doctors said it was a stroke. There was a clot blocking the blood supply to her brain, they reckoned, and that's what caused it.'

'So how is she now?' Georgia asked. 'I mean, she's going to get better, isn't she?'

Her parents exchanged a look. Her mum stared down at the cooling mug of tea and gave Georgia's hand a squeeze. 'We're not sure yet,' she replied. 'They operated to remove the clot, and that went okay, but the consultant said that some of the brain tissue is dead. Those cells won't work again, so . . .'

Mr Knight put an arm around his wife. 'It's early days yet,' he said bracingly. 'She's very tired still, and weak after the surgery. It'll take a bit of time before we know.'

Georgia's mouth felt dry. *Clot . . . blood . . . dead cells . . . surgery . . .* The words were like hammer blows. It almost didn't seem possible. She simply could not imagine sturdy, jolly Nan weak and tired in a hospital bed. It wasn't right. It wasn't how things were supposed to be.

She licked her lips. 'Can I see her?' Even to Georgia, her voice sounded scared.

Half an hour later, Georgia and her parents walked through the main doors of the hospital. London seemed a distant planet in the solar system now. A world away from this warren of scuffed-paint corridors, signs and arrows, wheel-chairs and trolleys pushed by whistling porters. She'd give anything to be back there, safe at her desk, phone on, PC humming, gossip and tittle-tattle streaming in from all her contacts, with the most pressing thing on her mind being whether or not to give into temptation and have a Mocha Choca from her favourite coffee bar on the Kings Road.

But no, here she was, feeling like she couldn't breathe as she followed her parents towards the lift. Everyone she passed seemed miserable and tired-looking, as if all the hope and energy had been sucked out of them. She could hear a baby crying somewhere and its wail reverberated around the corridor. The wall-to-wall beige décor didn't exactly help lift the atmosphere. If Georgia was in charge of the NHS budget, she'd at least make the places *look* nice.

A couple of girls chattering in the local accent walked

past and Georgia flinched. *Silly*, she told herself as she quickened her step. *They're only kids. Nothing to worry about.*

All the same, she felt vulnerable, out in public back here in Stockport. Daft, wasn't it, after so many years, to let it get to her, but there you go. Some things you couldn't help. Some things you never quite put behind you, however hard you tried.

They waited for the lift. The metal outer frame was dirty, the silver call buttons smeary. She'd forgotten just how horrible hospitals were. She hadn't been in one for years, not since . . .

She forced away the buried memory. No. She wasn't going to start thinking about *that* now. Not on top of everything else.

Nobody spoke inside the lift until it reached the fifth floor with a ping. 'Here we are,' Mr Knight said brightly, as if they'd come for a nice day out by the seaside.

Stroke Rehabilitation Unit, read the sign as they stepped out of the metal doors, with a long red arrow running along the wall. Georgia tried to pull her shoulders up, keep positive. She hoped her nan would recognize her.

'This is the ward,' her dad said, breaking into Georgia's thoughts.

She didn't want to go in to her nan's ward. She wanted to be home, curled up on her sofa with a glass of wine and a magazine. She wanted to be scanning a party for illicit celeb snoggers, gossip-worthy tantrums, who was wearing which designer frock. She wanted to be checking her emails, filing copy, RSVP-ing to invites at her desk. She wanted to be strolling through Covent Garden, her credit card burning a hole in her bag.

But in she went, through the swing doors and down the ward.

There was a little old lady asleep in the bed, her hair as white as the pillow, her skin like crumpled grey paper. Georgia was on the verge of walking right past until her mum went and sat down at the bedside, taking the old lady's hands between hers. 'Hello, Mum,' she said gently.

It was only then that it hit Georgia, only then that she realized that the old woman in the bed was Nan, and the ground seemed to shift beneath her feet.

Christ, how had it happened? How could it be that this frail-looking bedridden person was her booming, larger-than-life grandmother? Georgia's throat seemed to tighten; she couldn't speak or breathe for a few seconds. It was as if her childhood memories had been an optical illusion, a trick of the light. *She's gone*, a voice said in her head, and it was painfully true. That woman from Georgia's youth, she'd vanished. This old lady breathing so shallowly in her sleep – she was an impostor. She wasn't Nan.

Georgia could feel the stink of disinfectant sharp in her nostrils. Could hear the sound of a peevish quavering voice further down the ward ('I said to our Reenie, he's not good enough for her, you mark my words'), a muffled beeping from a nearby piece of equipment, brisk footsteps from the corridor behind. God, she hated hospitals. There was no window in sight in this particular ward, no natural light whatsoever. She realized she was shivering suddenly, her arms prickling with goosebumps.

Mrs Knight turned and looked up at Georgia. 'See if you can find some chairs for you and your dad,' she said. 'There's never enough in here.'

Georgia didn't need telling twice. She was more than happy to turn on her heel and walk away from her grandmother's bed with something practical to do. She didn't want her parents to see the shock-horror on her face, the jolt of fear that had kicked through her. Nan was going to die, wasn't she? How would she ever recover from this? Oh God. Georgia half wished she hadn't come at all…

No. That was cowardly. That was a cop-out. But she couldn't bear the way the feelings of guilt were churning through her body. She hadn't visited, hadn't been there. And while she'd been detached from her family, in her own London world, her nan had been deteriorating, shrivelling, withering. Her nan had become *old*, without Georgia stopping to notice.

She sighed, feeling bereft. What had seemed like a great escape not so very long ago already seemed like carelessness now. Why had she ever . . . ?

'Hey! Watch it!'

Her head down, lost in thoughts, Georgia had just walked straight into someone. All she could see was the white coat before her eyes for a second before she straightened up and blinked. 'Sorry,' she mumbled, raising her gaze to the cross-looking man she'd barged into.

He had dark eyebrows, olive skin, brown eyes, a dimple in one cheek. He gave her a curt nod and went on his way.

Mardy arse, she thought, pulling a face behind his back. Why did people have to be so bad-tempered, anyway?

Right. Chairs. There were two at the far end of the ward, grey plastic chairs like the sort she'd sat on at school. She stacked them up and carried them back towards her nan's bed. *Best foot forward.* She'd just get through this ghastly day and go home. Faster than a speeding bullet.

Nan was still asleep when Georgia returned to the bedside. Her mum was talking softly to her, holding her hand, but the lined old face on the pillow hadn't moved.

Georgia set a chair down for her dad, then sat on the other. What now? she wondered. Did they sit there until her nan woke up? Or was the whole exercise one of reassurance that her nan wasn't going to die while they weren't looking?

Her gaze fell on her handbag and, by reflex, she couldn't help wondering how many emails she had banked up for her by now. There was no harm in looking, was there, while her nan dozed? Might as well keep busy.

She reached her hand in and pulled out her phone. Forty-seven new emails already – well, the news didn't stop just because it was the weekend. In fact, with all the parties and premieres taking place, the gossip quota always shot up on a Saturday. One email with a red exclamation mark by it caught her eye. It was from Isabella, her boss. KEIRA'S NEW MAN! the subject read.

Ooh, photos too – excellent. Georgia couldn't resist having a quick squiz to check out the new love-interest . . . Phwoooarr, not bad actually. Out of ten, she'd give him one any day.

'Hi, I'm just coming to do Mrs Hatherley's obs here . . . Oh. Excuse me. I said, excuse me!'

A doctor or a nurse – someone in a white coat – had come over to Nan. Was he talking to her?

'Just a sec,' Georgia muttered, scrolling down to get a good look at all the totty pictures.

'No – *now*, please. You have to turn that off. Can't you read? There are signs everywhere!'

She looked up, irritated by the man's hectoring tone. Oh God, it was that grumpy bloke she'd bumped into a few minutes ago. Might have guessed. 'All right, all right,' she muttered, rolling her eyes. 'It's just something for work—'

'I don't care,' he snapped. 'The signal interferes with the hospital equipment. You need to turn it off now.'

Bloody hell! What was his problem? She narrowed her eyes at him in her best withering glare as she switched her phone off. Not exactly what you would call a bedside manner. Still, that was the NHS for you. She began mentally planning a journalistic exposé of NHS failings as he went over to her nan and held her wrist, checking her pulse against his watch. Oh, she could ruin this place if she wanted to, Georgia thought, gazing around for signs of dirt or dust. Any cobwebs in the corners of the ceiling? Any spillages on the floor? Super-hack Georgia would spot them. She'd lay the place bare with some scornful, insightful prose.

Damn. The area around her nan's bed seemed to be spotless. The curtains that stretched on rails around the bed were rather aged, but well-washed at least. And the floor looked clean enough to eat your breakfast off. Still, she could try and get some swabs, couldn't she, and get them tested for MRSA and other nasties. This could be a new direction for her journalism – campaigning and political. She might even get taken seriously at the Press Awards for a change.

The man – a nurse, she guessed – set Nan's hand gently down on the bed and made a note in a file he was carrying.

'Her pulse is fine, so that's good,' he said. 'I'll just take her temperature, then I'll leave you in peace.' And he smiled at Georgia's parents – a proper, sincere smile like he meant it, like he actually cared.

Georgia's anti-NHS rantings melted away suddenly and she felt a rare prickle of shame. He was only doing his job, she supposed, old Grumpy Guts. And he was being nice enough to the rest of the family. *Just me he has to have a pop at*, she thought petulantly.

'I'll go and get us some coffee,' she announced. 'Back in a minute.'

She stuck her nose in the air and walked out of the ward. How long was Nan going to sleep for? she wondered. She felt she had to stay long enough to speak to her, and for Nan to see that she'd come, that she'd made the effort to visit. That was the main thing, wasn't it? As long as Nan knew she cared, then ...

Georgia froze. Her heart thudded painfully and she felt her face flood with sudden heat and colour. Oh my God.

No. No way.

It was *her*. The stuff of Georgia's nightmares.

Michelle Jones, high-school bitch, coming down the corridor towards her in a nurse's uniform.

Michelle Jones, who'd ruined Georgia's teenage years, who'd crushed her spirit to a pulp, who'd made life unbearable. Of course, she was Michelle Finchley now – if the marriage had lasted, that was.

She had to get away. She had to run, fast. This was exactly what she'd been dreading, the person who'd haunted her childhood memories for all these years. But it was hard to breathe, suddenly. She leaned against the wall, shielding her face so that the woman wouldn't see her. Oh God, she could hardly breathe. Her heart was racing, the corridor seemed to be spinning.

She clutched at the wall beside her, her palms slick with sweat. She couldn't hear anything. Her chest felt so tight she thought she might faint. Was this it? Was she dying, right here in a hospital corridor?

'Are you okay?'

Someone was speaking to her, but she couldn't register who. Everything blurred and swayed in her field of vision. She wanted to say, *Help me!*, but couldn't get the words out. Not enough air . . .

'Okay, I think you're having a panic attack,' the voice said, calm and measured, somewhere in her vicinity. 'I'm going to cup your hands around your mouth to help you breathe, all right?'

Michelle Jones! Michelle Jones had just walked right past her!

Someone was lifting her hands up, positioning them in front of her face. She could smell the alcohol gel she'd cleaned them with. Sharp and acid, it made her nostrils tingle unpleasantly.

'You're okay,' the voice said. 'Keep breathing into your hands, that's it. I'm right here next to you.'

The world around her swung back into focus. She felt hot and cold all over, sweaty and damp. 'Oh,' she managed to say. It was all she could get out. 'Oh.' She blinked. 'I . . . I don't know what happened.' She'd been staring at the wall, and it was an effort to raise her eyes to her rescuer.

It was him, of course. Misery Guts. Who else? They seemed to be on some kind of collision course, the two of them, destined to keep crashing into one another. 'Come and sit down for a minute,' he said, his hands still on hers. She felt embarrassment sinking through her as he led her along to a nearby waiting area and guided her to a chair.

'Thanks,' she said. Her chest was starting to loosen, her breathing less short and painful now, thank goodness. She took her hands away from her mouth and leaned against the chair back feeling exhausted, as if she'd just run for a cab, heart-rate subsiding, legs weak and jelly-like. 'I saw — someone I used to know. That was what—' She stopped short, before she said any more. If Michelle Jones — Finchley, rather — worked here, chances were she and this bloke would know each other. They might even be best mates, lovers. Knowing Michelle, the latter was more than likely. She hadn't exactly been backwards about coming forwards at school. Especially when other people's boyfriends were at stake.

'It's all right, you don't need to explain. Do you want me to get you some water, or anything else?'

She shook her head. She wanted to go home now, let the train rattle her back down to the safety of the capital, where she was Georgia Knight, Somebody, not Georgie Knightmare, Victim. 'No,' she said. 'Thank you. Sorry about this, I—'

'Don't be sorry,' he said. 'There's nothing to apologize for. Panic attacks can be terrifying to experience.'

'I couldn't breathe,' she said, looking down at her fingers, limp in her lap. 'I thought ... I thought I was dying.' Why had she just confessed to that? She didn't dare glance up at him for his response, he'd think she was a right hypochondriac. Not that she cared what *he* thought, of course.

He was nodding. 'People do say that,' he said. 'It's like your body exaggerates its response to danger — or stress — and the adrenalin sends you a bit haywire.'

Georgia managed a smile despite her light-headedness. 'That's the medical term, is it?'

He grinned. 'Not exactly.' He glanced at his watch. 'Listen, I'd better go, I'm meant to be doing observations in Cardiology now, but ... well, I don't want to leave you here on your own. Can I walk you somewhere? Are you with Mrs Hatherley's family?'

Georgia hated being fussed over. Hated the thought of being walked anywhere, as if she were a dog, or an imbecile. But she was still feeling so weird, so trippy, she didn't dare say no. Besides, what if she bumped into Michelle out there in the corridor? She wouldn't get away with not being spotted twice. She could already imagine the light of triumph in Michelle's eyes. 'Well, well, well, look who it is,' she'd say, rubbing her hands together. And then it would all begin again.

She couldn't let that happen. She could *not* become a victim again. *Would* not, rather. It had been what she'd vowed all those years ago, when she'd run from Stockport at the first chance she'd got.

'Yes,' she said to the man now. 'Would you mind?'

'Not at all,' he said, helping her to her feet. 'Not at all. I'm Owen McIntosh, by the way. I'm part of the team looking after Mrs Hatherley.'

'Georgia,' she said. 'Nice to meet you.' She was surprised to realize that she actually meant it.

Chapter Six

Another Crack In My Heart

Monday, 16 June 2008

'So I thought we could make some house pictures, all right?' said the earnest-looking mum, coming over to the sticking table with a sheaf of papers and spreading them out. 'I've cut out shapes for windows here, and these rectangles could be doors ... There are some flower pictures I've snipped out of magazines, and we can use these green paper shreddy bits for bushes and shrubs ...'

It was Monday morning, and Alice was at the local Mothers and Toddlers group in the parish hall, with Iris. She'd seen the sign pinned up in the village shop the day after she'd moved in, and had been the first one there when the doors had opened at eleven o'clock. She'd been desperate for conversation and contact with other human beings whose vocabulary wasn't limited to 'gah!' and screaming.

Already she was finding it strange, not being with her parents after living with them again for so long. The first night, Saturday, she'd hated having to lock the cottage up all alone, and had then lain in bed, unable to sleep, wondering who else in the village might have keys to her front door. She didn't even dare leave a window open, despite it being a sultry night. It would have been easy for anyone to scramble up the honeysuckle trellis on the back wall and slither through the window. No thanks, thought Alice with a shudder.

It was just so quiet living in the village! She was used to the late-night noises of her parents' house – the neighbours' dog, the burble of the TV as her dad stayed up to watch *Newsnight*, the occasional car zooming by. Here, Alice felt smothered by the deep silence that swallowed up the cottage, punctuated only by the occasional symphony of peculiar creaks and squeaks from the floorboards. It made her feel alone, so alone, to be lying there in the gloomy bedroom, with acres of farmland and woods behind her. No lights were visible from other houses, no cars passing, no signs of life whatsoever. It gave her the creeps. If someone broke in and murdered her and Iris in their beds, how long would it be before anyone found them?

After a sleepless night, she'd caved in pathetically the very next day and gone back to her mum's for Sunday dinner. She couldn't bear the silence of the cottage for a moment longer, felt as if the walls were closing in on her.

Still, she wasn't on her own now, was she? She was out and about, surrounded by other people and their conversations. Babies grizzled, toddlers rampaged around on bright plastic cars, or rammed miniature buggies with balding dolly passengers at each other, mums sipped coffees and swapped stories. She had all the life and chat a single person could ever wish for. So why did she still feel so alone?

From her position on an uncomfortably dinky little chair at the sticking table, Alice listened obediently to the earnest woman who was now showing them all how to assemble a house picture, even though Iris was fast asleep and not actually au fait with glue pots and collages yet. Come to think of it, she wasn't strictly a toddler, as she showed absolutely no signs of walking yet, just crawling. Was that allowed? Alice wondered with a sudden lurch of nerves. Would they be asked to leave?

Alice hadn't really done much on the mum scene yet. She didn't know what to expect. Previously, she and Iris had done little other than accompany Alice's parents as they tramped around endless National Trust properties (Iris had witnessed more examples of Palladian stonework in her eight months than most of the population ever did,

Alice reckoned) and potter about the house and garden, not really engaging with the real world.

Alice looked around, worried now that it had crossed her mind she might have broken a rule, coming to a Mother and Toddler group without an actual toddler. Would she be turfed out and told to come back in a year's time?

Nobody was coming to tap her on the shoulder, though. Anyway, the mum running the show at the door, who'd taken her pound coin and told her to help herself to a coffee, hadn't asked to see Iris's birth certificate or made any comments about her being small for a toddler, had she?

For crying out loud, relax! she told herself. Crazy, wasn't she, to feel nervous about walking into the Mothers and Toddlers group. Laughable! She could imagine her old friends teasing her about it — *Ooh, into the lions' den, eh? They're a terrifying lot, those Mothers and Toddlers!* Georgia would have scoffed.

But Alice wasn't like Georgia. She couldn't just waltz into a room, brimming with confidence, and introduce herself to whoever she liked the look of. No. Alice stayed at the edges, casting nervous glances, hoping someone would come over to *her*.

So far, nobody had.

They all seemed to know each other, these mums, that was the problem. They were engrossed in huddles of chat, private islands that Alice didn't seem permitted to access. They were discussing each other's love lives, each other's children, and local gossip about their fellow villagers — none of which Alice felt qualified to comment on.

'So he says to me, I thought you *knew* I had sensitive nipples!' one woman was relating to a group of friends around her on a carpet area scattered with soft toys. Her audience screeched with laughter. 'And I said...'

No, Alice couldn't really join in there. What could she say? 'Mind if I listen? I love a good nipple anecdote.'

Definitely not. She'd be chased out of the village with pitchforks and flaming torches.

Next to an overflowing dressing-up box, a buxom woman was fitting a glittery tiara to a small girl's head whilst narrating a different kind of story. 'And I could smell this horrible smell, right, so I looked round and there was this great big turd on the carpet, with Alfie just about to step in it with his bare feet. And I went mental, I did, I just...'

Oh, *please*.

Alice didn't want to join *that* conversation either. She tuned out rapidly and stroked Iris's back, wondering if she should leave, give it up as a bad job. She couldn't bear the thought of sitting there in her plastic chair for another hour with nobody speaking to her. She'd come here for adult company, but she just felt invisible. Today was supposed to be the first day of the rest of her life, wasn't it? Today she'd emerged from her post-Jake limbo, like a shy butterfly from a cocoon, wings weak and crumpled. She felt as if she were still blinking in the light, not yet able to fly.

No one would notice if she just went home, by the looks of it. No one would care, would they?

But then she might get a name for herself in the village. *Oh, there's that weird mum who never talks to anyone.*

Yeah, she was at Mothers and Toddlers the other week, never said a word to anyone else, then just buggered off home!

Probably thinks she's too good for the likes of us! Snobby cow.

She didn't want that. She didn't want people getting the wrong idea about her. If no one was going to speak to her, she'd have to make the first move. She was just going to have to catch someone's eye, strike up a conversation. Oh God! But who with? This was really difficult!

Come on, Alice, she told herself. *Be brave. Just do it!*

Across the table, two mums were sipping coffee and half-heartedly supervising their children's glue-stick man-oeuvres. 'So she thinks she's got a chance with Dom again, apparently,' one said, twisting a long strand of honey-coloured hair between her fingers.

Alice's ears pricked up. Dom? Was that her Dom they

were talking about? She blushed at her own phrase. 'Her Dom' indeed. The over-friendly guy who'd barged into her cottage was what she meant.

'What, Dom Fletcher?' the other woman asked the first, with a scornful pursing of her lips. She tossed her red hair. 'She must be barmy, then. A glutton for punishment.'

The words sank into Alice's mind. A glutton for punishment? What was so awful about Dom, then? Was he a cheater, a heartbreaker?

She felt her mouth tightening. Weren't they all? She should have known!

'Mummy, Mummy!' The little girl sitting next to the blonde woman grabbed a handful of the green shredded paper. 'I want to make a tree with this. And a bush! I want a bush!'

The blonde mum winked at her friend. 'You'll get one when you're older,' she said, deadpan.

The redhead convulsed into giggles. 'She won't be so keen on the idea then,' she said meaningfully, helping her little boy splodge some glue onto his sugar paper.

'No,' the blonde agreed, and turned to her baffled-looking daughter. 'And whatever you do, love, if a bloke asks you to wax it off, tell him where to go!'

They were both rocking with giggles now, and Alice couldn't help laughing too. Then the blonde woman gave her a friendly smile. 'Sorry,' she said, 'we're not always like this.'

The red-haired woman gave a snort. 'What are you on about? Yes, we are,' she laughed.

The blonde woman shrugged. 'Shush, she doesn't know that yet,' she replied in a mock-whisper, indicating Alice with a tip of her head. 'Try and give a good impression, Mags, all right?'

Alice smiled back. And took a deep breath. 'I thought it was funny,' she said. 'I'm Alice, by the way. New to the village.'

The women exchanged a look. 'We know,' the red-haired woman – Mags – admitted. 'You can't fart round here without someone getting to hear about it. I'm Mags and this is Jen. And who's Sleeping Beauty, then?'

They all considered Iris, who was still dozing with her head resting on one of Alice's shoulders. 'Iris,' Alice said. 'I know she's a bit young to come here, but . . .'

Jen waved a hand dismissively. 'Never too young,' she assured Alice. 'I came here when Poppy was – what? Five weeks old, I think. I was just so bored of being in the house, I was desperate to get out and have a chat.'

Mags nodded. 'This is the right place to come, Alice,' she said. 'This is where you get to hear what's going on.' She rose to her feet. 'I'll just grab you a drink, then you can tell us all about yourself. Tea or coffee?'

'Tea, please,' Alice said gratefully. 'Thank you.' She felt faint with relief that these women were talking to her. Thank goodness!

'So,' said Jen conversationally, after breaking up some of the green shredded-paper clumps for her daughter's foliage, 'I hope you realize all the men in the village are talking about you already?'

Alice coloured, feeling horribly embarrassed. 'They what? Who?' she asked.

Jen grinned. 'My dad for starters,' she replied. 'Stanley. White hair, nosy old bugger, door-opener adviser...'

Alice blushed an even deeper red. 'Oh yes,' she said, realizing who Jen was referring to. 'So that's your dad? He ... um ... helped me get in the cottage. I couldn't...' She faltered, feeling an idiot in describing her incapability. 'Small world,' she said with a faint smile.

Jen rolled her eyes. 'Very small,' she agreed. 'Too small. It's like living in a goldfish bowl, isn't that right, Mags?'

Mags was back with a chipped mug of tea and a chocolate digestive for Alice. 'Oh yeah,' she said breezily. 'And everyone's very excited about the new fish in the bowl – you, I mean,' she said, raising her eyebrows at Alice.

Alice dunked her biscuit, glad of the opportunity to turn her gaze away. She wasn't enjoying this conversation so much now. 'Yeah?' she asked, trying to sound casual about it.

'Too right,' Jen said. 'They were discussing you in the pub last night. Dom Fletcher was telling them all about you.'

'He was?' Alice asked, startled. A hot flush stung her cheeks. 'What ... what did he say?'

Mags grinned. 'Ooh, now that would be telling,' she replied, her eyes glittering.

'Something about the two of you being up in your bedroom was what I heard,' Jen put in suggestively, raising her severely plucked eyebrows. 'You're a fast mover, Alice!'

Alice forced a laugh but inside she felt queasy. 'It wasn't like that!' she protested.

Mags leaned forward. 'What *was* it like, then?'

'Mum,' her son said, putting a gluey hand on her arm. 'Can you help me?'

Mags seemed irritated by the interruption. 'Oh, Ollie!' she cried, shaking him off her. 'You've made me all sticky!'

Jen was leaning forward too, considering Alice with narrowed eyes. 'You know ... there's something dead familiar about your face, Alice. I can't think where I've seen you before.'

In the tabloids, Alice thought, feeling a lurch inside. She certainly wasn't going to fess up as much, though. No way!

Her hair was much longer now than when she'd been papped and that image of her standing in her old doorway, hand on her rounded belly, blinking in the camera flashes, had been plastered all over the press. She'd been hoping to go incognito here, hoped nobody would remember the headlines.

She forced a laugh now, wanting to change the subject and distract Jen. 'Oh, lots of people say that,' she said lightly, her stomach churning. 'I've just got one of those faces. Common as anything, me!'

Jen wasn't put off the scent so easily, though. 'Hmmm,' she said, cocking her head on one side. 'No, it's not that. I've seen you somewhere, I'm sure of it.' She shrugged. 'It'll come to me.'

I bloody hope not, Alice thought, feeling her smile slip. The last thing she needed was the village to know the truth, to dredge up all the stuff with Jake. She'd been hoping this place would be a bolt-hole, somewhere she could get over her broken marriage in private. But if the truth came out, there'd be no chance of that. If everyone knew that Iris was actually Jake Archer's daughter ... Christ, she'd never hear the end of it.

Iris stirred in Alice's arms just then, stretched up her chubby little arms and opened her round blue eyes. She was silent for a moment, staring at the bustle and chaos of the room, then looked questioningly at Alice.

'Hello sweetie,' Alice said, stroking her cheek.

'Awww, what a poppet,' Jen said. 'So, what were you saying, Alice? You were about to tell us about your little ... how should I put it? ... *encounter* with Dom.'

'Brief, was it?' Mags giggled.

'Who said anything about briefs?' Jen tittered. 'I heard he wears Y-fronts.'

Mags burst into a laugh. 'Where did you hear that? Did Natasha say that? Or Cathy?'

Alice listened with a growing sense of horror. She'd only talked to Dom for about two minutes, yet news of their meeting seemed to have rushed around the village like wildfire. And who were all these girls Mags and Jen were referring to, who knew Dom's underwear situation so well? He was sounding more like the village Lothario by the second. 'Blimey,' she said, rather shakily. 'Seems like he gets around a bit.'

Mags and Jen exchanged a look. 'You could say that,' Jen said after a moment. 'Anyway, we're only teasing you, Alice. Don't mind us.'

'Mummy, help!' Mags's son cried, tugging at her again, and she rolled her eyes and dabbed some glue on his picture.

Iris had reached across the table and snatched up some of the shredded paper, which she was now posting into her open mouth. 'Oh, Iris!' Alice said, taking it gently out again. 'Are you trying to tell me something? Are you hungry?'

She was glad of an excuse to get to her feet and go, even though she knew Iris wasn't really that hungry yet. The conversation with Mags and Jen had cheered her initially — hooray, friendly mums talking to her! — but her feelings had quickly turned to dismay. She didn't like everyone knowing her business. And what did Dom think he was playing at anyway, telling everyone in the pub that he'd been in her bedroom?

'Cheers for that, mate,' she muttered crossly, wheeling Iris down the lane in her buggy. 'Now I'm the village slapper, and I've only been here two days. Thanks a bunch!'

The cottage seemed particularly joyless when she returned to it, with its small, mean windows and dusty front path. She had to unclip Iris from her buggy outside because it was too big to wheel into the cottage. Or rather, you *could* wedge it in, just about, but it took up most of the living room like some kind of looming Mothercare-esque art installation. Not terribly practical.

She carried Iris inside, her spirits sinking. Now what? What else should she do for the rest of the day? There was lunch to make, sure, and Iris would need a nap, but she had nothing else planned. And tomorrow was similarly empty, too, and the day after that . . .

Iris was mouthing wetly on her shoulder. Hungry now. Alice put her in the high chair and tried to think where she'd unpacked the bibs. Oh God. It all felt too much, suddenly. What had she done, coming here in the first place? Getting back on her feet after the double whammy of Jake's betrayal and Iris being born had felt such a monumental effort, she'd barely thought beyond actually moving in. For so long, she'd concentrated on coping from day to day, one step at a time, not daring to look any further ahead. She'd been so intent on trying not to dwell on the past and what might have been, that she'd forgotten to make plans for the future.

And now here she was, in this hotbed of gossip where everyone knew everyone else, and they were all talking about her. *You're a fast mover, Alice,* she heard Jen tease in her head, and felt like crying. They were so wrong about her! Fast mover? Hardly. She was at a complete standstill, not moving anywhere.

What, exactly, had Dom said about her, anyway? She'd thought he was nice when he'd come round on Saturday. Should have known there was an agenda. He sounded as if he was the kind of bloke who liked to make conquests, and boasted to the lads about them afterwards. Ugh. It sent her cold, that sort of thing. So ungentlemanly. So unchivalrous! He certainly wouldn't be getting a welcome if he showed up round here again.

She put her head in her hands at the small table, dimly registering that Iris was whacking a plastic spoon against her chair, but not actually feeling able to do anything about it. She wished she could rewind the last few days and move in all over again – confident and assertive, this time, able to open her own front door without help – and locking it afterwards, so that Dom hadn't been able to wander in of his own accord. It clearly didn't take much to get the tongues wagging around here.

Maybe she should have moved to a city, where she could have been more anonymous. If she'd gone to Bristol, she would have been near Katie and she'd have had an ally at least, rather than feeling like Alice No-mates out here in the sticks.

Her mobile phone trilled, jerking her out of her reverie. It would be her mum, no doubt, checking up on her, making sure things were okay. Just the thought of that act of kindness brought tears to Alice's eyes and she reached into her bag for her phone.

The caller display read *Katie* and Alice blinked in surprise. How peculiar, just as she'd been thinking about her, too. They'd always had a bit of a telepathic thing, her and Katie, back when they were students and did everything together. But these days ... well, these days the closeness was gone, inevitably. These days Katie never called her in the daytime. Daytime was school, wasn't it? And Katie was always in teacher mode then, one hundred per cent. Gossip breaks were not scheduled into the timetable.

'Hello?' she said into the phone.

'Oh, Alice! You're there!' Katie sounded hugely relieved.

'Is everything all right?'

A sigh came down the receiver. 'I don't know. No. I don't think so. It's a long story. I was wondering ... Are you doing anything today?'

Alice couldn't help a hollow laugh. 'No.'

'Oh good. In that case, can I come over?'

'What – here? I mean – yes, of course! I've moved, though, I'll have to give you directions—'

'Great, let me grab a pen. How's it going?'

'Um ...' Alice tried to distract Iris from spoon-banging by opening a drawer and giving her a few random objects. The tea strainer, a faded wooden peg, a plastic blue egg cup. Alice clattered the objects down and tried to concentrate. *How's it going?* Katie had asked. Ahh. The million-dollar question. 'Well,' she said, gazing out the window as a tractor juddered past. The farmer behind the wheel saw her looking and waved a hand in a friendly gesture. Alice raised her own hand back, feeling embarrassed to be caught staring. 'Well,' she said again. 'It's early days, I guess. We only got here on Saturday, so ...'

Something struck her. 'Hang on a minute, why aren't you at school, anyway? Is it an INSET day or something?'

There was a hesitant pause before Katie replied. 'I called in sick,' she said.

'Are you all right?' Alice said, surprised. Off work? Katie was the fittest person she knew.

'No, I'm not,' Katie replied forlornly. 'Not really.'

Chapter Seven

Why Can't I Wake Up With You?

Monday, 16 June 2008

Katie had never pulled a sickie before. She liked her job too much, couldn't understand people who spent all that time working when they hated being there. Besides, the guilt had always stopped her from skiving, even if she had a hangover or felt ropy. If she didn't turn up at school, it meant complicated reorganization of her lessons, as well as payment for a supply teacher out of their budget. So usually she'd have to be bedridden and hallucinating with the pain before she'd ever phone in ill.

The thing was, she hadn't slept the whole weekend. Barely a wink. It was just too damn weird without Steve there, breathing beside her in bed at night, making coffee in the morning, singing tunelessly in the shower. Obviously she and he did their own things at the weekends – he liked to go running or bike over to the gym on Saturdays, whereas she preferred to spend her free time in a slightly more laid-back fashion, sauntering into town with a girl-friend or two, shopping and coffee-ing. It wasn't as if she and Steve were joined at the hip when they weren't working, but all the same ... This weekend, she had been constantly aware of his absence, couldn't stop wondering where he was, what he was doing. And how would things be when he came back?

More importantly, *would* he come back at all?

On Saturday afternoon she'd had a long-standing arrangement to meet a couple of friends, Becky and Sam, in Broadmead. They were meant to be buying bikinis together for forthcoming holidays, and had decided an event so traumatic called for mutual moral support. They were all part of the same crowd – Katie and Steve, Becky and Rich, Sam and Andy. But how could she go and meet them now this had happened? How could she try on bikinis and chit-chat about the minutiae of their lives without mentioning the new Steve-shaped hole in her life? It would be like Chinese whispers, the talk flashing along the grapevine. She wasn't ready to go public about it yet, not when things still hung so precariously in the balance.

She'd lied on the phone about having a tummy bug.

'Oh, poor you,' Becky had said sympathetically. 'Hope Steve's looking after you.'

Katie had squeezed her eyes shut at the words. 'You know what he's like,' she'd replied lightly, not wanting to embellish with any more detail than she had to.

And so, while in a parallel universe another Katie tried on tankinis in Oasis and asked, 'Does my bum look big in this?' as she peered over her shoulder to inspect her rear reflection, here in the real world Katie had taken to the sofa and lain there numbly for hours on end, staring up at the ceiling and wondering what to do with herself. For once, there was no master plan. All she wanted was to be there when the phone rang. But it didn't.

By the time Monday dawned, her eyes felt red and sore from lack of sleep, and she had played and replayed the hotel scenes in her head so many times, she felt as if she were in danger of losing her marbles. She'd meant to go into work all along and then, at the last moment, she'd changed her mind.

Impulse. She never usually acted on it. Katie was always one for reading from the script – never did the improvisation thing. But today ... today she couldn't act as if everything was all right. She couldn't go through with the charade of school, teaching her Year 8s trigonometry, and revising probability and stats with her Year 10s. Not when her head was swimming with thoughts of Steve, not when she felt riddled with confusion and doubts. The kids would make mincemeat out of her; they could sniff out weaknesses from a mile off.

She really needed someone to talk to. Someone to give her advice. Becky, Sam and the rest of the crowd wouldn't do, of course. If push came to shove, Katie knew they'd be on his side. They were his friends, at the end of the day, however much they'd welcomed her into the gang.

And Georgia hadn't been a lot of help when Katie had phoned her on Saturday. In fact, she'd actually made Katie feel worse than ever. But there was always Alice. She was kind, wasn't she? Kind and good to talk to, with the sensitivity and all-round general niceness about her that Katie really craved right now. Alice would understand.

That was why at 1.30, when by rights Katie should have been on lunchtime playground duty, bawling out the Year 9s she always caught smoking round the back of the biology labs, she was instead driving out of Bristol along the Wells Road, towards Alice's village. Steve hadn't taken her car to be serviced at all it turned out – she'd found it parked neatly outside the house when she'd got back on Saturday afternoon. He really had planned the whole thing thoroughly, hadn't he?

Katie blinked at the thought, trying to concentrate on the road. She'd necked a double espresso before getting in the car in the hope that the caffeine would shock her into alertness behind the wheel, but it was making her very jittery and she kept braking nervously when anyone tried to overtake her.

She hadn't seen Alice for ages — absolutely months. Their friendship had waxed and waned over the years, from best-friend status in that brief time they'd had together at uni, to the odd weekend catch-up and emails when Katie was in Wiltshire, and then as close as sisters for a while again when she'd turned up at Alice and Georgia's flat in London after walking out on Neil.

Alice had been brilliant in that particular crisis, producing a stream of biscuits, cups of tea, glasses of wine, chocolate, and boxes of tissues. 'You did the right thing,' she said over and over again, until Katie started to believe it. 'Me and Georgia will look after you. You're staying with us, for as long as you need to.'

Katie had ended up moving in when their other flatmate, Helen, had moved out to live with her boyfriend. And there she'd stayed for the next four years, going back to finish her degree and passing with flying colours.

More recently, Katie had stayed awkwardly on the sidelines when all hell had broken loose between Georgia and Alice, trying not to get too involved, although privately she thought Georgia had been well out of order. And then, when Alice's marriage had broken down as a result . . .

Katie jumped as a white van blared its horn behind her, and she realized she'd left her indicator flashing since the last roundabout five miles or so back. She stuck two fingers up at the van driver who sailed past, making naughty-naughty finger-wagging gestures at her. 'Oh, sod *off*,' she said loudly, hoping he could lip-read.

Damn it, she hadn't been the most brilliant friend to Alice lately. She'd listened to her plaintive calls when Jake had done the dirty on her, but hadn't rushed to be by her side, as she would have done in their student days. She'd only visited her once at her parents' place during the fallout period, even though they were a mere forty-minute drive or so away.

Selfish cow, she said to herself now. Why hadn't she made more of an effort? It was partly her guilt, knowing that she was having a fantastic time with Steve in Bristol, happy with work and friends. The thought of visiting pale, wan Alice, with those leaking boobs and unwashed hair, grizzling baby in her arms, still agonizing about Jake, still so upset about Georgia ... Well. It hadn't been the most enticing of weekend jaunts.

She flicked the radio on, trying to ignore the bad feelings that were washing through her. No, she hadn't been a good friend at all. And yet, the first sign of trouble and here *she* was, calling up *Alice* and asking her for help. She was quite surprised Alice hadn't told her where to get off actually.

Instead, she'd sounded grateful for the call; delighted even that Katie wanted to visit. That made Katie feel ten times worse.

Christ, Alice lived in the middle of nowhere. The Bristol streets were long behind her now, and she was winding her way through smaller villages with golden Bath-stone cottages and picture-postcard churches. It was still and hot, and Katie opened the windows and sang along to Squeeze on the radio, trying not to think about the fact that 'Up the Junction' was one of Steve's all-time favourite songs.

She hoped Alice would have some good advice for her, know what to do. Ha, there she was being selfish again, wrapped up in her own problems. Her voice wobbled as she tried to hit the high notes in the song and suddenly she felt tears in her eyes.

Ahh, there was the turning to Alice's village – and not a moment too soon.

Katie gave a sniff as she indicated left and pulled into a lane, wondering why on earth Alice was hiding here, in deepest Somerset countryside. Chichi Chelsea or Theatreland this was not. Although perhaps that was the point.

Two minutes later, she parked outside a small whitewashed cottage, its garden in full bloom, its low thatched roof and tiny square windows the stuff of chocolate-box photographs. Gorgeous! Absolutely gorgeous – and perfect for daydreamy, romantic Alice. No wonder she'd sounded chuffed on the phone that Katie wanted to see her – she was probably dying to show off this new place.

It was dead quiet, Alice's road. Well – she said road, but really it was only a straggle of cottages on the outskirts of the village. A lane.

Oh, fancy living on a country lane! Katie thought of her own busy street with a wince as she went up the front path. The afternoon sun was warm on her face as she admired a peacock butterfly flitting up from a scruffy buddleia bush, and a couple of bees that were humming amidst the lavender. Lucky old Alice!

There was a pushchair outside the house – how relaxing to live somewhere with no crime problems, where you could leave stuff outside without a second thought. You didn't get that where Katie lived, sadly – didn't really get that in many places in Britain now, of course, but this … this was like being in the 1950s.

She rapped on the door with an old-fashioned brass knocker, tarnished with age. Ahh. Footsteps. And then the door was opening, and …

'Katie!'

'Alice!'

Christ, but she was skinny. What had happened to those round cheeks and dimples Alice had always had? Was she ill?

'Come in, come in,' she was saying. 'It's a bit of a state,

I'm afraid – we only moved in on Saturday and haven't quite got things sorted yet . . .'

The front door opened straight into the living room, and Katie pushed it shut before following Alice in. She could barely pay attention to what her friend was saying because she couldn't keep her eyes off her bottom. Alice in jeans! She had always been one for long floaty skirts to cover herself up, self-conscious as she was about her curves. But now . . . blimey. Jeans and a vest top. Alice-in-bare-flesh-and-tight-fitting-clothes shock! 'Nice jeans,' Katie mumbled, out of curiosity as much as anything else.

'What, these?' Alice said dismissively. 'Mmmm, they're great, jeans, aren't they? You can get away with not washing them for ages . . . Sit down, anyway,' she went on. 'Iris is having a nap thank goodness, so we can have a chat.'

Katie took in the surroundings for the first time – the living room which felt rather like a cave with its low ceiling and dingy atmosphere. There were colourful plastic toys all over the floor, and the walls were bare except for a single framed print of a beaming baby with one white tooth visible. *Okaaaay*, she thought. So the inside of the cottage didn't quite live up to the promise of the outside façade, but . . . hey, Alice had only just moved in. She could get on with the decorating soon enough.

Katie lowered herself into a squishy armchair that let out a small sigh as her bottom reached the cushion. A musty smell rose from the fabric and she looked at the shiny patches on the chair's arms before deciding to put her hands in her lap. *Potential*, Sarah Beeny would say about this place. *Bags of potential*. But you'd need a skip for all the crappy old furniture and carpet in here.

Still, at least the baby was asleep. Katie couldn't help a sneaky sigh of relief. She wasn't good with babies, she never knew what to do with them; whenever she held one or even smiled at one, it always seemed to start crying.

Alice brought in tall glasses of water – 'I haven't had a chance to do a proper shop yet, this is the only cold drink I've got, I'm afraid,' she said as she passed one over – and perched on the saggy sofa.

Katie was starting to feel really bad about inviting herself over on a whim. 'Sorry,' she said. 'I hadn't realized you'd literally just moved – I'm sure you've got enough to do without me barging in . . .'

'Oh no, it's fine,' Alice replied. 'To be honest, it's nice to see a friendly face here after this morning.' A shadow passed across her face and then she gave herself a little shake. 'So,' she went on quickly, before Katie could ask what she meant, 'what's been happening? What's with all the bunking off?'

Katie sipped her water thankfully. It was stuffy in the small room. 'Well, in a nutshell, Steve asked me to marry him . . .'

'Oh! Congratulations!' Alice cried, spilling her drink as she jumped to her feet. 'That's—'

'And I said no,' Katie put in.

Alice had got halfway across the room, arms out as if to hug her, but as Katie finished the sentence, her arms flapped down again. 'You said no? But why?'

'Because...' Katie ducked her head, shying away from Alice's look of bewilderment. 'Well, I've been there before, haven't I? Marriage, I mean. And it doesn't suit me. Once bitten, and all that. Besides, he started talking about wanting children, too. And that is *so* not going to happen. Not with me, anyway.'

Alice eyed her. 'Why not? You'd be a great mum.'

Katie didn't say anything, but the words pricked her. *Whatever you do, take precautions*, her mum had ordered Katie and her sisters, almost as soon as they had their first periods. *Don't mess up your life like I did, getting pregnant too young.* Katie's mum had been a pretty crap role model but that was one piece of advice Katie had followed to the letter. There was no way on earth she wanted to turn into her own mother and wreck an innocent child's life. Not likely.

Obviously she wasn't going to say as much in front of Alice, though. 'Let me ask you something,' she said, to change the subject. 'We don't have to talk about this if you don't want to,' she went on, choosing her words carefully, 'but … what did you like about being married to Jake? I mean, wasn't it just the same as going out with him?'

Alice shook her head. 'Oh no, totally different,' she replied. '*Totally* different. And I hadn't expected it to be so at all, but when he said he wanted to marry me … Oh! Honestly, Katie, I was so so happy. I felt as if I was just brimming with love for him. And when we'd actually got married … well, I just felt as if we would be together for ever, lives entwined. That's what I liked about it – that it's the ultimate commitment.'

A tear rolled down her cheek and she pushed it away.

'Oh, honey!' Katie said, getting up and hugging her. 'Oh, Alice, sorry. I'm so insensitive, aren't I? I shouldn't have asked.'

'No, you're all right,' Alice said, with a catch in her voice. 'I've got to toughen up and face the fact that it's over. I just …' She sniffed. 'I just feel sad, especially when I think of us making those vows. 'Til death do us part … More like "'til Victoria bloody Hartley do us part". That snake!'

Her voice was thick with melancholy, and Katie held her until she had stopped sniffling. 'What I was trying to get at – in a totally crap, insensitive way—' Katie went on, 'was that when Steve proposed to me, I didn't feel happy at all. I panicked. All I could think about was Neil cheating on me, and being trapped in that house with him. And I just wanted to run away, to push Steve away—'

Before Katie could finish, there was a knock at the front door, and they both turned to watch as the latch was lifted and it was pushed open. Alice's eyes narrowed and she folded her arms across her chest. 'Bloody hell, I'm sick of this!' she hissed to Katie. 'Come in, why don't you,' she said in a louder, rather sarcastic voice.

A man had appeared – somewhat comically to Katie's eyes, as he had to duck his head and stoop to enter the small cottage doorway. He stood there like a rather ungainly giant, blinking as his eyes adjusted to the light, then gave them both a friendly smile and walked across the room, holding his hand out. 'Hi, I'm Dom,' he said to Katie. 'Alice's sort-of neighbour.'

Katie rose from the sofa to shake his hand. He had a nice, honest way about him, she thought as his tanned fingers gripped hers. No guile. 'Katie,' she said, liking him. Alice's sort-of neighbour, eh? Interesting.

'Alice, I—' he began, then he peered closer at her face. 'Oh. Are you all right?'

He had noticed the tear tracks down her cheeks. *Observant for a bloke*, Katie thought.

Alice fixed him with a very bright, very fake smile. 'Of course,' she lied. 'Is there anything I can help you with?'

Katie was surprised at the stiffness of her tone. Alice

was usually so warm, so accommodating – but not to this sort-of-neighbour bloke. What had *he* done to rattle her cage, then?

Dom seemed taken aback too. 'Not really, I was just passing, thought I'd pop in and see how you were doing,' he replied. His eyes were concerned as he gazed at her. 'Are you sure you're okay?'

'Absolutely fine,' Alice replied, her smile starting to resemble a rictus type of grimace.

Bang. Nail in the conversation coffin. It would be clear to even the most thick-skinned of souls that everything about Alice – her body language, her fixed false smile, her curtness – was shrieking *Go away!*

Katie turned to Dom. Had the message got through?

He was shrugging, with rather a hurt expression. Yes. 'Okay,' he said. He was trying to catch Alice's eye, but she was looking away. 'Okay,' he repeated. 'Well, I'm only down the road if you need me, yeah? Nice to meet you, Katie. Er . . . I'll see myself out.'

'You just do that,' Alice muttered through gritted teeth as he left.

Katie could barely wait until he was out of earshot to ask the obvious question. 'What was all that about?' she hissed. 'I thought he seemed really nice.'

Alice raised her eyebrows and looked scornfully at the spot where Dom had been standing just moments earlier.

'Well, I did too, at first,' she said, 'but now I know differently.'

'Oh, right,' Katie said, wondering what on earth the guy had done wrong. Was he some kind of child molester? A peeping Tom? 'So what—'

A plaintive cry came from upstairs just then, and Katie broke off. 'That's Iris,' Alice said, and the life seemed to go out of her for a moment, as if someone had pulled out her stopper and she'd deflated. Then she scowled. 'Bloody idiot must have woken her banging the door,' she said with unusual vehemence. 'Let's listen. She might go back to sleep if we're lucky.'

They sat as if frozen, in silence. Tick, tick, tick went an ugly-looking clock on the mantelpiece.

Alice let out a sigh of relief after thirty seconds or so had passed. 'Phew,' she said. 'She often stirs like that. If we're lucky we'll get another half-hour before she's properly awake.'

'How's it going, then?' Katie asked. 'Motherhood, I mean. Are you managing all right on your own?'

Alice pulled a face. 'It's a bit scary,' she admitted. 'I'm dreading her being ill in the night – having to deal with that sort of thing alone. I've never had to do that before – Mum was always there to dish out advice, tell me what to do.' She sighed. 'It's lonely, too, just being the two of us here. Honestly, Kate, it seemed like a good idea at the time, moving to this place, but now...' She squared her shoulders and gave another of her fake smiles. 'Anyway, we'll manage. And you didn't come here to talk about me. Go on, carry on about Steve. Tell me everything.'

Katie didn't need asking twice, and the details poured out. 'I can't help thinking that Neil was right, you know – that I'm just cold inside,' she finished miserably. 'That there's something wrong with me. How come everyone else seems to want to play Happy Families, but not me? What's wrong with me?'

Alice put a hand on hers. 'Nothing's wrong with you,' she replied. 'You're brilliant. Steve thinks so too, right? Otherwise he wouldn't be trying to get you up the aisle.' There was a pause. 'So anyway ... what next? Have you phoned him?'

Katie shook her head. 'I don't know what to say,' she confessed. 'I thought he'd call me. And now it's been two days and ... I almost feel as if we've split up, you know. Which is ridiculous, isn't it? And just goes to show it must be a pretty flimsy relationship if we can't survive a conversation about the future without falling to pieces.'

They were both silent for a few moments. 'He's probably feeling a bit crushed,' Alice said. 'There he was, building up to this nerve-racking proposal, thinking of every detail, by the sound of it. Apart from the possibility that you might say no. I bet he feels pretty crap now. Maybe even embarrassed.'

'Yeah,' Katie said. 'I guess he wasn't expecting a "no".' She sighed, feeling muddled and tired. 'What a mess. Bloody marriage proposals wreck everything, if you ask me!'

Hindsight was a wonderful thing. Katie looked back at her teenage self now and knew that meeting Neil had been nothing more than a convenient means of breaking free from her home life, cutting the ties from her flaky mother, her absent dad. It was a something-for-me moment, a relief to step into his arms away from her chaotic family.

It wasn't the worst childhood in the world, to be fair, yet you wouldn't call it an ideal one. As a fourteen-year-old, while all her mates were hanging out, experimenting with make-up and practising the Lambada together, Katie would be stuck indoors babysitting her younger sisters because her mum was off down the White Horse and may well not come home for twenty-four hours. Or she'd be making tea for them all because Mum had passed out cold on the sofa again. Or she'd be suffering the charity of 'Aunty' Sylv next door who took it upon herself every now and then to do their washing – until Katie had heard Sylv gossiping in the mini-mart about it ('Poor little mites! I've a good mind to call social services, get them taken away from that woman!') and stoutly refused all offers of help from then on.

No wonder Dad had walked out, Katie would think, as her mum shambled from day to day, seemingly uncaring of how her daughters fared. Sometimes she wished her mum had been the one to go.

Katie leaned against the steering wheel as she sat in the rush-hour traffic, steeped in memories. It was hardly surprising that when Neil had sauntered into her world and picked her out, Katie had fallen head over heels. She was so desperate for some love and closeness, so grateful and delighted that anybody wanted her, that anybody found her attractive! It would have been pathetic if it wasn't so bloody sad, her trotting after Neil like an adoring puppy.

She stared out of the window, unseeing, as she waited for the traffic lights to change. Ironic really, wasn't it? While most of her friends were rebelling against their parents by drinking and smoking and throwing wild house parties behind their backs, Katie's act of rebellion had been to get married – a teenage bride. How tragic was that? And how spectacularly it had backfired on her!

Katie drove the rest of the way home on automatic pilot, trying not to think about her failed marriage any more. At last she was able to turn into her road, and she slowed as she approached her house. Then she almost stalled the engine in surprise as she saw the metallic blue Ford Focus parked neatly outside. Steve's car. He was back. He'd come back!

So what the hell should she do now?

Chapter Eight

Pray

1987

'Oh look, girls. Here she comes, the walking Knightmare herself!' Michelle Jones' voice had a ring of delight, and Georgia flinched as she heard it. Oh, no. Not again. She clutched her school bag defensively against herself as if it were a shield that would repel Michelle and her cronies. No such luck.

'Done your homework, then, Knightmare?' That was Gayle Fisher, dumb sidekick, with a bleached-blonde mullet and studs all the way up her ears. She was rock hard, Gayle, everyone knew that. And now she was advancing on her so that Georgia had to back away against the grey metal lockers.

'Yeah,' Georgia replied, eyes cast down to the ground. 'Course she'd done her homework. It wasn't worth her while *not* to do it when this lot wanted copies every day.

'Hand it over then.' That was Lindsey Newton, chewing on a wad of pink Bubblicious, holding out a stubby-nailed hand expectantly. Not as hard as Gayle, but with such an expert line in catty remarks she could make you cry within seconds if she put her mind to it.

Georgia scrabbled inside her bag for the English essay she'd spent hours labouring over last night. 'Macbeth's Downfall', it was called. She knew how he must have felt, poor old Macbeth, with these three witches breathing down her neck.

Michelle grabbed the book out of her hands and flicked through it. 'Oooh, what long words,' she mocked. 'Think you're better than us, do you?'

'No,' Georgia mumbled. It was true. She felt worthless pretty much all of the time. The only thing that kept her going was walking home with Carl Finchley. He was so nice, Carl. Different from the other boys. He made her laugh, too, and forget about Michelle Jones for the short distance from the school gates to her house.

'Good, 'cos you're not,' Lindsey said, leaning closer to Georgia so that she could smell the sickly waft of strawberry gum. The lockers were cold against her back, she could feel the metal chill on her shoulder blades. 'You're shit. You're nothing. Everyone hates you, you know. 'Specially us.'

'Watch out,' Michelle murmured just then, and they

turned to see what she'd noticed. Georgia raised her gaze slightly too and saw, to her great relief, that Carol, her sister, was striding down the corridor towards them with her best mate, Susie Leigh. Carol took in the scene – the three girls crowding around Georgia, pinning her against the lockers – but didn't comment. Her gaze flickered over Georgia's face disinterestedly, and she walked on. Georgia could hear her telling Susie about the new shoes she'd seen in Chelsea Girl as they disappeared down the corridor.

Michelle gave a hard, spiteful laugh. 'Well, whaddya know? Big sis Knightmare thinks you're a freak, too. She doesn't care what happens to little Georgie!' She grabbed Georgia's wrist and wrenched it in a Chinese burn. 'Looks like you're on your own, eh?'

Saturday, 14 June 2008

The scene flashed back into Georgia's mind as she walked along the hospital corridor with Owen. The shame – the years-old shame – spread through her like a rising tide. It had gone on for months and months, the bullying – years, actually. How ironic that Michelle Jones was now in the health profession. Healing, rather than crushing. Was that some kind of karmic penance? Or the universe's little joke?

She clutched her bag to her now, just as she'd done back

then in the school corridor all those years ago. Only now her bag was Balenciaga, glossy black and expensive, not a canvas rucksack with The Cure and Style Council drawn over it in marker pen. And now her hair was thick and sleek, not the ponytail it had been back in those days – the ponytail that Michelle had pulled on so hard at times, Georgia thought her roots would be ripped out.

It was disconcerting how she could be here with her glamorous bag, her salon-styled hair and her expensive designer shoes, and yet after just one glimpse of Michelle Jones, she'd felt as if her trappings had melted away to nothing, leaving her as gawky Georgie Knightmare all over again, vulnerable and bare.

She trembled at the thought, and Owen put his arm around her to steer her as they walked. 'Are you okay?' he asked.

Her teeth chattered and she was unable to speak. Then she took a deep breath. 'Yes,' she said. 'Just ... thinking about something. It was a long time ago.'

They were back at the ward now, and he stopped outside the swing doors. 'Here you are,' he said. 'Will you be all right from here?'

She nodded, trying to smile at him. She'd got it wrong about Owen McIntosh, he wasn't so bad. She was glad her nan had him looking after her. 'Thanks,' she said. 'Thanks a lot.'

'No problem,' he said. Then he hesitated. 'I guess I might see you again here?' he ventured. 'I mean, if you're visiting Mrs Hatherley. She'll be with us for a while, I think.'

Georgia didn't answer immediately. She'd planned to go straight home tonight, after all — I'm A Londoner, Get Me Out Of Here! — and the hospital had already proved itself to be a dangerous place, with the sighting of Michelle. Why would Georgia want to come back for more?

But then she remembered Nan lying so feeble and pale in the bed. And she felt Owen's dark eyes upon hers as he waited for her reply.

'Yes,' she said, surprising herself as the word fell out of her mouth. 'Yes, I'll be back tomorrow. Will you ... will you be around, then?'

He smiled at her. She liked the way his eyes were so sparkly when he smiled. He was actually rather handsome, now she came to look at him properly. 'I can be,' he said. He glanced at his watch. 'See you tomorrow then, Georgia.'

'See you,' she said. And away he went down the corridor, his white coat flapping behind him. Mmmmmm. Interesting.

Carol barged through the swing door then, almost knocking her over. 'There you are!' she said impatiently. 'What the hell are you playing at?'

Georgia started at the sound. 'Oh, hi,' she replied after a

moment. 'Nice to see you too.' Her voice dripped with sarcasm, and her eyes narrowed. Carol, who'd never come to her rescue. Carol, who'd turned a blind eye, pretended not to notice the bullying. It rankled even now. So much for sisterhood. So much for We-Are-Family!

'Where have you been? Nan's awake, you know. We told her you were here and now she's all upset because she thinks she's missed you.' Her voice rose an octave. 'And where's the frigging coffee?'

Georgia pushed past her sister, letting the door fall on Carol. Where's the frigging coffee, indeed. Who did Carol think she was, anyway? Some kind of charlady?

She walked down the ward still bristling, but the sight of her nan's face, eyes open, confused expression, sobered her immediately.

She dropped into the empty chair by the bed and took her grandmother's gnarled fingers in her own. The tired old skin moved over the tired old bones. 'Hi Nan,' she said. 'It's me, Georgie.'

It was hard to doze off that night. On the rare occasions that Georgia visited her parents she had to sleep in the bedroom she'd shared with Carol throughout their child-hood, and it always seemed to be the case that as soon as she lay down on the thin single mattress again, a whole host of shadowy memories would drift out from the faded striped wallpaper and hang above her like a mushroom cloud, choking her until she had to pull the duvet over her head.

So many times she'd lain here on this bed, weeping into the pillow, while Carol snored across the other side of the room. So many times she'd poured her heart out into her diary, all her fears about Michelle and her gang. All her wishes too that she would one day be in with the in-crowd; that one day she'd be liked by other girls, part of a group.

Over the years since then Georgia had wondered many times if Michelle, Gayle or Lindsey ever bought her newspaper, saw her byline. Did they feel guilt when they recognized her face staring out at them? Envy?

Both, she hoped. She hoped it turned their stomachs to read about her and her glamorous showbiz life. She hoped they felt ashamed. In reality, though, they probably felt nothing other than glee as they recalled all the times they'd made her cry.

Georgia had tried so hard to put those horrible teenage years behind her when she escaped down to London, and for a time, it had worked. She'd shaken the memories off and plunged into student life with abandon. It was only as the Christmas holidays were looming that she realized just how much she dreaded going back up north. The thought of seeing Michelle Jones' sneering face again made her feel ill.

And then, as term drew to a close, she'd lost it one night at the union bar. She'd had way too many cheap shots, and — so embarrassing — she'd burst into tears when that Slade song, 'Merry X'mas Everybody', started booming from the loudspeakers. Everyone was bellowing along with the words, except Georgia, who sat there with her head in her hands, weeping fit to bust. Alice — kind Alice — had taken her back to the hall of residence, made her hot chocolate and hugged her. 'I just don't want to go back,' Georgia had sobbed. 'I can't face it again.'

Alice — saviour Alice — had stroked her hair. 'What happened?' she asked.

And then it all came out — the story she'd never told anyone properly before, not even her own mum. How she'd been madly in love with Carl Finchley, her first-ever boyfriend, but how Michelle kept picking on her, because *she* fancied him too. And how the bullying had gone on for weeks and weeks, months and months, until one day, just before Christmas, Michelle had beaten the shit out of her. Georgia had been hospitalized for two weeks with broken ribs and internal bleeding. 'And I'm afraid you've lost the baby,' the consultant had said, pity in his eyes.

The baby. She hadn't even known she was pregnant.

Alice — lovely Alice — had listened while Georgia sobbed her way through the whole sorry tale. She'd insisted on sleeping on Georgia's floor that night, just in case Georgia couldn't sleep and wanted to talk some more, and then, the very next morning, she'd got on the phone to her parents and arranged for Georgia to spend the whole Christmas break with them. That was what you called a good friend. And how had Georgia repaid her again?

Georgia shivered despite the warm night, not wanting to think about that. She punched her pillow into a more comfortable position and tried to sleep, but her mind wouldn't shut down. What a day. Gob of the North and Michelle Jones, plus the terrible sight of her nan lying like that in the hospital bed. And it wasn't just *seeing* her that had been upsetting. Hearing her talk had been absolutely heartbreaking. Nan's strident no-nonsense tone had been replaced by a quavering stream of gibberish. Georgia had had to lean closer to try to make out the strangulated vowel sounds and muffled consonants, but it was as if the old lady was speaking in a foreign language – one that she couldn't understand.

While her nan spoke with such difficulty Georgia's glance had flicked across to her mum. She was close to tears, Georgia could tell. Horrible for her, Georgia thought, with a stab of sympathy. Horrible for them all, seeing this beloved woman reduced to such a state.

Still, it had comforted Georgia to be able to say to her nan 'See you tomorrow' when she'd left. Nan seemed to understand, and had seized Georgia's hands again, her eyes brighter than they'd been all afternoon. Her mum had clutched at Georgia too, eagerness lighting her face. 'You're staying, then? You're not dashing back off to London?'

'I'll stay tonight,' Georgia had replied. It wasn't as if she had anything pressing to do back home, after all. Once she'd filed her copy for Monday's edition of the newspaper (a cut-and-paste job, generally – she saved things up for it during the rest of the week), she tended to catch up on her sleep and telly on Sunday, give herself a breather after the hectic schedule of her week. 'If that's all right, of course.'

'Oh, Georgie! We'd love you to stay, wouldn't we, Bob?'

Mr Knight patted her on the back. 'Smashing,' he said. 'We can have a proper chat over tea, can't we?'

A proper chat no doubt meant goal-by-goal analysis of the football season, plus the rumours he'd heard about the manager's forthcoming sacking. Or maybe an in-depth discussion on the current Corrie storylines from her mum, or a wallet full of new photos of the gurning grandchildren that Georgia was supposed to admire.

Oh well. So be it. It was only one night, after all. She could see it through; she'd survived worse evenings in her time.

As it turned out though, they'd actually had quite a laugh, Georgia and her parents, sitting round the old table in the kitchen with their bangers, mash and beans, remin-iscing about camping holidays in North Wales, and what-have-you. Georgia had forgotten just how much she loved her mum's mashed potato; she tended not to do potato full stop, she knew what it did to the waistline – but tonight it had seemed like the comfort she needed. She'd forgotten just how infectious her dad's roars of laughter were, too. It had felt cosy, just the three of them, without Carol sticking her disapproving oar in every few minutes. And Georgia had drunk enough of her dad's whisky to send her spark out tonight – or so she'd hoped.

She sat up in bed and switched on the old bottle-green anglepoise lamp, the one by which she'd slaved over her homework in the evenings all those years ago. Despite the Scotch, she still felt too wired to drop off yet. She pulled her phone out and started checking her emails and texts. Got to keep in the loop. Got to stay in touch with her world.

She chuckled as she read an email from one of the reporters from the *Sunday Herald* – their sister paper – about the incriminating footage they'd been sent of a supermodel getting lairy after too much coke. Fantastic – she couldn't wait to see that. Then she raised her eyebrows as she read the goss about one of the Man United WAGs, Layla Gallagher, who was rumoured to be pregnant. Interesting.

Layla made regular star appearances in Georgia's column due to her wild antics – she was a party girl through and through, always in the clubs, dancing on tables, showing her arse. She had a background similar to Georgia's – working-class girl made good – and was blinging it up with her boyfriend's wages in hilarious style now. And boy, was she value if you ever got her on tape. Great quotes and one-liners tumbled from her lips with reliable frequency. She was especially accomplished at embarrassing her man, Carlos Ramirez, Man United's current star.

So a baby for Carlos and Layla was big news. Despite a temporary curbing of Layla's partying, there'd be plenty of mileage to be gained from belly shots, and speculations about Baby ... The public always seemed to lap up such snippets.

Polly Nash, a junior hack, had been doing some research for Georgia, and had emailed some copy over for her to check (on Saturday! That was a bit keen), so Georgia spent a while tweaking it and rewriting, before replying to her other emails. It was only when she'd done that, re-established her connection with her London life, that she was able to lie back down on the bed and close her eyes.

Just as she was about to sink into sleep, an image of Owen McIntosh floated into her mind and she smiled. Yes. Owen. She'd quite forgotten about him. She was rather looking forward to meeting him again tomorow.

It was ridiculous how jittery Georgia felt the next day about returning to the hospital. Nervous about another near-collision with Michelle and that Nan might have taken a turn for the worse, but also intrigued about meeting Owen again. Had he been coming on to her when he'd said he'd see her today? Or was it some kind of pastoral-care thing, where he wanted to check she hadn't had another panic attack?

Either way, she was looking forward to it. And thank heavens she'd had the foresight to stuff a change of clothes in her bag yesterday; you could never tell with Carol's kids if they were going to puke on you, or scribble on you with felt-tip or something equally vile. And there was no way she would risk travelling back to London in that sort of a state.

It was a good choice, too, the dress she'd brought with her: a red summery one which actually made her look as if she had something resembling a cleavage. She considered her reflection in her mum's full-length mirror. It was rather a look-at-me dress, the sort she'd wear to summer parties or receptions, with red stilettos and a sparkly bag. Was it too much for a visit to a Stockport hospital?

She shrugged. Oh, sod it. She didn't have anything else with her, and Nan did like bright colours. And Owen ... well, bless him, he was only a bloke after all. Either he wouldn't notice (in which case he wasn't a real man in the first place) or he'd assume the effort was all for him and get above himself (in which case, she'd have to take him down a peg or two). She found she was actually quite curious to see his reaction.

Nan was awake when they arrived at the hospital this time. Her eyes sparkled at the sight of Georgia and she stretched a withered arm in her direction.

'Hello Nan,' Georgia said, leaning over to kiss her face. It felt as dry as parchment. Poor thing. Georgia knew her grandmother had sunk countless pots of Pond's cold cream into that face over the years to keep her skin soft, and now it was like kissing a piece of bark. She delved into her handbag and brought out her own jar of Crème de la Mer – a freebie she'd snitched from the beauty editor's desk at work – and dabbed some onto the old lady's cheeks. Four or five dabs – probably twenty quid's worth. If it had been anyone else, Georgia might have made reference to the sum. She might even have joked about charging them. 'There,' was all she said, though. 'That feel better?'

Nan nodded and made a noise that might have been yes. She took Georgia's hand and pressed it to her face, then kissed it. Definitely a yes, loud and clear.

'Thanks Georgie, that was lovely of you,' her mum said now, sitting down and stroking the old lady's hair. 'Shall we give this mop a brush, then, eh, Mam?'

Georgia felt choked as her mum did her nan's hair for

her, gently and tenderly. With her nan's incoherent speech and inability to do these things for herself now, it was as if she had slipped back into a toddler existence, dependent on her descendants. And there were still so many conversations Georgia wanted to have with her, so many things she wanted to ask — about her nan and granddad falling in love, her nan's experiences in the war, her hopes and aspirations as a young woman, her take on the feminist revolution . . .

Tears stung her eyes. Already it was too late. Short of a minor miracle where her nan's powers of speech came back, Georgia had missed her chance.

Her nan was patting her skirt, trying to say something. 'Ni-i-i eh,' it sounded like.

'Nice dress?' Georgia guessed.

Her nan nodded, her mouth curving at one side to form a saggy smile.

'Thanks, Nan,' she said. 'It's a great colour, isn't it? I'll look out for some flowers that shade of red to bring you next time, if you want?'

Next time? Why had she just said that?

But her nan was nodding again and mangling another word through her slack, sloping lips. 'Ow-er.'

'Flowers, yes. I'll do that. I'll bring them in tomorrow, yeah? Brighten this place up a bit.' What was she saying?

She was meant to be back at work tomorrow, she'd said as much in her email to Polly last night. But another glance at the happy light in her nan's eyes told her she had done the right thing.

Oh well. It was only a day. She'd phone Isabella, the editor, later and spin her a story about having to stay up north in an attempt to nab a big interview with the new Corrie starlet. Or she'd ring in sick; Isabella would never need to know.

There was a movement behind them then and Georgia turned to see Owen approaching. Ahhh. Yep. That was definitely a once-over he'd given her, eyes flicking over her dress, a small smile on his lips. He gave her a meaningful nod, then assumed a professionally brisk air and turned his gaze to his patient. 'Good afternoon, Mrs Hatherley! You're looking cheerful. I'm just here to do your obs, if that's all right. Won't take a minute.'

Georgia watched him as he chatted away to her. She was intrigued as to what — if anything — Owen would say to *her*. Surely it would be naff of him to ask her to have coffee with him while she was sitting at her grandmother's bedside? In front of her parents, too! Would he have the bottle?

Owen finished his observations and jotted them down in the folder that was kept at the end of the bed. Then he smiled at them all and tucked his pen back in his jacket pocket. 'Everything's stable,' he announced. 'Is there anything anyone wants to ask me while I'm here?'

Cheeky bugger. Was that for her benefit? Was he passing the buck, expecting her to put her hand up and ask, Please, Doctor, may I buy you a drink at the coffee bar?

He could dream on, if so. She wished she hadn't worn this dress now, if he thought she was an easy target! It was almost laughable, how wrong a man could be.

She raised her eyebrows but said nothing. Her mum, meanwhile, launched into a series of probing questions about her nan's mental health which Owen was now obliged to answer. Ha! Served him right.

Finally the lengthy Q-and-A session came to a close. 'Right then,' Owen said, trying to catch Georgia's eye. 'I'll be off.' He hesitated for a moment, but Georgia deliberately ignored him. Let him sweat, she decided. She wasn't going to have any bloke thinking they could have her, just like that.

'Thanks very much, love,' Georgia's mum said to Owen, bestowing a bright smile on him.

With one last, puzzled look at Georgia, he walked away.

Georgia rose to her feet with an unhurried air after a few moments. 'I'm just going to stretch my legs,' she said. 'Anyone want anything from the café?'

With orders for two teas and some biscuits, Georgia

sauntered down the ward. Now then. Where was Mr McIntosh? Was he loitering, or had he given up?

She smiled to herself as she went through the swing doors and saw him studying a noticeboard nearby. *Pretending to study it, more like*, she thought, for he turned almost immediately and smiled at her. 'Hello again,' he said. 'How are you doing today?'

Oh, like that, was it? Doctor and patient? She'd always liked a game of doctors and nurses as a kid, but this was a new one on her.

She took pity on him, gave him a bit of encouragement. 'Fine, thanks,' she said. 'I'm going for a coffee. I don't suppose you fancy one, do you?'

She half-expected him to say, *What, a coffee?*, like she'd been offering anything else, but he merely winked. 'Love one,' he said. They started walking along the corridor and he laughed. 'Well, I say "love" one, but the coffee in this place ... There's not much about it to love, if you know what I mean.'

'Tell me about it,' Georgia said. 'Where I work, the canteen is so dire, we're forced to leave the building and get our coffees from the Italian place down the road.'

'Where do you work, then?' he asked. 'In Stockport?'

She nearly scoffed contemptuously – as if! – but remembered at the last second that *he* worked in Stockport. 'London,' she said airily. 'I'm a journalist.'

'Oh yeah?' He didn't seem as impressed as she thought he might. 'Muckraking and gossip-spreading, that kind of thing?'

She arched an eyebrow at him. 'No, I'm the current affairs editor, actually. Hardline politics and Westminster diaries, if you must know.'

Now he was impressed. 'Really?'

She smiled. 'No. Not quite. Maybe next year.' And maybe never, if she was being strictly truthful. She wasn't going to have her job dissed though, so said no more. People were quick to turn their nose up at what Georgia did. She didn't want to give Owen the opportunity.

They'd reached the coffee bar now. Georgia had a precautionary flick round for Michelle, but the place was practically empty. Behind the counter there were two elderly ladies, a huge silver urn of tea and a nasty-looking coffee machine. 'Hmmmm,' Georgia said, considering the choice. 'Maybe I'll just have a sparkling water.'

'Spoken like a true Londoner,' Owen teased. 'I can't stand that stuff.'

'What are you having then, a mug of Bovril?' she flashed back. 'Or perhaps a can of Irn-Bru?'

He grinned. 'Touché,' he conceded. 'The tea's not bad, here. If you like it well-brewed, that is.'

'Well, you know what us soft southerners are like with

our delicate palates,' she replied tartly. 'I think I'll give it a miss, thanks, and stick with my water.'

He held his hands up. 'All right, all right!'

'I'll inflict the tea on my parents instead,' she said. 'Hi,' she went on to one of the silver-haired ladies. 'Two teas to take away please and a sparkling water. Oh, and some of these biscuits, please.' She dumped a handful of miniature packets on the tray, then a thought occurred to her and she turned to Owen. 'Oh, and do you want me to get your disgusting tea, too?'

He grinned again, and the dimple deepened in his cheek. 'I thought you'd never ask,' he said.

They sat down at one of the Formica-topped tables and she poured her water into a dishwasher-battered glass. She hadn't meant to stay long – she had her parents' drinks cooling, after all – but somehow or other, the conversation flowed from one topic to another – his job, her job, his flatmate, her ex-flatmate horror stories, their favourite TV shows, their favourite books...

He was just so easy to talk to. So nice. For the first time since she'd met Harry, she found she was actually hanging on his words, really listening, really wanting to hear about him. It was a strange sensation. Not one she was used to.

'So what brought you to Stockport, then?' she asked.

He'd already mentioned he'd grown up in Manchester. 'Don't tell me ... the football. No, the nightlife. No – I know. It's got to be the shopping and culture?'

He laughed. 'The job,' he answered simply. 'It's a really good hospital, this. Best one I've worked in yet. Manchester is great – but it started to feel too in-my-face. I fancied somewhere a bit smaller and quieter.'

Georgia shook her head. 'And that's where we differ,' she told him. 'That's exactly why I left. I love London precisely because it's so in-your-face.' She glanced at her watch. 'Damn, I'd better go. I'm going to have to get new teas for my mum and dad now – these are stone cold.'

'I'll walk you back to the ward,' he said. 'Just in case you get lost.'

She giggled, feeling like a little girl suddenly. 'Owen, it's only down the corridor,' she said.

'Ahh, good point,' he said. 'In that case, I'll walk you the long way round. Then we'll have more time to chat.'

He was flirting with her, he definitely was. She turned to go up to the counter, trying to hide her smile.

'Right, off we go, then,' he said, once she'd bought two new scalding hot cups of tea. 'The magical mystery tour. This way!'

He led her in the opposite direction from the stroke

unit, and through a warren of clinics. She had a brief palpitation at the thought of seeing Michelle somewhere en route, but did her best to block out her former tormentor from her head. No. Don't let that cow spoil things.

It wasn't long before Georgia was completely lost. 'I feel as if I should be dropping a trail of crumbs so that I can find my way back,' she said. 'I might have to start crumbling these biscuits up, you know.'

He smiled. 'Here – we can go outside for a bit,' he said as they came to a door. 'It's a gorgeous day.'

'Don't you have work to do?' she asked.

He shook his head. 'It's my tea break,' he said. 'And if you're going back to London tonight, I'm going to spin it out for as long as possible.' He paused. 'You are going back to London tonight, aren't you?' he asked.

There was something about his dark eyes that made Georgia feel ... liquid inside. Or was that all the sparkling water sloshing about? Yes. Must be.

'Well ...' She hesitated. 'I'm not sure now. I was planning to, but I've kind of promised my nan I'll come back tomorrow too, bring her some flowers.'

He smiled. A proper smile. 'Great,' he said. 'I'm in tomorrow too. So maybe ...' He hesitated. Was he about to ask her for a drink? Georgia wondered with a hopeful surge inside.

'Maybe we could do this again tomorrow?' Owen asked after the briefest of pauses. 'I'll take you round the X-ray department if you're really lucky.'

They were walking in the sunshine now, and she shielded her eyes to look up at him. A handful of witty bantering remarks fizzled on her tongue and she found that she was blushing. No. Not blushing. Just hot in the sun. Should she ask him for a drink instead? Or would that be jumping the gun? 'Thanks,' she said in the end. 'I'd like that.'

Oh God. This was ridiculous. She'd just told a bloke that she'd like him to show her round the X-ray unit of a hospital in Stockport. Get a grip, Georgia! But for a second, it had seemed the most appealing offer she'd had in ages.

She blinked, feeling dazed. Was she coming down with something? This was so unlike her. Was this the first sign of MRSA or some other nasty, that you started getting soft in the head?

She was just about to change the subject to something more neutral and safe, when an ambulance wheeled around the corner, siren wailing. 'Mind out the way,' Owen said, stepping back from the A&E entrance.

The ambulance stopped and a paramedic jumped out from the driving seat and flung open the back doors. Georgia could hear a woman crying and another female voice saying, 'Calm down, Layla. Everything's gonna be all right, I promise . . .'

Layla?

Georgia's brain clicked into work mode. She dumped the cardboard tray of tea on the ground and snatched her phone from her bag, just in case. Layla Gallagher and Carlos didn't live that far from here, did they? Cheadle way, she was pretty sure. Could it really be Layla Gallagher in the ambulance? What a scoop, if so! What a glorious scoop!

One of the paramedics was now assembling a wheelchair. The other stepped out of the ambulance with – yes! – a pale, sobbing Layla Gallagher in his arms.

'Oh my God,' Georgia hissed, holding up her phone to get the photo. The stupid paramedic had swung round though, blocking Layla's face. Georgia willed him to turn back so she could have a clear view of the girl. She had to get those tears in the picture – talk about a money shot!

'What are you doing?' Owen asked.

She'd all but forgotten him, so exhilarated was she at this unfolding drama. Was Layla losing the baby? She couldn't see any blood, but that didn't mean anything . . .

'I said, What are you doing?' Owen asked. His voice was cold – and then he grabbed the phone from Georgia's hand.

'Hey!' Georgia yelped. 'Give that back!'

He was looking at her with revulsion, as if she were a slug he'd just stepped on. 'I was right first time about you, wasn't I?' he said in that same icy voice. 'You're a muckraker, aren't you? A tabloid bully, preying on other people's misfortunes. Well, not here you don't. Have a bit of respect!'

'I only—' Georgia started, but he was stalking away from her, stopping only to toss her phone into a bin.

Chapter Nine

Babe

Tuesday, 17 June 2008

'Just these please,' Alice said, putting the wire basket in front of Mrs Smithers. Mrs Smithers ran the village shop and by all accounts considered you a traitor if you went to the Tesco a few miles away, despite stocking the mankiest, knobbliest fruit and veg Alice had ever seen, and glaring gimlet-eyed at any children who dared put their grubby fingers on her pick 'n' mix selection.

Mrs Smithers rang up the purchases slowly on the old till, a rheumaticky finger jabbing at the buttons. No rush. Nobody ever rushed in this village, Alice was starting to realize.

Her gaze wandered to the newspaper rack and fell on the front page of the *Herald*. Georgia's paper. GIRLS

ALOUD – GOSSIP SPECIAL! screamed a headline in bold black print. By Polly Nash, Showbiz Reporter.

Alice gave her usual shudder at glimpsing the tacky headlines of the *Herald* – it was a reflex action for her – then blinked as a thought struck her. *Polly Nash*, Showbiz Reporter? What had happened to Georgia's Knight on the Town column, then? Had she been axed?

A prickle ran down Alice's spine. Had Judgement Day finally arrived? She had been wishing for the guillotine to fall for such a long time. Could it actually be true that karma had paid Georgia back at last? She stretched out a hand for the newspaper, curious to find out.

'You'll have to pay for that if you want to read it,' Mrs Smithers barked, without moving her eyes from the till.

Alice thought quickly. She had boycotted the *Herald* on principle ever since Georgia had run the back-stabbing story that had wrecked everything. She would not pay a penny towards its future while that evil bitch still worked there. But if Georgia had *gone* . . .

'Well? Do you want it or not?' Mrs Smithers persisted.

No wonder people shopped elsewhere, Alice thought, hackles rising. Rude old cow! But she forced a smile and passed the paper over to the shopkeeper. 'Yes, please,' she said as sweetly as she could manage. She'd already had her reputation tarnished by Dom and his mates in the pub. She didn't want Mrs Smithers joining in the Alice-bashing with rumours about any perceived bad manners.

'Right. Eleven pounds seventy-two, then.'

No please, no thank you. Mrs Smithers was not exactly going for it on the customer-service front. It drove Alice into a sarcastic frenzy of over-politeness to make a point. 'There you are. Thanks. Thanks very much. Goodbye now!'

Miserable trout. Alice turned the buggy with some difficulty to avoid knocking over the ageing bottles of pop lining the wall, and left the shop. Then, as soon as she was out in the sunny street, she pulled the newspaper from her bag and turned to the showbiz page, propping it on the buggy hood to read it.

Oh, rats. The page was still headed Knight on the Town – and there was Georgia's face sneering out at her. But hold on ... What was this?

'Brought to you today by Polly Nash, Showbiz Reporter.' And then, in smaller letters, 'Georgia Knight is away.'

Damn. Damn it! False alarm – and now she'd gone and paid good money for the wretched newspaper. Georgia was probably stretched out, oiled and glistening, on a sunbed in Barbados, sipping cocktails in between being ravished by willing studs and concocting new bitchy stories with which to destroy other people's lives. Pah. And there Alice had been hoping her old enemy had been fired and reduced to gloomy stints in the jobcentre. Huh. She should have known. Georgia was made of tougher stuff. People like Georgia didn't get pushed out of their job, did they?

'Checking your horoscope?'

She looked up at the voice. Dom, of course, astride a bike. Did the man never have any work to do? She'd have thought this time of year there would be plenty of stuff to be done on the farm, or wherever it was he worked. She shook her head and stuffed the newspaper unread into the nearest litter bin. 'Nope,' she said.

His gaze flicked curiously from her face to the newspaper. Oh great. So what would the next rumour be? *Weird new-girl Alice has money to throw around! She bought a newspaper — and didn't even read it!* Well, she'd look forward to hearing the Chinese-whispered edition of *that* breaking-news story at the next toddler group session. She could hardly wait.

In the meantime, though, she wasn't going to hang around. Lecherous Dom would only get the wrong idea again. 'Bye then,' she said dismissively, and wheeled Iris straight past him before he could reply.

She could feel his gaze on her back. He was probably rolling his eyes and saying 'Women!' or something equally patronizing. Well, sod him. And sod Georgia bloody Knight, too!

*

It had been Alice's worst nightmare come true, the newspaper article. Of course, ever since Jake had landed a plum role in the big new prime-time BBC drama, he'd appeared in a few tabloid columns, but mostly only saying things like *Spotted in Covent Garden* – *Flying High's Jake Archer buying a latte!* Or *Watch out for* Flying High, *the new series on BBC One starring sexy newcomer Jake Archer as trainee pilot Leo Stone* ... That sort of thing, a mention. A small compliment at the most. Only a few words, but he'd cut them out all the same, stuck them in a folder. He'd laughed at himself for doing it – 'I know it's a bit train-spottery,' he'd said when she'd seen him there with his scissors, 'but I'm just dead proud, Alice. I'm dead excited!'

Then, as the series gained in popularity, the column inches grew longer. There were accompanying colour photos, and the words 'sexy' and 'hot' were bandied around with increasing frequency. And it wasn't long after that that he began appearing in the glossy celebrity magazines. 'You're in *Now* magazine!' Alice had screamed down the phone to him, the first time she'd seen it. She'd been flicking through the pages while she was waiting in the dentist's surgery and felt a huge jolt of excitement race through her at the shot. Her husband! Famous!

He'd chuckled down the line, sounding very pleased. 'I know – and my agent just called to say that *OK!* want an interview for next month, too. We're on the up, babe!'

That was when he'd still said 'we' and 'our', of course. Before it all became 'I' and 'my'.

She'd had no warning, Alice, when the storm broke. Jake was away filming – they shot a lot of the series in Suffolk – and Alice was on her own, her belly getting rounder by the day. What was she? Five, six months' pregnant? You'd think she'd know the date, but she'd blanked it from her mind, locked it away in a space she didn't often revisit. She'd been just about to leave the flat for some milk and chocolate on that particular morning. But as soon as she opened the front door, she'd been dazzled by the camera flashes.

'Over here, Alice! That's it, darlin'!'

Flash, flash!

There was a crowd of cameramen and journalists with notepads there, pressing in around her. She stepped back, blinking and confused, clutching the door jamb for support. Were they after Jake? Didn't they know he was filming?

'Can we get a comment from you, Alice? How are you feeling today?'

Flash, flash!

Stupidly – so stupidly! – she'd thought they were referring to her pregnancy. (She still cringed when she remembered that bit. As if they cared!) 'Well … fine,' she said, her hand covering her belly. She found herself wishing she'd washed her hair. It had been so greasy ever since she conceived, it was like an oil-spill disaster. And if the paparazzi were chasing *her* now — a celeb by proxy, like the WAGs you saw in all the magazines — well, she'd have to start making more of an effort with her appearance.

Someone laughed from the crowd but she couldn't see who.

'What do you think about Jake and Victoria, though? Any comment for us, sweetheart?'

Jake and Victoria?

Jake and Victoria?

Alice had stared in shock, flashbulbs popping like fireworks before her eyes. *Flash, flash, flash!*

'Don't tell us he hasn't broken the news to you yet?' one of the hacks yelled. 'What a swine! You wanna get a look at today's *Herald*, love. Here!' And a newspaper was shoved into her hand.

Alice had heard enough. She stepped back into the hall and slammed the door on them. The letter box opened straight away and a business card was posted through. 'My mobile number's there, Alice. Give us a bell when you want to talk. We can set the story straight, put your side across, all right? When you're ready.'

Her legs were shaking. She thought she might very well faint there and then in the hall. It was only the fact that someone was peering in through the letter box at her that propelled her to the safety of the kitchen, away from the vultures.

Once there she had leaned against the table and stared in shock at the front page. SEXY JAKE'S MILE-HIGH ROMPS! *Jake Archer and his leading lady in secret love trysts – full story by Georgia Knight, Showbiz Reporter, on page 3.*

That was the precise moment her world fell apart.

'Alice!' He was coming after her. 'Alice, wait!'

Oh, now what? She didn't feel like waiting. Not for Dom. He was another ladies' man like Jake, wasn't he? Cut from the same cheating cloth, no doubt. Well, she wouldn't be making that mistake twice. No way. She held the handles of the buggy so tightly that her knuckles paled. She'd ignore him. He'd get bored of her soon enough, and would move on to someone else. Just like Jake had done.

It had shocked her, his reaction to the pregnancy when she'd broken the news to him last year. 'But if we have a baby, you'll love it more than me,' he'd sulked.

The 'if' jarred. She *was* pregnant. In her mind, there was no 'if' whatsoever. She'd stared at him, wondering if he was joking. He wasn't. 'It's a different kind of love,' she'd countered. 'You're my husband. I'll always love you. And I'll love our children too.'

He'd recoiled. '*Children*? How many do you want?'

He wasn't looking at her, was fiddling instead with the PlayStation controls, his character on screen charging through a jungly scene, machine gun in one hand.

'Well ... I don't know,' she'd replied. 'I guess we have to see how we get on with this one first.'

He made a grunting noise and shot someone through the head. Alice winced at the blood explosion on screen. *Right*, she thought. *Like that, was it?*

That had just been the start of it. He was as indifferent to the pregnancy as she was delighted. He refused to be drawn into discussions of names, what colour they should paint the spare room, what the baby might look like ... She felt as if a chasm had opened up between them – almost that she'd lost her husband, her companion. In her darkest moments, she even wondered – she could hardly bear to think this now – she even wondered about aborting the baby. Just to get back the closeness with Jake.

Incredibly, he seemed to have lost interest in having sex with her too. That was unheard of. Unheard of! Alice found herself miserably examining her thickening waist in the bedroom mirror, her expanding thighs and bottom. Didn't he find her attractive any more? Not even with the huge bazoomas wobbling around on her chest?

Clearly not. He stayed out later and later at night, while Alice was so knackered she just wanted to sleep earlier and earlier. She felt a terrible ache of guilt that she was somehow to blame for this, that it was her fault relations had broken down between them.

Days went by without them having sex. Then a whole week! It had never happened before. Jake had always wanted sex round the clock previously – during hangovers, illnesses, Alice's period – nothing had ever put him off. But something had now.

'Alice, wait!' Dom's voice dragged her back to the present. It was a relief, actually, to find herself here in the leafy green lane, rather than in the claustrophobic and depressing confines of their old flat, sunk in anxiety for her marriage and baby.

She stopped walking and turned to face him. The sun was so bright she had to shield her eyes with her hand. 'What is it?' she asked.

He caught her up, the bike between them like a barrier. 'It's just ... I was wondering, have I done something to offend you?'

His brown eyes were wide with innocence and she almost wanted to laugh. Why did he care, all of a sudden? A show of thoughtfulness *before* he started discussing her in the Duke of York – that would have been the decent thing. But afterwards – too late, pal. The damage had been done.

She stood her ground and looked him in the eye. What did she have to lose by telling a few home truths? She'd never had the chance to say such things to Jake — he'd done a bunk by then. She'd wished and wished afterwards that she could have given him a piece of her mind.

'Actually, you have,' she replied, folding her arms across her chest. 'I don't like people gossiping about me behind my back. Especially in a village like this, where news spreads fast.'

He looked baffled. 'I'm not sure ... What do you mean?'

She put her hands on her hips. 'I *mean*, I heard what you were saying to your mates in the pub the other night.' She glared. 'Telling them you'd been up in my bedroom!' She blushed violently at the words, and the accompanying image that had just popped into her head. 'What did you say a thing like that for? I don't want people getting the wrong idea about me, I've only just moved in! So I'd appreciate it if you could keep that sort of remark to yourself next time!'

She swung away from him and tossed her head. Her hands were trembling and she clenched them into fists so that he wouldn't notice. 'Not that there will *be* a next time,' she added icily. Yeah. Good one, Alice. So there!

She risked a sideways glance at him. He looked annoyed. Well, not as annoyed as *she* had been! She stalked off, waiting for him to follow her and defend himself. He didn't bother.

Huh. Guilty as charged – she might have known. He could at least have put up a fight, though. She'd expected him to call after her, apologize even. But no.

She was surprised to find that she was just the tiniest bit disappointed.

Later that day, Alice was in the front garden, pulling up weeds in the sunshine. Iris was napping and it was so warm out, she couldn't bear to stay in the cottage to wash up the lunch things, or do anything housewifey. There was nobody but her own sweet self to tidy up for these days – Iris didn't care if they lived amid chaos. So maybe she'd muddle along in a mess for a while. It didn't really matter, did it?

She was just unwinding thick ropes of bindweed from a shrub and enjoying the heady fragrance from the rambling sweet pea whose flowers hung in perfumed bunches around the front door of the cottage, when she heard a voice.

'Hi there. Have you got a minute?'

Alice looked up from where she was crouching. At the end of the front path, leaning over the gate, was a tall, smiling woman with wayward dark curls. Alice straightened up and walked over to her. As she got closer, she could see that there was a pushchair just in front of the woman with a dozing baby inside. 'Sure,' she said. 'Hi, I'm Alice.' She smiled back expectantly.

'I know,' the woman said, and Alice's heart sank. Not

again. Was there anyone in this place who didn't already know who she was?

Her feelings must have shown on her face, because the woman smiled. 'Sorry. It's a nightmare, this village, for the gossips. I'm a single mum, so you can imagine they've had a field day with me.' She rolled her eyes. 'I'm Cathy, anyway, and this is Joe, who's nine months. We're only round the corner down from you, so if you ever fancy a coffee sometime—'

'Yes,' Alice blurted out without thinking. Then she blushed, embarrassed at sounding so keen. Desperate even! 'I mean ... that would be really nice. Er ... Are you doing anything now?'

Cathy shook her head. 'Nope,' she said. 'Well, obviously there's a mountain of washing back home with my name on it, and all the cleaning to do, but if you're offering...'

Alice grinned. 'I'm offering,' she said.

'Sod it, then, the housework can wait,' Cathy replied.

'Great,' Alice said. 'Come on in!'

It was too hot for coffee, so they sat in the back garden with glasses of iced water. Cathy wheeled her pushchair into a shady spot under the cherry tree, and as the babies slept, she and Alice chatted. *Cathy*, Alice kept thinking. Why did she know the name Cathy? Who in the village had mentioned Cathy to her? She was feeling fuzzy though, after a bad night up with Iris, who was teething, and the answer didn't come to her immediately.

'It's the evenings that are the worst, I think,' Cathy was saying. 'When you come in from the day and close the front door, and you know that's it, you won't see anyone else until you go out again the next morning.' She wrinkled her nose. 'I hate that, always makes me feel a bit gloomy.'

Alice nodded. 'Me too,' she said. 'I was staying with my parents after . . . after my husband left, so I was with them for the end of my pregnancy and while Iris was tiny. But now I've come here . . . well, it's so much harder on my own. It feels like the walls are closing in in the evenings, when it's just me and the telly night after night.'

They sat in silence for a moment and Alice worried that she'd been too downbeat. She'd only just met Cathy after all – she didn't want to come across as a total doom-monger. 'So, are you from the village, then?' she asked quickly.

Cathy nodded. 'Born and bred,' she replied. 'Left for a while to go to college in Exeter but somehow ended up back here again. It's a lovely place but . . . kind of small-minded, unfortunately.'

'Mmmmm,' Alice said. 'I can't believe everyone seems to know who I am already. It's a bit freaky. I was hoping to come here and keep my head down a bit, until I'd sorted myself out, but . . .'

Cathy looked sympathetic. 'But then you get here and realize that you're living in the gossip-centre of the West Country,' she said. 'There are a few people here with nothing better to do than bitch about their neighbours. The Duke of York? More like the Duke of Talk.' She shrugged. 'But you get used to it. And people do rally round, once they know your face. You wait, Stanley Middleton will get pissed and crash his tractor at the weekend again, and they'll all be talking about that instead of you. You'll be old news.'

Alice managed a smile. 'That sounds good. I just want to be left alone to get on with my life. Oh – I don't mean left alone by you,' she added hurriedly, 'but ... well, by *men*, basically. I've given up on them. And I've met this guy in the village who seems to have told everyone down the pub that I'm some kind of slapper and...' She grimaced. 'I mean – it's not true, for starters. And for seconds, what a cheek! Just because I'm on my own, it doesn't mean I'm gagging for a bloke.'

'What a prat,' Cathy said, shaking her head. 'Well, they're not all bad here, honest.'

Cathy's baby stirred at that moment and she took him out of the pushchair to cuddle him. 'He's so sweet,' Alice said, leaning over to stroke his cheek. And then something clicked in her head. Joe had a mop of dark hair, big brown eyes, and a wide friendly smile. He was the spitting image of Dom! And then she remembered where she'd heard Cathy's name before — down at the Mother and Toddler group on Monday.

I heard he wears Y-fronts, Jen had said, making a joke about Alice and Dom's so-called brief encounter.

And Mags had laughed, hadn't she? 'Where did you hear that?' she'd asked. 'Did Natasha say that? Or Cathy?'

The words spun in Alice's head now as she looked from little Joe to Cathy, and the penny dropped. Oh my God. Was Joe Dom's *son*? Clearly Dom wasn't with her any more, though — she'd said herself she was a single mum. So what had gone wrong with Dom and Cathy, then? And oh, how awful! There he was coming on to *her*, Alice, when poor Cathy lived in the village too! Did the man have no shame? No wonder he'd got himself a name around here. Alice could hardly believe Dom Fletcher's cheek. She despised him more than ever.

It had been on the tip of her tongue to ask Cathy about Dom, but as the afternoon passed, Alice decided not to. Why rake it all up? She'd only come across as being as inquisitive as the other village gossips if she started questioning her new friend about her love life. And she liked Cathy too — she didn't want to jeopardize anything by poking her nose in. They'd only just started getting to know each other; there was plenty of time for ex-husband confessionals further down the line.

It was half past eight in the evening now, but still warm and light outside. Cathy had gone home to give Joe his tea ages ago, but they'd arranged to meet up later in the week. Iris was fast asleep upstairs, arms outstretched above her head.

Alice hummed to herself as she shook the grass off her rug and brought it back inside. She loved this time of year. It made her think about the first summer she and Jake had been together. They'd both been skint, her with her job in the theatre as costume assistant, him trying out for endless stage and TV roles that always came to nothing. But they hadn't wanted for anything back then – it hadn't mattered that they barely had enough money for bus fares into London. They spent hours just lolling around in Jubilee Gardens, holding hands as they lay on the grass, kissing and laughing about stupid things. Alice couldn't remember feeling so happy to be doing nothing. The world was a wonderful place.

Still. That was then, of course, back when she was young and stupid. These days she knew better.

She poured herself a large gin and tonic, then flicked on the telly and sank into the saggy armchair. Thank goodness she was coming to terms with what had happened, she thought to herself bracingly. Positive thinking, that was the secret.

The picture appeared on the screen, and then her jaw dropped. All positive thoughts vanished instantly.

'Oh, Amelia, you know it'll only ever be you,' Jake said, his face glowing on the old TV, his pixelated eyes dark and intense. 'Say that you'll marry me!'

'Oh, Leo!' Victoria threw her arms around his neck. 'I am the luckiest woman in the world!'

The image of them kissing seemed to burn itself onto Alice's brain. Her hands shook as the credits began rolling up the screen in large white letters.

LEO STONE – JAKE ARCHER
AMELIA SANDERS – VICTORIA HARTLEY

'*Flying High* returns next week at the same time,' a hearty BBC voice announced. 'Tune in to see if the wedding of the year goes ahead, or if . . .'

But with a strangled cry, Alice had already switched the TV off, unable to bear seeing her husband and his mistress for a second longer.

Chapter Ten

A Million Love Songs

Monday, 16 June 2008, 5 p.m.

Katie's mind had gone blank. She leaned her head against the steering wheel, trying to think. She felt totally unprepared for the big conversation with Steve, despite her pep talk from Alice earlier. She'd panicked and driven right past her house in the end, parking up round the corner instead.

Think, think, think. She had been so engrossed in old memories all the way home, it seemed a struggle now to shake them off and reconnect with the real world. But Steve was back. That was a good sign. All she had to do was say the right words, talk through the situation calmly and stay in control of her emotions. No crying or big scenes – she knew men hated that sort of thing. She pulled down the sunshade and flipped open the mirror there to try out a few lines from the safety of her car.

'Can't we find some middle ground that we're both happy with?' she said to her reflection. 'I don't want to lose you, Steve.'

No. The bit about losing him was pure TV drama. Maybe a straight-out apology would be a better opener?

She gazed at the slice of her face that stared back from the mirror. Her eyes looked bloodshot and droopy, as if she'd been up all night on the lash. The skin around them was blotchy and pink. Not a good look. It was more a Suffering-From-Hay-Fever look than Stand-By-Your-Man.

'Steve, I'm sorry I didn't say what you wanted to hear,' she tried instead. Hmmm. That was the sort of sentence she might trip up on if she wasn't thinking straight. She'd get muddled up with the 'hear' and the 'say', knowing her.

Try again. 'Steve, I'm sorry,' she said instead.

Yes. To the point. Easy to remember. 'I'm sorry things went a bit wrong on Friday,' she went on, warming to the theme. 'It was a surprise, that's all. I didn't mean to hurt you.' Good, all good.

She pondered for a moment. 'The thing is, I just don't think I'm the marrying type – but that doesn't mean I want us to split up. I don't. So . . .'

Sighing, she pulled out her lipstick and rolled some colour onto her mouth, then applied some mascara in the hope of making herself slightly less haggard-looking. You never could tell, *Steve* might actually have a speech all lined up. She might go in the house and he'd be there, apologizing to *her* for putting her on the spot, of course it didn't matter about marriage and children, the main thing was that they were together. That was what counted...

She felt relieved at the idea. They could talk it out, resolve their differences, and all would be well again. She raised her eyebrows at her reflection. 'Well, let's find out,' she said to herself, starting the engine.

Katie's heart thumped as she parked near the house and opened the car door. Cool, calm, collected, she reminded herself, reaching over to grab her cardigan and bag from the passenger seat. Apologetic. Nice. Rational.

Her fingers felt clammy on the door key; it took her a few goes to get it into the lock and twist. She pushed the front door open and stepped inside. 'Hello?'

Dead silence greeted her. 'Steve?' she called into the empty hall. Dust motes swayed and danced in the shaft of light streaming in from behind her. But there was no sound or sign of him.

She turned on the spot and looked out at the road. Had he gone? Her eyes searched for his car but it wasn't there. Oh no! He must have driven off while she was parked round the corner, plotting her speech. And now she was too late!

Katie felt a wave of dismay break over her. Just as she'd

been all geared up for reconciliation and UN peace talks as well! Blindly, she dumped her cardigan and bag on the little table in the hallway and kicked off her shoes, feeling as if all the life was draining out of her. She couldn't believe she'd missed him. If she'd known he was in such a hurry, she'd have rushed here quicker, ad-libbed the whole scene.

But then a thought struck her. *Hold on a minute*. The fact that he'd come back was a good sign, sure, but where had he gone now?

Her mouth went dry. What if he'd come back for his stuff, then gone away for good?

Her legs felt like jelly as she pounded up the stairs. Their sunny bedroom at the front of the house looked different, she could tell at once. His alarm clock had vanished. There was a stray black sock on the floor. And ... Oh God. His suitcase had disappeared from its usual place up on the wardrobe.

She sank onto the bed, trying to take it in. He'd moved out. He'd actually left her! He'd sneaked in when he thought she'd be at work, packed some stuff and gone again, without so much as a note. What a coward. What a bastard!

She put her head in her hands, too shocked to cry. She felt numb, just trying to absorb the shock. But then anger began to rise through her steadily — anger that he'd run out on her in such a crap way, ducking the problem. Probably embarrassed that she'd turned down his proposal, as Alice had suggested. But there was no need to take such drastic action, was there? Bloody hell!

That was men for you. Emotional retards, the lot of them. And to think she'd been all set to try again with him, patch things up. To think that just a few days ago, he'd wanted to marry her — and now he'd buggered off. Honestly! How pathetic could you get?

Well, good riddance to him. Yeah! Good bloody riddance, Steve. She gave a hollow laugh, her fists clenched. She didn't need him anyway. She didn't need anybody!

An hour later, Katie was convinced she was a complete sadomasochist. Why else would she have heaved out all the holiday photo albums to leaf through, stopping to wipe away tears and blow her nose every other page?

There they were, her and Steve outside the Grand Palace in Bangkok. Their first holiday abroad together last autumn. They'd bought return flights to Bangkok, with Steve insisting that rocking up in the hectic capital with no accommodation booked would be much more exciting and fun than having everything arranged. Katie, of course, hadn't been able to resist poring over the Internet and her

Lonely Planet book, and had secretly booked them into a B&B just off the Khao San Road. That was the difference between them, you see.

Steve had roared with laughter at the airport in Bangkok when she'd sheepishly produced the plastic wallet she'd packed with maps and tourist information. 'What are you like?' he asked, hugging her to him and kissing the top of her head when she fessed up. 'Katie Taylor, Intrepid Explorer ... not!'

She'd laughed self-consciously. 'Sorry,' she said, burying her face in his new blue holiday T-shirt. 'I just couldn't help it.'

He'd kissed her again. 'So where are we going, then, oh Organized One? Lead me to our destination. I am in your capable hands.'

What had it been called, that place? The New Siam Guesthouse or something. Their room had had a simple wooden bed with white cotton covers, and a view over some back alleys where Katie imagined all sorts of wheeling and dealing took place. And oh yes, there had been that incredible tacky black marble bathroom which had had Steve whooping when he'd first seen it. 'Hey, it's like *Hollywood Wives* in here!' he'd called to her.

Woozy with jet lag, they'd sipped Singha beers in the bar downstairs, stunned by the mid-afternoon heat. Then they'd wandered along the Khao San Road together, marvelling at the tattooists and hair-braiders, the stalls selling tie-dyed sarongs and jewellery, the noodle bars with white paper tablecloths, the hustlers, hippies and total headcases all mingling on one dusty road...

Katie snapped the photo album shut. Why was she torturing herself with this? Why was she rubbing her nose in all these lovely memories?

'Wise up,' she told herself. 'It's over. So get used to it.'

Her phone bleeped at that moment and she snatched it up. A text message from her sister Laura:

Oi slag where r u?

Oh God! It was Monday night, wasn't it? She always met up with Laura for drinks on a Monday – 'It's the shittiest day of the week, only cocktails make it bearable,' Laura had decided – but somehow or other time must have slipped by. Was it really six already?

She checked her watch. Yes, it was – ten past, even. Oh ... bollocks. Well, she'd have to blow Laura out. She was so not in the mood for cocktails and chit-chat, much as she loved her sister. Laura would chew her ear off for not going, but it was a small price to pay. Tonight was a night to stay in and cry over old photos. Maybe neck some wine. And definitely scoff through the packet of Bourbons she had in the cupboard. That was if Steve hadn't packed them with the rest of his stuff, of course.

She dialled her sister's number and Laura answered after

one ring. 'So where are you?' her sister asked without even a 'hello'. 'There's a Sloe Comfortable Screw waiting here for you and it's getting all warm.' She gave a dirty chuckle. 'I suppose you could say it's better warm than – Eww, some pervy minger is looking at me now. Oi, nosy, this is a private conversation, thank you very much!'

Katie held the phone away from her ear as her sister barked at the pervy minger. 'Er Laur, the thing is, I—'

'So are you on your way or what? Only I'm really hungry, I was wondering, should I order us some food now, or—'

'Laura, I'm not coming out tonight.' There. She braced herself for the response.

'Oh Ka-ate! You could have let me know! Here I am sitting like Nelly No-mates on me tod, with nosy creeps all round me, and two drinks ... *and* I nabbed one of the tables out the front, too. So what's up? Why aren't you coming?'

Good question. Katie took a deep breath. 'Because ...' Her voice wobbled. 'Because Steve's left me.'

There was a shocked silence before Laura replied. 'NO!' She sounded incredulous. 'He's done what? No, I don't believe it. He's madly in love with you, what are you talking about?'

'Well, he *was* madly in love with me,' Katie admitted, trying not to sniffle. 'But now ...'

'Oh Kate, no, I'm not having this, I'm not letting you sit in all by yourself getting weepy. This is what I'm going to do, are you listening? I'm going to order you a cab to come and pick you up, and then I'm going to buy you nice drinks and food, and you're going to tell me all about it. Then we can make a plan. Maybe find a voodoo doll and stick some pins in its bollocks. Yeah? So blow your nose and put some slap on. Taxi is on its way.'

And before Katie could argue, Laura had clicked off.

Bloody hell. Since when did her little sister get so bossy and assertive? Katie tried ringing back but the line was engaged. No doubt Laura would be on to a cab firm already, dishing out her orders.

Katie sighed and looked over at her reflection in the living-room mirror. Pasty-faced, blotchy around the eyes and nose, plus a grid of worry lines etched deep in her forehead. How attractive.

She could always send the cab away again, she told herself. Just because Laura had spun into Emergency Rescue mode, it didn't mean Katie had to go along with it. And oh, this whole taxi thing was just reminding her of Steve's proposal at the hotel all over again, that ridiculous farce outside school with the cabbie asking her all those stupid questions ...

She squeezed her eyes shut, trying to stop herself crying. *Come on, deep breaths.* If she didn't go and meet Laura, she'd be stuck in all evening, moping and weeping. That was not a good option. Mind you, the prospect of moping and weeping in public wasn't exactly doing it for her either.

Oh sod it. Laura was good at cheering people up, she was one of those naturally ebullient types who managed to make you laugh whatever mood you might be in. She was straight-talking too – called a spade a spade. Out of everyone Katie could think of, Laura was probably the best person to be with tonight.

Okay. Decision made. She'd better trowel some make-up on as Laura had instructed. Hell, she'd even put on something nice to wear too, rather than the frayed old denim skirt she'd worn all day.

Just ten minutes later, the taxi was beeping outside her door, and she was off.

Katie and Laura always met at the same place on Monday nights: a bar on Whiteladies Road in Clifton, the nicest, poshest part of Bristol. Laura lived round the corner (lucky thing) in a leafy Georgian street – her small flat ('bijou' she liked to call it) was worth way more than Katie's house, despite it being about half the size. But then Laura was a high-flying PR woman who seemed to know all the Bristolian celebs – well, the Holby actors and actresses anyway – and earned the sort of salary that maths-teacher Katie could only dream about. Katie often thought that go-getting Laura should have been the oldest sister of the three Taylor girls — she'd probably have coped a lot better than Katie had with all the responsibility.

'Oh, at last, here she is,' Laura said as Katie got out of the taxi. Laura was sitting on the terrace outside the bar, two lurid orange cocktails on the table in front of her, one half-drained. 'I was starting to think you'd chucked yourself in the river or something.'

Katie paid the taxi driver and smiled wanly. 'That's a cheery thought,' she told her sister, rolling her eyes. 'Thanks for the sympathy.'

Laura pushed the full glass across the table. 'Sit down. Drink that. And tell Aunty Laura all about it,' she instructed.

So Katie began, uncertainly at first, feeling as if she must be some kind of loser to be pouring out her love-life woes at the age of thirty-four to her younger, sassier sister. The truth of it depressed her. 'How come I still can't do relationships?' she burst out, when she'd finished the update. 'I'm the oldest sister, yet you and Charlotte seem to have it all sussed. I'm the only crap one. What am I doing wrong?'

Laura snorted. 'I wouldn't exactly say *I've* got it sussed, mate,' she pointed out. 'I'm not about to go up the aisle any day soon. Charlotte — okay, so she's married with a couple of sprogs. But who's to say that's the most desirable thing in life? Honestly, Kate, I'm not being mean, but her life does sound kind of *dull* these days. She's gone all housewifey; can't talk about anything other than our lovely nieces. And they are gorgeous, of course, but ... well. Nappies and vegetable purees don't exactly rock my world in the conversation stakes.' She pursed her lips suspiciously. 'So are you really telling me that's the Holy Grail to you, all of a sudden?'

'No,' Katie replied, 'but the thing is, she's happy doing that, isn't she? In her eyes, she's got everything she ever wanted – husband, kids, farmhouse in Devon, Labrador, blah blah ...' She sipped her drink and winced at the sharp citrus tang. Charlotte had done what Katie had done – got married quick, to the first person who'd offered to look after her. The difference was, Charlotte had made a better choice. 'And then there's you – all sorted with your brilliant career, your swanky flat and famous mates. You know what you want, you know where you're going ...'

'Yeah, speed dating at Po Na Na's on Saturday,' Laura told her, pulling a face. 'That's where I'm going – I must be mad.'

Katie was barely listening. 'But me ... I thought I was on track, doing all right chugging along, you know? Suddenly I've swerved off the rails and don't know where I'm supposed to be any more.'

Laura raised an eyebrow. 'Nice analogy, Kate, but this

doesn't have to be complete derailment, does it? You can still mend things with Steve. He might just have gone off to get some space for a few days, clear his head. He's probably trying to phone you right now!'

Katie glanced down at her mobile, which remained reproachfully silent. 'No, he's not,' she replied. 'He's more likely out with his mates, drinking good-riddance pints and getting lairy.' She gazed up and down the street. 'We'll probably see him in a bit, doing the Whiteladies pub crawl on his hands and knees.'

'He'll get a Sloe Comfortable Screw over his head if he is,' Laura told her bracingly. 'Oh cheer up, Kate. Steve's not like that anyway, I bet you'll straighten things out with him. And if not, well, then, you can always come speed dating with me on Saturday, can't you? Twenty-five quid and there's a wine-tasting session too, so booze is thrown in for the price. I'll get you a ticket if you want, I know the manager there.'

The thought of speed dating made Katie feel old. And afraid. She didn't relish the idea of a conveyor belt of sneering men sizing her up then marking contemptuous black crosses on a scorecard; rejection after rejection. 'Thanks for the offer, but . . .'

'You think about it,' Laura interrupted. 'We'd have a laugh, you know we would. You don't have to take it seriously or anything, it's only a bit of fun.' She glanced past Katie's shoulder suddenly, then lowered her voice. 'Although if we play our cards right here, we might be in for something a bit sooner...'

Before Katie could look behind her to see what Laura had noticed, a couple of guys had plonked down a large jug of bright red liquid swimming with clinking ice cubes and lime wedges on their table. 'Evening, ladies,' the first bloke said. He had a white T-shirt and jeans, and tanned, hairless arms and face. 'I'm Gary and this is Mick. Just wondering if you'd like to have some Sex on the Beach with us?'

Katie stared at confident Gary's smooth forearms – had he put baby oil on them? They had some kind of sheen – and then at Mick, just behind – blond and sweet-faced and about ten years younger than her – oh Christ! – and was just about to say a polite *no thank you*, when Laura got in first.

'Sure, the more the merrier,' she said blithely. 'Pull up some chairs, lads. I'm Lulu, by the way, and this is Roxie. Cheers!'

Katie woke up the next morning feeling as if she'd been run over by the 41 bus. Her arms and legs ached. Her head pounded. Her mouth was dry, her tongue seemed cumbersome and unwieldy, and she could feel last night's make-up still on, tight and uncomfortable across her face. She peered at her watch through her thick, crusty-mascaraed lashes. Six in the morning. Ugggghhh … And she had school today, too! She'd have to squeeze in another hour's shut-eye and hope that a shower before breakfast would make her feel semi-human again.

She was just about to drift back into sleep when she heard an unfamiliar snore rumble behind her, and her blood ran cold. Oh no. Oh *no*! Suddenly she was wide awake and fearful. Who was she sharing a bed with? She opened her eyes again and blinked. And whose *bed* was it, anyway? She definitely wasn't on her own clean sheets.

She shut her eyes hurriedly, hoping it was a dream. A bad, couldn't-possibly-happen dream. But vague shadowy images of the night before were taking shape in her mind now, like a horror show flickering before her eyes. Necking that jug of Sex on the Beach with Mick and Gary – oh, and *Lulu*, of course. (Bloody Laura, what was she like?) Oh, and then they'd bought another jug of … what had it been that time? Tequila Sunrise. Ugh. She couldn't do tequila any more, she always lost the plot on it. And then …

The flimsy memories melted away to nothing. What had happened then?

It was a blank. She just couldn't remember. *Please don't let me be in bed with Gary*, she prayed under her breath. *Or Mick. I'll be arrested for child molestation if it's Mick. Probably be struck off as a teacher, branded a pervert …*

She opened her eyes again in a fit of boldness. She had to know the truth.

Oh. Duh. She was in Laura's bedroom. Of course. White walls. Fairy lights around the mirror on the dressing table. A framed Frida Kahlo print on the far wall. Wardrobe door flung open, revealing Laura's colourful clothes and shoes, handbag handles spilling from the bottom shelf in bright snaky coils. Her own clothes dumped all over the floorboards. Oh Gawd. Did that mean she was lying here stark naked?

She peeped under the cover. Still wearing knickers. That was a good sign at least. Then, taking care to move stealthily so as to go unnoticed, she turned over so that she could see who she had been sleeping with.

Laura. Just Laura. Thank God for that.

Katie had never been so relieved to see her sister's face in her life, her auburn hair curled on the pillow, cheek slightly flushed. So she hadn't ended up in bed with Mick or Gary then, thank goodness. And presumably she hadn't done anything too awful, no 'tampering and fumbling', as Laura would put it.

Although she did vaguely remember Gary – or was it Mick? – leaning in close to her, face looming as he tried to kiss her . . .

God. Please let me not have kissed him. She wasn't even sure if she had or not. How teenage was that?

She sat up carefully, wincing with the hangover as she levered herself upright. Ouch. She hadn't been so drunk for a long, long time. And on a Monday night, too! What had she been thinking? It had seemed such a good idea at the time, *yeah, another jug, let's do another jug,* and she'd been in a fuck-you-Steve kind of mood, so was up for complete debauchery.

Yes, but now here she was, stuck in Clifton, a good mile from her own place, with school to prepare for and . . .

An awful thought slammed into her. Oh shit. Shit! It was the Year 7s' parents' evening tonight at school on top of everything else, wasn't it? Hordes of parents to whom she'd have to talk coherently about their son or daughter's progress (or lack of). Even Katie – super-organized Katie – found parents' evening a long slog of a day, and that was when she'd spent the night before preparing and writing notes. Which – obviously – she'd neglected to do this time.

Why oh why had she drunk so much?

She padded off to Laura's monsoon shower filled with self-loathing and despair as she remembered the pile of marking she'd left at the school too, back on Friday afternoon before everything had gone so horribly wrong.

'Standards are slipping!' she heard Matt Dawson, the head, say in her ear. Yes, and he was right, too. Skiving off yesterday, having left her unfinished marking in school the whole weekend, no preparation for parents' evening, and, worst of all, suffering the mother of all hangovers on a Tuesday morning.

Standards had plummeted, worryingly quickly. Any moment now and the standards would reach rock bottom.

She bit her lip, feeling ashamed and queasy all at the same time. This was just not like her. Katie Taylor was usually fully in control, hands tightly on the steering wheel, knowing exactly which direction to take. Steve teased her for her conscientiousness, and she was known for it in the staffroom too – a professional through and through, with her spreadsheets and highlighter pens mapping out every occasion in glorious detail.

But now look at her! Hungover, waking up in her sister's flat presumably because she'd been too sloshed to make it home in one piece, whole hours of the night before a complete mystery, and totally unprepared for the working day ahead.

What had happened to her? How had she let her life get so messy so fast?

She stood beneath the shower spray and hung her head as the water rained down on her.

Chapter Eleven

Patience

Tuesday, 17 June 2008

Georgia was fuming. It was Tuesday morning and she was on the train heading back down to London. She'd already been in a pretty foul mood by the time she got to Stockport station to set off for home, but this was the icing on the cake. The cherry on the icing on the cake, in fact. Georgia had picked up a copy of the *Herald* to while away the journey, and had nearly keeled over when she'd seen the front page: GIRLS ALOUD – GOSSIP SPECIAL! by Polly Nash, Showbiz Reporter.

Er ... *hello?* Polly Nash was *not* the showbiz reporter. That was Georgia's job, thank you very much. Which moron in the subs team had cocked that one up, then?

But then, when she flicked through to her page, there

was Polly's ugly mug splashed at the top of it for all to see. And worse – *Georgia Knight is away.*

'No, I'm not!' Georgia had muttered furiously, gripping the pages so tightly the newsprint marked her fingers. 'I'm on my way back to the office right now, and you bloody know it!'

The cheek of Polly Nash, muscling in on her territory like that! Talk about dog eat dog. She'd have that little mutt for breakfast next time she saw her in the office, with ketchup on.

Georgia glared out of the graffiti-etched window as the train rattled down the track. She hoped this wasn't Isabella's idea of edging Georgia out. As editor of the paper, Isabella would have undoubtedly given the front cover her approval before it went to print. *She* clearly thought it was all right for Polly Brown-Nose Nash to be labelled 'Showbiz Reporter', didn't she? So where did that leave Georgia?

Hmmm. Georgia didn't like to think about that too much all of a sudden.

'Well, when can we expect you back?' Isabella had asked, in a rather chilly way, when Georgia had phoned her on Sunday to say she'd be out of the office for a couple of days. Isabella didn't like having surprises sprung on her. But then control freaks never did.

'As soon as possible,' Georgia had assured her. 'Wednesday at the latest. I'm going onto the *Coronation Street* set first thing tomorrow and I'll try to sew up the interview there and then. Hope you don't mind, it's just I bumped into one of my connections in Manchester yesterday and thought it was too good to turn down.'

'Right,' Isabella had replied. Deadpan, as if she were suspicious of Georgia's motives or something. Mind you, she was quite right to be suspicious, seeing as Georgia hadn't been anywhere near the *Coronation Street* set, and had had no intention of heading in that direction either.

Isabella didn't have to know that, though. These things fell through all the time. Georgia could pretend the teenage actress had thrown a hissy fit and changed her mind at the last minute about being interviewed. 'Pain in the arse,' she planned to grumble once she was in the office again. 'She's a right diva by all accounts – but I'll pay her back in the gossip column, you wait.'

And her boss would just have to swallow that. In the meantime, Georgia vowed to chase up some of her Granada contacts, see if they could get her a snippet of gossip that might conceivably have come from an on-set visit.

She sighed and closed the newspaper, folding it so that she didn't have to look at Polly's name any more. Tomorrow's column was sure to run with Polly's face on it again, much to the glee of that little amateur. Polly was probably already planning to move into Georgia's nice corner desk just as soon as she could get her Topshop-skirted bottom into Georgia's swivel chair.

Well, she could forget *that* idea. Georgia was going to work from home this afternoon, taking back her page with a mountain of articles and snippets that she would bash out. And she'd be back in the office proper first thing tomorrow and she'd bloody well stand over the layout person if she had to, making sure that her name and photo were back where they should be for Thursday's column, and for every column from then on. *And* she'd make a point of reminding Polly Nash exactly where her place was by dumping some dreary admin stuff on her: updating their celebrity database or something equally tedious and time-consuming. That would shut her up for a while.

Shit. This was all Georgia needed. She scowled out of the window feeling bad-tempered.

It had been heartbreaking saying goodbye to Nan the night before. She'd planned to go back to London on the last train yesterday but had ended up staying and staying at the hospital, not quite able to bring herself to go. Just in case it was the last time, although even *thinking* that was unbearable.

Georgia had brought flowers as promised, but she knew that flowers didn't make up for leaving. And oh, the twist of guilt at the sight of those tears leaking from her grandmother's eyes, it had made Georgia wince.

She sniffed, just remembering, and blew her nose. She was all muddled inside, as if someone had stirred her up with a big stick. She didn't feel the same Georgia who'd travelled north along this line just a few days earlier. She'd been so cocksure, so confident about her life then. In her mind, her family had been shut firmly in their own compartment, quite separate from Georgia, as if they were an accessory she could put on and take off at will. But now she felt as if it wasn't quite so easy to shrug them away, or put them back in their box. The family ties seemed suddenly to be tight around her, like bindweed.

No, not bindweed. That was the wrong word. That made it sound as if the ties were a bad thing and, to Georgia's great surprise, they didn't feel like that any more. For the first time in years – perhaps ever – she didn't have the usual upsurge of relief about saying goodbye to her family and leaving them behind. Instead, she just felt ... sad. Sad, and a tiny bit lost. Which was very peculiar, and not at all pleasant.

As a student, she'd been envious of the relationship Alice had had with her parents – an easy-going, uncomplicated love. Her own family dynamic felt much more difficult – she'd always felt like the wild one in the family alongside sensible Carol; Georgia was the one who'd champed at the bit to be different and get away. She'd felt scornful of her parents – what did they know about anything? And what good were parents when they didn't even realize you were so miserable you couldn't wait to escape?

But now ... now she was older and maybe even wiser too. She'd realized just how much her parents and nan were ageing, how much more fragile they'd become. She didn't feel that desperate need to run away from them any more. It was very odd.

Still, everything considered, it was hardly surprising she felt peculiar. Since arriving in Stockport on Saturday she'd seen her grandmother, old and dying in a hospital ward. She'd suffered a panic attack over Michelle Jones walking past her in a corridor. And she'd had her job rubbished by Owen, just when she was starting to really like him, too ...

She bristled. Owen was another reason why she felt mixed up inside. He hadn't shown his face at the hospital yesterday. Not that she'd been looking out for him or anything – she so *hadn't* – but all the same, she was half-expecting him to seek her out and apologize for his temper tantrum the day before. Flinging her phone into the bin like that – her expensive prized-possession phone, thank you very much! – sheesh, talk about a strop. Just because she was trying to do her job! How would he have liked it if she'd chucked his stethoscope into the bin, or his stupid clipboard?

Idiot. She'd been annoyed ever since. Who did he think he was anyway, speaking to her like that? Some morality crusader? Layla Gallagher was public property and so was her unborn baby. Didn't Owen Goody-Two-Shoes McIntosh know anything about celebrity life? That was how it worked: if someone had done their utmost to secure tabloid column inches in the past with their footballer boyfriends and dirty-dancing nightclub displays, then they were fair game. Law of the red-top jungle, wasn't it? He was naive if he didn't know that much.

All the same, something had prevented Georgia from filing any copy on the story. For some inexplicable reason, even though she knew a juicy headline about Layla Gallagher miscarrying would sell another few thousand copies of the paper and therefore earn her Isabella's praise and thanks, Georgia hadn't quite managed to press the Send button on the scoop email that lingered, unwritten, in her mind.

Not because of Owen. No way! But because . . .

She fiddled with her music player, flicking past a mournful song that had just come on. *Oh all right, perhaps a little bit because of Owen, then*, she admitted to herself. She had felt so judged, so criticized, the way he'd yelled at her. What was it he'd called her, in that horribly cold voice? A muckraker and a bully. Her, Georgia! *Have a bit of respect!*, he'd shouted before stalking off in his huff.

Her skin prickled as she remembered. A bully – he'd actually called her a bully! Georgia knew about bullies – oh yes, she knew all about them. And she was certainly *not* a bully. She despised bullies after everything she'd been through at school. Loathed them. And for Owen to turn around and lump *her* in with the likes of Michelle Jones...

Well. It took her breath away. It was pretty much the worst thing he could have called her.

That wasn't the only thing that had shocked her. It was the unexpected surge of empathy she'd felt for the pampered model afterwards, remembering her vulnerable and frightened, crying in the ambulance like that, when she was usually dolled up to the nines and flicking her hair around for the snappers. Sure, Georgia knew that celebs were real people too, with feelings and fears, she wasn't *completely* dehumanized. But in her job, it was easy to see these people as meat on a rack. Puppets manipulated by their PR maestros. All players in a game.

Owen's words had broken the spell. And what had been front-page headlines suddenly became a woman in pain, a frightened, crying woman who thought she was losing her baby.

Tears pricked Georgia's eyes. She of all people should have known not to dehumanize a person in that situation.

She'd been there herself, same spot, bleeding and scared in an ambulance. How had she become so numb, so desensitized?

She found a tissue from the depths of her bag, wiped her eyes and then slid her shades down to cover her damp lashes. A tricky weekend, that was what it had been. Everyone made mistakes, didn't they? And now she was going home, thank goodness, and back to normal life.

She stared out the window, feeling numb, not particularly looking forward to being back in London. And wishing she could stop thinking about Owen for five bloody minutes.

Two hours later, Georgia was there. She lived in an airy top-floor flat in a large Victorian house overlooking Clapham Common, a stone's throw from the bars and restaurants of the High Street and Old Town. She'd bought the flat a few months after splitting up with Harry, once she'd got her head together again. That had been a mad, mad time — one that she didn't like to think about too much. By then, Katie had tired of London and was studying for a PGCE in Bristol, but Alice was still in town, designing costumes at the theatre, having worked her way up from skivvying, and her flat in Streatham was the first place Georgia thought to take refuge.

'Of course you can stay,' Alice had said when Georgia

had appeared in tears on the doorstep. 'Oh, honey! Look at the state of you. Come in, let me take those bags. Everything's going to be all right.'

It had been a sanctuary, Alice's flat, the perfect place to mend a broken heart. Georgia had slept on a camp bed in what Alice called the 'sewing room', where swatches of fabric were pinned up on the walls, half-made costumes were hung on a rack, and a hotchpotch of outfits were stuffed into the wardrobe – everything from Caliban's mask to Cinderella's ball gown. It was like sleeping in a strange dream.

Georgia felt a twang of remorse thinking about it as she unlocked her front door. Alice had really looked after her, had listened to her vent all her hatred of Harry, hadn't moaned once when Georgia had wanted to sit up talking until dawn for nights on end, had kept the fridge full of wine and dark chocolate. And then had come that day when Alice arrived home practically glittering with excitement. 'There's this gorgeous actor in rehearsals at the moment,' she'd sighed. 'Jake Archer. Oh my God, George, he's absolutely lush...'

Georgia banished the memory instantly and stepped into the hallway. It felt cool and quiet after the hot pavement bustle outside, and she dropped her bag and kicked her shoes off as soon as she'd shut the front door on the rest of the world, grateful to be back in her own space at last.

She picked up the post, then walked across the honey-coloured stripped floorboards of the open-plan living space and into the kitchen area, where she poured herself a tall glass of water and sat at the table. She stared around her kitchen, as if seeing it for the first time. Her clear, cold granite surfaces, clean lines and reflected light – such a contrast to her mum's peeling beige worktops overrun by sticky spice jars, the fingerprint-marked toaster, piles of mail and old newspapers, recipes snipped from magazines . . .

Thank Christ she was back here now, where it was all in order. No children's paintings Blu-Tacked to the wall, no overflowing bread bin (a dieter's nightmare) and no naff mug tree complete with full set of football mugs.

The thought prompted her to phone home. Unexpectedly she found herself wanting to make that connection. Just so her mum didn't worry, or anything, that was all.

'Hi, it's only me,' she said when her mum picked up. 'Just . . . letting you know I got back all right.'

Her mum sounded slightly bemused. 'Oh. Right. That's very nice of you, Georgie. Did you have a good journey?'

'Not bad,' she replied, leaning back on the chair and putting her feet up on another. She wiggled her bare toes – must get a pedicure booked in soon. You couldn't have too many in the summer. 'How was Nan this afternoon?'

'She was a bit drowsy, they're trying her on some new

medication.' Her mum sighed. 'Couldn't get much out of her, to be honest. Maybe tomorrow.'

Georgia hesitated. She wanted to find out if Owen had been round, but hated herself for even wondering about it. No. She wouldn't lower herself to ask. This phone call was not about him. 'Well, give her my love when you see her next, won't you?' she said in the end.

'I will, pet. It was a real tonic for her, seeing you. We're all ever so grateful that you came up.'

Georgia squeezed her eyes shut. The words made her squirm. It wasn't right that her family should be so grateful for one measly little visit when the rest of the time she'd deliberately stayed away. 'I'm glad I did,' she said, surprised by the truth of her words. 'And ... I'll try and visit again soon.'

'Oh, great!' Her mum's surprised joy almost lit up the phone. 'She'll look forward to that – well, we all will. Me and your dad were saying it was just like old times having you home. Ever so nice to catch up properly.'

'Yeah, it was, wasn't it?' She meant it as well, she was taken aback to realize. She'd felt so relaxed on her parents' old sofa, so comfortable.

She stood up and gazed out of the window. Five o'clock now, and the first few office types were sauntering their way gladly into the pubs and bars. Down on the common, women were pushing prams in slow convoys while bare baby legs kicked in the late afternoon sunshine. Studenty types were sitting in big groups on the grass, newspapers, books and cans of lager dotted between them. *Home*, her mum had said. But this flat, this city, was Georgia's home now, had been for a long while. If she felt like it, she could be down there too within five minutes, choosing a table on the roof terrace of the Sun pub and sipping a cold white wine while she read a book. Or she could call a girlfriend about meeting for tapas in Carmen, or buy herself a vodka in Revolution and hang out there eyeing up the talent. If she felt like it.

She dragged herself back to the conversation. 'Okay, Mum. Love to Dad and Nan. Speak to you soon, bye.'

She pressed the red button to end the call. *Right*, she thought. *Now what?* She didn't actually want to go to any of the places that had just popped into her head. She wanted to . . .

No. Don't be ridiculous. Of course she didn't want to sit at a Formica-topped table in a Stockport hospital and drink fizzy water with Owen McIntosh. Why the hell would she want to do that, when she had the best bars and restaurants in south London right on her doorstep?

She groaned out loud and sank her head onto the table. What was *wrong* with her? Was she ill? She hated feeling like this – weak and muddle-headed. Why couldn't she snap out of it, the way she usually did? Why couldn't she get that man out of her mind?

Two seconds later, she banged a fist down on the table. Enough, Georgia. Enough wallowing in this weird mood. Time to move on, yeah? She sat up and steepled her fingers together, putting together an action plan.

First, she told herself, *I'm going to take a shower and have some proper food. Then I'm going to call the office, kick Polly Nash's butt and write some fabulous copy for tomorrow. Who gives a monkey's what Owen McIntosh thinks anyway?*

Georgia felt fired up with energy and enthusiasm the next morning. She got up early, went to a BodyPump class where she squatted and lunged with the zeal of Paula Radcliffe, showered and blow-dried her hair, then threw back a vile wheatgrass concoction, followed by a latte and Danish on the tube (hell, she was only human). She strode into the office at eight thirty, feeling ready for action, swishing her hair behind her like someone in a Pantene advert. Make sure Isabella had clocked her early arrival ... check! Isabella didn't seem to need any sleep, she pretty much lived in her office. No wonder she was onto her fourth marriage by now. Georgia waved a hand at her editor, standing in her glassed-in box, hand on Armani-clad hip as she barked at somebody over the phone – she liked to be able to see her minions, did Isabella — then stalked smartly along to her own, slightly less glamorous, corner of the office.

Right then! To work. She switched on her PC and slid into her chair, her bottom aching slightly from the exertions of her gym class as she lowered it to the seat.

She grabbed the day's paper to flick through while she waited to log on — but didn't get past the first page before her jaw dropped open with an almost audible clunk. *Win your very own Knight on the Town — with Georgia!* screamed a caption to the left of the main headlines. And there was a mugshot of her — not the most flattering one of her either — and a *See page 5 for details!*

Christ. What the hell was this? *Nice of the editorial team to bother telling* me *about it!* she thought sarcastically, as all the poise and energy she'd had two minutes ago deserted her. She whipped through to page 5 feeling hot with indignation.

Our new competition — win a Knight on the Town! she read. *Do you love celebrity gossip? Do you have what it takes to party with the best of them? If so, this competition is for YOU. We're offering one lucky reader the chance to see and be seen in some of London's most exclusive haunts. Imagine yourself drinking cocktails in the West End's premier bars. Perhaps you'd like to dine where the A-list hang out? And then you can round off the evening by partying with the hippest crowds at one of London's trendiest nightclubs! Best of all, you'll be with our super-scooper Georgia Knight, as she gets the low-down on all your favourite celebs and stars. It'll be a Knight to remember, and that's for sure!*

Great. Bloody great. Whose bright idea was this, then, to offer Georgia up as a competition prize? And which joker had dared describe her as a 'super-scooper', for crying out loud? It made her sound like some nasty dog-care accessory used for cleaning up turds on the pavement. Just the image she'd been trying to build – not.

Her phone rang just then and she snatched up the receiver, feeling agitated. 'Yes?'

There was a moment's pause and then Isabella's voice snaked into Georgia's ear. 'I'd like to see you in my office,' she said. That cold tone again. 'Now.'

Georgia flinched as the line went dead, then frowned. What was Isabella in a stew about, then? She got to her feet a little shakily (and ouch, her bottom was really starting to feel as if someone had whacked it with a bag of spanners), and brushed down her skirt in case any telltale Danish pastry flakes still lingered there. Isabella noticed these things, and always let you know she'd noticed them, too.

She's probably just going to explain this ridiculous competition, Georgia thought to herself as she wound her way back through the desks towards Isabella's office. *Or brief me about some new premiere or interview she's lined up for me. That would be nice . . .*

She knocked on her editor's door and went in.

'Georgia, did you or did you not have an interview arranged at the *Coronation Street* set on Monday?' Isabella snapped without preamble.

'I . . .' Words failed Georgia momentarily. She wondered whether or not she should sit down, but Isabella was still standing, and Georgia didn't want to give her boss the advantage of height. She drew herself up and looked her editor full in the eye. Time to lie, she reckoned. 'I'd set up a meeting with Anna Tate, the new Rovers' barmaid, yes,' she said coolly, crossing her fingers behind her back. 'Unfortunately, it was cancelled at the last minute. Annoying, but one of those things. The good news is—'

'Georgia, I'm not an idiot,' Isabella said crisply. 'So don't mistake me for one.'

Georgia stopped talking abruptly. Shit. What did Isabella mean by that? Her heart raced and her palms felt clammy. She'd have to try the innocence card in the hope that Isabella would explain. 'I'm sorry, I'm not sure—' she faltered.

'I was at a dinner party with Isaac, Anna Tate's agent on Saturday night,' Isabella went on smoothly. 'And coincidentally, I mentioned to him how we'd love to do a piece with Anna for the paper. Unfortunately, he told me he'd just signed up a big exclusive interview with Anna to go in the *Mirror* next week. All about her abusive foster parents, apparently. Dynamite stuff, he reckoned.' She gave Georgia a long, disdainful look. 'So imagine my surprise when you called the next day to tell me *you'd* got an exclusive with her. I double-checked with Isaac just to give you the benefit of the doubt but . . .' There was a delicate pause, and then Isabella shrugged. 'He didn't seem to know anything about it.' She left the words hanging in mid-air and stared expectantly at Georgia. 'So . . . would you like to explain yourself?'

Georgia thought fast. Her reputation was at stake here, job possibly at risk, even. Whatever she said had to be slick and convincing. She could *not*, for instance, make excuses that she'd been visiting her ill grandmother. Isabella would probably hurl a BlackBerry at her head if she came out with that line of defence. She could always wheel out her secret weapon, Layla Gallagher, she supposed, but did she really want to go there?

'My contact let me down over the Anna Tate interview,' she bluffed instead, just about managing to meet Isabella's gaze. Sweat trickled down in a channel between her shoulder blades. 'A false promise. It sometimes happens. But fortunately, I got something even better.'

The dangled carrot got Isabella on the back foot at last.

'What's that?' she asked. *This had better be good*, was the unspoken subtext.

Sod it. Sorry, Layla, Georgia thought. But it's your neck or mine on the line here. 'I've got an exclusive on Layla Gallagher,' she said. 'She was rushed to hospital on Sunday with—'

Isabella let out a contemptuous snort and tossed that day's edition of the *Sun* at her. Georgia had to scrabble to catch it and even so, Mystic Meg's page broke free and floated to the floor, the clairvoyant's eyes staring into her as she fell to earth. Georgia tried to reassemble the newspaper, adrenalin coursing through her. And then, as she saw the front page, she felt a sinking sensation of doom.

Layla: My Baby Scare — an exclusive report by Chloe Wells, our Showbiz Reporter!

Shit. Oh shit. Georgia had missed her chance. Even worse, she'd rocketed right into Isabella's blacklist of hacks behaving badly. Bollocks. This was possibly the worst moment of Georgia's professional career — worse, even, than when a member of a chart-topping boy band had puked cider and black all over her in The Ivy. How on earth was she going to dig herself out of this hole?

'Thank goodness we've had Polly here to keep *our* showbiz page running,' Isabella said after a few moments' excruciating silence. She raised her hand and smiled in greeting as someone walked past her glass wall outside, and Georgia turned to see the brown-noser herself smirking back with a little wave in reply to Isabella's. Polly had new shoes on, Georgia saw with envy – high, strappy, petrol-blue new shoes. Damn her. Had she been given some kind of bonus? Junior hacks couldn't usually afford such niceties on the pittance the paper doled out to them.

'As you know, Polly's been covering for you while you were . . .' (deliberate pause for effect) '*away*, and she also came up with the brilliant idea for our new competition in the Monday meeting,' Isabella said, turning her gaze back to Georgia. 'I've decided to send her to the Film Festival Awards on Friday, see how she gets on.'

Georgia felt very small, as if she were five years old and had been hauled up in front of the headmistress at her old primary school. Ouch. That hurt. She could no longer meet Isabella's fierce stare and looked down at her feet in their rather shabbier black wedges instead. She was surprised they hadn't been transformed into T-bar Start-rites, scuffed at the toes from too much skipping at playtime. 'Yes, I saw you were running a competition,' she replied, trying not to sound too sullen about it.

'Georgia, you know I've always been a fan of your work, but Polly's snapping at your heels,' Isabella went on in a brisk, no-nonsense manner. Every word made Georgia's spirits plunge even lower. 'Don't give me good reason to switch your positions over, will you?'

What a snub. Isabella had all but rubbed Georgia's nose in the stinking mess she'd made. 'Of course,' Georgia managed to say. 'It won't happen again, Isabella.'

'Hmmmph.' And with that final snort, Isabella turned away from Georgia and buzzed through to her secretary. 'Get me Samantha Cameron on the line, Hester,' she ordered.

Chastened, Georgia left Isabella's office. Well, that had gone about as badly wrong as it could have done. She scowled as her eyes alighted on Polly, who was cooing merrily to someone on the phone. 'Of course I'd love an invite to the wedding, Casey,' Polly simpered. 'I'll bring a photographer along too — make sure we get some lovely shots in the paper, yeah?'

Pah. Since when had Polly gotten so chummy with Casey Holland, the bitchy new nurse on *Casualty*? Georgia couldn't bring herself to listen to any more. She stormed over to her desk and started typing as if her life depended on it. She would not be pushed out of the job that she'd worked her arse off to get. No way!

Two hours later, Georgia was feeling slightly better. She'd dashed off a piece about Candi's birthday party, composed a thinly disguised 'Mystery Whisper' about Adam Tennant which implied he was impotent, and she'd even humoured Page Three stunna Aimee Morello with a bitchy snippet about Warren Blake's so-called chipolata and his love of being spanked. That would get the away crowds taunting the poor lad at the Emirates Stadium next season, she thought, putting in the final full stop with a savage stab.

She'd also heard that Layla Gallagher hadn't lost the baby, after all. This comforted Georgia more than she wanted to let on. Partly because it demonstrated that the doctors and nurses in her nan's hospital were doing a bloody good job. And also because what had been a scoop the other day was now a non-story. Chip papers already.

Her phone chirruped to let her know that a new text message had arrived and she checked it at once, hoping for a juicy titbit that Polly wouldn't have got. It was from Katie, though.

Y r men all such wankers? her friend had typed. *Fancy running away to lezza commune with me?*

Georgia was curious enough to be tempted out of Efficient Work Mode for a moment. *Wotsup?* she speed-texted back. *Lovely Steve not behaving?*

Lovely Steve has left me, came the reply seconds later.

O fuck! Georgia typed, taken aback at this news. *Will ring u 2nite 4 chat. Chin up. Xxx*

Her phone rang two seconds later – caller display: *Katie*

Mobile — and Georgia answered, hunching over her desk, not wanting to be spotted by Isabella on a personal call after this morning's dressing-down. 'What happened, then?' she asked her friend. 'Last you told me, he wanted to marry you?'

Katie sniffed. 'He did,' she replied. 'And now he's gone. Talk about all or nothing.'

She exhaled loudly, and Georgia frowned, recognizing the sound. 'You're not ... you're not *smoking*, are you?' she asked in shock. It was like finding the Pope snorting coke off a Bible.

'Yeah,' Katie admitted dolefully. 'I'm sitting in my car smoking. Just bought a pack of ten B&H for the first time in fifteen years. Morning break-time,' she added, as if that made it all right. 'Oh Georgia,' she wailed suddenly. 'Why are men such shits? Why?'

'Well...' Georgia paused. She was still too surprised at the smoking confession to think properly, and her reply spilled out without caution. 'Not all of them are, you know. Some are ... good.' She closed her mouth hurriedly, but it was too late. Katie hadn't missed her words.

'Oh yeah?' Suspicion laced her reply. Drag, puff, puff. 'Something you're not telling me about?'

Georgia felt flustered. Yes, all right, Owen's face *had* popped into her mind at Katie's why-are-men-such-bastards question, but she really didn't want to explain. She caught a movement out of the corner of her eye and turned to see Polly standing there as if butter wouldn't melt in her mouth.

'Are you going to be long?' Polly hissed. 'Only I've got Elliot Drake on the line, wants a word.'

Georgia held up a finger to signal one minute, hoping that would send Polly buzzing off again, but, to her annoyance, the goody two-shoes stayed right where she was, rocking back on her new blue heels as if she hadn't a care in the world.

Georgia gritted her teeth but knew she'd have to end her call. Elliot Drake was number one in the charts this week, gorgeous, gay and always full of gossip. Polly had no doubt already tried to tap him for information but if he was holding out for Georgia, she owed it to him to be quick. 'Sorry babe, gotta fly,' she said into the phone. And then, because she knew Polly was earwigging, she added, 'Let me know what Jordan says after your lunch together, yeah? Ciao.'

Katie would know there was an eavesdropper — Georgia had had to hang up in similar ways before, and she rather enjoyed pairing up her friend with the least likely fictional lunch-mates. And it was convenient, too, not having to fess up to anything about Owen right now.

She flashed a dazzling smile at Polly. 'Thanks, I'll take that call now,' she said, and pressed the Hold button on her office phone. 'Elliot! Hi! How's it going, sweetie?'

She listened, scribbling quickly, while Elliot reeled off tales of Soho shenanigans that would make her readers' hair curl. Her mobile chirruped again and, during a particularly filthy fisting anecdote that Georgia knew was totally unprintable, she pressed the messages button to see a new text from Katie.

U r SO not off the hook mate — who is this bloke then? + wot's so good abt him anyway?

Rats. She was never going to hear the end of this now.

Chapter Twelve

Shine

Thursday, 19 June 2008

There was a teddy bears' picnic organized that week for the village toddler group, all mums and little ones invited as long as they brought along their own food, picnic blanket and teddy. 'Not forgetting the vino of course,' Jen had muttered, reading the sign pinned up on the church-hall noticeboard.

'Now you're talking,' Mags had giggled in reply. 'And the ice bucket, too, dahling.'

Alice had dithered over whether or not to go – it would probably be horribly cliquey, she'd thought, imagining the miserable scene of herself and Iris sitting on their own little patch of grass feeling left out and shy, a small island set apart from the sea of other picnic blankets, where the rest of the village mums chatted about their primary-school allegiances and thirty or so years' worth of other shared nostalgia. And she'd be stuck there, Alice the Loser, silent and embarrassed on public display. Not a very tempting prospect.

But then Cathy had said that she would be taking Joe to the picnic, and was Alice going along too? And in a fit of bravery and must-try-to-be-sociable feeling, Alice had found herself saying yes. Safety in numbers and all that. Besides, she was curious to know more about Cathy and what had happened with Dom. There was definitely an untold saga there waiting to be revealed.

The gathering was to take place in Ellingham Woods, over on the far side of the village. 'I think "woods" is a bit of an exaggeration, seeing as there are only about ten trees,' Cathy said as they pushed their buggies that way on the day of the picnic. 'But at least it'll be shady. Pfff! It's so hot today.'

Alice nodded. It was practically unheard of in England, such a long, dry spell. She barely had the energy to speak, with the sun blazing down again on the back of her neck. She'd tied her hair up to keep cool, but a few rogue strands had escaped and were clinging wetly to her skin. She found herself longing for the soft wet mist of summer rain to dissipate the sultry heat. She glanced over the buggy's sunshade to see that Iris was asleep with flushed cheeks and sweat prickles on her nose, despite being dressed in just a thin cotton vest and nappy.

Phew! It was almost unbearable. Alice wiped her brow with her bare forearm, praying they were nearly there. The cheese sandwiches she'd made would be molten by now, squidgy and liquid in their cling film. As for the pot of veggie mush she'd brought along for Iris's picnic lunch — that was probably fermenting unpleasantly at the bottom of the bag.

'Here we are,' Cathy said, manoeuvring her buggy through an old iron kissing gate with some difficulty. 'Let's get in the shade before we evaporate. This way.'

Alice followed, grateful to escape from the sun under the leafy, shock-headed trees where the air felt fractionally cooler. In a clearing ahead, she could see bright picnic blankets spread out like a patchwork, with shrieking sun-hatted children chasing each other around the tree trunks.

As she and Cathy drew nearer, she realized that a series of eye-poppingly elaborate picnics had been laid out for all the world to admire — a large bowl of Caesar salad, complete with croutons and parmesan shavings, on a Cath Kidston picnic blanket (label up, obviously, just in case anyone didn't recognize the print), flanked with cold chicken legs and slabs of ham enrobed in glistening pink jelly on white china plates. Someone else had arranged a platter full of carrot, cucumber and celery sticks in circular patterns around an earthenware dish of what looked like home-made hummus, with drizzles of olive oil around the edges. One person had brought along a whole fruit cake, with a veritable flotilla of pink-iced fairy cakes, like attendants, in its wake. It was like a round of *Picnic Idol*, Alice thought despairingly, or the Bath and West Country Show she'd attended as a child, with all the farmers' wares proudly laid out.

Her thoughts turned again to her pathetic Mother's Pride cheese sarnies and she felt her cheeks flush even hotter. Mother's Shame, more like. Mother's Embarrassment. She hadn't realized this was a Domestic Goddess Picnic Showdown, Tupperware containers at dawn. She glanced around, hoping for some other mums to keep her company on the crap picnicker front, but all the others — ten or twelve women, she estimated — were unpacking and displaying arrays of goodies as if they were contestants in some kind of Stepford Wives gourmet lunch contest.

She swallowed miserably as she and Cathy parked the babies in the shade.

'I haven't got a picnic blanket,' Alice realized, too late. *Or a proper picnic*, she wanted to say, but she could feel some of the mums watching, and didn't dare voice it out loud.

The woman nearest them, an elegant Scandinavian-looking type with long blonde hair and slim brown shanks, was unpacking a cool-bag onto a tartan travel rug. Out came a lidded jug of juice, clinking with ice cubes. Out came bowls of strawberries and grapes, glossy and plump, heaped high like colourful, nutritious hillocks. Out came a selection of cheeses and a butter dish. It was rather like Mary Poppins' carpet bag, Alice thought, with a sickening fascination, unable to tear her eyes away. Any moment now, she'd pull out a hatstand and set it down neatly on the ground.

'I've been baking all morning,' Mary Poppins – or whatever her name was – announced to no one in particular, opening up a large Roses tin and producing what looked like a moist lemon drizzle cake. 'Now, where did I put those cranberry flapjacks?'

Alice turned back to Cathy, not wanting to see any more. 'I feel such a failure,' she muttered. 'I hadn't realized it was going to be so . . .'

'Competitive?' Cathy replied, rolling her eyes. 'Welcome to my world, Alice. Don't worry, I've just brought along some Hula Hoops and an egg roll from the bakery.' She grinned conspiratorially. 'Oh yeah, and some Bakewell tarts – Mr Kipling's finest.'

'A cheese sarnie is my lot,' Alice confessed in a low voice, not wanting Mary Poppins to hear. She knew already that she'd rather starve than eat that sandwich in public now, she was so ashamed of it. 'And some lukewarm mush for Iris. Oh God. I'm rubbish, aren't I?'

Cathy spread out a blanket and gave a snort. 'Sit down. And of course you're not rubbish! You're just normal, that's all. Not mad, like these people.' She said it in a quiet voice, but all the same she jumped with guilt when Mary Poppins called over.

'Hi there!'

Alice and Cathy both turned. The blonde woman was kneeling up, smiling at them, with her perfect lunch spread out all around her, like a photo shoot for a magazine. *Beat that if you can, ladies*, Alice could read in her smug expression.

'Hi Natasha,' Cathy replied politely. 'Alice, this is Natasha Willocks. Natasha, this is Alice. She's just moved to the village.'

Natasha's cornflower-blue gaze seemed to take in Alice's frazzled hair, her sweat-marked vest top, the sick stain on her skirt and her beaded flip-flops that already had half the beads missing, all in one damning swoop. Then she gave a dazzling smile. 'Alice. Nice to meet you. I've heard so much about you, of course.' Her voice was treacle-rich, but not so sweet. There was an edge to her words that Alice couldn't decipher. What did she mean by the 'of course'? Was it just to rattle her, or what? Something about the way Natasha's top lip had curled gave Alice the impression that it wasn't out of politeness.

Alice forced a smile in return. 'Nice to meet you too,' she said warily.

'And Cathy,' Natasha purred. 'I hear the lovely Dominic's back in town. How long will he be sticking around this time, then? Do we have the pleasure of his company for very long?'

A muscle twitched in Cathy's cheek and she folded her arms across her chest. 'Yes, he's back,' she replied evenly. 'I'm not sure what his plans are, though.'

Natasha snorted. 'What a surprise,' she said softly.

A coldness entered Cathy's voice. 'Why are you so interested, anyway?' she asked. 'Still carrying a torch, by any chance?'

'Don't make me laugh,' Natasha sneered. 'Carrying a torch? He wishes.'

'Ha! No he doesn't,' Cathy retorted contemptuously. 'In your dreams, love.'

Alice realized she was holding her breath. The air was charged with tension, as the two women locked gazes. Natasha reminded her of a snake rearing, poised to strike. Cathy had gone very pale. Then Alice remembered what Mags had said the other day, about Dom Fletcher's choice of underwear: *'Where did you hear that? Did Natasha say that? Or Cathy?'*

Ahhh. All was clear now. Crystal clear. Alice sat down on the rug pretending to be looking for something in the back of the buggy, but her mind was spinning. So Natasha and Cathy had *both* had relationships with Dom – no wonder sparks were flying! *Ouch.* That was the downside of village life, all right – having to rub along with rivals and enemies, everyone knowing your histories. Thank *goodness* she'd turned down Dom's advances! Imagine if she'd walked straight into a fling, with these two ex-girlfriends (ex-wives?) living in close proximity! Not that he had specifically *offered* her a fling, of course, but . . .

Alice pulled out a bottle of water and took a drink, trying to appear unobtrusive. She didn't want to get involved in this eternal triangle, no way. She wanted to blend into the background, not be pulled in to take sides.

Luckily Natasha's attention was caught just then by a small tousle-haired girl who was shrieking like a banshee as she rampaged around the trees barefoot. 'Sophia!' she yelled at the girl. 'Where are your shoes? Put them back on this minute, young lady!'

Alice couldn't help a guilty moment's *schadenfreude* as Sophia blithely ignored the command and continued chasing a little boy, squealing at the top of her voice. The soles of her feet were already filthy. *Good for you, kid*, Alice thought, trying to hide a smile.

'Excuse me a moment,' Natasha said, her eyes flashing with irritation, and stalked after her recalcitrant daughter, long pale fingers clenched at her sides.

Cathy let out a strangled-sounding groan. 'God, I hate that woman,' she muttered. 'She is pure poison.' She sank down onto the blanket and rubbed her eyes. 'Maybe this was a bad idea, us coming along. I should have known

243

she'd be here too. Never misses a chance to...' She broke off as two more women approached. Mags and Jen.

'Afternoon, ladies!' Jen carolled, pushing her sunglasses on top of her head as she wheeled her pushchair over to join them. She parked up on the other side of Cathy's blanket, and Alice felt hemmed in all of a sudden. No chance for a quick getaway now, she thought with a fleeting feeling of despair.

'Phew, it's a scorcher,' Mags put in, fanning herself with a copy of *Hello!* magazine. 'Who fancies a glass of vino plonko, then? I brought along my plastic wine glasses specially.'

'Count me in,' Jen said at once, spreading out a huge red blanket next to Cathy's. She unfastened her little daughter – Poppy, was it? – from a buggy and started unpacking boxes full of sandwiches. 'Pops, why don't you go and play while Mummy sorts out lunch?' she suggested. 'Look, I can see Sophia and Aunty Tasha over there.'

Aunty Tasha? Alice thought. Did that mean ... Ahh yes. She was surprised she hadn't noticed the resemblance before. Jen had the same colouring as Natasha, although she didn't have quite the same forbidding glare.

Mags was sloshing straw-coloured wine into glasses and handing them around. 'Here, Alice, one for you, get it down you while it's still cold,' she instructed, and Alice found herself raising the glass to her lips obediently. *From*

Mother's Pride to Mother's Ruin in one single movement, she thought. Ahh well.

'Thanks,' she said. Clearly she wasn't going to be able to ask Cathy about the exchange she'd just had with Natasha – not now the cavalry had rocked up with their provisions and gossip-radars.

'Cheers, everyone!' Mags said, knocking back a huge gulp.

Alice looked at Cathy, who was still staring in Natasha's direction with a scowl on her face. 'Cheers,' she replied weakly. Life in this village just got more and more complicated. She was starting to think things would be more comfortable living in a nest of vipers.

Thankfully, Sophia kept Natasha busy for much of the afternoon, fighting with the boys, then falling out of a tree and screaming blue murder. Alice wasn't at all sorry when Natasha eventually packed up her (largely untouched) picnic spread and dragged her daughter off home. 'Wanna go to McDonald's!' Sophia screamed at the top of her voice and Alice had to stifle a giggle at the look of fury that appeared on Natasha's face.

'Ding dong, the witch has gone,' Cathy sang under her breath, joggling little Joe on her knee as they watched them go.

'She's horrible,' Alice agreed in a low voice, casting

furtive glances around for Mags and Jen. Luckily both were attending to their children, well out of earshot. She nibbled on her second Bakewell tart, dabbing a wet finger to pick up the pastry crumbs at the bottom of the silver foil dish. 'So what was all that about when we got here, anyway? Why was she so bitchy about Dom?'

Cathy turned in surprise at the question and Joe let out a squawk at the sudden movement. 'I didn't realize you knew him?' she said, and Alice blushed, immediately regretting asking. That was daytime drinking for you – it made you blurt out all sorts of things you were meant to be keeping shtum about.

'I don't really,' she confessed. 'He popped round the day I moved in. Then, next I heard, he'd told the whole village he'd been up in my bedroom and I had Mags and Jen over there giving me knowing looks, as if . . .'

Cathy looked hurt and Alice closed her mouth hurriedly. Oh my God. She could have kicked herself. What was she saying? This was the last thing on earth Cathy wanted to hear, what with Dom having previously dumped all over *her*.

'I mean . . .' Alice tried to backtrack quickly. 'I don't know the guy from Adam, so . . .' Thankfully, Iris chose that moment to stir, having slept through the entire picnic thus far, and let out a wail. Saved by the yell. 'Ahh. Are you hungry, pickle?' Alice got to her feet (rather woozily) and located the pot of veggie mush for her daughter's lunch. Perfect timing, Iris, she thought, turning away from Cathy and hoping that their awkward conversation about Dom would now judder to an abrupt halt and die of natural causes.

Cathy had other intentions, though. 'Well, take it from me, he's lovely,' she said defensively. 'Natasha did her damnedest to ruin his life but he got away from her, thank God. She just can't bear it that he wised up to her and told her where to go.'

Alice bit her lip. She really *really* wished she'd kept her mouth shut now. Dom was clearly too painful a subject, judging by the jut of Cathy's chin and the drawn look on her face. 'Sorry,' she said. 'I just ... I just didn't know why she was being so frosty.'

'I think Natasha was born with an icicle up her bum,' Cathy said with a small smile. 'She's trouble. Stay away from her.'

'I will, don't worry,' Alice said truthfully. She had no wish ever to meet Natasha again after this first encounter. She put a bib on Iris and spooned some food into her mouth. There — subject closed, she hoped. Next time she'd know better. Cathy was obviously still very loyal about her ex and blind to all his faults. Alice did not want to make her new friend feel any worse by talking about him. All the same, she couldn't help feeling intrigued. What on earth had *happened* between Cathy, Natasha and Dom?

Later that evening, the heat became oppressive. The sky, which had been a bright, cloudless blue the entire day, was now invaded by dense, dark clouds which blotted out the sinking sun. There wasn't a breath of wind in the air any more, just rising heat from the baked earth.

Iris was tired and grouchy and took a while to settle when it was her bedtime. Alice felt drained too after drinking wine in the sun, and found herself leaning on the side of the cot, willing her daughter's eyes to close. She'd often wished Jake could be there to help out at times like this, when she was already dog-tired and ready to crash out herself. Imagine if she could kiss Iris's warm up-turned face, then creep out and ask her husband to do the bedtime honours for a change. Or better still, imagine if he were to come into the room at this very moment and put an arm around her shoulders. 'Here, you look knackered,' he'd say. 'Go and pour yourself a glass of wine. I'll take over now.'

Imagine!

'It's not going to happen, is it?' she murmured to Iris, who was chewing sleepily on her cuddly bear's ear. 'It's just us two, soldiering along together. But don't you worry. Everything will be all right.'

Iris's round peachy face lit up with one of her sudden beaming smiles as if she'd only just noticed Alice there, and the rush of love that surged up inside Alice swamped all wishes of husbandly help and glasses of wine. Maybe it was better this way, anyway. You only had to look at the women of the village to know that Happy-Ever-Afters were few and far between – her, Cathy, Natasha – they'd all been dumped on by various men. And even Capable Katie, who was always so together about everything in life, had recently stumbled on the relationship front. Maybe it was better just to wash your hands of it and make do the best you could alone.

As if to prove a point, Iris's eyelids suddenly drooped shut, like blinds being pulled down, and her breathing deepened. The soggy bear fell out of her fingers and lay face-down on the sheet.

There. Jake wasn't needed after all. Alice stood for a moment gazing at the way Iris's eyelashes fell in such a perfect sweep across her plump cheeks, at her rosebud lips slightly apart, at the soft dark hair that was just starting to curl at the ends. 'Sleep well, sweetheart,' she whispered into the semi-darkness.

Then she went to pour her own wine, all by herself.

Curled up on the sofa an hour or so later, with a paper bag full of raspberries leaking slightly on her lap, Alice was so engrossed in a fat romantic novel, it took her a moment or two to hear the gentle tapping at the door. She jumped up in surprise, knocking over the glass of wine balanced next to her, and sending the raspberries scattering all over the carpet.

'Bollocks,' she muttered, putting the book down and picking her way through the squashed fruit to answer the door. She caught sight of the clock on the mantelpiece as she went – eight thirty. Who would be coming round at this time of the evening? She had a sudden yearning for the safety chain and fish-eye spyhole she and Jake had had in their front door in London, feeling vulnerable on her own here now.

She hesitated before opening the door. 'Who is it?' she called through the wood, her fingers around the handle.

'It's Dom,' came the unexpected reply, and she twisted her mouth in a helpless grimace. What did *he* want? She hadn't seen him since she'd snapped at him in the lane for gossiping about her. He was persistent, you had to give him that.

She pulled open the door, conscious that she still had her grubby vest top on, and that she hadn't plucked her eyebrows for about a year. If Dom liked his women to be as flawless as Natasha, or as pretty as Cathy, he was really lowering his standards to be calling on her.

'Hi,' she said, feeling disconcerted as a memory of the

catfight there'd been over him at the picnic earlier flashed into her mind. She paused, wondering what he was doing there. Should she shoo him off the premises before any more rumours sprang into life?

'Hi,' he said. He had a bottle of red wine in one hand and a bunch of wilting sweet peas in the other. He took a step forward, thrusting his offerings towards her, and she caught the flowers' sweet heady fragrance with the movement. 'Look – I come in peace,' he said baldly. 'I feel like we've got off to a bad start. May I?'

Oh Christ. Now what? Was this how he'd collected his other bedpost notches, charm and perseverance, doorstepping unsuspecting victims and plying them with booze and posies? Well, she could see through his tricks! She wouldn't be impressed by such niceties. She drew herself up taller and looked him in the eye. 'Sure,' she replied coolly, with a dismissive shrug. *If you must,* was the subtext. 'Come on through.'

Her heart thumped uncomfortably as he walked into the cottage and shut the front door behind him. His fingers brushed hers as he handed her the flowers and she stepped into the kitchen away from him to get a vase so that he wouldn't see her blush. Stupid Alice! The blood was rushing to her face – all that wine, presumably. Village life was turning her into a right old lush.

He followed her into the kitchen and the room felt

absurdly small with him in there, leaning against the worktop while she found a glass stem vase and filled it with water. The scent of the sweet peas was intoxicating but she felt determined to keep a cool head. He probably didn't realize she knew all about him and his former conquests. Decided he'd try it on before the word had spread to her — well, too late for that, sunshine, she thought.

'Have you got a corkscrew?' he asked, and she felt herself flush a deeper pink. Impatient or what? What was wrong with the man, why was he so desperate for a drink?

'Sure,' she said, pulling one out of the utensil drawer and getting down a single glass for him. She remembered, just then, her fallen glass in the living room — oh, and all those raspberries that had spilled everywhere like blood spatters after a murder. Great. It would look as if she'd been having a food fight all on her own in there. 'Can I leave that with you?' she asked, handing it over, along with the corkscrew. 'I'll just get my glass from the other room.'

She went quickly past him before he could reply and darted through to the living room where she got down on all fours and began gathering raspberries as if fruit-picking in a field. They were soggy and battered now, staining the old carpet with scarlet juice. Bloody hell! She was so clumsy! Her wine had seeped into her rug too, so that would stink of alcohol now for the rest of its days and . . .

'Everything all right?'

Oh, great. There was Dom in the room — and there *she* was, bottom in the air, trying to gather the last few runaway raspberries from under the sofa. She straightened up, accidentally putting her hand on a stray berry and squishing it, feeling mortified that he'd caught her in such a position. What would he think? Knowing his Casanova ways, he'd probably take it as some kind of come-on.

'Fine,' she said, forcing a smile and trying to ignore the pulped fruit between her fingers. She picked up her glass and the bag of carpet-hairy raspberries and bustled out to the kitchen. Sod worrying about becoming a lush. She definitely needed a top-up now. 'Do have a seat,' she called through, rinsing the scarlet juice from her hand and sloshing wine into her glass. *Can anything else go wrong?* she wondered, rolling her eyes and feeling flustered. Maybe she'd fall over when she went back into the living room and splash her drink in his face. Oh, and land in his lap or something equally embarrassing. Or maybe . . .

A sudden cool breeze whipped through the window and she glanced outside. And then, all at once, the rain started to pour — pattering down like silver needles, noisy and rushing, spattering the dusty patio slabs. A jagged scribble of light flashed in the sky and she found herself counting beats, waiting for the rumble of thunder.

One . . . two . . . three . . . four . . . five . . .

There it went — a low, warning growl in the distance. She shivered with pleasure. She'd always liked thunderstorms — there was something so primitive and dramatic about them.

She returned to the living room and pushed open the small cottage windows to let in the fresh air. Water was already running down the panes, dripping from the wooden frame. 'I love the smell of rain,' she told Dom conversationally and then cursed herself for sounding like a flake. 'I mean,' she added, trying to explain, 'I mean, I like the way the plants smell when they've been rained on. And the earth. You know.'

Worse and worse. She wanted to giggle suddenly at the stupid things that were coming out of her mouth. Dom would be out of the house in a flash, storm or no storm, if she kept up such a stream of inane wittering. 'Anyway.' She tried to pull herself together. Being giggly might be construed as flirtatious, and that would never do. 'Anyway,' she repeated feebly, not knowing what else to say.

He took up the cue, thankfully. 'Anyway, yes,' he said as she sat on the sofa, taking a demure sip of wine so as to shut herself up. 'I came here to make peace. This village is a small place and . . .' He wrinkled his nose. 'Well, frankly, Christ knows I've got enough enemies already here so . . . it would be a shame for us not to get on, seeing as we're almost neighbours and are going to be bumping into each other everywhere.'

Alice stiffened at the mention of his enemies – was he referring to Natasha and Cathy? – and she was just trying to think of something suitably cool and dismissive when he added, rather disarmingly, 'I love the smell of rain too.'

She narrowed her eyes. Was he teasing her?

'It's great, that freshness you get from the soil, I mean,' he said. He waved his hands expressively when he spoke, she noticed. 'So pure and earthy. They should bottle it – I'd wear it.'

Oh, of course. He was a farmhand or something, wasn't he? Wasn't he? God, Alice had drunk far too much for one day, her thoughts were starting to slur into one another.

He was looking at her oddly and she felt alarmed. Had she just said that out loud, the bit about him being a farmhand?

'So . . .' he said, his voice earnest and steady. 'I know you were angry because you thought I'd been gossiping about you, but I swear I hadn't. I'm not like that – in fact, that's why I left the village in the first place, because I couldn't stand everyone talking about everyone else's business.' He shook his head. 'It still does my head in, to be honest, but you know, sometimes you have to put up with it, don't you? Anyway. What do you think? Can we be friends?'

She felt slightly as if he'd taken the wind from her sails with this information. And there she'd been, wrongly accusing him of rumour-mongering about her, too, all but shrieking at him in the lane. Good one, Alice. How to win friends and influence people – not. Then her thoughts slid to Cathy. 'Well,' she said, stalling for an answer. How was she going to explain this to her? Sorry, Cath, but I've only gone and chummed up with your ex, you know, that git who left you holding the baby ... She frowned. 'The thing is, Dom, I'm friends with Cathy, so ...'

'Oh!' His eyebrows shot up into that mop of hair. 'Oh, I didn't realize you'd met her.'

No, I bet you didn't, she felt like retorting. She put her nose in the air, trying to carry off her best Narnia queen impression. She hadn't been married to an actor for four and a half years without picking up a few tricks herself. 'Yeah,' she said. 'She's really nice. And so ...' This wasn't easy. Was it a bit teenage of her to say no, she couldn't be friends with him because he'd upset her new mate?

Well ... possibly. Probably. But ...

'Yeah, she's fab, isn't she?' he said warmly. 'And Joe is such a cutie. Oh well, that's good, then – you're getting to know people round here.'

She eyed him suspiciously. Did the man have no guilt, no conscience? How could he sit there and say Joe was cute when he'd all but abandoned the little tot? The wine made her impulsive all of a sudden. 'Don't you think you should sort things out with her, then? Help her a bit more? It must be really tough for her being on her own.'

He seemed baffled at the remark. 'Well – that's why I came back to the village,' he said slowly. He was staring at her in a defensive sort of way. 'I know it's hard for her and I'm helping out as much as I can but ... well, you know ...'

She waited for him to finish but he left the words hanging in the air. Then he scratched his head and said, 'You've lost me, Alice. I'm not sure what you're getting at. You're looking all accusatory and I don't know why.'

'Look,' Alice said. Sod it, she might as well just come out with it now. 'I don't want to upset Cathy – especially after what happened today with Natasha. It's not like I'm taking sides but – oh well, all right, then. I *am* taking sides. Us single mums have to show a bit of solidarity. And I don't know what happened between you two but until you've sorted it out ...'

'What happened between me and Natasha?' He still looked somewhat bewildered.

'No! Between you and Cathy!' Did she have to spell it out to him?

He stared at her, a small frown creasing his forehead. And then his expression changed, like a light being switched on, and he smiled. 'Nothing's happened between me and Cathy,' he said slowly. 'Apart from that time she grassed me up to our mum about scrumping apples from Mr Daley's orchards and I pushed her in the river. But somehow I doubt that's what you're referring to?'

Now it was Alice's turn to stare. *Our mum?* Did that mean...? 'Hang on,' she said. 'Did you just say...?'

He nodded. 'Cathy's my sister,' he said. 'You thought I was her traitorous ex, didn't you?' He laughed, his eyes twinkling. 'You thought I was Joe's dad.'

'Well, he does look like you!' Alice burst out, her cheeks flaming. Oh help. What had she done? What an idiot! She put her head in her hands. 'So you're his uncle ... oh God! Sorry. I just thought...' She shook her head. Why was she so stupid? She could hardly look at him. 'Well, now I feel a *complete* pillock. I'm so embarrassed. Aaarrrgh.'

'Oh, don't be,' Dom said, grinning. 'I think it's funny.'

She bit her lip. 'Well, I'm glad we've got that straight, anyway,' she said, blushing furiously. 'And I'm sorry I got it all wrong.' She managed to look him in the eye again. 'Does the offer of being friends still stand, or are you about to make a run for it, now you've found out what a nutter I am?'

He laughed and pretended to consider the question. 'Let's drink to friendship,' he said after a few moments.

'I'll second that,' she agreed. She got up to clink glasses with him and he caught her eye as she did so. Not just caught it – held it, his gaze locking hers. Something about the way he was looking at her so meaningfully made her catch her breath. The atmosphere seemed to change; tension thickened between them.

'Cheers,' she said, feeling flustered.

'Cheers,' he echoed, smiling. He touched his glass gently to hers and the chinking sound seemed to break the spell.

She stepped back as if released from an enchantment. Lightning flashed again, and thunder boomed a split second later. Rain was pouring down now and wind swirled in the chimney breast.

'I don't think you'll be going anywhere for a while,' she said, glancing outside to where large marshy puddles were forming in the grass. The words sounded like a bad line from a film and she blushed again.

He raised his eyebrows. 'Well ... if that's all right,' he said. 'I don't want to be responsible for any more gossip in the pub ...'

She wrinkled her nose at his words. A strange tingly sensation had been stirred up inside her and she felt reckless all of a sudden. 'Who cares about the pub?' she said. 'More wine?'

Chapter Thirteen

Promises

Still Tuesday, 17 June 2008

Katie was not having a good day. Alfie Stewart, one of her problem Year 10s, had been lippy and aggressive throughout the entire double lesson that morning. Usually she had him on a very tight rein, not letting him get away with a single word out of line. Usually she was more than a match for his oafish comments and rudeness, and could put him in his place with well-practised ease.

But today he seemed to sense she was struggling. Today he'd got right under her skin, drawling too-loud comments about her hair, her outfit, even the way her arse jiggled slightly as she was writing up a series of equations on the board. And today, she just didn't have the wherewithal to stop him in his tracks with the curtness he deserved. She'd snapped at him for his remarks but her face had reddened at the class's giggles — and from that moment on, she was undone. He had the upper hand and she, for once, was on the losing side. God, she felt like wringing his fat, unwashed neck. The bell for break-time could not peal fast enough and she let out her breath in a gust of relief when it finally did.

At lunchtime she tried to make notes for the parents' evening later that day in the staffroom, but her thoughts kept returning to Steve, and the empty house. She hadn't been able to help a tiny spark of hope when she went back that morning to pick up her school things. She'd opened the door and called his name, only to hear it echo through the stillness. Nobody home.

For all the bravado she'd felt last night as she and Laura made their way through cocktail after cocktail, now she just felt hollow. She tried Steve's mobile for the millionth time, but it went straight to voicemail, and she couldn't bring herself to leave a message. She felt great remorse for the way she'd behaved with Laura too — like a pair of silly schoolgirls, encouraging those blokes who were only in it for a leg-over. What if Steve had seen her? She could imagine the hurt and disappointment shining from his eyes, the disapproval at her giggling and flirting with Gary and Barry, or whatever their names were.

'This is what you call a bad day,' she muttered to herself as the lunch bell rang, signalling a return to the classrooms. 'Nine hours to go, then I'll be in bed, and it'll all be over.'

Annie French, one of the PE teachers, overheard and gave her a wink. 'One of those, eh?' she said, patting her on the back. 'Think yourself lucky. I've got the Year 8s for athletics all afternoon. Let's hope one of them manages to impale themselves on a javelin.'

That afternoon, it was Katie's final lesson with her Year 11s before they were due to take their Maths GCSE the following week. She wanted to cover the bases one last time, instil in them all the knowledge and problem-solving skills they'd need for the exam, and fire them up with abundant confidence. She was evangelical about education being the one big salvation for all kids, especially those who, like her, hadn't had parental support. But were they interested? Were they heck. Unfortunately, the summer heat was glaring through the windows over their greasy teenage heads, sending them into a sluggish, somnolent state. As the lesson ended, Katie wished them the best of luck in the exam but couldn't help a queasiness on their collective behalf. Even her brightest pupils had stalled on some of the revision questions – subjects she'd hoped they would know off pat by now.

Let's hope it's raining on exam day, she said to herself as they jostled out, a few of them remembering to say goodbye Miss and thank her. *Otherwise we'll all be roasted.*

Sometimes she wondered why she bothered. She'd had those kids for five years — had seen them enter the school as nervous Year 7s, wide-eyed and relatively attitude-free, and watched them erupt into hormonal, leggy youths, taller than her, some of them. All those homework books she'd marked, all those lessons she'd planned for them. She'd done her best, but was it enough? 'Over to you, guys,' she'd said helplessly at the end of the lesson. 'Try your hardest in the exam, and make me proud, yeah?'

She sighed again, as the classroom door swung shut after the last student. 'Don't let me down,' she said into the warm, chalky air.

Now then. One hour to go before the first parents were due to arrive. She had to do some serious cramming if she was to get through this evening without too many cock-ups.

Four thirty. Show-time! The school hall looked like a rehearsal for next week's GCSEs, set out as it was with rows and rows of small tables, a teacher at each one, with two empty parent seats before them. Katie looked to her left where her friend Liz, head of art, sat fiddling with a paper clip, a resigned look on her face. 'Who've you got first, then?' Katie asked in a stage whisper, conscious that the initial consultations were due any moment.

Liz pulled a face. 'Joshua Wakefield's parents,' she

moaned. 'Competitive as hell, I seem to remember – even about art. Last time they were here, they kept asking about tests and grades, and whether Joshua was in the top group … in art, for fuck's sake!' The paper clip pinged out of her fingers as her voice rose. 'Let's hope they've chilled out a bit this time. Who've you got?'

Katie glanced down at her list. 'Kelly Stevens,' she said. 'I don't remember meeting her parents before, though. Can't wait to break it to them that Kelly is the class fidget and more interested in applying herself to love-texts and graffiti on the desks than to solving equations.'

Liz grinned. 'Ahh, if anyone can, it's you, Katie. Oh – parents at twelve o'clock, I spy. Our evening of fun starts here …'

Katie drew herself up straighter in her seat, trying to present the right image to the approaching mums and dads: professional, smart and caring, rather than hungover, knackered and wishing-she-was-at-home. So … now to play Spot Kelly Stevens' Parents. Kelly was small and skinny, with lots of brown hair, pale freckled skin and a nervous energy that seemed to channel itself through her mouth. She liked to chat, did Kelly.

Katie scanned the room. Big bald bloke, man-boobs jiggling as he strode in, dragging a dumpy wife behind him … nah. Surely they wouldn't have produced a live wire like

Kelly. She was right — they were heading towards Wendy Grey, the elderly music teacher.

Next up: an extremely smart-looking couple — him in an elegant suit, her with swishy shampoo-advert hair ... nope. Too posh to be Kelly's. Off they strode to Lucas Walker, one of the chemistry teachers.

Ahh. Here came a woman with bobbed brown hair, a red short-sleeved top and cropped jeans, walking confidently in Katie's direction, checking the table numbers. She had the same slim build as Kelly ... and there was something vaguely familiar about the way she walked, too. Hmmmm. Katie couldn't put her finger on it. Had they met before?

The woman drew nearer, searching the rows of tables, head darting from side to side as she looked. Then she paused, clocking Katie's number — 28 — and slid into one of the empty seats in front of her. 'Hi,' she said breezily, smiling as she held out a hand across the table. 'I'm—' She broke off, and stared at Katie. 'Oh my gosh,' she said, whitening suddenly. 'Katie — is it you?'

Katie stared back at the woman in surprise ... and an image flashed into her mind — of them both sitting around a T.G.I. Friday's table years ago, her with that hen-night tiara slipping in her hair ... 'Oh my *God*,' she said, losing every shred of professionalism in one breath. 'Nicki?'

Could it really be her, her ex-sister-in-law? Katie hadn't seen her since that disastrous Watkinson Christmas when Neil had presented her with a Kenwood Chef mixer and she'd just wanted to heave it up from the torn red wrapping paper and brain him with it. Nicki was married by then – yes, to Anthony Stevens! – and had seen fit to scold her brother for the gift. 'Neil! That's not very romantic! Honestly, Katie, what is he like?'

And here she was now, Nicki Stevens, née Watkinson, sitting here in front of her, fourteen or so years later. Kelly Stevens' mum. Yikes.

'I can't believe it's you!' Nicki said. She was pale, her eyes never leaving Katie's. 'I thought you'd fallen off the face of the earth. And here you are, Ms Taylor, teaching maths to my Kelly. Wait till I tell Neil!'

Katie winced at the words. It was madness that after all these years her ex-husband's name could still send a shaft of guilt piercing her skin. Crazy that her instinct had been to blurt out 'Don't tell Neil!' as if she was worried he'd want to track her down and marry her all over again. Because they both knew *that* wasn't going to happen.

She tried not to squirm in her chair, wondering what to say, then checked herself. This ten-minute slot was meant to be about Kelly, not ancient history. All the same, she found she needed to defend herself. 'I don't know if you heard what happened with me and Neil, but . . .'

Nicki's eyes were soft. 'I heard,' she said. 'Linda O'Connor, wasn't it? And the rest of them. What a prat.'

Katie stared down at the table, pained at that casual 'the rest of them'. Right. She didn't know exactly how many times Neil had been unfaithful – didn't want to know either – but clearly word had got round that there had been several conquests. Katie had even heard a rumour that he'd tried it on with someone – Amy Phillips, was it? – at the actual wedding itself. How lovely. How very tasteful. 'Maybe we should talk about Kelly now,' Katie said, steering away from the subject.

Nicki waved a hand, dismissing her daughter's mathematical offerings from the conversation. 'I haven't seen you for about five hundred years,' she said. 'So how *are* you? How's it all going?'

Katie looked at her warily. She hadn't anticipated a cosy little chat about 'how it was all going'. And how could she reply to that, anyway? *Oh, well, my latest boyfriend just walked out on me because I couldn't commit, and I might have snogged someone last night but I can't remember because I was too pissed, and...*

Not bloody likely. She couldn't let that sort of detail get back to Neil. He'd probably laugh his head off. 'What a hypocrite,' he'd say. 'After all the grief she gave me for putting it around, too!'

'Fine, thanks,' she said cautiously. 'You?'

'Oh, you know, married, three kids, working part-time

at the big Toys R Us in Brislington...' Nicki reeled off. 'We moved to Bristol just after Kelly was born. I still can't believe I'm sitting here opposite you! It must be ... how long? Years, anyway.'

'Fourteen years,' Katie said, nodding. 'How ... how is he? Neil, I mean?' There. The question had been hovering unspoken between them ever since Nicki had sat down and gasped in recognition.

Nicki rolled her eyes. 'Oh, well, you know Neil,' she said. 'Can't make his mind up, that one. He was with Louise for a while – and they've got Harry, who's twelve. And then they broke up and he started seeing Tracey. Had Grace – she's ten now. And then he married ... what was her name? Carla. Didn't last two minutes. No kids, luckily. Now he's with Marianne and she's up the stick. Poor woman. You'd think she'd have heard about his track record, right?' She shrugged. 'You're lucky you got away when you did, Katie. I don't want to diss my brother but ... well. Fact is, he's a git. My own brother and I wouldn't trust him as far as I could throw him.'

Katie gulped. All those women ... all those children. Neil certainly hadn't wasted any time pining over her. 'Blimey,' she said faintly.

'I know,' Nicki said. 'Bet you're glad you dumped him when you did, eh? I just hope he didn't put you off men for life!'

She was laughing, saying the words lightly, but Katie felt a wrench inside. The truth was ... he *had* put her off, for a long time. Too long.

'Just as well they're not all like Neil, right?' Nicki was saying.

Katie managed a smile in return. 'Just as well,' she agreed. And suddenly, she was longing to see Steve again. Steve, who'd never mucked her around. Steve, who'd never done the dirty on her, or bailed out.

Until now, of course. Until she'd gone and lost him in the blink of an eye.

Something shifted in the periphery of her vision, and she noticed that another couple were waiting at a polite distance behind Nicki. The next parents on her list of consultations. 'Oh God, sorry, Nicki,' Katie said, trying to sound too thankful. 'We're going to have to finish here – and I've not even talked to you about how Kelly's getting on with her maths.'

Nicki wrinkled her nose. 'She's not going to be a mathematician, is she?' she asked.

Katie shook her head. 'She's not, I'm afraid,' she replied. 'But if she could just concentrate a bit harder ...'

Nicki laughed as she got up from the chair. 'I know my Kelly. Too much concentrating on boys and eyeliner. But I'll have a word. See what I can do.'

'Thanks,' Katie said. She swallowed, feeling awkward

again. 'And ... it's nice to see you, Nicki. Say hi to Anthony for me. And ... er ...' She stood up and suddenly hugged her, her ex-sister-in-law. 'All the best,' she said.

Nicki squeezed her back. 'Lovely to see you, Kate,' she said. 'Really lovely. I'm glad things have all worked out for you. Wait 'til I tell Neil you're a maths teacher!'

It almost sounded mocking, the way she phrased it, as if being a maths teacher was something to poke fun at. But before Katie could protest and throw in a few more post-Neil achievements – 'Yeah, and tell him I got the highest marks in my year for my teaching degree while you're at it, won't you? Tell him I've got my own house! Tell him walking out on him was the best decision of my life!' – Nicki was waving and walking away.

Maybe it was just as well she hadn't had the chance to say all of that, Katie thought, watching her go. It might have made her sound rather ... well, desperate, if she was honest. And Nicki wasn't the sort to mock, it was just her getting on the defensive.

She glanced down at her list and gave the waiting parents a bright smile. 'Mr and Mrs Lovell – nice to see you again. Come and sit down. I'm pleased to say Bradley has made *excellent* progress in maths this year ...'

She could hardly think straight for the rest of the evening. Neil and his harem of women, eh? It made her feel better about her failed marriage, in a funny sort of a way. No one else seemed to stay married to Neil very long either. So perhaps it wasn't some failing in her, Katie. Perhaps the fault was all down to Mr Lover-Lover himself. It made her all the more relieved she'd taken the pill secretly throughout their brief marriage, when she heard about all those children he'd fathered. Well, that figured, too. He had been gutted when she couldn't – or rather wouldn't – produce one for him, had made her feel shit about it, as if she was a failure, a freak of nature. She'd wanted to wait a few years, have some fun first before she thought seriously about mother-hood, but then, when she'd found out he'd been playing away, she'd left the marriage feeling hollow. Good, she'd told herself. Who wanted kids anyway? She'd probably only turn out a rotten mum, as useless as her own had been. She didn't need a man *or* kids, she could get by on her Jack Jones – for now and for the rest of her life.

It had been terrifying, sure, rocking up to the station and getting the London train on her own, just that one bag of possessions to show for herself. Her bravado had shrivelled away to nothing by the time the train had hissed into Paddington. Could she really go through with this? Did she really have the bottle? But the thought of her husband gripping Linda O'Connor's podgy shoulders as he heaved himself into her was enough to propel Katie through the station and onto a bus to find the house Alice and Georgia were renting. And then, thankfully, they'd greeted her with open arms, a box of wine and the start of a new life.

Georgia had never liked Neil, had always looked down her nose at him for his stonewashed jeans and taste in music ('I've never met a bloke into Level 42 and Dire Straits who wasn't a crap shag'). Alice wasn't quite so vocal about her dislike, but she was quick to tell Katie she'd done the right thing. With a little help from her friends, Katie had her life back again, and the lid had closed tight shut on Neil Watkinson.

Until now, when the memories kept seeping out. It made her shudder. *You're lucky you got away when you did, Katie,* Nicki had said. How true was that!

She tried to concentrate on the matter in hand, discussing Zoe Eldon's trouble with getting homework in on time with her earnest, mousy-looking parents, but her thoughts kept sliding back to Neil and his line of conquests. What a sleaze. He was like an animal, moving from one mate to the next.

'Ms Taylor?' Zoe Eldon's mum asked, puncturing her thoughts. 'Are you ... all right?'

Katie jumped back to the here and now. Christ, how long had she been lost in her reverie? She shoved Neil to the back of her head with great force and pulled herself together. 'Sorry,' she said. What a space cadet she must seem to them! 'As I was saying, Zoe is very bright in lessons, confident to have a go at solving a problem in front of the rest of the class, and . . .'

She broke off as Nicki went through her field of vision once more, lining up to see Peter Barton, head of science. What had she been talking about again? 'So that's about it, really,' she finished lamely. 'Tell Zoe to keep up the good work!'

The Eldons walked away and Katie all but put her head in her hands and groaned. Why couldn't she get a grip and concentrate? Her reputation would be in tatters by the end of the night if she didn't sort herself out.

She shook herself. She was not enjoying this evening at all. Ten short minutes of chat with Nicki and she was all over the place.

Concentrate, Katie. Not long to go. Concentrate!

The next parents on her list were those of Conor Graham. Ahh. Conor, and his brilliant mind. One pupil she'd actually enjoyed having in her class, with his lightning-quick brain, the way he sat there, soaking up everything she said, relishing homework, really loving being challenged and stretched . . .

Well, until recently, that was. 'Conor is very able,' she told his parents with a smile. 'He's got a genuine talent for maths – a fantastic problem-solving brain.'

Mrs Graham was puffed up with motherly pride. 'He's

always been like that, right since he was a littl'un,' she couldn't resist confiding, her eyes glistening. 'I don't know where he gets it from. Nothing to do with me or his dad, is it, John?'

Mr Graham shook his head, smiling. 'Definitely not,' he agreed. 'He can run rings round the both of us when it comes to numbers, can't he?'

'He can,' Mrs Graham confirmed, nodding so violently her fleshy chin wobbled.

'The only thing is,' Katie went on carefully, 'I've noticed a change in Conor recently.'

That took them by surprise. The nodding stopped, as did the proud smiles. 'A change?' Mrs Graham repeated uncertainly.

'Yes,' Katie said. 'He didn't score as well as he might have done in a test a few weeks ago – it was when he was very hay feverish, and I'm sure that's the only reason he slipped up.'

'He *was* suffering with it,' Mrs Graham put in. 'I tried to keep him off school, but he wasn't having any of it . . .'

'Ever since then, it's as if he's given up,' Katie went on. 'He's stopped trying – he seems to have lost his confidence. And it's a real shame because it was only one test. It would be terrible if he gave up just because things went wrong for him once.'

She felt oddly dazed as she finished her little spiel and

wasn't sure why for a moment. Then the truth resonated through her like a note from a tuning fork. Everything she'd just said about Conor Graham and him giving up on maths after one bad result was exactly what she'd done with her marriage. One negative experience, and she'd written it off for life.

She forced a smile and bid goodbye to the Grahams, her mind spinning.

The house felt hot and airless when she got in that evening, even though it was almost dark. It was messy in there — she hadn't felt like tidying since Steve had packed his stuff and gone. Not like Control Freak Katie to let standards slip, but there you go. Right now, housework was not number one priority.

Katie padded through the rooms, pushing up the swollen, resistant sash windows to let the building breathe. She turned on a couple of lamps in the living room, creating soft pools of light, and sank into the sofa feeling unsettled. Her mind was still churning with thoughts about Nicki, Neil and Steve.

She dragged a chair from the kitchen to the bookcase and climbed up to reach down one of the boxes from the top shelf. There was dust on its top — she hadn't looked inside for a long time. Now the thought of opening it up made her heart skitter.

She took it over to the sofa and lifted the lid. Packets of old photos were piled inside, hidden away in the dark like flashes of memory. She'd had to leave the fat wedding-photo album behind, of course, when she'd walked out on Neil (did he still have it, she wondered? A nice collection of wedding-photo albums he'd have amassed so far), but on impulse she'd grabbed a single packet of photos. Just for sentiment.

She rummaged through the pile, looking for it now. Katie being Katie, the packets were all carefully labelled and dated. *School trip – Isle of Wight*, she read in her girlish, rounded handwriting. *First term at Uni. Charlotte's wedding. Georgia's hen night* – God, there was some incriminating stuff in that lot! And finally . . . *Wedding, March 1994.* There.

She took it out, feeling shifty. What would Steve say if he walked in right now and found her going over her old wedding photos? She sat very still for a moment, breath held, listening, but there was no noise in the house. Don't be daft, Katie. Steve's gone, remember? Gone off in his hissy fit. He doesn't care what you look at now. Probably finding someone else to marry him instead, just like Neil. Out with the old, and all that . . .

Full of a sudden *who-cares?* feeling, she opened the packet and took out the photos. She felt an ache inside as she saw the first few. There she was, just nineteen, looking serene and calm in her old bedroom, as Georgia pinned up her hair in one photo, and Alice put on her make-up in another. She was a baby, really — they all were. So fresh-faced and hopeful. Nineteen, though! What did anyone know about relationships at nineteen?

She felt a smile twist her mouth as she remembered the chaos of that wedding morning. *She'd* been organized, of course, taking deliveries of the flowers and arranging last-minute changes to the seating plan, but everyone else was running about flapping like headless chickens. Laura and Charlotte had had that ridiculous mix-up over their brides-maid shoes, while her mum was at the sherry before mid-day, surprise surprise ('Just getting into the party spirit!'), and almost had to be carried out to the wedding cars when they arrived.

There was a great photo of Katie and her bridesmaids — Georgia, Alice, Laura and Charlotte — all beaming into the camera. Katie in white, of course, with flowers garlanded in her long brown hair, and the four bridesmaids in dark pink with big puffy sleeves.

She flicked her way through a few more. Off they went in the cars, click click!

There was the church, and crowds milling about outside, click click!

There was Neil and his best man Rob looking shiny-faced and dapper in their morning suits. Neil looked endearingly nervous in one shot, where the photographer had caught him unawares, glancing towards the road, as if he was worried Katie wasn't going to come. Although, knowing him, he'd probably been eyeing up the talent, wondering where Amy Phillips was.

She sighed. Why was she looking at these anyway? What was the point of raking up ancient history? Just a few more photos, she decided, then she'd put them away for another fourteen years.

There was her car arriving, with its white ribbons and flowers on the bonnet, click click.

Oh – and there she was, about to enter the church. She loved that photo. She was smiling, looking absolutely radiant with happiness, face upturned like a flower to the sun.

Katie blinked at the sudden wetness in her eyes. She could remember that moment as if it were yesterday. Her heart thudding underneath the tight bodice of her dress. Her fingers around the bouquet of white roses, the smell of the freshly mown church lawns. The bells were pealing and she was excited and nervous all at once, like an actress about to go on stage.

Her mum was already red-faced and loud, her breath so alcoholic it was practically a fire risk as she sat there making catty remarks about one of Neil's cousins. Laura had nipped inside to try to shut her up, while Charlotte resolutely ignored her, head down, absent-mindedly pulling petals off her posy.

And then the organist had struck up the music, dah dah da-DAH! as she entered the church, terrified she was going to fall on her high heels in front of everyone, her eyes seeking out Neil's as he stood there waiting for her, smiling at her . . .

She shoved the photos away abruptly and pushed away the tears that were sliding down her cheeks. What was the point of reliving the whole day? It was in the past now, same as the rest of their relationship. Nicki's voice rang around her head: *I hope he didn't put you off men for life!*

Maybe not. She'd fallen in love with Steve, after all. But Neil had certainly put her off *marriage* for life. And who could blame her for feeling that way?

Chapter Fourteen

It Only Takes a Minute

Friday, 20 June 2008

It was a struggle to get out of bed on Friday morning. For the first time since Georgia could remember, the thought of being at her desk didn't fill her with excitement. Usually, she was eager to get out and into action, digging up dirt, teasing out secrets and hot gossip, giggling over the pap shots from the night before as they came in. Usually, the ring of her phone was music to her ears, the promise of a new story, a new headline.

But today . . .

Today she felt kind of sluggish. Something she'd eaten? Not enough sleep? Aching muscles from yesterday's strenuous BodyPump class? Hmmm . . . No, to the lot of them. She wasn't quite sure what was causing this inertia, this reluctance to shake off the duvet, but there was definitely a feeling of *Thank God it's almost the weekend* floating in her mind today. It was only the thought of beating Polly Nash into the office that finally saw Georgia stumbling from her bed and into the bathroom.

No gym this morning — she couldn't be bothered. If she didn't get a move on, she'd be late to her desk and she couldn't bear to have the brown-noser smirking across at her from her corner. As it was, she was going to have to put up with Polly's excited boasts about going to the Film Festival Awards that evening. Great.

She showered and dressed, grabbing a black coffee and a croissant from the deli on the corner before catching the bus into town. The newspaper office was in South Kensington, thank goodness — she'd cut her journalist teeth over in Wapping, the most soulless place on earth. The *Herald* wasn't such a high-profile tabloid, but at least she could hit the Kings Road in her lunch hour and catch a minimum of five celebs by the time she'd reached Dino's. And the number of times Georgia had got a scoop just by slipping on her sunglasses and earwigging discreetly in Mimi or Gloss or any of the other boutiques ... well, she'd lost count by now, put it like that.

The bus was packed as usual, with suit-wearing slickers, rowdy schoolkids and the token bus nutter, in this instance, a woman wearing a red bobble hat and voluminous black mac, despite it being a warm summery morning. Georgia managed to get herself a seat upstairs by a window in front of someone playing thrash metal or something similar at top volume on their iPod, although the screaming electric guitar and thunderous bass sounded more like annoying buzzing insects in a tin can.

She slumped against the window feeling weary. She hadn't even checked her phone for overnight emails and texts yet – was that a record? Usually it was the first thing she looked at every morning, before her own reflection in the bathroom mirror even. Today she just felt ... jaded with it all. So what if another celeb had drunk too much in China Whites and flashed their knockers? So what if a soap star had thrown a strop at a too-keen fan and smashed their phone to the pavement? Such stunts, such people felt tiresome this morning. She had heard it all before, a billion times.

She gazed out of the window as the bus rumbled over the Thames. The river glittered in the morning sunshine, a thousand reflected sparkles twinkling like sequins on a dress. What was wrong with her, being so glum on such a gorgeous day? Come on, Georgia. Pull yourself together. No more moping. No more tickings-off from Isabella. Best foot forward, as her nan would have said.

She thought of her nan then, waking up in her hospital bed. She hoped the old lady's fight was coming back now

– hoped she had enough strength to start moaning about the hospital breakfasts they served up. Nan always made Scott's Porage Oats at home – the proper way, thank you very much, with water, none of this faffing around with milk for her – and a mug of brick-coloured tea, two sugars. Georgia could imagine the pale soggy hospital toast with nasty margarine and felt sad. Well, next time she visited, she'd jolly well poke her nose into the standard of the food there and . . .

She stopped herself. Next time? She'd only just got back from a stay up north. It was way too soon to be planning another visit. Wasn't it?

She wished she was closer to the hospital, suddenly. Just so that she was able to pop in after work some evenings. Drop round there with some marmalade for her nan's toast (Frank Cooper's, of course), or a flask of proper Tetley tea, just because she could. And *while* she still could, more to the point. It had been a wake-up call, seeing her nan so frail and fragile there in the hospital. A reminder that she wasn't actually immortal after all. That one day, those papery eyelids would close for the last time and that would be that.

But anyway. On with the show. First email check of the day – and what glories would there be for her to discover this morning on her phone? Illicit snogging from already-married-to-other-people pop darlings at a gig last night? A Hollywood B-lister back in rehab after an amphetamine binge?

What-evah, Catherine Tate drawled in her head. *Does my face look bovvered?*

She waited for her inbox to appear ... then her eyes widened as the screen filled with tiny writing, and she saw the subject line of the very first email. Oh God. Okay. She took that back. She *was* bothered. This really was news.

JAKE ARCHER – LOVE SPLIT she read. The stylus felt slippery between her fingers suddenly, and her heart thudded at the words. Jake Archer had split up with that actress bird? *Alice's* Jake?

She hunched over her phone, desperately trying to find the full story. Ahh – just in on the entertainment wires. She scanned the details apprehensively. Yep – it was all over for Jake and posh skinny Victoria, according to this report; the gist being that he'd got sick of her jealousy and clingy behaviour. *Miaow.*

Adrenalin skidded through her as it always did at a big new story. And this was a whopper. Massive. Breaking the news of Jake's infidelity to Alice had sent sales of the paper rocketing last year. And now that *Flying High* was such a smash in the TV ratings, Jake Archer sold bucketloads of newspapers and magazines just by having his sexy chiselled mug on the front cover. This would be on every one of the front pages tomorrow, all right . . .

She turned away from the screen suddenly as a dart of guilt struck her. She remembered the tearful, hysterical phone call she'd had from Alice the day the storm had broken first time around. *Two-faced*, Alice had shrieked at her, voice catching with sobs. What else? Oh yes – that she was a bitch. And that Alice hated her guts and hoped she rotted in hell . . .

'Well, that's pregnancy hormones for you,' Georgia had muttered when Alice had finally slammed down the phone, but her voice was shaky. 'The woman's gone completely bonkers. I've done her a favour, really, showing her what a two-timing cheat her husband is – and she goes and has an epi about it!'

A monster, Katie had called her. 'That job's turned you into a monster,' she'd shouted at Georgia down the phone. 'How could you *do* that to Alice? You're supposed to be her friend!'

Yes. But somehow the size of the story, the lure of that front page . . . somehow, caught up in the thrill of the exclusive, Georgia had overlooked the friendship. The story had won.

At the time, Georgia had managed to kid herself that by exposing Jake's infidelity, she'd actually helped Alice in the long run. And that she'd only been doing her job at the end of the day. But Alice hadn't seen it like that, of course. Alice had taken it as a stab in the back, a betrayal. And when you looked at it in black and white, it was true.

Still. She wasn't a monster. And yes, okay, Georgia had wished, more than once since then, that that particular morsel of gossip hadn't reached her first. If Chloe Wells from the *Sun* had had the scoop, say, everything would have been different. Georgia might have been able to winkle a sympathetic interview out of Alice and keep her sweet for comments on any future developments (*Jake and Victoria's new love-nest: read what ex-wife Alice has to say . . .*).

No. God, that made her sound even worse. Mercenary as hell. Only caring about her career. It wasn't like that. *Really*, she said defensively to herself, really, it wasn't. She just . . . missed having Alice in her life. Since Georgia's article, there had been nothing but a frosty silence from her. Understandably. Their friendship down the pan after just five hundred words.

She sighed as the bus rumbled past the distinctive red-brick Chelsea Royal Hospital, and Owen's face popped into her mind. What would Owen McIntosh say if he knew what she'd done, stitching up Alice the way she had?

She gazed unseeingly out of the window, feeling a prickle of shame. He'd have stared at her with contempt again, stalked away from her, no doubt. The worst thing was, she knew deep down that she'd have deserved it. What kind of a friend had she been, anyway, running the story about Jake without giving Alice any kind of heads-up beforehand? Her job had come first, without doubt. Alice had been the collateral damage.

Hmmm. And here she was again – Groundhog Day! – with a big new story about Jake. So what should she do this time? It felt like a second chance, somehow, possibly even a means to put things right. The paper would run the story, that was a given, but perhaps this time she could . . .

She frowned to herself, unable to think coherently, as London blurred before her eyes, the bus lurching away from the changing traffic lights. Why was she so sluggish today? Usually she'd have mapped out half a dozen snippets of feature ideas by the time she'd got out of the shower in the morning. Today, she felt about as much enthusiasm for going to work as she did for her smear test.

Once she got into the office – result, arriving five minutes before Polly's new blue shoes tip-tapped across the floor – the newsroom was humming with variations on the Jake Archer split. Georgia being the paper's showbiz reporter, this was her stomping ground, and almost as soon as she had sat down at her desk, Hester, Isabella's assistant, buzzed through with the news that they were holding tomorrow's front page for the story.

'Excellent,' Georgia said briskly, but inside she felt nauseous. She couldn't help her thoughts swerving to Alice. Did she know yet about Jake and Victoria? Was she over him by now, or still heartbroken and pining? Knowing Alice, it would be the latter. She'd always been one of those devoted one-man woman types, even as a student when everyone else was hopping in and out of bed with whomever they fancied. And Alice had been crazy about Jake ever since the day she'd met him. Georgia could still remember how blissfully happy Alice had been at her hen night at that chilly spa place, stuck out in the middle of nowhere. She'd positively glowed with excitement as they'd lounged around in their white waffle robes, hadn't stopped smiling once, it had seemed. Georgia had found all the mushy stuff rather nauseating, to be honest. There was only so much gooey-eyed wittering that a hardened hack could stomach.

Jealous? a cynical little voice piped up in her head now, remembering this, and Georgia scoffed at it. Jealous, what – her? Georgia Knight, jealous of Alice the Mouse? As if!

All the same ... it had been a lovely wedding, Alice and Jake. If you liked that sort of thing, of course. Smiling into each other's eyes, holding hands at the altar, Alice with that beautiful velvet cape, like something from a fairy tale. Jake with a tear rolling down his manly cheek, even! Mind you, he was an actor, wasn't he? They all knew he could cry like a tap if need be. But even so ... there was something moving about it. And when she compared it with her own wedding day, with Harry coked off his head, buzzing around the ridiculously over-the-top reception like an over-excited hyena, then ...

But anyway, this was all past history. Come on, Georgia! Work to do! And if Isabella had trusted her with the big front-page showbiz write-up after Wednesday's humili-ation, then she had to nail it.

So. Decision time. What angle should she take on this story? *Jake Jilts Again*? Not dramatic enough. *Archer's Shot to the Heart*? Nah – too corny.

She leaned forward on her elbows, thinking hard. She could always work in some goodwill towards Alice, by skewing the story so that it reflected her in a good light: *Victoria: A Mistake, Says Jake*. Would she be able to get away with that kind of an angle?

Hmmm. Maybe not. He might get nasty and sue her for blatant fibbing.

Unless ... Perhaps she could use this as an opportunity for some more solid bridge-building. She, Georgia Knight, could reunite Alice and Jake for the big happy ending. Amends would be made. Her conscience would be clear, Alice would forgive her, and, more importantly, she'd have a piece of tabloid dynamite to set off in Polly Nash's face. Who needed film-award ceremonies anyway?

She picked up her phone and buzzed through to Jacquie, the features secretary, her mind spinning with good intentions. 'Jacquie, get me Jake Archer's number, would you?' she asked.

Jake Archer had gone to ground, unsurprisingly, and the incoming news wires were thick with rumours about where he was hiding out. A luxury yacht in Marbella, claimed one source. A secluded hunting lodge in the Highlands of Scotland, reported another. A third tip-off was that he'd been spotted in the lobby of the Four Seasons Hotel in New York, although Georgia's US sources had had no word on that.

Georgia had her own private theory. What if he'd gone back to his and Alice's old apartment? Or, even better, what if he'd tracked down Alice, wherever she lived these days, and was begging for her forgiveness?

The problem was, getting hold of Alice had proved almost as hard as locating her famous ex-husband. She was ex-directory these days and despite Jacquie's best digging around, no number could be found. Katie hadn't been forthcoming either. 'I saw on breakfast telly that Jake's dumped his new woman,' Katie had said with her usual candour when Georgia had called her mobile. 'So no, you can't have Alice's number. I know you too well, Georgia Knight.'

That stung, more than Georgia cared to admit. Even her best friend thought she was a troublemaker, bent on stirring things up. When, actually, she was trying to do something rather selfless, thank you very much!

Finally, she'd managed to track down Alice's parents (they were ex-directory too, just to make life more difficult) and had fibbed a line to Alice's dad about her being an old friend from the theatre where Alice had worked. At last she'd been able to scribble down the sacred digits and dial.

Throughout her life, Georgia had made all sorts of telephone calls that lesser mortals might have quailed at: she had phoned David Beckham pretending to be a call girl hoping to get a story (he'd hung up on her); she'd managed to wangle a direct line to Prince William once and had put on an American accent and impersonated Britney Spears, hoping he'd fall for her trap (no such luck); she'd even tried a phone scam on Elton John, pretending she was his long-lost love-child (he'd laughed and said 'Pull the other one, darling' before cutting her off). She'd done all that and millions of calls like them without batting an eyelid. So why the hell was her heart pounding now as she waited for Alice to answer?

Ring-ring

Ring-ring

Ring-ring ...

Then a click, and Georgia took a deep breath. But

instead of Alice's sweet voice, there came a robotic auto-mated one, telling her to leave a message at the tone. BEEP!

'Alice, hi, it's me, Georgia,' she said, hoping the briskness in her voice was enough to cover any hint of nerves. 'I'm ringing up with some news. It's about Jake.' She hesitated. Should she drop the bombshell into Alice's answerphone? Best to tell her properly, in fairness. 'Could you give me a ring, please? No catch.' She swallowed. 'Oh, and Alice? I'm sorry about what happened. Truly. I owe you one. So give me a ring and we can talk.'

Now she just had to wait and see how badly Alice wanted Jake back.

'So, are you telling me you've actually got photographic evidence of that?'

Polly's voice was more high-pitched than usual, and Georgia's ears pricked up. What had Goody Two-Shoes got her paws on this time?

'Oooh ... sounds very juicy. Will you email me that, Clare? ... Of course! You can trust me. You're a star. This is hot, you know, babe! Isabella is going to love it!'

Georgia gritted her teeth at Polly's excited twittering. But it wasn't just Polly. Everyone, it seemed, was gossiping around her.

'What, Kate Moss really said that? Can I quote you on that?'

'Yep, got that, nervous breakdown, Priory, overdose. What is he like? Cheers, sweets, I owe you...'

'Oh God! Have you seen Popbitch today? She is such a slapper, isn't she? ... yeah, we've got a photo of it... 'Course we're printing it! Slag deserves all she gets, if you ask me...'

Georgia lifted her head and stared around at her colleagues as if seeing them clearly for the first time. There was Sandra, in her fifties now, a peroxide blonde with a vicious tongue and a heart of steel. Three divorces she'd been through, no kids, currently a twenty-something toy boy on the go. Then there was Lola, spoilt little Daddy's girl, who'd only got her job because she was in with all the Chelsea it girls and brought in loads of fabulous gossip from Boujis and the other poshos' hang-outs. And Leon, who read every single celeb mag going as if it was part of his religion, who could spot a WAG or wannabe from fifty paces, and who had a real knack for hunting down exclusives.

They were all good journalists who could bang out 200 words' witty copy at the drop of a hat, who could winkle out interesting morsels from even the most guarded of interviewees, but ... Georgia rubbed her eyes. Today, she couldn't help seeing the tawdry side of what they all did for a living: selling papers on the back of others' misfortunes.

She shook her head. She mustn't think like that. Mustn't go soft. She'd lose her job within seconds if Isabella detected any weakness in her.

She got to her feet and went over to the kitchen to make herself a coffee. One of the assistants was in there waiting for the kettle to boil, a sweet-looking thing with wide eyes and a mane of red hair.

'Hi,' she said timidly, dropping a tea bag into a Battersea Dogs' Home mug. Georgia could see she'd put a sticky label around it saying 'Lily's mug!!!!!' 'You're Georgia Knight, aren't you? We've had loads of entries for your competition, you know. Over a hundred already!'

Your competition indeed. Like she'd had any say in it! 'Really,' Georgia said tightly. 'Lucky old me.'

Steam gushed from the kettle's spout and the girl switched it off. 'Some of them sound really nice,' she said defensively. 'One even phoned up, he was so keen to win, you know . . .'

Georgia pulled a face. 'Oh Gawd,' she said. 'Sounds a bit stalker-ish to me. I'll have to scan them for weirdo potential before I choose anyone.'

The girl blanched. 'Um . . . well, actually, Isabella said . . .' She bit her lip as if steeling herself to finish the sentence. 'Isabella said not to show you the entries. Said it would be more . . . fun that way.' Her voice had become a whisper and she lowered her eyes.

Georgia snorted, feeling furious. Was Isabella trying to make a monkey of her? 'We'll have to see about that,' she retorted, to save face as much as anything, and stormed out of the room without making her drink. She'd pick up a coffee from the deli on the corner instead, she decided, grabbing her purse and stalking through the large glass doors. Suddenly the office felt a very toxic place to be.

South Kensington was heaving – crowds of tourists en route to the V&A, fevered fashionistas on shopping missions, open-top buses rumbling along bound for Hyde Park, black cabs patrolling the streets. The sort of quintessential London scene she'd loved being caught up in not so very long ago. Today it felt too noisy, too fast. She wandered up to her favourite deli on Brompton Road to get herself a latte and was about to go inside when a stick-thin woman with big hair and even bigger sunglasses barged past her, almost knocking her over.

'Watch it!' Georgia growled.

The woman turned and then raised her eyebrows to peer at her. 'Oh, it's *you*,' she said scornfully. 'I was about to apologize but I won't bother. Not after the lies you've been printing about my daughter!'

Georgia stared, not recognizing her accuser. Whose mother was she? 'I don't know what you're talking about, darling,' she replied coldly. Passers-by were casting curious looks their way and the guy from the deli was blatantly leaning over the counter so he could listen. Oh Christ. Who had she offended now, then? She was so not in the mood for this.

She took a step towards the door but the woman grabbed her arm. Red nails like talons; polished and buffed in the best Chelsea salons no doubt. 'If you print another word about Sasha, I'm calling the lawyers,' she hissed. 'Got that?'

Oh, right. Sasha's mum? That figured. 'Get stuffed,' Georgia snapped, throwing the witch's claws from her arm and striding into the deli. 'Latte, please,' she said crisply, hoping the guy behind the counter wouldn't notice how badly her hands were shaking. Sasha Withington-Jones was one of this season's it girls and a right royal pain in the arse, if you asked Georgia. Famous for nothing but being blonde, photogenic and minted, Sasha had made regular appearances in the tabloid pages and celeb magazines until she'd been photographed clambering awkwardly out of a cab, and Georgia had given her a new nickname. Unfortunately for Sasha, the nickname had stuck and Sasha the Flasha was now an object of mirth, rather than anything else. But for goodness' sake ... what did the girl expect?

She rubbed her arm where Sasha's witch-mother had dug in her nails. Just for that, the old bag deserved a horror story of her own. If Georgia had had the energy, she'd have gone back to the office and dug up all the dirt possible on the Withington-Joneses. She always rather enjoyed having a battle in public – it was great publicity for the paper, Isabella said, plus it invariably made the celeb in question look ridiculous by the end of it.

Today, though, she lacked the firepower for a scrap. Her mojo seemed to have disappeared, along with her enthusiasm for the job.

'Cheer up, doll, sun's shining, the world's a great place,' the deli guy said, handing over her coffee.

'Really,' Georgia said flatly, dumping some coins on the counter and walking away.

Back in the office, Georgia trudged across the newsroom with her latte. Sandra was eyeing her curiously. 'Everything all right, kid?' she asked.

Georgia glanced around the room before perching on the edge of Sandra's desk. She could see that the words *Why We All Love to Hate* had been typed on Sandra's Mac and pointed at them. 'Who do we all hate today?' she asked.

Sandra chewed hard on her nicotine gum. 'Haven't decided yet,' she replied airily. 'Maybe Lily Allen. She gets right on my wick. Or Sienna Miller, perhaps. She's always annoying. Why, got anyone in mind you'd like to see publicly dissed?'

Georgia glanced down at her bare arm where the red crescents from Mrs Withington-Jones' nails were still visible. 'Well ...' she began thoughtfully.

'Ahh – got it. Jake Archer,' Sandra said, interrupting. 'Very topical. Why we all love to hate ... Jake ... Archer,' she said as she typed, and then smiled to herself. 'Prepare yourself for a flaying, Jakey,' she said with a Benson & Hedges chuckle.

Georgia cringed. She wanted Jake handled with kid gloves until she'd had a proper crack at sorting things out between him and Alice.

Sandra looked more closely at Georgia. 'Sorry – you were about to say something, before I went off on one. You're not all right, are you? Aunty San can tell. What's up?'

Georgia hesitated. Would Sandra understand? She didn't even understand how she was feeling herself. How was she supposed to explain her muddled thoughts to this seasoned old hack, with her hide like a rhinoceros? Sandra would laugh at her, say she was going soft. And then word might get back to Isabella and ... game over. Goodbye, Georgia. Have a promotion, Polly.

She forced her brightest fake smile. 'Nothing. Just ... just wondering how to blag myself into the Sugababes party next week, that's all. Nothing I can't fix.'

'Ahh,' Sandra said, her eyes a shade narrower. Georgia

could tell she didn't buy it for a second. 'Let me know if there's anything I can do to help, yeah?'

'Sure,' Georgia said casually, sliding off Sandra's desk and making her way back to her own. She could feel Sandra's gaze, heavy with curiosity, on her the whole way.

She sighed as she sat down at her desk. What was wrong with her? She'd hardly done a stroke of work this morning. Alice hadn't called her back and there was still no word on Jake's whereabouts. She began half-heartedly sorting through the images that had come in from last night – a nice one of the latest *Big Brother* evictee's birthday party in the Zed Bar, yeah, she could probably do something with that – when her direct line went.

'Is that Georgia Knight?' A breathy, female, northern voice, slightly muffled as if the caller had her hand cupped around the mouthpiece.

'Speaking.'

'Oh hi. First off – I love your column. Always read it.'

Georgia continued flicking through the images. 'Cheers,' she said, slightly impatiently.

'And second,' the girl went on, 'I work at Malmaison in Manchester – the hotel, yeah? – and I were just ringing to say, you'll never guess who's checked in here in the last few minutes . . .'

Georgia's ears pricked up at once. 'Tell me.'

'It's that Jake Archer – you know, from *Flying High*?'

Georgia gripped the phone so hard she thought it might shatter. 'You're sure? You're one hundred per cent sure?'

'Oh aye, yeah, it's definitely him. I heard him signing in at the front desk. He's up in one of the posh suites.'

Georgia scribbled down a few more details, her spirits soaring. Jake Archer in Manchester – exclusive tip-off! It was a sign, it was definitely a sign. Fate had stepped in and was helping her with her bridge-building. Fate was sending her home.

Just over an hour later, she was boarding the Manchester train in Euston, feeling lighter and more alive than she'd done all day. She was booked into Malmaison on the same floor as Jake. She would somehow or other bring about a resolution with him and Alice, she'd get to see her nan again, and then, she'd track down Owen McIntosh and persuade him he'd got it all wrong about her.

She leaned back in her seat as the train's engine started up, and watched the Euston platform slip away. Yes. This weekend was crunch time. She was going to make sure that everything – absolutely everything – ended up all right.

Chapter Fifteen

Relight My Fire

Friday, 20 June 2008

Alice woke up on Friday morning with a smile on her face. Iris had slept brilliantly – waking at six for a brief feed, then dozing off again. The storm had passed, the sun was shining and the birds were twittering in the ash tree outside her window. And, best of all, she'd had a great evening with Dom the night before. How could she have got him so wrong? He was lovely. Really funny and charming and good-looking . . . and not Cathy's ex! He wasn't a farmhand either, she'd discovered to her mortification – he was a freelance photographer, who'd been working abroad for the last few years, specializing in landscape and wildlife shots. He'd come back to the village to support Cathy when her husband left her, and was currently doing some work for *Somerset Life*, one of the local magazines.

It had been the first evening for months and months — over a year actually, now that she thought about it — that she'd spent alone with a man, chatting and laughing and getting to know one another. Not that anything had *happened* between them, she reminded herself. He was only being neighbourly, calling on her like that. It was just the kind of person he was — friendly and nice and . . .

She was smiling again. There was a skittery feeling that leapt inside her whenever she thought about him. She felt like a schoolgirl, daydreaming about her first crush. A silly crush, that was all it was. It wasn't as if she was going to *do* anything with him. It was just nice to spend some time with a man. A handsome man. A handsome, charming, really rather lovely man.

Thank goodness for that storm, though! It had rumbled on for at least an hour, by which time they'd managed to drink nearly all of his peace-offering wine. And by then, they'd got over the initial awkwardness and she felt as if they were old friends. Oh yes, and nothing was going on with Natasha either — Alice had asked him outright after the second glass of wine, and he'd told her it had been a stupid teenage thing years ago, but now he couldn't stand the woman. Alice had all but danced on the spot, she'd been so pleased. Because Natasha was clearly not good enough for Dom, that was all. No other reason whatsoever.

He'd kissed her on the cheek when he'd said goodbye

and she'd wobbled slightly on tiptoes trying not to lean into him. Oh! It was just nice to be held by a man again, a man who wasn't her *dad* . . . She'd held her breath, wondering if he would go any further. She'd be up for it, if he tried to kiss her properly, she knew it.

He *hadn't* tried to kiss her properly, though. Just as well, she supposed. She might have tried to snog the hell out of him, and then where would they be? He probably didn't fancy her in the slightest anyway. But that was all right. Yes – it was really all right. Alice was fine just swooning and smiling from afar, nursing her secret crush.

Humming cheerfully, she went to dress Iris and make them both breakfast. Village life was certainly looking up, after its shaky start.

Later that morning, Alice needed to stock up on essentials, so wandered down to the village shop. She left the buggy outside and carried Iris on her hip while she negotiated the aisles, dumping milk, baked beans and Red Leicester cheese into her wire basket. It was slow and tricky going about carrying Iris *and* the basket, and she found herself wishing she'd lunched it and gone to the Tesco instead. She wished that even more a few minutes later.

She rounded the corner and saw Jen and Mags browsing the rack of magazines, completely ignoring Mrs Smithers' belligerent scowl. 'All right, Alice?' Jen asked, pausing her thumbing through the pages of *Heat* magazine to glance her way.

Annoyingly, Alice found herself turning pink at the question as an image of her and Dom laughing about something or other the night before flashed into her mind. 'Fine,' she said, not quite meeting Jen's eye. 'You?'

'Oh yeah, not bad, ta,' Jen replied. 'Just catching up on the latest goss, you know.'

Mrs Smithers gave a loud, deliberate cough from behind the counter. This too was ignored.

'Ooh, look, they've got a photo here of that gorgeous Leo off *Flying High*,' Mags said, jabbing at one of the glossy pages of her magazine. 'He's lush, isn't he?'

Alice's heart seemed to skip a beat at the words. All of a sudden her mouth was dry. 'Anyway, nice to see you—' she began, wanting to get away from the conversation. She tried to squeeze past Jen, but the aisle was narrow and there wasn't room.

Jen was busy leaning over to see the picture. 'Phwooar, he's lovely,' she agreed. 'I'd join the Mile High Club with him any day. Hey, did you see the news about him this morning on GMTV?'

'No? What?' Mags looked up in interest.

Iris let out a squeal as Alice gripped her too tightly. *What* news about Jake on GMTV?

'Well, do you remember, there was all that scandal when

he dumped his wife and got it together with what's-her-name—' Jen ducked her head back to the magazine to double-check '—Victoria Hartley, who's Amelia in the TV programme?'

Alice was finding it hard to breathe. Did she remember? Ha ha. Would she ever be able to forget, more like.

'Oh yeah, vaguely,' Mags replied. 'That poor cow. Up the duff, wasn't she? I remember.'

'Well, apparently he and that Victoria were seen having a huge row. The reporter on GMTV was saying they've split up, and everything. I bet it's tense on set there right now.'

'God, yeah, you wouldn't want to be working with them, would you?' Mags said. 'What's his name again, the actor?'

'Jake,' Alice said, her fingers shaking uncontrollably on the wire handles of her shopping basket. 'His name's Jake Archer.' The basket of food fell to the floor with a crash and Iris let out a yell of surprise, but Alice barely noticed. She pushed a hand through her hair wildly, Jen's words still ringing around her head, echoing over and over. *Jake and Victoria splitting up?* Oh my God. This could be major. This could be seismic. Did it mean . . . ? Could it possibly mean . . . ? She let out a gulp. Might there be a chance that Jake would actually come back to her?

'Are any of you ladies going to pay for your goods any time soon?' Mrs Smithers barked, flinty-eyed.

This time they all ignored her. Alice was dimly aware of Jen looking strangely at her. And then Jen clapped a hand to her mouth, her eyes wide. 'Oh my God!' she screamed, pointing a triumphant finger straight at Alice. '*That's* where I know you from! I knew I recognized you, didn't I say? You're her, aren't you? You're the wife!'

Alice nodded dumbly, feeling as if she might very well faint. 'Yes,' she managed to say. 'I'm the wife. I'm the poor cow.'

It was like a weird dream, the next few minutes. Alice turned on her heel and ran out of the shop – 'Excuse ME!' she heard Mrs Smithers call shrilly – and then Mags and Jen were running after her, both agog with this breaking news – speechless for at least five seconds, before launching into a series of breathless questions. 'So you were *married* to him, you were married to Leo? I mean, Jake?'

'Oh my God, I can't believe it, Alice, is this a wind-up?'

'Is it true, he's hung like a carthorse? Only I've always thought he *looks* like he is, from when he's been on telly, you know, the way he stands . . .'

'So is Iris his daughter? Oh my God – she is, isn't she? Jake Archer's daughter in this village!'

Alice was trying to strap Iris back in the buggy but she was all thumbs. At the last words – almost shrieked with excitement — she felt sick. 'Leave Iris out of this,' she said, anger thumping through her.

But Mags and Jen were staring at her daughter now, their eyes wide. 'She does look like him,' Mags said in a hushed voice. 'Sorry, Alice — I'm just stunned. I mean — what if he's split up with this Victoria to come back to you?'

Alice swallowed. *Don't say it, Mags*, she wanted to wail. She still couldn't actually believe it was true. Jake and Victoria finished, the affair over? It hadn't sunk in yet. She was stunned at the idea. Speechless. And oh, she couldn't stop her heart from pounding, her hands from trembling, whenever she dared dwell on the possibility of Jake coming back to her . . .

'I've got to go,' she said abruptly, wiping her eyes with the palm of her hand. 'I can't think straight. I need to get back to the house in case he rings, or tries to get in touch. I mean, I know it might be nothing . . . They might still be together, but . . .'

'Good idea,' Jen said, nodding enthusiastically. 'Want me to come with you?'

'No,' Alice replied. No *way* did she want nosy Jen hovering over her, grilling her with more questions and earwigging on any phone calls.

'Are you sure you'll be all right on your own?' Mags

asked. 'I mean ... if you change your mind ... This must be a big shock.'

'I'll be fine, honest,' Alice said, avoiding their gazes. 'I just need to go home.' She felt light-headed as she got to her feet and gripped the buggy handles. Thank goodness she had them to cling on to – she didn't think she could walk anywhere on her own right now. 'I'll ... I'll see you soon. Please – please don't tell anyone about this yet.'

They exchanged glances. Like they'd be able to keep quiet about such a huge piece of news! ''Course not,' Jen assured her. 'Bye Alice,' they chorused.

She could feel their eyes upon her as she stumbled through the trees towards the cottage. It would be all over the village within seconds, she knew that already. She could almost hear the high-pitched excited voices.

You know Alice? You'll never GUESS who she used to be married to. You'll never guess!

Have you heard? Alice – you know, the new one in the village? Her daughter was only fathered by Jake Flipping Archer! Yeah – the fit one off the telly!

Oh Christ. Just what she didn't want. The whole village knowing the truth about her failed marriage with love-cheat Jake. She could already imagine the meaningful looks she would get from now on. The whispers behind her back, the stares into the buggy, all the intrusive personal questions . . . Oh God. So much for her quiet rural existence. Iris would never be able to grow up free from glances and raised eyebrows. Would Jen and Mags go to the papers, even, she wondered? Would the village be invaded by journalists? Her stomach clenched at the thought of the long-range cameras and hard-eyed hacks shouting questions at her, Georgia Backstabber Knight leading the pack, no doubt.

But then again, if that was the price she had to pay for Jake coming back . . .

Well. No question. She'd suffer it like a shot. She'd put up with the lot of it, if it meant that she'd be back with him — husband, wife and daughter together, one happy little family. Tears rolled down her hot cheeks. Oh, if only. She'd give anything for that, anything.

She could hardly see where she was going through the tears, and stumbled blindly through the village. She didn't care if anyone saw her like this, crying in the middle of the day. They'd be talking about that too, no doubt. Barmy, heartbroken, jilted Alice. She was certainly making her mark on this place, you had to give her that. So much for blending into the background.

She all but ran the rest of the way home, ignoring the curious stares of the old couple she saw in the main street, aware that she looked a state, tear-streaked and wild-eyed.

Why hadn't she brought her mobile out with her? For all she knew, Jake could have been trying to call her. Oh, what was going on in his head? She was desperate to know!

A thought struck her then. Had she even connected her home phone yet? There were still so many things she hadn't got around to unpacking and sorting out yet. Wouldn't it be typical if she'd missed a call after waiting for so long for one?

Her heart leapt into her throat as she burst through the front door of the house, leaving Iris stranded in her buggy as she ran to the phone. Yes, it was plugged in . . . but the sound was off. Oh no! So calls had been coming in all week but she'd not heard them! Her mouth dry, she checked the display panel . . . and let out a cry. Thirty-seven messages, it said. *Thirty-seven messages!*

Oh my goodness. Her fingers trembled as she slid the ringer switch to on. Had she accidentally turned it off when she'd packed the phone, she wondered, or—

Realization dawned. Of course. The last time she'd used that phone had been way back when the news had broken about Jake, last year, when she'd been living in London. She'd switched the bloody thing off for the last few days of being in the flat, when she'd got fed up of it ringing round the clock with grasping journos all wanting to get their pound of flesh. Then it had been packed up with the rest of her stuff, in a box in her parents' garage for all the months in between. She hadn't thought to check the ringer when she'd unpacked it again. And all the while, people had been trying to get through to her!

She pressed the Play button and sat back on her heels.

'You have ... thirty ... seven ... messages,' the machine announced. 'Message one.'

'Alice, this is Pete again from the *Sun*. Come on, sweetheart, pick up, we know you're in there. We're offering you a very nice deal on an exclusive, so ...'

She pressed the Delete button before he could go any further, and grimaced. Talk about a blast from the past. There were twelve more similar calls from the press and they made her skin crawl. It was weird to think their voices had been logged on her phone for over a year.

Then there was a leap forward in time: message fourteen was from her mum. 'Hello, love, just seeing how you're getting on in your new home. It's strange here without you! We've found a couple of Iris's vests and socks in the laundry, so I'll iron them and have them ready for you next time we see you. Speak to you soon.'

There were another six messages from her mum, getting increasingly concerned. Was Alice all right? Why wasn't she returning her calls? Alice's mobile didn't seem to be switched on either – was everything okay?

Alice felt stricken with guilt as she skimmed through them. She'd been so caught up in her new life that she'd barely thought to consider her poor old mum, waiting to hear how she was getting on. And she wasn't even sure where her mobile was now. It must have run out of charge. Had Iris stashed it somewhere, she wondered uneasily?

'Hiya, it's Katie. Just to tip you off that Georgia's been asking for your number. I didn't give it to her because I wasn't sure if you wanted to hear from her, but I've got her mobile number if you do, so just let me know. By the way, I saw the news about Jake this morning. Hope you're okay. Ring me soon for a chat, won't you?'

Alice felt her hackles rise. Georgia had been asking for her number? Of all the nerve!

'Message twenty-five,' the robotic answerphone voice said. Beep!

'Alice, hi, it's me, Georgia.' Talk of the devil. Alice flinched at her old friend's voice – brisk and business-like. The bitch. 'I'm ringing up with some news. It's about Jake.' A pause – for dramatic effect, no doubt. Too late, Georgia. She'd already heard. 'Could you give me a ring, please? No catch.' Another pause. 'Oh, and Alice? I'm sorry about what happened. Truly. I owe you one. So give me a ring and we can talk.'

Sickening. Absolutely sickening. Alice jabbed the Pause button of the machine, feeling furious. Who the hell did Georgia bloody Knight think she was anyway? She went to let Iris out of the buggy, not wanting to listen to any more messages for the time being, but saw that her daughter had nodded off, her sun hat drooping over one eye, her baby chest rising and falling with deep sleepy breaths. Just the sight of her was calming, and Alice stood for a few moments watching her, letting her heartbeat subside. There was a bad taste in her mouth and she flicked on the kettle before remembering too late that there was no milk. Duh.

God. What a day this was turning out to be. What a mad day. Alice put her head in her hands, Georgia's words echoing around her head. What got her most was that tacked-on apology at the end. That *Oh yeah, sorry by the way that I stabbed you in the back last year. Truly.*

Truly, indeed. Truly! As if Georgia even knew the meaning of the word. God! What was she like? Did she really think Alice was stupid enough, forgiving enough that she'd fall for that? Did she really think that throwing in a sorry now, a whole year too late, was going to swing it?

Not bloody likely.

She pressed the Play button again, warily, as if she was putting her finger into a tank full of piranhas.

'Hi Alice, Chloe Wells from the *Sun* here. Just ringing for a reaction to the news about Jake … He's not hiding out with you, is he? Give us a call, we'd love to talk to you …'

'Alice, hi, it's Georgia again. I guess you're out. I'll keep trying you, okay?'

'Hello, message for Alice, this is Jessica Miller from the *Mail*. Just wanted to get your take on the Jake and Victoria split. Has he been in touch? How do you feel about him these days? The number here is ...'

'Alice, it's Dad. We've had a lot of people ringing up for your new number. Is everything all right, love? Should we come over?'

'Alice, it's Chloe again. Give us a bell, darling, we're very keen to speak to you ...'

'Mum again. Mrs Burton from down the road just told me the news about Jake. Are you all right, lovey? I'm starting to get a bit worried that we've not heard from you. Has he been in touch? Please call, just to let me know you're all right. I've been out all morning but your dad says the phone's been going mad here, lots of people wanting to get hold of you. The daft eejit has given out your number, I'm so sorry, love, I hope you've not been plagued by calls. Maybe that's why you're not answering? He won't do it again, anyway, my orders. Okay. Bye, then.'

And so it went on ... and on ... and on. But the one person she'd been hoping to hear from hadn't called. Well, there was a surprise. She should have known better. Because really, what on earth could he have said, to make things all right again?

I've been such a pillock. But I'm going to make it up to you, Alice, I swear!

No – she wouldn't believe that for a second. And how could you possibly 'make up' the first eight months of your child's life to them? Too late, mate. He'd never get that time back now.

I treated you so badly. I lost the plot. I would give anything for a second chance, Alice. Anything.

Hmmm. Better. But she wasn't a pushover – it would take a lot more than that.

I've had a year-long amnesiac episode. I have finally remembered that you – YOU – are the woman I love. And I can't wait to meet our little daughter. I'm going to give her the world!

Yeah, well ... Jake was a good actor, but even he couldn't pull off a *Dallas*-type stunt like that. Still ... it would be nice if he made the effort to try though. She had to find her mobile as soon as possible! What if he'd been trying to get through on that?

The phone rang again, and she nearly jumped out of her skin. Oh my God. It was Jake. It had to be. Alice was a great believer in psychic coincidences. She ran to pick up the receiver before it woke Iris. 'Hello?'

'Alice, it's Georgia.'

The words were like a sting in her flesh after her daydreams of Jake. 'Oh,' she managed to get out, wrapping her free arm around her middle defensively. 'What the hell do *you* want?' she spat, anger boiling up inside her. 'Let me guess – another little stitch-up? A quote for another scuzzy article you're writing? Well, here's a quote for you: get lost. I'm not interested.'

'Alice – wait.' Georgia sounded pleading and Alice hesitated. She'd been about to crash down the receiver but something stopped her. 'Look – I know you hate me. I know you've had a shit time—'

Alice barked a laugh – hard and angry. 'You know I've had a shit time?' she parroted. 'Oh well, let me see. How did that shit time come about, again? Oh yeah – 'cos you stabbed me in the back with your sleazy article. So thanks for that. Thanks very much!'

'I know, I know.' Georgia's voice was low. Humble, even. 'I wish I hadn't done that. Honestly. I was totally out of order, and I really regret writing it. But, the thing is . . .'

'The thing is, you're ringing up to dig some more dirt now that Jake's dumped Victoria,' Alice interrupted tartly. 'What a coincidence you're ringing up to apologize *now*. How sincere and convincing!'

'Look, I know you hate me,' Georgia said again. There was an edge to her voice now as if she was getting pissed off. *Join the club*, Alice thought scornfully. 'But the thing is, I'm on my way to see Jake. I've had a tip-off about where he is, so I'm going to check it out. And—'

'Oh right, I get it, so you're going to hound him, the way you and the rest of the hacks have been hounding me,'

Alice put in. 'What a nice way to earn a living. You must sleep really well at night, Georgia.'

There was a pause. 'I'm trying to do the right thing,' Georgia said in a quiet voice. 'Honestly. I'm trying to repair the damage. This is not a stitch-up, there's no catch. I'm just letting you know, that's all. If you want, I can pass on a message to him from you, or act as a go-between, or—'

Alice snorted. The woman was unbelievable. 'What, out of the goodness of your heart?' she asked mockingly. 'Sorry, Georgia, but I don't buy it. There's always an ulterior motive with you. If Jake wants to ring me, nothing's stopping him from doing so all by himself. He doesn't need you as a go-between and neither do I. Trying to weasel another little story out of me, are you? What a surprise.'

'No – I promise!' Georgia cried. 'Alice – I'm not doing this for a story. I'm—'

'Oh, don't give me that,' Alice snapped. She'd had enough of this. 'You'd sell your own grandmother for a story. You've never bothered apologizing before for splashing my marriage breakdown all over your horrible paper – why the hell would I believe you want to do something for me now?'

'But—'

'And you'd better not print this conversation in your nasty little rag or I'll sue,' Alice declared. And hung up.

Chapter Sixteen

I Can Make It

Friday, 20 June 2008

By the end of the week, Katie was feeling low on energy, and low on smiles. It was seven days since she'd been picked up by the cabbie and taken on the mystery trip into Bristol which had culminated in the Hotel of Proposal Doom. A whole week since her life had swerved off track, seven days of thinking, remembering, agonizing. Seven days of loneliness.

She missed Steve. She really missed him. She felt as if her life had gone to pot without him. The house seemed hollow, too empty, too quiet. The bed was wide and cold. There was no one to share a bottle of wine with, no one to discuss the small, funny things of the day with. She missed hearing his key in the door, his 'Hallo-o!' when he came in from work.

Mind you, if he did come in now, he'd be shocked. She hadn't bothered picking up after herself lately. Her marking was scattered all over the table. Magazines and books littered his side of the bed. Clothes lay where she'd dumped them, crumpled in piles, waiting to be washed or hung up.

She just didn't get it. She just didn't get why he had given up on her so easily. 'Doesn't he think I'm worth fighting for?' she moaned to Georgia on the phone, pouring herself a Friday-afternoon G&T. 'Doesn't he care?'

The phone line was crackly and it sounded as if Georgia was in a room full of people, but her answer came through loud and clear. 'Well, what about you? Do you think *he's* worth fighting for? And if so, why aren't you doing something about it?'

'Well...' Katie hadn't been expecting that. What was going on with Georgia these days, anyway? She was becoming increasingly unpredictable. Katie was distracted by a hoot of someone else's laughter that spilled down the line. 'Where are you?' she asked. 'Are you in the office? It's very noisy.'

'Ahh.' Georgia sounded pleased at the question. 'Top-secret assignment actually. I'm on the train, off to track down a certain someone up north. Can't say any more right now, but hopefully you'll read all about it very soon. Hang on – we're approaching a tunn—'

And that was that. Katie waited a few moments then

dialled again, but Georgia's mobile just rang through to voicemail. She sighed. Four o'clock on a Friday afternoon. She hadn't bothered finishing her marking at school today, couldn't be arsed with the supermarket run either. All she felt like doing was moping around.

The phone rang at that moment and she picked up the handset quickly. 'Georgia?' she asked.

There was a pause and Katie held her breath. Was it Steve?

'Katie? It's Mum.' Her mother's voice was slurred and stumbling. No surprises there.

'Hi Mum,' Katie said, her heart sinking. Calls from her mother were few and far between. Not your usual mother–daughter chit-chat scenario either. 'How are you?'

'Bloody bookcase, shoddy thing, gone and fallen on it, juss wondering . . .' The words always tumbled from her mother like beads off a string. The only pauses came for cigarette pulls. 'Juss wondering, 's Steve around? Need it fixing. Iz'e busy?'

Right. She should have known. Her mum only ever phoned when she wanted something. Money usually, or some favour or other. She'd cringed the first time Steve had seen her mum rock up at the house, pissed, tottering about on those scuffed white sandals, jabbering a stream of incoherent nonsense. Talk about scare a man to death. Steve had been polite and courteous though, treated Katie's mum as if she were the Queen, rather than some half-cut overweight alcoholic. Since then, Steve had fixed half a dozen things for her, sorted out her car when she'd pranged it, and given the gas company an earful when they'd cut her off for non-payment.

'Areyouthere?'

'Yeah, sorry, Mum. Um ... Steve's not around this weekend, so ...'

A wheezy cackle. 'Left you, has he? Had enough of Little Miss Perfect?'

Katie's fingers tightened around the handset. God. To think that this woman had given birth to her, held her as a baby. Dressed her and fed her, held her hand to cross the road ... and now seemed to think she had carte blanche with the insults. 'What's your problem?' she asked, suddenly angry. 'Why do you have to be so horrible?'

That cackle again, like a witch. 'Ahh, I was right, then? Face it, love—' a brief pause to suck on the B&H '—you're like me. Not the settling-down kind.'

'Whatever,' Katie said tersely, and hung up. She bristled with indignation at her mother's words. *You're like me* indeed – what an insult! Being like her mum was what she'd fought against her whole life, the very last person on earth she would ever want to emulate. God!

She glared around the room, noting all the mess and chaos, the tall glass of gin on the table that had left wet interlocking circles like a Venn diagram, where she hadn't bothered finding a coaster.

Then she stared down at her hands, twisted together in her lap. Okay, so she'd let things slip lately and yes, she was drinking gin in the afternoon, but that didn't make her her mother's daughter, did it?

Did it?

The thought was like a shot in the arm. No way. No bloody *way*. Katie would rather die than follow in her mum's footsteps, skidding all the way down to rock bottom. She was better than that. Way better.

She leapt to her feet and began a whirlwind assault of the room, stashing the old newspapers in the recycling, books back on the shelf, CDs into their boxes with an angry, ferocious energy. Into the bin went the faded old roses on the mantelpiece along with all the dried petals they'd shed. Into the dishwasher went the cold coffee mugs and sticky juice glasses, the smeared plates and cutlery from last night. Gross! How had she let everything get so dirty? How come she had managed to give up so quickly?

What next? Clothes. There were clothes everywhere. She swept through the house gathering them, bundling them up from where they'd been dumped. What a mess! What a slut she'd been! Well, no more. This worm was turning — and getting out the fabric conditioner as it did so.

Into the washing machine went the clothes, in went the

powder, on went the button. Water whooshed into the drum – a pleasing sound, she always thought – and then, as she moved away towards the sink, something inside the machine caught her eye. There was something white tucked in with her pale blue cardigan – damn, had she managed to mix her colours in the rush? She knelt down for a closer look … and stared as she saw what it was. Not a white item of clothing at all. An envelope. With her name on it. Steve's writing.

She tried to wrench open the washing-machine door but of course it was locked now that the water was pouring inside, the level rising through the tumble of clothes, seeping into the envelope, making the inked letters of her name run. Oh my God. A letter from Steve. Where had that come from? And how long ago had he written it?

She tugged at the dial, all the way round to STOP, and tried the door. It still wouldn't open. Duh – because the water was still in there. Aaargh! She felt so flustered she could hardly think. Where was the DRAIN bit on the cycle? How could she get the water out before the letter went too soggy? And what – WHAT – had Steve written in it anyway?

Ahh – DRAIN, there it was. She yanked the dial round and the water glugged out of the drum. Back round to STOP with the dial, before the wretched thing went into the spin cycle. Now would the door open? No. There was a minute's delay on it, she seemed to remember. So now she had to sit there for a whole minute, wondering and waiting.

She couldn't believe there had been a letter from Steve in the house all this time. Where had he left it? And when? She tried to think clearly, to stop her mind darting from one question to the next. So ... the envelope was tucked in with her blue cardigan. It therefore stood to reason that perhaps it had been *under* that cardigan somewhere in the house. Now all she needed to do was think when she'd last worn that cardigan ...

Bingo. Alice's house. Yes — of course. The events unfolded into her head like a jack-in-the-box springing out.

Coming back from Alice's. In a spin, about what to say to Steve. She'd come into the house and dumped her cardigan and bag down on the table in the hall, before searching for him in the house. He hadn't been there, of course, and she'd sunk into despondency, never knowing that he'd left her a letter ...

God. What did the letter say? What did it SAY?

She tugged at the door again — and mercifully this time it opened. She pulled out the wet envelope — oh, no, it was soaked through! — and peeled it open. The letter inside was stuck together and she pulled it out gingerly, trying to unfold it without tearing it. Her hands were shaking as she smoothed it on the table. Not all the words were legible, but she could make out some of it at least.

Hi Katie,

Hope you are okay, sweetheart.

Sweetheart! She couldn't believe how her heart soared at the word. She read on, hardly able to breathe.

I was hoping to catch you this afternoon but had to get my train for the conference.

Conference? What conference?

I still want to work things out between us even if [the writing blurred here for a few lines]

She had to sit down suddenly as she felt weak with relief. He wanted to work things out! That had to be good, didn't it? That had to mean he wasn't just bailing out on her.

If you do too, then [more blurred writing]

She frowned at the illegible words. There were some numbers there, but she couldn't make them all out. Was it a phone number? Was she supposed to call him on a particular phone number?

If I don't hear from you, then I'll assume you feel differently. But I hope we can sort this out.

   Love Steve

She read it through again, her mind in a whirl. So if he didn't hear from her, he'd assume it was all off, was that what he was saying? But how was she supposed to get in touch when she couldn't read this flaming number?

She put her head in her hands, unable to think. Where *was* he anyway? She vaguely remembered him telling her about this conference now, but it had been at the hotel, after she'd just turned down his proposal and her head had been all over the place, not able to process anything properly. London? Birmingham? Somewhere abroad?

Bollocks! What was she supposed to do? How could she find out? And — oh no! Was he now assuming the worst, because she hadn't called him on this illegible number?

She thought of Georgia's words again — *Do you think he's worth fighting for? And if so, why aren't you doing something about it?*

She thought of her mum too, so bitter and caustic, so quick to assume Steve had dumped Katie, tarring all men with the same poisoned brush.

Well, no. Steve was different. Steve *was* worth fighting for. But where the hell was he? And, more to the point, how did she start the fight?

Chapter Seventeen

Sure

March 1999

'Georgia, this is Jake.' Alice did a self-conscious flourish. 'And Jake, this is Georgia.'

Well, he was gorgeous, you had to give him that. Smouldering dark eyes and perfect cheekbones. He stood out a mile, even in this Soho bar full of beautiful people. Mind you, he knew it too, Georgia could tell. She held out her hand coolly. 'Nice to meet you. Heard a *lot* about you.'

He raised an eyebrow. 'Likewise. Love the column. Hoping you're going to give us a good review of the play.'

'It's probably a bit upmarket for our old rag,' Georgia told him. 'But I'll see what I can do.'

He eyed her over his beer. 'I suppose it's not exactly the *Guardian*, is it? Ahh well. Thought it was worth a try.'

His words stung. Oh, right. Like that, was it? They'd

only just been introduced and he was going for the one-upmanship.

'Georgia's writing a novel too,' Alice put in, noticing the way Georgia had responded with icy silence. 'You'd better be nice to her, Jake, otherwise you'll end up in it, as one of the villains.'

He gave her a measured look. 'Is that right?'

She could feel it then, something between them. She'd learned over the years that many men got confused by female journalists. They seemed to think that being interviewed by a woman, getting all that attention, that tell-me-about-yourself kind of conversation, meant the woman fancied them. Since realizing this, Georgia had always been careful not to give out the wrong signals, to keep things professional. But this was something different. She wasn't even interviewing him, she wasn't giving out *any* signals other than I-am-Alice's-friend, and yet he was looking at her, lips slightly parted, as if . . .

She turned away pointedly. Hopefully she was mistaken. But she could feel his interested gaze still upon her. Ugh. What a creep. This one really loved himself. Couldn't Alice see what he was like?

Obviously not. Alice was looking at him with adoration all over her face. 'Right, well, I'll just go to the bar,' she said. 'Anyone want anything?'

It had taken him ten seconds to press his knee against

hers under the table. 'Your photo doesn't do you justice,' he'd said, voice low and teasing. 'You're much more attractive in the flesh.'

Friday, 20 June 2008

Georgia felt shaken as Alice hung up on her. Alice the Mouse, threatening to sue! Alice the Mouse ranting and raving at her, so loud Georgia was sure everyone else in First Class had been able to hear. And Alice the Mouse twisting the knife with that comment about her nan. *You'd sell your own grandmother for a story!*

That was bang out of order. Way below the belt.

Georgia picked up her bag as the train hissed into Manchester Piccadilly, feeling slighted and indignant. Actually, Alice, she wanted to say, you've got it all wrong about me. I'm going to see my grandmother this weekend, thank you very much, and I wouldn't sell her for anything!

She realized, from the wary glances other people were giving her as they waited for the train doors to release them, that she was muttering under her breath. She shut her mouth hurriedly. Now of all times she had to keep it together. She had to stay totally in control and hope she could work a bit of magic with Mr Jake Archer, the sleazeball. She'd never liked him, but if Alice was mad enough to want him back, then Georgia would do her damnedest to make it happen.

She'd never told Alice about the way Jake had come on to her so arrogantly that first time they'd met. She'd pushed him away from her, feeling repulsed. 'Don't even go there,' she'd warned him. 'Or I'll tell Alice about this.'

'Tell her what?' he'd replied. 'I'm only being friendly.'

Right. Like Georgia was stupid. If she'd responded at all to his advances, she knew he'd have tried it on – if not then, at some other occasion. She'd debated telling Alice just what her new boyfriend was like, but Alice seemed so happy, so madly in love, Georgia didn't have the heart to burst the bubble. So no, she'd never liked Jake Archer, had never thought him good enough for her friend. And yes, when he'd done the dirty on Alice, Georgia had come down on him like a ton of bricks.

But hey. What did she know about love?

She walked through the station, remembering all the times she'd come here with her family to do their Christmas shopping. It had always been the big treat, coming in to the city for the day, seeing the enormous Christmas tree swaying with fairy lights in Albert Square, and eating hot chestnuts from one of the stalls.

The Malmaison hotel was only a minute's walk from the train station – perfect – and Georgia strolled up to its grand red-brick building feeling apprehensive. She'd read that it had been an old warehouse many years ago, but now the keyword seemed to be luxury, if the light, glamorous lobby was anything to go by. Impressive. She walked across the chequerboard tiles, breathing in the scent of expensive perfume and casting an eye around for any of the Manchester footballers who might be checking in for a secret afternoon rendezvous.

She signed in quickly at the desk and took her key. Jake was in the Moulin Rouge suite apparently, and the paper had paid for her to have a room on the same floor. *Neighbours*, she hummed to herself as she went up in a gorgeous old wrought-iron-framed lift in search of her quarry. *Everybody needs good neighbours* ... Her heart thudded under her shift dress as she wheeled her case along to her room.

Okay. She was here in Manchester. Jake was here in Manchester (she hoped – unless he'd already done a flit). She had a mission of reconciliation to accomplish, and, with a bit of luck, the *Herald* would sell another fifty thousand copies when she did the follow-up interview with them both. She could picture the headlines already: REUNITED! *'We're so in love,' says Archer. 'And it's all thanks to Georgia Knight!'*

Well ... you know. She didn't want to get ahead of herself or anything. She had work to do.

Georgia dropped her case off in her room – very nice –

and eyed the minibar for a split second. Not yet. She'd save that for when she'd sewn up the article. She hoped. A quick freshen-up in the enormous limestone-tiled bathroom – mmm, lovely toiletries, they'd definitely be going home with her – and a last touch of lippy, and she was ready.

She felt like Davina McCall, hounding a *Big Brother* evictee: okay, Jake, I'm coming to getcha! Only this would be a slightly more private affair, naturally.

She squared her shoulders and looked at the reflection in the mirror. 'No time like the present,' she said to herself. And off she went.

'Room service!' She knocked on the door of the Moulin Rouge suite, adrenalin spiking through her. *Please let him be in. Please let him be in.* She had her camera behind her back at the ready, although she wanted to bide her time before flashing it in his face. That gave all the wrong signals, didn't it?

The door opened. Jake Archer, unshaven and sexy, looking irritated at being disturbed. 'But I didn't order— Oh.'

She smiled sweetly and wedged a foot in the door. 'Hi Jake, long time no see. May I?'

He looked down at her foot, a black strappy sandal with her toenails painted scarlet. Surely he wouldn't slam the door over her bare toes, would he?

His head dropped. A beaten man. Good — just the way she wanted him. 'I've been talking to Alice,' Georgia went on before he could turn her away. 'She's tucked away in deepest Somerset, middle of nowhere. Ex-directory. Low profile. Although I've got her number if you're interested.'

He sighed. 'Georgia — not now, all right? I've got some thinking to do.'

'Obviously I'll be writing *something* about your split with Victoria,' she breezed on, fingers tightening around her camera. 'You're a hot ticket right now, Jake. Everyone's been trying to track you down. And you know what us hacks are like. If you don't *give* me anything, I might just have to use my skill and judgement to cobble something together. Maybe I could run a story reminding readers about how you abandoned your pregnant wife, and how you've never met your baby daughter, and . . .'

She paused, leaving her words dangling. She was braced for him trying to push her away and slam the door on her, and was ready with her camera for an angry face shot, if need be.

Surprisingly, though, he opened the door. 'Maybe you should come in, then,' he said.

'I could get used to this,' Georgia said, settling herself on an overstuffed plum-coloured velvet chaise longue, adorned

333

with silk and velvet cushions. 'Very nice, Jake. You've done all right for yourself, haven't you?'

He ignored the question and sat down in a huge wing-backed armchair, sipping a cold drink. He didn't offer Georgia one.

'So, how shall we do this, then?' she asked conversationally, gazing around and noting everything for her copy. The bed was huge with fat white pillows and a rumpled silky purple bedspread. There was a vast claw-footed bath in another area of the room, plus a massive plasma-screen TV and music system. Heaven.

He didn't answer and when she'd finished her sweep of their surroundings, she turned back towards him to see that he was staring at her. Not a pleasant stare – more a stare of contempt. 'Georgia – why are you here?' he asked. 'Why are you so keen to stir things up between me and Alice again?'

She folded her hands in her lap. 'Believe it or not, I'm actually trying to put things right, not stir them up,' she told him. For the first time, she lowered her gaze. 'I ... I guess I'm having second thoughts about what I do for a living. It grinds you down after a while, this way of life. So I just thought, wouldn't it be nice to ...'

He snorted. Rolled his eyes. 'You are so full of shit, did you know that?' he said coldly. 'Do you really expect me to fall for that crock? Jesus, I'm not a complete muppet. You didn't come here to be nice, or put things right. You came here to sniff around for a scoop, get some dirt on Love-Rat Jake, or whatever you're planning to call me. So fucking predictable, Georgia. You and the rest of the baying mob.'

'Now, now,' she said, trying to be breezy. Really, his words had cut her, though. 'You're not exactly being unpredictable yourself, mate. You lot are all the same – you love the media when we're building you up, but then you turn into a diva and stamp your little feet when we don't applaud your every move.' She shrugged. 'Alice would have done anything for you, you know. She adored you, worshipped the ground you walked on. And what? You just got too big and important for her, is that what happened?'

'No—' he started sulkily, but she hadn't finished.

'I think we're more alike than you care to admit, Jake,' she went on. 'We both treated Alice badly. We let her down – you, her husband, me, an old friend. We should have known better, but we both got a bit too cocky, didn't we?'

'Have you quite finished your sermon?'

'No. I haven't actually.' She crossed her legs, glaring at him. 'Now, Alice can hardly bear to speak to me, she hates me, but I bet she's still crying into her pillow at night over you. Don't you think you should show her a bit of respect and do the decent thing, Jake?' She was on a roll now, jabbing a finger at him, giving it all she had.

'Decent?' He snorted. 'That's a bit rich, coming from a

gossip columnist, isn't it? Since when did you get so high and mighty, anyway?'

Her eyes blazed. 'Since I got my priorities straight, mate,' she told him curtly. 'Look, I don't care what you think of me. I came here for Alice's sake, not for you. Here.' She scribbled down Alice's phone number on a business card and thrust it into Jake's hand. 'Call your wife. You owe her that much, I reckon, Love-Rat Jake.'

She turned on her heel and was about to march off when she remembered her camera that she'd tucked into her handbag. Screw it. This interview seemed to have come to an end, so why not? She pulled it out of her bag and aimed it at his face. 'Say cheese,' she told him.

Back in the safety of her hotel room, she called Isabella. 'I got him,' she said. 'Brief interview and a photo. I'll file some copy straight away.'

'Brilliant, Georgia,' Isabella told her. 'I knew we could count on you.'

Georgia poured herself a large gin and tonic before opening her laptop. Her fingers shook slightly as she began typing. She had to get this right. She had to make this article word-perfect. Just to show Alice that she *didn't* have a heart of stone. Just to show the world that actually, Georgia Knight was not the sort of person who would sell her own grandmother for a story.

HEARTBREAK FOR JAKE

*We all know him as the **sexy pilot** Leo Stone from BBC smash
hit Flying High. But in real life, Jake Archer is a **broken man**,
as we found out when we tracked him down to his **luxury** hotel
hideout. Not only is he reeling from the recent **love-split** with co-
star Victoria Hartley, we discovered that he is also racked with
guilt for the way he treated his ex-wife, Alice Johnson . . .*

Her fingers flashed over the keyboard, portraying Alice
with sympathy, but not patronizing her, nor giving away
anything too personal. The real thrust of the article was
saved for Jake, a call to arms, a rallying cry for action:

*. . . So come on, Jake! We've all seen what a man you are on
the screen, now it's time to show us that you can be a man
in real life, too. You're so good at flying to the rescue on TV
— but have you got the courage to admit you made a mistake
and fly back to your wife and daughter? We're crossing everything that a happy ending's on the cards for you — and your
family . . .*

She read her words through again, her heart thumping.
Was it too much? Would it make him dig in his heels?
Would it piss *Alice* off, dragging her name into it?

'Well, nothing ventured, nothing gained,' she said to
herself, and hit 'Send' before she could change her mind.

There. Job done. *First* job done, anyway. There were still a few more left to tick off on her list . . .

She rang down to the hotel reception. 'Could I book a taxi, please?' she asked. 'To Stockport.'

By the time Georgia finally got into her luxurious hotel bed that night, she was feeling pretty good. She'd hopefully engineered the foundations for some bridge-building between Alice and Jake. She'd paid a surprise visit to her nan, who was sitting up in bed, looking pinker in the cheeks, and flicking through *OK!* Magazine with her specs on. 'Look!' she'd managed to tut, jabbing a finger at Paris Hilton and Nicole Richie out on the town, and opening the packet of Crunch Creams Georgia had brought her.

A lump had risen in Georgia's throat at the comment. That was definitely a good sign, if Nan was enjoying slagging off the Z-list again. Like grandmother, like granddaughter, she'd thought, joining in happily.

Then she'd turned up at her parents' house to a squeal of delight from her mum and a huge bear hug from her dad. 'What a lovely surprise!' her mum had trilled, eyes shining with happiness. 'Oh, that's made my day, that has. Come in, love, come in! Kettle's just boiled.' Georgia was surprised how nice it was, popping in like that. For the first time in years, it felt as if she was home.

The only fly in the Germolene was the fact that she hadn't been able to see Owen while she'd been in the hospital. 'Sorry, pet, he's not in today,' a mumsy-looking nurse with curly hair had told her.

'Can I ... Is it possible for me to get a phone number for him?' Georgia had tried. 'Or find out when his next shift is?'

The mumsy nurse had gone all strict on her at that. 'No, afraid not,' she'd said at once. 'We can't give out information like that to the public.'

Georgia had guessed as much, but still couldn't help a wrench of disappointment. She hadn't realized until she'd got there how much she'd been hoping to see him again, to make him realize she wasn't the bad person he seemed to think she was. For the first time since her mad chemical attraction to Harry all those years ago, she had felt fluttery at the thought of being in his presence again. Fluttery ... and now flattened.

'Could I leave a note for him, then?' she tried, batting her eyelashes and trying her best to look sweet and nice and not at all mad-stalkerish.

The mumsy nurse pursed her lips. 'Go on, then,' she said. 'I can't promise anything, mind. The NHS employ me as a nurse, not flaming Cupid.'

'Thanks,' Georgia said, grabbing her notepad and pen. Mumsy Nurse was standing there waiting, big arms folded over her big chest. Blimey, talk about feeling under pressure to write the perfect note. She could almost hear the *Countdown* clock ticking down on her with its irritating background music.

Dear Owen,

Sorry not to see you here — I popped in to surprise my nan. I was hoping you'd be around so that we could clear the air.

She paused to think, but Mumsy Nurse was sighing and rolling her eyes skyward so she hurried on before her Cupid changed her mind.

I just wanted to say . . .

She paused again. This was really hard. Mumsy glanced at her watch. 'Sorry, pet, I'm going to have to go. You can leave a note for Nurse McIntosh at the ward desk if you want, all right?'

'Thanks,' Georgia said gratefully. She'd have a quick coffee, she decided. It was late afternoon by now and she'd had no lunch. Her adrenalin had kept her going all this time, but she was suddenly feeling jaded, and in need of a caffeine boost.

She made her way down the long windowless corridors to the café — and then froze in the doorway. Okay. Change of plan. Lightning-quick change of plan. There was Michelle Jones, her old enemy, sitting at a table, her head in her hands, sideways on to Georgia. She'd know that profile anywhere, that sheaf of dark hair, the slightly-too-large nose, the cruel eyes. But today those eyes were full of tears. Today, Michelle Jones didn't seem to have an ounce of fighting spirit left in her.

Georgia hesitated. Her instinct had been to flee, but now her journalist's curiosity had been provoked. Why was Michelle so upset? Who had managed to break the Stone-Hearted Bitch from Hell? This needed investigating. Very carefully.

Two other nurses were sat either side of Michelle, each making noises of comfort. 'Leopards don't change their spots, Shelley,' the blonde one with lots of make-up said, rubbing Michelle's back with long pink nails.

'You've got to walk away this time,' the other friend advised sagely, ripping open two sachets of demerara and pouring them into Michelle's mug. 'Here — have some of that for your shock. And one of my shortbreads too, if you want.'

'He's a bastard,' the blonde nurse said, shaking her head and tutting. 'A cheating bastard. You've got to tell him — enough's enough.'

Whew. Sounded nasty. Georgia edged away, not needing to hear any more. She was surprised at how hollow she felt, seeing her old enemy so miserable and beaten down. Shouldn't she be jeering, cheering, sticking the Vs up at Michelle, calling her a loser? She'd often imagined herself hearing of horrible things that had befallen Michelle and being filled with victorious joy. Ha! See how *you* like being a victim, love! Not much fun, is it?

Instead, she felt nothing. No triumph. Not even a twist of curiosity about what this so-called bastard bloke had done to Michelle, or who he was in the first place.

Blimey, you are *going soft, Georgia Knight*, a voice said in her head. Fancy passing up an opportunity to gloat over the old school bully.

Was that going soft, though, or just growing up?

She sat on the front wall of the hospital to write her note to Owen.

Dear Owen,

Sorry not to see you here — I popped in to surprise my nan. I was hoping you'd be around so that we could clear the air.

I just wanted to say, I made a mistake that day. I've become a bit desensitized, working as a gossip columnist for so long. I'm thinking of packing it all in—

She stopped writing, not sure how she felt, seeing the words in black and white. Where had they come from?

She ripped the page up and started again.

Dear Owen,

I'm sorry we fell out. My fault. But I'm not the bitch you think I am, honest. I've been seeing things differently lately and know that I was out of order that day.

If you're ever in London—

She sighed. What was she thinking? What was the point? He wasn't going to be in London, was he? So why bother?

She stuffed her notepad in her bag. Suddenly she needed a good cup of tea and a hug from her mum.

Chapter Eighteen

Once You've Tasted Love

Friday, 20 June 2008

The phone hadn't stopped ringing. Alice had felt harassed at first, but now that she'd polished off the last of Dom's wine, she was starting to be able to tune out the calls as they flooded in.

The *Mirror*, the *Sun*, the *Mail*, the *Express*, the *Telegraph*, the BBC, ITV West ... they all wanted a piece of her, they all wanted answers. 'It'll blow over,' she assured Iris, who looked startled each time the phone rang. 'They'll get bored and leave us alone soon.'

Jen had popped by. 'Any news?' she'd asked, and Alice had shaken her head. 'Not from him, no,' she'd replied. 'Jen – I really don't want anyone else to know about this, so—'

'Don't worry, I haven't said anything,' Jen replied. 'I

know I might seem like I've got a big gob, but I can keep a secret.' Then she handed over a bag of groceries. 'Here,' she said. 'I wasn't sure if you'd been up to finishing your shopping. Must have been a right shock.'

Alice peered into the bag. It contained milk, bread, Haribo Starmix, tea bags, three bottles of wine, a slab of Dairy Milk and *Heat* magazine. 'Th-thank you,' she said, almost lost for words. 'Oh – thank you.'

Jen shrugged. 'A girl needs her essentials when she's had a trauma,' she said. 'I've been there myself. Well – you know. Not with the celebrity high-stakes hiding-out thing, but...' She rolled her eyes comically. 'Anyway, if there's anything else you want, you just give me a shout. I wrote my number down for you, it's in the bag somewhere.'

'Thanks, Jen,' Alice said faintly, still rather taken aback. 'That's really kind of you.'

'No worries,' Jen replied. 'That's what friends are for, right? Me and Mags will get you through this.' She patted Alice's arm. 'Better get back to my rabble. But remember what I said – call me if you need me, okay?'

'Thanks, Jen,' Alice said again. 'Really – thanks.' She shut the door feeling touched. *That's what friends are for*, Jen had said. And all those goodies she'd brought round! How sweet was that? How thoughtful!

A small burst of optimism flared inside her again as she unpacked the bag of treats. She had Iris. She had friends.

Whatever happened with Jake, she would be fine, she knew it . . .

The phone went quiet at around six, thankfully. Even journos stopped their pestering for Friday night drinks in the boozer, it seemed. She had stopped picking up the calls long ago anyway, was screening everything on the answerphone. The only time she'd answered had been to assure her mum that yes, she was still alive and fine, and that no, she wasn't the cause of Jake's split with Victoria. Not as far as she knew anyway, although she couldn't help wondering and hoping. She'd found her mobile and had charged it up, trying not to jump every time the text-message alert sounded. But nothing from Jake either.

She'd just got Iris off to sleep and was trying to tear open the packet of Starmix when the ringing started up again. She knew the drill now. Six rings, then the answerphone would start. On came the automated voice. *There's no one here to take your call, so leave a message after the tone.*

BEEP!

'Hi . . . Alice? Hi. Are you there? It's me, Jake.'

The bag tore open and she dropped the sweets all over the kitchen floor with a start, then ran through to the living room. She stared at the phone as if it had just landed from Mars, not quite able to believe what she was hearing.

'I'm just ringing to say—'

She couldn't hold back. The one and only time he'd

phoned in over a year. She couldn't wait a second longer. He might change his mind and hang up, and then all would be lost again. She snatched up the receiver. 'Hello? I'm here,' she said, trying not to pant. Calm down, she instructed herself, but her head had turned to jelly.

'Hi,' he said, sounding slightly thrown at the interruption. 'Um ... hi. Georgia's paid me a visit,' he went on baldly. 'Gave me a bit of a bollocking, actually. Told me I should call you.'

Alice was silent for a moment, digesting this. Georgia was involved? Then surely there would be a catch. 'What — and that's why you're ringing? Because she told you to?' she asked, unable to help a scornful note creeping in. 'What *is* this, are you two cooking up some story for her paper together now?'

'No! God, no,' he said. To be fair, he sounded horrified. 'Sorry. Don't know why I mentioned her. Just ... nervous.'

Nervous? Ha. That would be a first then. And was he drunk? He sounded all over the place. She bit her lip. This wasn't quite the perfect make-up call she'd been hoping for.

'I don't know what to say,' she said after a moment's silence. She held herself very still, almost not able to breathe, trying to work out how she felt. Disappointed, partly. She had longed for him to make contact for so long, but now that he had, it was like talking to a stranger.

'Yeah, it's a bit weird, isn't it?' he said, and an ache started up inside her. She could picture him standing up with a phone to his ear – a flash new one, probably. His eyes would be soulful and melty, she guessed. His voice was as deep and rich as ever.

God, she had missed him.

'Yeah,' she said, a lump in her throat. She felt confused, torn in two. Part of her seemed to be dissolving to goo, a great thick slurry of emotion. Any second now she'd start begging him to come back. The other part still had a shred of dignity and managed to hold off. 'So ...' she said, then stopped. *So what happens now?* she wanted to ask, but left it unsaid. It was not up to her to do all the legwork this time.

'So ... can we meet?' he asked. 'Can I meet her?'

Wham. There. The words she'd longed to hear. And yet ...

'Who, your daughter?' She couldn't help the jibe. 'She does have a name you know.'

'I know. And she looks beautiful from the photos you sent. Gorgeous.' He sounded animated for the first time. 'She's got your eyes and chin, and oh, *definitely* your dad's nose.'

Alice fell into a grudging silence. It was true, all of it. So he *had* looked at the photos. He must have studied them, even, to pick out all of the resemblances. She tried

348

to play it cool but her heart was pounding. 'Yes,' she said lightly. 'Unlucky for her.'

He laughed, and she felt weak at the sound. 'So, where can I find you?' he asked. 'Georgia said you were hiding out in the West Country. Is it . . . is it all right if I come and hide out with you?'

They'd chatted for a while longer, and the whole time Alice felt as if she were filling up with air, floating almost. Jake . . . coming to see her! Coming to meet Iris! Oh, he would just fall in love with his little girl, she knew it. And hopefully . . . oh, she almost didn't dare hope! – but maybe, just maybe, he'd fall in love with her, Alice, again, as well. And then they'd all live happily ever after. The End.

She got the shivers just imagining. She actually felt sick with nerves. And then she looked at herself and the cottage and decided that if there was a chance for Happy-Ever-After, she had to pull out all the stops to get it. She had to give herself *and* her home a makeover to woo Jake into coming back to her. She had to give it everything she'd got.

No problem. She could do glam. She could do minxy. Hadn't done it since Iris had been born, admittedly, but she could pull something off. She'd lost loads of weight since he'd last seen her – hadn't Katie said how slim she was looking? – and she could slip into something tight that skimmed her flat belly. And she definitely had some sexy undies *somewhere* in one of her boxes – unless the moths had got to them first, of course.

Oh yes. Who needed Gok Wan anyway? Alice Johnson was going to make a big, big impression on Jake. He wouldn't know what had hit him.

Seconds later, she'd launched Operation Foxy. She tied her hair off her face in an old paisley scarf and began on her eyebrows. Goodness, she'd neglected them! They were so bushy, straggling over her eyes like unkempt caterpillars. She bet Victoria had hers threaded, or waxed at one of the top salons. She couldn't quite picture the leggy actress hunched over her own magnifying mirror, yelping and cringing like she was as she got to work with the tweezers.

But hey ho. Needs must. Next – a face pack. The tube of Clarins goo she'd always used back in the pre-Iris days, when she had still had longer than two minutes in the day to pamper herself, was crusty and slightly dried up, but she squidged the tube until it ran cleanly onto her palm. There. Dab, dab, dab. God, she'd forgotten how *nice* this was, applying unguents onto one's own skin, rather than Sudocrem onto one's infant's bare bottom.

Just as she was sliding the grey goo up the bridge of her nose, there was a soft knocking at the door, and her heart almost stopped. Christ! Was he here already? Did Jake have his own private jet these days, *à la* Leo Stone, his character?

She went to the door. 'Hello?' she called through the keyhole.

'It's only me, Dom,' came the reply.

She glanced at herself in the mirror — oh Gawd, what a sight! Her eyes looked big and frightened, circled as they were by the face pack. And it never really suited her, that hair-scraped-off-the-face look.

'Um . . . I'm just in the middle of something, actually,' she said cautiously.

He was jiggling the latch. 'Mind if I come in? I won't stop for long.'

She sighed. What the hell. Once he saw her, he'd probably run a mile anyway, and then she could start filling the bath and shaving her legs. And squeezing her black-heads and plucking her nose hair and all the rest of it.

She opened the door and he laughed. 'Ahh. Okay. Fair enough,' he said, his eyes crinkling at the edges. 'You really are in the middle of something.'

She grinned. 'Yeah — you'll never guess what?' she said, the words bubbling out in her excitement. 'I've just had a call from Jake — you know, my ex? He's coming to see me. And Iris too — he's never even met her before!'

Dom's face seemed to fall slightly at this news. Then he

smiled. Well, kind of, anyway. His mouth tilted up at the corners, but his eyes seemed anxious. 'Oh, right,' he said, in a polite way. 'And ... and you're pleased about this. Obviously.'

'Obviously,' she echoed, beaming again as she thought about it. 'Hence the beautifying and the cleaning and the ... everything else,' she said, waving a hand behind her.

He looked sad, then. 'Alice – you look beautiful in your jeans with baby sick down your top,' he told her. 'And raspberry juice all over your hands.' He pressed his lips together as if trying to stop himself.

She flushed. Thank goodness he couldn't see it through the face pack! 'Oh Dom, you are nice,' she told him. 'Thank you. But really – I should get on with making myself look presentable. I mustn't blow it tomorrow, it's really important.'

He nodded. 'I understand,' he said. He hesitated as if he wanted to say something else, then forced a smile. 'Well ... good luck.'

It was only as he walked away that she noticed the bunch of white flowers in his hand. A strange feeling swirled up inside her at the sight. He'd brought flowers again? Did that mean ... ?

She banished the thought at once, blocked the white flowers from her mind. Jake was what she had to think about now. Jake was coming back to her and Iris, and they were going to get their happy reunion at long last! Now ... was a home bikini wax going to be too painful?

Alice was half expecting to wake the next morning with a huge spot on her nose, or for Iris to have bellowed the whole night through, doubling Alice's eye bags to suitcase size. But no. Fortune was smiling upon her. Her skin looked dewy and fresh. Her eyes were sparkling with anticipation. Her hair fell just how she wanted it to as she blow-dried it and she didn't get a single breakfast splatter on her favourite pink top.

Perfect, perfect. Everything looked perfect. Even Iris didn't complain as Alice brushed her soft tuft of hair and put her into a cutie-pie peach-coloured dress with matching over-nappy knickers. This was an omen. It was all meant to be. Daddy's Homecoming ... Jake's knock on the door ... his eyes would light up at the sight of Alice and Iris waiting there for him ...

God, the tension was almost unbearable. When would he arrive? He had been vague on the phone last night, said something about his manager, Jed, helping him get down here incognito. Alice wasn't keen on Jed, whose real name was actually Jeremy, and who'd been born with a whole canteen's worth of silver spoons in his mouth. Jed was flash and shouty, all macho backslapping and braying haw-haws. But hey. If Jed was the means to the happy ending, then let the backslapping begin.

There was a knock at the door just after nine and Alice's heart went into overdrive at the sound. Oh my God. He was here. This was it. Make or break. She had to get it right.

A bloom of sweat prickled up on her back and she grimaced. Sweaty patches was not a good look. She stared at herself anxiously in the mirror. How did she look? Was this a face Jake could fall in love with all over again?

Hmmmm. She looked petrified.

She practised a smile. She looked crazy.

The knocking came again. Shit, he would give up and go away again if she didn't answer soon. 'Just coming!' she carolled, then hastily wet a finger and teased her eyebrows flat (the plucking hadn't been too successful after all), glanced over at Iris, who was playing the part of Ideal Baby like a pro, sitting on the living-room floor and patting experimentally at a Baby Music Centre, and . . .

And opened the door. She hadn't realized she was holding her breath until it all rushed out of her in the anticlimax. 'Oh. Hi Cathy,' she said, unable to prevent her shoulders slumping. 'Everything all right?'

'Yeah — but are you? Dom told me your ex is on his way back! I just wanted to . . .' She blushed. 'Sorry, is this really nosy of me? I'm chuffed for you, that's all. I just wanted to see how you're doing.'

Alice smiled. 'I'm good. No — better than good. Cathy, I'm so excited! This is what I've been dreaming about! I just can't wait to see him. I've really missed him, you know. Really, really missed him. And now ...'

'So what did he say? I mean, did he just contact you out of the blue?'

A car drove by just then and Alice's heart jumped at the sight. She froze as it passed — was it going to slow down, stop? — then relaxed as it went by. 'Sorry. What? I can't think straight. I'd ask you in but ... but he might turn up at any moment, and ...'

Cathy patted her arm. 'It's all right, I won't stop. I want to hear everything later though, okay? And if there's anything I can do — if you two want to go out this evening or something, I can babysit Iris, or ...'

Alice couldn't concentrate. Was that another car engine she could hear in the distance?

Cathy laughed. 'I'll leave you to it,' she said. 'Good luck, Alice. I hope it all works out for you.'

'Thanks,' Alice said, her ears almost on stalks as she tried to follow the sound of the car. 'Me too.'

Hours went by and Alice began to feel as if she were a prisoner in the cottage. She didn't dare go anywhere in case she missed his call. Even the back garden seemed perilous. She might not hear his knock, or him phoning, perhaps asking for directions. And to go out in the small front garden, even on the pretence of weeding, would appear desperate, as if she were waiting to pounce on him. No. She mustn't go all bunny-boiler-esque.

The phone was still ringing — the Sunday papers all trying to get a quote from her now. She didn't pick up the calls, but the messages on the answerphone seemed to rub salt in her wounds. 'Alice, have you heard from Jake?' 'Alice, do you know where he is?'

No. She didn't know where he was. She hoped he was on his way, but was starting to wonder if she'd made up the phone call the night before in a fit of madness. Or had it been some kind of a trick, orchestrated by Georgia and her rotten newspaper? A cruel wind-up, to get her going all over again?

Her spirits were sinking. Iris had pooed through her lovely peachy pants and had to be wrestled into a different outfit. And now the cottage would probably stink, and Jake might wrinkle his nose in horror and dash off again without staying very long, and . . .

Knock knock.

It was half past four in the afternoon. Alice's hair had gone a bit frizzy in the heat, her face was shiny and her pink top had got a splodge on it from lunch. Oh, and the place stank of poo now, knowing her luck. Damn, damn, damn. Still, chances were, it wouldn't even be Jake yet. Maybe he'd sent Jed to take a few photos of Iris on his behalf. Or it would be Mags or Jen, coming to see how she was doing.

She wiped her damp hands on her trousers, feeling queasy, and opened the door.

It was him, Jake, with an enormous fragrant bouquet of pink roses. He was smiling at her, his eyes soft and warm. 'Hello Alice,' he said.

She felt dizzy. Light-headed. She could smell his after-shave, clean and fresh. 'Hi Jake,' she managed to say. He was still as gorgeous as ever. Maybe even more gorgeous. *Stop staring, Alice. Act normally.* 'Come in,' she said, even though she felt as if she were going to stop breathing any second. 'What lovely flowers, thank you. Come on in.'

Chapter Nineteen

You Are The One

Friday, 20 June 2008

Katie was feeling defeated. Typical, wasn't it, that she hadn't seen Steve's note until right at the dog-end of the working week. She'd got on the phone to his office straight away but his department all seemed to have cleared off early. Or were they at this mysterious conference with him? Either way, the receptionist couldn't find a single person who could help.

She'd read his letter through until she knew it off by heart, had analysed each and every legible word. He'd gone to get a train for the conference ... well, that meant it was in the UK, surely? Otherwise he'd have been getting a taxi to Bristol airport. Unless, of course, it was a train for Heathrow because he was actually bound for New York, or Washington ... The telecommunications firm where

Steve worked had offices all over the globe. He could be anywhere. Shit.

His mobile didn't seem to be working when she'd called that. Ironic, really, given his line of work. She'd called his mum, asked if Steve had been in touch, had told a tiny lie about losing the hotel number and did Steve's mum have it? No. 'Where is he, then?' his mum had asked, sounding slightly anxious. 'First I've heard of this.'

'Oh, you know what Steve's like,' Katie had said uncomfortably. 'Always off somewhere! Thanks anyway, hopefully we'll see you soon...'

She'd got away with that one at least, but she knew Steve's friends wouldn't be fobbed off so easily. They were nice enough blokes, but she didn't have the sort of relationship with them where she could just ring up out of the blue for a chat. And what if they took Steve's side and closed ranks against her, refused to tell her anything? What if it was already too late?

If I don't hear from you, then I'll assume you feel differently, he'd written. So was there some kind of deadline going on here? Had he already written her off, assumed the worst? *Well, she hasn't phoned, so clearly she doesn't care...*

Her heart ached at the thought. She couldn't think about that now. Mustn't let the idea of it put her off. She just had to keep trying until she managed to get hold of Steve.

She scrolled through the names in her phone. She had the numbers of Rich, Andy and Dan, his three best mates. Had he stayed with one of them, that Saturday when he'd left her in the hotel restaurant alone, she wondered? Maybe he'd slagged her off to them, called her 'cold' just as Neil had done all those years ago.

No. She was getting paranoid now. He'd called her 'sweetheart' in the letter, hadn't he? And he wanted to make things work between them...

Come on, Kate! Stop dithering! She tried Andy first, but there was no answer, and she hung up without leaving a message. Damn it. Why hadn't she done this before, swallowed her pride and tried to reach Steve earlier in the week? But she'd been so angry when she thought he'd walked out on her, and the mixture of anger and self-preservation had stopped her picking up the phone.

Now, though ... oh God, she'd lose every last remnant of pride, she didn't care about embarrassing herself in front of Steve's friends, if it meant she could get hold of him, patch up the wounds.

Dan was next. Bit of a lad was Dan. Friday night, six o'clock, he'd probably be in the pub already, shouting, drinking, making everyone laugh. She felt apprehensive as she waited for him to pick up. But again it went through to voicemail and she didn't leave a message.

Third time lucky – Rich actually answered, but he

seemed rather distracted. 'Steve? I've not heard from him,' he told her. 'Isn't he in Birmingham this week?'

'I ... is he?'

She could hear the sound of traffic whizzing by. Oh God. Health and Safety nightmare. 'Rich, are you driving?' she asked sharply. Was she technically breaking the law, speaking to him as he drove?

'It's all right, I'm on the hands-free,' he said. 'Yeah, I think it's Birmingham. Wait ... how come you're asking me that though?'

'Um ...' She stalled, squeezing her eyes shut. 'I can't find the bit of paper with his number on, I've not been able to get through on his mobile and ...'

'Oh yeah, Dan said something about him losing it. His mobile, I mean. He's had to borrow a new one for work, or ... Hang on, roundabout coming up ...'

'Rich, I'll let you go,' she said, wincing at the sound of squealing brakes. Time to get off the phone before she caused a pile-up, hands-free or not. 'Cheers, mate. Bye.'

She clicked off the call, her brain spinning with all this new information. Steve was in Birmingham, at a conference, he'd lost his mobile – typical Steve! She should have guessed that from the start – and ... and suddenly she was energized. She could track him down, she could find him. All she had to do now was find out exactly where in Birmingham this conference was taking place.

She switched on the PC, poised for some major Goo-gling. And while she waited for the computer to load, she called Laura. 'Hi, it's me,' she said. 'I know it's Friday night, but I'm ringing for a favour...'

A whoop came down the line. 'Yay! I knew you'd change your mind about the speed dating tomorrow. So you're ringing to beg me for a spare ticket, are you?'

Katie smiled faintly. 'Not exactly. It's complicated. Would you mind coming over to help me with something?'

They worked well together, Katie and Laura. Between the two of them, Google and their phones, they went through a comprehensive list of hotels in the Birmingham area, one by one. 'I'm ringing on behalf of GeoComm, I gather you've been hosting our conference this week?' was their opening gambit. Unfortunately though, 'Oh – you haven't? I do apologize. Must have got the wrong number' tended be their closing line.

'Maybe the conference isn't at a hotel after all,' Katie said despairingly when they'd notched up twenty-seven misses between them. 'You know how flash GeoComm are, they might have hired a room at one of the football grounds, or ... I don't know, the town hall, or ... or maybe Rich got it wrong altogether about Birmingham. Maybe they're in Brighton, or Bournemouth, or ... I don't know. Bahrain!'

'Well, we'll try hotels in the Middle East once we've exhausted the West Midlands,' Laura told her bossily. 'Come on, let's make it a nice round thirty, then we'll dial out for pizza.' She punched in another number. 'Oh hi, I'm ringing on behalf of GeoComm...'

Laura was right. They had to keep plugging away. But what if the conference had finished that afternoon? What if all the delegates were already streaming homewards, striding to their cars or taxis, being ferried to the train station...? Katie sighed, feeling despair at the not-knowing. *Where would Steve head for?* she wondered. From what she could make out of his letter, it sounded as if he were leaving the ball in her court, expecting *her* to call *him*. What would he be thinking now that the week was almost through and she hadn't?

Bollocks. This was what happened when you let the control slip from your hands, she thought bitterly, dialling the number of her next hotel. This is what happened when—

Laura clutched her arm suddenly. 'Oh, right, yes, thank you,' she was saying. 'I was just ringing to find out how things had gone today and ... Actually, could you put me through to the conference room now, please?'

She was grinning like a kid at Katie but Katie couldn't grin back. She felt too tense, too wired up with nerves to respond. 'Oh, of course, silly me,' Laura went on smoothly, crossing her eyes. 'And so after dinner, it's the evening do, is it?'

She was guessing wildly, Katie knew, but God, Laura was doing well. If it had been Katie who'd struck gold with the right hotel, she'd have got in a flap straight away and blown her cover within seconds.

'Yes, thank you, and so . . . let's see what I've got here,' Laura went on, rustling some papers for a sound effect. 'Can I just confirm what time check-out is tomorrow? Eleven, thank you. Well, that all sounds fine. Thanks for your help. Goodbye.'

She put down the phone and rubbed her hands together. 'We've got him,' she said.

'This is actually really exciting,' Laura said half an hour later, accelerating down the slip road. She twiddled with the radio buttons, flicking through news and classical music to find a bouncy dance track. 'Don't you think?'

Katie raised her eyebrows. 'What, being on the M5 on a Friday night?' she said deadpan.

Laura indicated to overtake and nipped into the fast lane. 'C'mon! Seriously, it's kind of cool, isn't it? You dashing up the country to find Mr Lover Man in romantic Paris – I mean, Birmingham – on a relationship-rescue mission . . . It's like something from a film. Where's Hugh

Grant when you need him, eh? Hang on, we should have something more dramatic as background music . . .'

She reached out to fiddle with the radio again and Katie, who wasn't a natural passenger, pushed her hand away. 'I'll find something,' she said. 'You drive.'

'A big smoochy number,' Laura suggested. 'A bit of Whitney, maybe — *And I. I-I . . . will always lurvvvvve you-oo-oo-oooooooo . . .'*

'Oh shut up, Laura!' Katie was feeling too wound up to joke along. She found a travel station on the radio. 'We should probably listen to this, just in case there are any traffic problems . . .'

'Traffic schmaffic,' Laura scoffed. 'Bung a tape in instead. Look, I'm going to get you there, whether there's traffic or not, mate. Don't you worry about that. I won't let a few cars stand in the way of true lurve.'

Katie smoothed her dress for the tenth time since they'd set off. 'Don't say it like that — true love — it makes me feel nervous,' she replied, then sighed. 'Are you sure I look all right in this?'

'This' was a cherry-coloured dress she'd bought in the Jigsaw sale last Christmas in a fit of exuberance but had never actually worn. Laura had plucked it from Katie's wardrobe of sensible navy and brown immediately. 'You've *got* to wear this one,' she'd said, before rummaging through

Katie's shoes. 'X factor or what. Wow. Get it on immediately. And these sandals, too,' she'd added, holding up Katie's highest, strappiest pair.

Laura tutted from the driving seat at Katie's question now. 'Am I sure? Of course I'm sure! You look gorgeous. As soon as he sees you, he'll be running into your arms, you wait. Slow motion, just like on the big screen.' She giggled. 'Obviously *you* won't be running anywhere in those heels, but...'

'I know, I can hardly walk in them,' Katie fretted. 'I'll probably fall over, right in the middle of their swanky conference party, and go flying into the buffet table or something.'

Laura giggled again. 'Let's hope there's a nice soft trifle for you to land in then,' she said. 'Sorry! Your face! Honestly, Kate, just chill. It's all going to be great. I've got a feeling.'

It was still light when they parked near New Street a little before nine o'clock. The city was gearing up for Friday night – there were gangs of girls in short skirts and clompy heels with miasmic clouds of perfume in their wake, there were posses of lads with gel in their hair and clean shirts on, and there were clusters of office workers sitting outside the bars, laughing and joking, free from the shackles of the nine-to-five.

'God, I feel really nervous now,' Katie said, as she clip-clopped her way uncomfortably along towards the hotel. 'I feel sick, actually. What if he's not even there? Or what if they don't let us in? Oh Laura, I think this was probably a mistake. I think—'

'No way!' Laura sounded indignant. 'This was a brilliant idea. Coming to find him in person to say . . .' She paused. 'What *are* you going to say, anyway?'

Katie bit her lip. 'I was kind of hoping the right words would come to me at the time,' she said.

'So you don't know.'

'No.'

'Oka-a-a-ay. Well – good luck, anyway.'

Katie turned, almost stumbling into a lamp post in shock. 'What do you mean? Where are you going?'

Laura tipped her head sideways towards a small Italian restaurant on the other side of the road. 'In there,' she said. 'What? You didn't expect me to come in with you and hold your sweaty hand, did you? This is a conversation you and Steve need to have on your own. And I'm sure the right words *will* come to you. But at this moment, the words that are coming to me are "garlic bread" and "pizza". Sorry, Kate. I'm Hank Marvin, though, haven't eaten all day.'

Katie could feel herself drooping slightly at the thought of not having Laura there to prop her up, give her confidence and, more to the point, blag them both into the conference party. 'Okay,' she said uncertainly. 'But ... hang on. We need a plan. If Steve isn't there, or if I can't get in—'

'You will get in,' Laura told her firmly. 'You've got to.'

'Okay, but if Steve has already gone, then...'

'Then it's plan B. You come and find me in the Italian, we'll eat pizza and go back to yours and drown your sorrows,' Laura said. She glanced at her watch. 'I'll give you 'til ten o'clock, all right? And if I don't hear from you by then, I'll assume everything's going tip-top and I'll shoot off back to Brizzle on me tod. Okay? Best of British to you, then!'

And before Katie could reply, she was off, striding towards the Italian restaurant like a woman on a mission. A hungry woman on a mission.

Katie shivered, rubbing her bare arms. *And then there was one.* She watched Laura enter the restaurant, saw the dark-haired waiter hurrying over to her and lead her into the room ... and for a moment she was tempted to run in there too, sit down at one of the tables with red-checked tablecloths, listen to the cheesy Italian music, smell the garlic and pizza dough and rich, herby sauces...

No. Come on, Katie. Be brave. Think with your heart, not your belly.

With that in mind, she walked purposefully towards the hotel before she had time to waver any more.

Katie wasn't used to being unprepared for anything, but she felt vulnerable as she stepped into the hotel lobby – as if she were walking on stage without a clue what was in her script. She was really here, in Birmingham, on a romantic whim! It just wasn't her. She never acted like this – recklessly, without hours of forethought and planning. And yet, strangely, it felt kind of liberating as well as scary, to be there with just a toothbrush and clean pair of knickers in her handbag, rocking up to this hotel in pursuit of her man. Exciting, even. Her skin tingled. Anything might happen.

The reception desk was long, as if it was used to seating four or five members of staff at a time, but there was only one guy there now, with a pink scrubbed face and short sandy hair. He was frowning at a computer screen, with the wet red tip of his tongue sticking out of the side of his mouth.

She clopped up to him, trying to smile confidently. *Do as I tell you*, she instructed her feet, which felt perilous in their high sandals on the polished stone floor. *Do not skid or twist or anything else. Please.*

The receptionist was staring at her, tongue back in,

thank goodness. 'Hi,' she said quickly before she started blushing. 'I'm with the GeoComm party.' She was about to go off into an embellishment about how she was staying nearby in the Britannia, or how she'd brought Steven Patrick's notes with her and needed to deliver them urgently, or ... or anything, frankly, that she could pluck from her imagination. At the last second, though, she managed to stop herself. First rule of the blag, according to Georgia: keep it simple. Lie and fabricate only when you have to. She'd wait until he asked who the hell she was, or scoffed and said, *Oh yeah? Reckon? Don't think so, babe!*

'Certainly. Are you staying with us tonight?'

Oh. That was remarkably easy. She crossed her fingers surreptitiously by her side. 'No, I'm...' Again, the temptation to launch into a story. 'No,' she said firmly.

'Okay, if you could just sign in for me then, please?' he said, passing over a leather-covered book. 'They're all in the banqueting suite. If I could ask you to wear this pass, please? And follow signs to the Horton Suite. Any problems, come back and ask me, all right?'

She felt like kissing him after she'd signed her name. Kissing him on his pink, shiny cheeks, then punching the air in triumph. Ha ha, fooled you! I'm not really with the party, I'm an interloper! A gatecrasher! And you just let me in. YESSS!!!

'Thank you,' she said, clipping her plastic pass to her handbag with trembling fingers. 'Thank you very much.'

Horton Suite ... right ... okay, then. She wandered along a corridor, following signs to the Horton Suite. Her heart was thumping beneath her floaty dress. Another Friday, another city, another hotel. There was a neat kind of symmetry there that appealed to her, but she hoped this would be a flipside to last Friday's episode, not a repeat of it.

This corridor seemed to be never-ending — it was like being in a dream where you kept going and going along a road, and never actually arrived. Still, at least the carpet was so thick and dense it was anchoring her heels nicely with every step.

Oh God. Horton Suite. This was it. She was here. She hesitated for a second before the double doors, wishing there was a mirror nearby so she could check her reflection. Wishing she was more prepared, with a carefully planned script for guidance, the perfect lines all ready to trip off her tongue.

Deep breath, Katie. He probably wasn't even going to be there, was he? She knew it in her heart. He'd probably be on the train by now, gazing mournfully out of the window as the sun sank behind the Malvern Hills, wondering why Katie hadn't called him, when he'd specifically asked her to, given her a number and everything ...

The thought sent her forwards, made her push the doors open and step inside. Now or never. Here we go.

She found herself in a large room, with big round tables like you got at a wedding, Madonna booming from the speakers, disco lights flashing rather feebly, silver trays with a few curling sandwiches left on tired white doilies on one of the tables. Kicking nightclub this was not. There were clusters of people at the tables, at the bar, a few pissed ones on the dance floor even, mucking about and vogueing terribly. But where was Steve? Katie's eyes scanned the room anxiously for a glimpse of him.

There were at least a hundred people in there, all in their best gear, making small talk or cutting straight to the booze and chat-ups. Ugh. One bloke was leering right into the cleavage of a woman in a deep-cut emerald dress. Nice. Other blokes were guffawing loudly, puffing out their chests like apes, their bald scalps gleaming rainbow colours under the lights. One woman was giving it some on the dance floor, head and shoulders back, jiggling her bosoms for all she was worth. Christ. Didn't she have any mates there to lead her off to a dark corner and give her a black coffee? How did these people let themselves get so out of control?

Still. Maybe control isn't everything, eh? thought Katie. *Look at me, for example. I'm hardly a success story at the moment.* She gripped the back of the nearest chair as she continued her room-scan. Her spirits were sinking. She'd got so damn close. Within touching distance. And for him not to be there, not to know about this gesture . . .

Her heart gave a lurch suddenly as her eyes roamed the far side of the room. There . . . right there at the back . . . was a bloke on his own, sat at one of the tables, frowning over a mobile phone with a glass of red wine next to him. It was Steve.

Show-time.

Somehow she made it across the room without falling over on those heels. Her mum's scornful voice rang in her ears: *They're all bastards, men, every last one. All the same!*

No, they're not, Mum, Katie retorted under her breath. You're wrong.

She could hear Georgia's voice too – *Why aren't you fighting for him? Isn't he worth a fight?* Yes, Katie imagined herself replying. This is my fight – this is it, watch me go!

She was almost there. Three more steps . . . two . . . one . . .

'Hi,' she said, sitting down next to him at the table.

He looked up from his phone and gaped. 'Katie! When did you . . . How did you . . . ?'

Oh, it was so *nice* to see his face again. Like coming home. His eyes widened at the sight of her, he'd dropped his phone on the table with a clatter. And then he was staring at her in bewilderment. 'I just wanted to see you,' she managed to say. 'I've missed you so much. I only found your note earlier today, otherwise I would have called before, but . . .' She swallowed, suddenly nervous.

Laura's voice joined the crowd inside her head. *The right words WILL come to you.*

Steve opened his mouth to speak but she put a hand over his and looked him in the eye. 'Steve,' she said, interrupting him. The blood was thrumming around her body. This was it. She was going to do it. She imagined Whitney starting up a chorus inside her head.

'Steve . . . will you marry me?'

Chapter Twenty

Greatest Day

Sunday, 22 June 2008

The train pulled into Euston and the automatic doors flew open. All around Georgia, people were getting to their feet, taking bags down from the luggage rack, bustling off the train and down onto the platform...

She sat still, as if paralysed. Here we are again. London town.

Sighing, she dragged herself to her feet and left the carriage, the last person to do so. The weekend had gone well on so many levels – seeing her nan looking better, and catching up with her parents (amazing what happened in a week), and of course her bridge-building between Alice and Jake. Tick, tick, tick. Good work, Georgia.

Except the one thing she hadn't been able to do was see Owen. She was astonished how disappointed that made her feel. It wasn't as if anything huge had ever happened between them, after all. And he might have completely forgotten about her by now. He might be happily loved up with someone else for all she knew!

Yet ... there had been a connection between them, she was sure of it. A spark, a flicker. But then she'd blown it with the Layla Gallagher debacle and he'd despised her for it. She couldn't quite believe how desperate she felt to win back his approval.

She slid her train ticket into the slot at the barrier and pushed through into the main station. It was noisy and busy, people were criss-crossing in front of her, talking into mobile phones, eating smelly fast food, rush rush, hurry hurry. She'd lived with Harry in this area during their brief relationship: a first-floor apartment on the Marylebone side of the station. Many nights they'd wandered back from sweaty clubs along Eversholt Street together, both buzzing – him from his amphetamines, her from champagne and the latest morsel of celebrity gossip – before crashing into the flat and having hot, fast sex all over his expensive designer furniture. So long as the drugs didn't make his cock shrink as they sometimes did. *Often* did, actually, now that she thought back.

Harry Stone, eh. Harry Stoner, more like. She still half expected to see reports of his death come in on the wires – drug overdose or some alcoholic binge gone horribly wrong at a high-society party. What a mess their relation-ship had been. She'd thought it a charmed life at the time, mixing with his A-list friends in all the highest circles — yachts in Marbella, weekends in New York and Monte Carlo, dinner in all the most glamorous restaurants ... it was amazing she managed to get any work done — but back then, of course, the showbiz news had been handed to her on a plate. She was part of the in-crowd for a short time, where everyone was beautiful, thin and rich ...

She trudged down the concrete steps to get the Tube home. It seemed like a fantastical dream now, that time of her life. A blast of colour and light and heat. Parties, and catwalk shows, and paparazzi everywhere. But everyone knew that dreams didn't last. Everyone knew that when you'd flown so high there came a time when you had to crash down to earth.

'Big Isshooooo! Big Isshooooo!' A skinny girl with olive skin and greasy dark hair was sitting in the tunnel that led to the Northern Line, knees up protectively. She had tatty stained combat trousers and scuffed DM boots. One arm was outstretched in a plea. 'Big Isshoooo?'

God, London life suddenly seemed like hard work. Depressing. Georgia reached into her purse and took out a tenner, pressed it into the girl's palm. She was starting to wonder if she wanted to be here any more.

*

Monday morning at the office, and for once, Isabella had a smile for Georgia. 'Nice work with the Archer scoop,' she said. 'It looked great in Saturday's paper, and we've had a huge postbag, according to the secretaries – you struck a chord with a lot of single mums out there. Well done.'

Phew. 'Well done' was the highest praise Isabella had been known to dish out. Ever.

'Now then.' She narrowed her eyes and folded her arms across her tailored grey trouser suit. 'Any chance of a follow-up? Do we know Archer's movements now? Did he take your advice? Let's milk this while we can, yes?'

Georgia hesitated. She hadn't heard anything from Alice. Not a call, not a text. God knows what was happening with any reconciliation attempts. 'I'll see what I can do,' she said guardedly. Isabella was a difficult person to say no to.

'Look forward to it,' Isabella replied, as if the whole article was a shoo-in. And off she swished into her cubicle of power, leaving Georgia brimming with conflicting feelings – pleased that her work had merited praise, but not quite so thrilled that more of the same was expected. Hmmm.

Before she could think on it any further, Jacquie, the features secretary, was by her desk with a twinkle in her eye. 'We've got a hot date lined up for you tomorrow, Georgia,' she said, waving a piece of paper mysteriously.

Georgia eyed the paper, then Jacquie. Warily. 'What are you talking about?'

'Our little competition, remember? We've got a winner. We've arranged for him to come in to the office tomorrow, live the life of a showbiz columnist with you for the day. We've booked—'

'Oh, Jacquie, do I have to?'

'Yes. We've booked you lunch at the Wolseley and an evening do at—'

'Well, who is he? Has he been checked out? I don't want to end up with some weirdo on my back.'

Jacquie tapped her nose in an annoying fashion. 'Wait and see,' she said, setting the paper down in front of Georgia. 'There, that's your schedule. We've already sent him a copy. Lucky lad!'

Georgia gave her a look. 'Jacquie—'

'Boss's orders. Don't want to slip out of her good books again, now that you've only just got yourself back in, do you?'

Georgia gritted her teeth and snatched up the paper. 'Thanks. For nothing,' she muttered.

The next day, Georgia made an effort to look her best. She was going to have a photographer by her side all day with this wretched prize-winner, so this was not the time for bad hair or skin – not unless she wanted to go begging to the art department for some major photo retouching, that was. So in went the big rollers for a proper blow-dry, on went the foundation, powder, mascara and lippy, on went a foxy fuchsia dress that cinched her body in all the right places, on went the matching heels. There.

She eyed herself critically in her full-length mirror. Not bad, although she said so herself. Most hacks her age hadn't the stamina or looks for the gossip-girl thing once they hit their thirties. Georgia prided herself on keeping up appearances, not letting herself become fat and bloated on the free booze, or wrinkled and haggard from the late nights, like *some* columnists she could (and did) mention. She could still do femme fatale with the best of them. But she'd made other sacrifices along the way, of course. The job had changed her on the inside, even if her outward appearance remained relatively unscathed.

The itinerary Jacquie had put together covered just about every in-place to be seen around the West End. As well as their lunch date, Georgia and her shadow would be taking in an afternoon movie premiere, sipping cocktails at the opening of some new Cuban bar in Piccadilly Circus, and going to a record company party in Soho that evening. The usual suspects would be out, no doubt, the WAGs and the pin-up girls, the Chelsea boys, the pop darlings and perhaps even a few minor royals for good measure. The line from Isabella was that they had to dazzle the winner – and the readers, of course – with the A-list lifestyle of Georgia Knight.

Dazzling. Ha. She'd once thought it dazzling, too, of course. But the shine had gone from that world lately. Five years, she'd told herself when she landed the job. Any more than that and you lose it. She'd seen it happen to colleagues who'd turned into alcoholics or had let the party circuit take over their lives. She hadn't meant it to happen to her, but somehow or other, she was still here, ten years on. It was a long time to do any job, let alone one as exhausting as this.

She sat at her desk trying to write up some copy about Jude Law's alleged new squeeze, but the words were hard to find. She took a call from her *Emmerdale* mole who was always feeding her secret scandalous titbits about the rest of the cast – God, she was starting to despise that woman – and then half-heartedly chased up a story about one of the Holby actresses from a PR woman in Bristol.

'Oh – Georgia Knight! You're my sister's friend,' the PR woman said after Georgia had introduced herself. Her voice was bubbly with enthusiasm. 'Katie Taylor? I'm Laura, her sister. What can I do for you?'

Georgia had a vague memory of Laura, auburn-haired and quite loud, she seemed to recall. 'Oh yes,' she said slowly. 'When did we meet? The wedding, was it? Or Katie's hen night?'

'Both I think,' the reply came. 'Hey, talking of which . . . have you spoken to Katie lately?'

'No, is she all right?'

'Ooh, yes, I'd say so,' Laura said. 'But I'll let her tell you about it herself. Anyway, down to work. You're ringing about the Patsy story, are you?'

Georgia ended the call feeling curious. What was Katie up to, then? No point ringing her on a Tuesday, she'd be teaching algebra or some other god-awful thing to spotty teenagers, but she'd have to get hold of her later for sure.

'Here she is,' came a voice just then. 'Georgia! Here's our competition winner, who's going to spend the day with you. Meet Owen.'

She was rising from her feet automatically at the words, hand outstretched, but when she saw who was standing there with Jacquie, she promptly sat down again, her legs giving way. Oh my goodness. Two worlds colliding. Owen McIntosh was standing in the office. Smiling disarmingly at her.

'Right,' Jacquie said, smirking. 'I'll leave you two to get to know one another, then. Taxi's booked for half eleven, okay? Lily's just bringing you both some coffee.'

Georgia realized her mouth was hanging open and promptly shut it with a snapping sound. 'How . . . how . . . ?' she began, but she couldn't get the question out.

'How come I won the competition? I fixed it, of course,'

Owen said, perching himself on the corner of her desk. He looked smart and sexy out of his hospital uniform, in dark jeans and a crisp white shirt. 'So, how are you?'

'Wait . . .' Georgia couldn't get her head around it. 'You fixed it? How?'

Owen grinned. 'Better ask her,' he said, looking at the red-haired girl who was walking towards them bearing two mugs of coffee.

Georgia sized up the redhead – it was the girl who'd been talking about competition entries the Friday before. Lily, was it? 'What do you mean?' she hissed curiously. 'What's she got to do with it? Do you *know* her?'

Owen didn't answer because Lily was there in front of them, holding out the coffees. Georgia gave her a beady-eyed stare and the girl blushed violently, her spattering of freckles vanishing completely. 'Cheers, Lily,' Owen said, as if it were the most natural thing in the world for him to be there, drinking coffee in the *Herald* office. He had balls, you had to give him that. *Cojones*, as Gordon Ramsay would say.

Lily looked up at Georgia through her long fair lashes. 'Taxi's coming in—' she began in a timid voice.

'I know,' Georgia snapped. Feeling Owen's gaze upon her, she managed a gracious, 'Thank you.'

This was all so weird. Was she dreaming? Was this actually happening? 'Sorry,' she said after a moment, shaking her head. 'I just . . . I'm just a bit stunned, that's all.' *Was this some big wind-up?* she suddenly wondered, eyeing him suspiciously. Was it him proving a point about her shallow London life or something? But surely he wouldn't go to so much effort to score one over on her, would he? *Would* he?

Georgia got to her feet, not looking at Owen. She didn't want to give him the satisfaction of thinking he'd triumphed in any way until she'd sussed out his motives. 'Come on,' she said. 'We can't talk here.' For the benefit of the others in the room, who were no doubt earwigging madly, she added loudly, 'I'll show you the office bunker where all the hush-hush stuff takes place.'

She felt incredibly self-conscious as she led him through the newsroom. Leon gave a piercing wolf whistle that made her feel even worse. How she wished she'd worn something looser fitting, rather than going for the all-out siren look! Her bottom wiggled like a bag of melons in this dress, and wearing these shoes only accentuated the shimmy. God. She couldn't get her thoughts straight, she felt scrambled inside. Owen McIntosh was in London. He'd fixed the competition and here he was, walking right behind her. Any minute now, her nan would bowl in on roller skates, then Georgia would wake up.

She glanced over her shoulder to check he wasn't some kind of mirage. He was definitely there, having a good old nosy around as they went along. 'Where's this place you're taking me, then?' he asked. 'The bunk-up, did you call it?'

She was about to glare and make some haughty remark, but he was grinning at her so cheekily, the words melted away. 'That's very forward of you, Ms Knight, if you don't mind me saying,' he added wickedly.

She could feel her cheeks flushing at his words. And her legs were going wonky and weak at his smile. And then suddenly, she laughed. She couldn't help it. 'I think you've got the wrong idea about me, sunshine,' she said, trying as hard as she could to put on a snooty voice, but spoiling the effect by smiling.

He arched an eyebrow, then took her hand. 'I don't think so,' he said.

Ba-boom. Ba-boom. Her heart was beating wildly and a fizzing sensation spread through her, like sherbet on her tongue. 'I . . .' she started, but words failed her. She was drowning in his eyes – no, not drowning, she corrected herself, that was a terrible cliché, one that only a wet-behind-the-ears hack would ever use . . . But oh, sometimes clichés worked so well . . .

She cleared her throat, aware that other members of staff were looking at them curiously. 'I'm not sure if the bunker can match the thrills of the hospital canteen . . .' she started – but then he was leaning in to kiss her, right there in the newsroom, with all the hacks whooping and cheering around them.

'Get a room!' someone yelled. But Georgia didn't care. Owen was holding her and kissing her, kissing her, kissing her, and she was oh, just kissing him right back . . .

'Welcome to London,' she managed to say when they came up for air. Then she grinned at him and crooked her arm. 'Shall we?'

It felt like the very best kind of skiving, leaving work with Owen, stepping into a purring black cab together and kissing feverishly as they were driven to the Wolseley. He had just a hint of stubble on his chin, and mmmm, his arms were so hard and muscular, just the way a man's arms should be . . .

'Here we are, lovebirds! The Wolseley, right?'

Georgia managed to disentangle herself and sign the chit. 'Thanks,' she said, taking Owen's hand and dragging him along the seat. 'This way, northern boy.'

She was spinning with excitement now that the realization was sinking in. She had a whole day out in London with Owen McIntosh. A date that he'd somehow wangled. Never in her wildest dreams had she thought this might happen!

The Wolseley was right on Piccadilly, a beautiful old listed building with stone arches at its front and high-vaulted ceilings and magnificent columns inside. 'Wow,' Owen said, gazing above his head as they walked in, and almost bumping into a grey-liveried waiter.

'Wow, indeed,' Georgia smiled. It felt nice to impress him, to show him a bit of her city. She'd make the most of it while it lasted. 'We've got a table booked,' she said to the waiter. 'Georgia Knight?'

The waiter seated them quickly – good, at one of the nicest tables by the window – and brought them water. Georgia leaned over the table and took Owen's hand. It seemed such a natural thing to do and yet so extraordinary at the same time. 'So,' she said. 'Come on. Tell me what you're doing here. Apart from snogging all my lipstick off.'

He put his other hand over hers. 'I couldn't stop thinking about you,' he said. 'I didn't just imagine it, did I? There was something between us.'

She nodded. 'Yes,' she said. Oh *yes*, she sighed inside. *Yes, Owen, yes!*

'And...' He looked down at the starched white table-cloth for a moment before gazing up into her eyes. 'And I felt awful about the way we parted. Me storming off in a huff, and...'

'You were right to,' Georgia said quietly. 'I was ... an idiot.'

'We were both idiots,' he told her. 'I couldn't believe I'd

let you go back to London without anything happening. I was gutted. And so . . .' He cocked an eyebrow. 'I had to think of a plan. And then I saw the competition in your paper.'

'You actually *bought* the *Herald*?' Georgia couldn't help laughing.

''Course not! It was hanging around one of the waiting rooms. Like I'd spend my hard-earned money on that kind of tat!' He gave a snort, then smiled a little sheepishly. 'All right, I bought it,' he admitted. 'Only because I saw your name on the front cover. And then I read about the competition, and . . .'

'And what? I'm genuinely intrigued here. This is the sort of stuff that *Blue Peter* have been done for, you know, competition-fixing. Did you slip a bung in a brown envelope to Isabella or something?'

'Kind of,' he said. 'A bung in a brown envelope to Battersea Dogs' Home. That was what did it . . .'

Georgia frowned — then it clicked. Red-haired Lily's Dogs' Home mug . . . 'You bought her off,' she laughed. 'You bought Lily off with a pledge to Battersea Dogs' Home!'

He nodded, a little shamefaced. 'I did,' he said. 'Very corruptible, that Lily. You want to watch out for her.'

She leaned across the table and kissed him. Several times.

'Wiles like that, you're wasted in the NHS,' she told him throatily. 'Ever thought about working as a journalist?'

'Nah,' he replied. 'But I have thought about working *on* a journalist...'

She kissed him again, laughing. Several more times. She felt giddy and excited, tingling all over with anticipation. He'd come all this way to find her, he'd wheedled and wangled, he'd pulled strings to get her.

'I looked for you in the hospital last week, you know,' she told him between kisses. 'Then I tried to write you a note, but I couldn't get the words right. I wanted to say sorry. What I did – it was horrible. This job – it's not good for me any more. I know that now.'

He looked into her eyes. God, he was so lovely. 'Ever thought about relocating?' he asked. 'I've heard the best thing about being a writer is that you can work anywhere ... even up north.'

She flushed. 'I've always wanted to write a novel,' she said. 'Maybe I should just take the plunge and leave...'

He held her hand. 'Maybe you should.'

Was this really happening? It was all so, so romantic. And then she was kissing him again, and...

'Blimey, Georgie, don't eat the lad,' came a voice just then, and Georgia turned to see Malcolm, her snapper for the day, there with his camera. He raised his eyebrows at the sight of their flushed faces and their hands tangled together on the tabletop. 'Cor, is this the story, then? Showbiz girl about town falls for her prize-winner? Fatal attraction at the Wolseley?'

Georgia exchanged a glance with Owen. 'Something like that,' she said. 'But we're keeping that bit private, all right?'

Malcolm winked. 'Got it. Are you ready for your close-up, then, darlings? And . . . smile!'

Chapter Twenty-One

Back for Good?

Saturday, 21 June 2008

He looked out of place in the cottage, Jake, as he ducked to enter the low doorway and go into the living room. He was too handsome — high-definition handsome — with his hair in a different style so that it flicked over one eye in an insouciant sort of way, and his clothes definitely a step up from Primark. He smelled different too. Back when they'd been together, he'd smelled of Adidas deodorant, Fahrenheit aftershave and, frequently, sex. Now he smelled rich, of fame and Hollywood castings, of money, money, money.

He was looking around politely. 'So . . . have you bought this place, then?'

Was he looking down his nose at her, at the cottage? It was hard to tell. Seen through his eyes, it was probably poky and dismal. He probably wasn't used to being in such a small room, after the all-star lifestyle he'd been leading for the last year. It must seem like a cupboard to him.

'No, just renting,' she said. And then, bluntly, because she didn't want to put it off any longer, she scooped up her little daughter and said, 'This is Iris.'

This is Iris. Like there was any other baby in the room, any chance of him not realizing who the small person on the rug had been all along.

Iris was squawking because she wanted to get back down to the plastic stacking pots she'd been banging together for the last ten minutes, her chubby arms flailing, her eyes mutinous.

'She's tired,' Alice said, plopping her back down again, feeling a needling irritation that Jake hadn't said anything, that she'd felt she needed to defend her daughter.

He crouched down. 'She's gorgeous,' he said softly. 'Hello, Iris. Hello little one.'

It choked her up to see him talking to Iris, and her eyes swam with tears suddenly. There they were, father and daughter, looking at one another for the first time. It was just so . . .

'Ow!' said Jake, recoiling. 'She just whacked my nose!'

Iris gave a chuckle. 'Ba, ba,' she said conversationally, waving the pink plastic beaker in mid-air.

'Iris!' Alice said, coming to kneel next to Jake. 'Gently with that.' She felt mortified. Jake was going to think his daughter was a right biffer now. 'Sorry,' she said. 'She doesn't know what she's doing.'

But he was smiling. 'Cheeky monkey,' he said, tickling her under the chin. 'Are you bashing Daddy, hey? Are you bopping Daddy on the nose?'

Iris's face lit up in a toothy beam and she gurgled at the tickles. Alice had a lump in her throat. He'd said 'Daddy'! He'd actually used the word 'Daddy'! And he was talking to her properly, as if he'd known her for months, unlike some of the blokes you saw, who seemed nervous of babies, as if they would break them just by speaking to them.

'I bought you some things,' Jake was saying to Iris now. 'I did! Some jim-jams.'

'Bo,' Iris said conversationally.

'Yeah, bo, exactly,' he replied. 'You are so cute, you know. Nearly as cute as your mum.'

He grinned up at Alice and she felt as if her heart was melting. *Nearly as cute as your mum* ... Oh! But she had to take it with a pinch of salt, of course. She must. A whole bag of salt. Once a liar and a cheat ...

'I'll leave you two to get to know each other,' she said, feeling sniffly and sentimental. 'I'll just make you a coffee, Jake.'

Biting her lips together so that he couldn't see the happiness that was flooding across her face, she turned and went through to the kitchen. She filled the kettle, humming.

He liked his coffee milky with one sugar, she remembered. And now here she was, making him a coffee with one sugar again, as if the year without him had passed in the blink of an . . .

She leaned forward and stared through the window at the sleek silver Mercedes she'd just noticed parked outside the cottage. A fat-necked bloke in shades was reading the newspaper in the front seat. Oh God. Was it the press? Had they followed him here?

'Jake?' she called. 'Jake — there's a car outside. Do you think—?'

He cut in before she could finish. 'Oh, it's just Jed,' he replied airily. 'He dropped me off here.'

'Oh,' Alice said, getting down a couple of mugs and spooning coffee into both. Her hands were shaking. 'But . . . why is he still there? Have you got to rush away somewhere?' She felt shattered at the thought. So this was a flying visit, after all, then. Nothing more. No Happy Families. No Happy-Ever-After. She should have known. 'You're welcome to stay as long as you want to,' she added quickly, trying to sound casual. But she found herself clutching the worktop as if hanging onto it for dear life while she waited for his answer. *Stay, stay!* she wanted to shriek. *Don't rush away — you've only just got here! And we've been waiting for you for so long!*

'Well . . .' He came into the kitchen with her and almost

made her jump with his presence. God, he was so handsome in that ever-so-slightly dishevelled sort of way. Rumpled, as if he'd been lounging around having sex all morning, before throwing on a pair of jeans and shirt to come and see her. *Don't think about that, Alice.*

'Well, to be honest,' he said, with disarming frankness, 'I wasn't sure what sort of reception I'd receive. I didn't know if you'd throw crockery at me or something, once you clapped eyes on me. Not that I'd have deserved any less, of course – the way I treated you was so atrocious . . .'

She blushed as he stepped nearer. The kitchen felt warm and he was just a fraction too close for comfort. Deliberately, no doubt. That expensive cologne was making her feel dizzy. 'I would never throw crockery at you,' she said softly, not quite able to raise her eyes to look at him.

'You're so lovely, you'd never throw anything at anyone,' he agreed, and placed a hand over one of hers. 'Alice, I can't believe I'm standing here with you. You look amazing.'

She opened and shut her mouth but no sound came. She felt swoony and weak from his words. *Come on, put up a fight, at least,* a voice chided in her head. *Don't just fall back into his arms as if nothing's happened!* 'Jake, I . . .' she began falteringly. 'I missed you,' she said. Did that sound desperate? She knew he didn't like desperate or clingy. She pulled away suddenly as the kettle reached boiling point, hissing out plumes of steam, then subsided. 'But anyway,' she said, not wanting to plunge any deeper into the subject. Not yet. She didn't feel ready to go there yet. 'Anyway. Coffee?'

'Lovely,' he said. 'No sugar for me, thanks.'

Her hand had been on the sugar packet in the cupboard and she let it go, feeling as if the world had tilted on its axis. Oh, right. She wondered fearfully if Kenco instant would still do him, or if he only drank the real stuff these days. Probably only ever saw lattes or cappuccinos with perfect froth and a dusting of chocolate powder. 'Um . . . is instant okay?' she asked.

'Yeah, anything,' he said carelessly. 'I'll just go and send Jed packing, shall I? Tell him he can have a wild night out in Yeovil or somewhere. Yeah?'

She smiled. So Jake was staying. That was good. That was *really* good. 'Sure,' she replied. 'You tell him.'

Somehow the time just passed. She'd worried the conversation might be stilted, awkward – because, really, what did she have to talk about other than Iris and life in the village? – but it flowed between them with barely a moment's silence. He was full of stories about celebrities he'd met, places he'd been, funny moments on set (thank goodness he didn't ask her if she watched the show) and plans for the future.

'I think everything's opening up ahead of me now,' he

told her. His face looked almost boyish with the excitement, and she could see the light of optimism in his eyes. 'Hollywood, I mean. The big time. I've been to a few castings over there, got a few studios sniffing around after me, according to Jed. This could be it, Alice. This could be what I've always dreamed about.'

She was pleased for him – she couldn't *not* be when he looked like a kid who'd been promised his first Chopper bike – but at the same time, she could feel him slipping away from her; she felt a gulf opening up between them. Because, of course, there was no competition. The domestic life she was living in the quietness of the countryside versus the tits-and-teeth world of Tinseltown. No contest.

A while later, Iris went to bed in the cute shortie pyjamas Jake had bought for her (Baby Dior no less. Baby DIOR!), and once Alice had settled her, she came back downstairs to discover that Jake had opened one of Jen's bottles of wine and was pouring them each a glass. He drank half of his in a single gulp, smacking his wet lips afterwards. 'I needed that,' he said, and had another huge mouthful.

'Must have been a strange few days,' Alice said, watching him. He did look jaded all of a sudden, as if he hadn't slept for a while. His eyelids had a bruised tinge about them.

He nodded and pulled out his phone. 'Sorry – just need to check in with Jed quickly,' he said.

'No problem. I'll make us some food.'

Alice retreated into the kitchen and made them a Spanish omelette and salad. She was conscious of how small the cottage was, and how Jake had dined in all the best London restaurants recently but was now eating his tea from a tray on his lap, crammed into her tiny living room. Still. He didn't seem to mind – he was tucking in with gusto, drinking and eating quickly as if he were half-starved.

'Oh, proper food,' he said after a few minutes, topping up his wine glass – blimey, the bottle was empty already – and wiping his mouth. 'This is so nice, Alice, eating proper food after posh hotel stuff, all with *jus* and *coulis* and served in little towers so that you spend ages fiddling around with the stuff before you can actually get any of it in your gob...'

Alice looked down at the chipped china plate she was eating from, the mismatched cutlery, and felt a pang of longing. 'Oh, I dunno,' she said. 'I always quite liked the posh places we went to in London. Seeing how the other half live, and all that.'

He turned to her, his eyes slightly glazed from the wine. 'Then I shall take you there again. To all of them, each in turn!' he declared. He leaned over and grabbed her hand, almost sending his glass toppling. 'What do you think?'

'Well...' *Well, we'll have to sort out a babysitter, obviously,* was the first thing that sprang to her mind. But that was probably a deeply unsexy, sensible sort of thing to actually say. 'Sounds wonderful,' she replied instead, although she felt as if she were betraying Iris in some way. 'And if we go there for lunch, we could take Iris too,' she added boldly.

He seemed to deflate at the mention of their daughter but nodded. 'Absolutely,' he said. 'Why not?' He swallowed the last of his wine. 'Mind if I open another?' He stopped himself. 'Have you got another, rather?'

Alice nodded. 'Help yourself,' she said, but wished he wouldn't. She wished he would stop now. Merry and jovial, fine, but he was necking the booze alarmingly fast. Too fast. She didn't want to go all prim and virtuous on him – it wasn't as if she didn't like a drop herself – but at the same time, she wanted to be able to talk to him properly without him being pissed.

Maybe he was just nervous. That was probably it. He was nervous, and needed a bit of Dutch courage. All the same, she watched him fill his glass and it made her feel stone-cold sober to see him do so.

'You know,' he said, as he sat down next to her again, 'if I do get one of these Hollywood jobs, you should come out there with me. You and Iris. What do you think?'

I think you're drunk, she wanted to say. But she smiled even though her insides were churning with disappointment. 'Sounds great,' she said lightly, not meeting him in the eye.

By half ten, Alice was done in. The whole build-up to Jake's arrival, the adrenalin and whirl of emotions she'd felt as he'd stepped back into her life, the confusion and doubt that had seeped through her during the evening ... she was exhausted. Jake didn't seem to have noticed it was dark outside. He was still chatting away, his eyes brighter now that he'd eaten, his face more animated and relaxed.

Oh, Jake. It felt so natural to have him by her side again, but he had changed. He seemed harder, somehow. Spikier. She couldn't imagine ever feeling as if she were his equal again, now that he had his film-star haircut and expensive clothes. Mind you, she had never felt his equal even when they first got together; she'd always been in his shadow, always felt in his thrall.

But what had she expected? That he'd walk in here untouched by his fame and money, the same affectionate Jake, the same horny, couldn't-take-his-hands-off-her Jake? This seemed like a cloned copy of her husband. A badly cloned copy. His voice had become a shade more London, his look had become sharper, classier ... and somehow his normalness had vanished.

Maybe she was being unfair.

'Alice? You look very faraway there.' He put a hand on her arm and she jumped at his touch.

'Me? No, I'm . . .' She felt goosebumpy as he leaned closer. Was he going to kiss her?

'You're so beautiful,' he went on, not seeming to notice that she'd spoken. 'Why did I ever let you go, Alice?'

The big question. *Yes, why, Jake?*

'I must have been mad,' he said, tracing a finger very slowly down the side of her face. 'Stark, raving mad. But I've come to my senses, Alice. I really have.'

He smelled strongly of wine. Alcoholic fumes were pouring from his mouth with every word. *Don't think about that, Alice.*

'You have?' she said, feeling shivery at the way he touched her skin.

'Mmmm,' he said. And now his palm was cupping the side of her face and he was drawing her in towards him. His mouth met hers and he kissed her. Gently at first, then harder and more passionately.

She pulled away. 'Jake, I—' Her heart was hammering and she felt giddy, unsure of herself.

'Sorry,' he said. His mouth was wet from the kiss, his pupils huge pools of darkness. 'I've drunk too much and I couldn't resist you sitting there, so lovely and perfect.'

She wanted to cry. This was all going wrong. Why was it only now he was calling her lovely and perfect? Why hadn't she been lovely and perfect enough for him to resist getting tangled up with Victoria? The worst thing was, she didn't even believe him. She looked at him and felt let down.

'I'm going to bed,' she said, trying to make it clear that it wasn't an invitation. She needed space to think straight, without him drunkenly pawing at her knickers. 'I'll get you a blanket and pillow. You'll be all right on the sofa, won't you?'

The next morning, Iris woke with the dawn as usual and Alice took her into bed with her. She'd barely slept, listening out for Jake's tread on the stairs – would he come up and try to get in bed with her? – but then, when it became clear he wasn't going to attempt anything of the sort, she'd tossed and turned, feeling utterly thrown by the whole encounter.

Jake was back. Jake had kissed her. Jake had talked all sorts about life in LA together and dinners in expensive restaurants. So why – WHY – didn't she feel happier? Why wasn't she snogging the face off him, overjoyed at his return?

It just didn't feel right. Something about him jarred with her. She couldn't imagine how they'd ever fitted together as a couple in the first place now. She certainly couldn't imagine how they'd fit together in the future.

But ... he was Iris's dad! So surely if he was talking about trying again, she ought to give it a whirl? Maybe in time they'd click back into their easy intimacy. Maybe in time he'd prove his devotion again and she'd feel able to trust him.

Time. That was what they needed. Time together, with Iris, doing normal things, getting used to each other again. But could she really bring herself to give up her life in this country for a fresh start in the States with Jake?

'I just don't know, baby,' she murmured to Iris, tracing her daughter's eyebrows as they lay together in the bed. Iris gurgled a reply and grabbed one of her own feet to chew.

'Hungry, hmmm?' she said, stroking Iris's little body. Bless her, she looked so cute in the pyjamas Jake had bought her. She wondered if he'd chosen them himself or if some dogsbody assistant had been sent to buy them.

She shut her eyes. Wondering such things made her feel disloyal. He was trying, wasn't he? He was here, at least. That counted for something.

'Come on, sweetie-pea,' she said, pulling on her dressing gown and scooping up Iris in one arm. 'Let's get some breakfast. But try not to wake Daddy up, okay? He's probably a bit tired.'

It was lovely to say the words. Just like a real family, she thought, as she carried her daughter downstairs.

The door to the living room had been pulled to, and

she tiptoed through to the kitchen, feeling a wave of optimism about the future. She'd expected too much from this visit, really. You didn't just click back with somebody after being away from them for a whole year – you couldn't! – and it was stupid of her ever to have imagined it might happen that way. But given time, things really might work out. One step at a time.

She plopped Iris on the floor and pulled up the blinds to let the sun stream in. Another lovely day. Perhaps they could take a picnic and go out somewhere, she thought cheerfully, as she got out the Weetabix for Iris and the tea bags for herself. Maybe drive to the Mendips, or . . .

She heard a scuffling sound and looked around on the floor for Iris, just in time to see her daughter's big nappy bottom crawling away from her. 'Hey you, cheeky girl,' she said. Iris went faster at her voice, giggling. So cute. So unbelievably lovely. Alice went after her, smiling. It was only a couple of steps to the living room but Iris was so fast on all fours now, she was already there, pushing at the door with her little fingers.

'No, come on, Daddy's asleep in there,' Alice hissed, bending down to scoop her up. But Iris had already got the door open and squirmed between Alice's hands like a little pink eel.

Alice had expected the room to be in darkness, but only one of the curtains had been dragged over the window, and sunlight was pouring in. Jake was slumped on the sofa, spark out, the blanket half off his body to reveal his bare chest. She swallowed at the sight. He looked so handsomely dishevelled, even in his sleep.

Then she saw what was on the coffee table. White grains of powder and a credit card. Drugs. Drugs in her house!

Oh my God.

'Iris, no!' she cried, making a lunge for her daughter, who was making straight for the coffee table. Alice snatched her up quickly, her skin crawling with disgust, and backed away, unable to believe what she'd just seen.

Oh my God. She couldn't stop staring. Iris could have dabbled her fingers in that stuff, swallowed it, died, even!

Iris let out a yell at being captured but Alice barely heard her. She felt so angry, she wanted to scream at Jake, still lying there on her sofa, the selfish idiot! What was he thinking? What was he *doing*? Why did he feel the need to snort coke, or whatever it was, in her house? It wasn't exactly a nightclub!

A low moan had emerged from her lips. Was that why he'd been so talkative last night, was he some kind of addict?

God. It shook her – right to the core when she thought what could have happened to Iris. A trip to A&E, a stomach pump, a visit from social services ... the events unravelled before her like a horror movie. All because of Jake!

She started to cry with the shock. It could have gone so badly wrong. What if she hadn't followed Iris in there? What if Iris had died?

She held Iris close as she stumbled back to the kitchen, then strapped her safely in her high chair. And oh, she was so bitterly disappointed in Jake, it was indescribable. Just like that, all her dreams of starting over had evaporated and were gone.

Of course, she'd sent him packing as soon as he woke up. He'd cried – he'd actually cried! – tears leaking from his bloodshot eyes, head in his hands, the works. Nice performance, if you liked that sort of thing. She didn't. She could do without that kind of drama in her life.

'I'm sorry, Alice,' he'd said, scrubbing the heels of his hands into his eyes like a boy. 'I'm going to get some help. It's all got a bit much for me lately, I . . .'

Pathetic. It had all got a bit much for Alice too, being a single mum, but she hadn't turned to chemicals to prop herself up. She didn't say as much, though, just watched him weep into his uneaten toast and felt . . . nothing.

'You can't stay here,' she'd said. 'Don't you understand? I've got to put Iris first. She comes first.' *I've got to protect her from druggie Daddy who leaves his cocaine all over the table.* She softened a fraction at the mournful look in his eyes. He looked as if he'd been whipped. 'Look. We can be friends, can't we? For Iris. I'd like that. She would too, I'm sure. We'll come and see you in LA, we'll keep in contact, yeah?'

It was amazing how poised she felt, how in control of the situation. She was at the helm of the relationship now, deciding the direction it would take. It was a good feeling.

And after she'd watched him shamble down the path to Jed's car half an hour later, and waved him goodbye, her eyes fell upon the sweet peas in the front garden. The flowers were so pretty with their papery petals, their leggy green stems, and the wonderful fragrance that spilled from their heads.

Later, she decided, she'd cut some and take them round to Dom's house. Just as a friend, of course. Now that Jake had left in disgrace, she felt free, light and free, like a bird spiralling joyfully up into the sky. The sun was on her face, and she felt sure there was still a happy ending out there for her somewhere.

Chapter Twenty-Two

Beautiful World

Katie's Hen Night, November 2008

Katie sat on the high stool at the bar, twisting her fingers nervously in her lap. She was here first, of course. She was always everywhere first. She'd have to make a real effort to arrive at the registry office *after* Steve next month. Punctuality was fine on one's wedding day, but being an early bride was definitely uncool.

She put her phone on the bar, half expecting it to buzz with an apologetic text. *So sorry, can't make it . . .* She wouldn't be surprised. She'd had to beg Alice and Georgia to come out tonight, after all. A reunion could go horribly wrong. But still. It wasn't every year that a girl got married, was it? The least they could do was show up and have a dance with her.

She sipped her drink, smiling at the thought of the

wedding. Just two weeks to go now, and she couldn't wait. After all her angst, the proposal had slipped from her lips as easily as if she'd planned to say it all along. What was more, it had felt right. It was going to be so different this time around.

Steve had stood up and held her and laughed into her hair, his arms tight around her, and said, 'Yes. Yes!', and it had felt brilliant, like fireworks going off all around them. It had been such a fantastic night from there on. The two of them had taken over the dance floor, swinging each other round to 'Come on Eileen' and 'Blame it on the Boogie' and 'Dancing Queen' and all the other greats, laughing and doing stupid moves and then smooching like teenagers to the slow songs ... She wasn't even drunk, but she felt high as a kite, bursting with exuberance and happiness.

And oh, it had been so romantic after that. Steve had ordered champagne to be sent up to the room and they'd made love all night, unable to take their hands off each other. God, he was just lovely. Definitely the marrying kind.

'Let's stay here the whole weekend,' he'd suggested the next morning as they sat in the tangled white sheets feeding each other bits of croissant.

She'd dipped her finger into the raspberry jam and put it into his mouth. 'Mmm, that would be nice,' she said as he licked it off. 'But I don't have any clothes.'

He'd grinned and given her breast a gentle squeeze. 'Who needs clothes?'

Who indeed. They barely surfaced from the bed that day, just ordered in room service and made the most of the facilities. It wasn't as posh as the Bristol hotel room they'd stayed in the week before, but it was definitely more intimate. Sure, it was something of a squash, both of them fitting under the drenching shower, and they had to stay pressed pretty close together throughout – but that was okay. (That was *more* than okay, actually.) And the bath wasn't as gargantuan or elegant as the one last week, but Katie didn't care. Full to the brim with the steaming water and the entire contents of the complimentary bubble bath, it left barely any room for her and Steve to get in together, but they'd managed it (and very erotic it was too).

So no, Katie hadn't actually been too fussed about clean clothes in the end. It was only when they got home to Bristol on the Sunday night, still glowing from their Birmingham shagathon, that she remembered what else might have come in handy. 'Oh shit,' she cried that evening over a takeaway curry. 'I forgot to take my pill. That's two days I've missed!'

She couldn't believe it. She was like a robot with the contraceptive pill every morning, never missed one, having always been so terrified of the consequences. But in the excitement and drama of the Birmingham jaunt, in the happiness of her reunion with Steve, the sureness that yes, she wanted to be with him for the rest of her life ... somehow the clockwork had clicked to a stop.

There was no mistaking the hope that flared in Steve's face at this news. He stared at her, opening his mouth to say something, then closing it again. 'What does that mean?' he asked carefully after a moment.

Katie tried to make the calculation, but her brain seemed to be on a slowdown. To her surprise, she wasn't gripped by the sick panic she thought she might have been over-whelmed by. She actually felt quite ... excited. 'I don't know,' she replied, looking into his eyes. 'I guess it might mean I'm pregnant.'

Everything seemed to go into slow motion as she said the word. Their eyes were locked on one another, food forgotten, each weighing up the possibility.

'And ... would it be such a bad thing?' Steve was hesitant, as if he wasn't sure he wanted to hear the answer.

Katie thought about it. Really thought. For so long – for ever – an automatic 'no' had come up in her mind, like a number popping up on an old-fashioned cash till, whenever she'd thought about babies. Ching-ching! Babies and motherhood had always been tied up with her feelings about her *own* mother. But it didn't have to be like that, did it?

'If we had a baby...' she began slowly, then blinked at

what she'd just said. The words were half shocking, half thrilling to hear from her own lips. 'I can't believe we're having this conversation,' she said faintly, more to herself than Steve.

He reached over the table and took her hand. 'If we had a baby,' he repeated, 'we would do things our way. We wouldn't be like our parents.'

She nodded. 'And ... and we wouldn't change, would we?'

'No,' he said. 'We'd still be us.'

She squeezed his hand. Statistics were returning to her. The average couple took at least six months to conceive. And Katie was thirty-four now – didn't a woman's fertility plummet once she was thirty-five? Chances were, she wasn't pregnant and life would go on as before. But if she was ...

She smiled at Steve. 'Let's wait and see, then.'

She hadn't expected to be pregnant, deep down. She'd never been pregnant before – didn't even know if she could physically conceive in the first place. Maybe she was infertile. Maybe he was. But, as it had turned out, neither of them was.

Now she was four and half months' pregnant, and her belly was showing. Just yesterday, she thought she'd felt the baby move inside her for the first time. She was so, so happy that this was happening, that she and Steve were going to be parents together. It felt such a big adventure.

Mind you, there was the wedding to get through first. They were having a small do: no penguin suits, no meringue dresses, no feeding of the five thousand relatives. Just close family and friends, a small registry-office affair and then food and dancing at a pub in Clifton. The only thing that was troubling Katie was wondering how Georgia and Alice would get along tonight. She hoped they could let bygones be bygones now and edge back towards friendship again. She'd been counting on Laura being there as a buffer zone, neutralizing any bad feelings, but Laura had phoned to say she was running late and wouldn't be there for a while. So it would be the three of them all together at first — well, if the other two showed, of course . . .

Meanwhile, half a mile away, Georgia was walking into a different pub and trying to remember when she'd last felt quite so apprehensive. Maybe when she was bracing herself to tell Harry she was leaving him and the marriage was over? No. The words had burst out in a tirade of hatred with barely a tremor of fear. Maybe when she'd been trying to blag her way into the MTV Millennium Eve party? Nah. She'd had enough Dutch courage to quench any nerves. Or possibly when she'd been about to break the news to Isabella that she was quitting her job? Well, that had been daunting, but she'd been so excited at the prospect, she'd managed eye contact and everything. *Start spreading the news, I'm leaving today* ... Polly had all but jumped up and down with glee.

But this ... this was proper nerves. Meeting up with Alice, burying the hatchet after all these months. Georgia hoped the hatchet wouldn't end up buried in her head. The fact that Alice had agreed to meet her at all gave Georgia slight hope, but things changed, didn't they? People bottled it, or decided that actually, they didn't feel quite so conciliatory after all.

Still. Here she was, right time, right address. 'You'll feel so much better once you've seen her and had a chat,' Owen had said as she'd kissed him goodbye that morning. 'You're doing the right thing.'

She'd put her arms around him, not wanting to go any more. She'd only been living with him for three weeks, and had never felt happier. She felt ... complete. Was that too corny? She didn't care. It was true. Leaving London, her home for the last sixteen years, had been terrifying, but exhilarating too. She was letting her flat now with a view to selling it at some point in the future, and she and Owen had found a place to rent together in Manchester's trendy Northern Quarter. Everyone was so friendly there, she couldn't believe it! And the bars and shops were fab, too –

she'd almost forgotten there were any other cool places outside London.

Since making the move, she had thrown herself into freelance opportunities, pitching an idea for a column to the *Evening News* and feature ideas to various magazines, plus she'd written some blog posts for one of the big Manchester websites. She'd also set up her PC on a desk and typed CHAPTER ONE in a new Word document.

'I'm going to miss you,' she told him that morning, kissing his neck. He smelled so nice it made her insides flip and she slid a hand under his T-shirt.

'Georgia Knight, you dirty cow,' he said thickly as she unbuttoned his jeans.

'You love it,' she replied, groaning with pleasure as he pulled up her skirt and pressed her against the radiator. 'Ohhh . . .'

She'd had to peg it for her train, but God it had been worth it. Her love life had been parched and pathetic for the last few years, but now it felt like monsoon season and she couldn't get enough of him. The thought was enough to put a smile on her face as she cast an eye around the pub – no sign of Alice – and went up to the bar. 'Vodka tonic, please. Actually, make it a double.'

Alice was running late, having missed her bus after a last-minute wobble about leaving Iris overnight for the first time ever. She knew very well that her parents would lavish her with love and care and that her little girl would be absolutely fine but it still felt awful, the thought of not being able to kiss her goodnight at seven o'clock. And how would Iris react the next morning when Alice wasn't there? She squeezed her eyes shut, not wanting to think about it, as she hurried up the road, limping slightly in her high heels. She was out of practice with such shoes – hell, she was out of practice when it came to nights out full stop. But still, Katie's hen do, eh? She wasn't going to miss that one for anything.

Her phone bleeped and she fumbled to get it out of her handbag, heart skipping a beat at the dread of a call from her mum: *Iris has had a fall. Iris has stopped breathing. Iris has got a very high temperature . . .*

No. Stop it. The caller display read *Dom* and she pressed 'Accept'. 'Hiya, are you okay?'

'Hi, yeah, fine, just wanted to say, I hope it goes well tonight. Have you met The Bitch yet?'

'No, not yet, on my way now. I think she'll be all right. She was incredibly contrite on the phone.' Almost embarrassingly so, actually. Laying on the apologies and we-are-not-worthy stuff so thick, Alice had half wondered if Georgia had suffered some kind of head injury. Or was this an impostor she was speaking to? Georgia had never been one for 'sorry' unless it was dragged out of her.

'Yeah, well, quite right too,' Dom said. 'Anyway, don't let her give you any grief, will you? No being sweet-talked into an interview about Jake or anything.'

Alice gave a little shudder. 'Don't worry, I'm not going there. I've already said he's off-limits. This is for Katie's sake. Georgia and I are just going to clear the air, then we can join Katie and . . .' She pulled a face. 'Oh God. I'm nervous now.'

'Don't be.' He was as calm as ever. He should have been in the emergency services, Dom, he was always so steady. 'I'm sure it'll be fine. Let her apologize and move on. I bet you'll have a good laugh once you're all together.'

'Yeah. Hope so. Anyway, I'll see you tomorrow. Thanks for ringing. Bye.'

'Bye, sweetheart. Love you.'

She pressed the phone against her cheek as the call ended, wishing he could be there with her. She spent so much time with him now, it was strange to be someplace he wasn't.

Ahh. Here was the pub. She gave a deep breath and pulled back her shoulders. She could do this. She could definitely do this.

The thing about Georgia, thought Alice as she pushed open the door, was that she'd always been so dazzling, so full of life, energy and attitude, that she made you feel a little brighter, just being near to her. She had this presence, always had done, even when they were first years at uni together. Alice had been gawky and square, had never had sex, never tried any drugs, only ever been mildly squiffy on cider a few times before. But as luck would have it, her room in the hall of residence was right next to Georgia's — this loud, glamorous creature who seemed hard as nails, fearless. And amazingly, Georgia had been really nice to Alice, had looked after her a bit, always asked her along to pub nights or whatever. Then, a few months in, when Georgia had revealed herself to be so bruised, so fragile about the baby, and the attack . . . it had broken Alice's heart.

After that, there had always been a closeness, despite the differences in their personalities. She'd trusted Georgia — as she'd felt Georgia trusted her. Which was why it had all been so shocking, the betrayal. Almost worse than Jake's cheating.

Tears pricked her eyes suddenly. *No. Don't start getting emotional.* She needed to stay in control for the next few hours.

She stood in the doorway, her hand still on the handle. The thing was, Alice thought to herself, what she'd come to realize in the last few months was that she actually missed Georgia. Despite everything that had happened in the past, she missed all the vibrancy and sparkle that came with having Georgia in your life. And so if Georgia was ready to say sorry, then she, Alice, was ready to listen.

She scanned the room — it was trendy-scruffy, with mismatched chairs and tables, old leather sofas, lamps shining soft circles of light. And there, sitting in a pink brocade armchair, legs crossed, reading a magazine, was Georgia.

God. Just the sight of her made Alice feel twisted up inside. Georgia had had her hair cut shorter, in a choppy, shoulder-length bob, and had a fringe — very Cleopatra — and was wearing dark jeans and a low-cut red top. Cool as a cucumber, as ever. Alice suddenly felt overdressed in her black trousers and spangly top.

Still. She was here now. She crossed the room and stood next to her old friend. 'Hi,' she said.

Katie shifted on her bar stool, feeling uncomfortable. Where were they? Had they blown her out? It was nearly half eight now, and she'd said eight to them both. Bloody hell. And Laura wasn't due until nine ... could she really sit here another half an hour on her own? She was starting to feel self-conscious all by herself. *It's my hen night as well*, she thought miserably. Didn't her friends care about her?

The music in this place was starting to get on her nerves now. It was tinkly piano music, but the melody didn't seem to be getting anywhere, as if it were on a loop. The lights were too bright and starting to give her a headache. She was beginning to wish she was at home, with her feet up, and some comfort food to tuck into. Maybe it had been a bit ambitious, this whole hen-night thing.

But then – at last. In came Georgia ... closely followed by Alice. Oh my God. They were together! They were speaking! She held her breath as they made their way over. They weren't scratching each other's eyes out – wahey! Had peace finally broken out?

She clambered inelegantly from her stool and stood there, a hopeful smile on her face. 'Hi! Have you two just bumped into each other, or ...?'

Georgia grinned and hugged her. 'Hiya,' she said. 'My God, the belly on you. Phwwwoooar, let's have a stroke of it!'

Alice kissed her and managed a sideways hug while Georgia was oohing and ahhing over Katie's bump. 'We thought we'd meet up first,' she said. 'We've been in a pub down the road, talking things through.'

'And ...?' Katie hardly dared ask. 'Is everything all right?'

Georgia and Alice exchanged a glance. 'Yes,' they said in the same breath. 'Water under the bridge,' Alice added.

'I've been hearing all about the lovely Dom,' Georgia teased, raising an eyebrow meaningfully. 'Sounds like he's a bit of a catch and a half.'

'And she's been boring me to death swooning over this Owen bloke,' Alice put in. 'Joke,' she said quickly, but Georgia was smiling.

'And here's you, our Katie, up the duff and looking amazing,' Georgia said fondly. 'We've done all right, us three, haven't we? Another hen night, and we're all grown up and happy.'

'Grown up?' Katie snorted. 'Speak for yourself, love. I was hoping for a bit of silly dancing to Take That tonight.'

'God yeah,' Alice agreed. 'And cocktails. And I really hope you've got *Pretty Woman* on video back at your place...'

'Too right,' Georgia said. 'Girls, I think we need a toast. Can we get some service around here?' she asked the barman. 'Bottle of bubbly, please.' She turned back to Katie. 'What are you drinking?'

'Lemonade,' Katie said. 'But I reckon I might manage a sip of bubbly. Just to be polite.'

The barman uncorked the bottle with a pop and poured them each a glass of the fizz.

'Here's to us, girls,' Katie said, feeling a rush of happiness as they stood there together, all smiling at one another.

'Definitely,' Georgia agreed. 'Cheers to the blushing bride,' she said, raising her glass, her eyes twinkling.

Katie grinned. 'I'll drink to that. And to you two, as well, my hens and best friends, all back together again. Cheers to the hens!'

Lucy Diamond
exclusive interview

Q&A

Did you have a hen night yourself? And if so, what did it involve?

I did have a hen night, yes, but as a thirty-something with three children, I felt rather more 'mother hen' than 'cool chick', so it wasn't a completely debauched affair! My partner took the kids away for the weekend, so I invited 'the girls' and my sisters to our house in Bath. We hit the shops, went out for dinner and then on to a club for cocktails and dancing. And yes, I *did* have a list of challenges (thanks a lot, girls) but fortunately for me they weren't quite as outrageous as the ones that feature in Georgia's hen night. (That's what I've told my husband anyway – and I'm sticking to the story!)

Do you have a favourite character in Hens Reunited?

Ooh, that's a hard question. I love all three of my main characters, and would hate to choose one over another. Perhaps to be diplomatic, I'll choose Laura, Katie's sister. She's an ideal ally, I think – great fun and a bit of a party animal, but supportive too, when it comes to the crunch. Maybe Laura needs a novel of her own, now that I come to think about it.

Do you think female friendships are more prone to complications and fallings-out than male friendships?
I do, and I think you can see that right from girlhood. Without wanting to generalise too much, I think friendship on an emotional level matters more to girls and women, which is probably why it can all go a bit pear-shaped sometimes.

Who are some of your own favourite writers?
I'll happily read anything by Rose Tremain, Jonathan Coe, Kate Atkinson, Maggie O'Farrell, Anne Tyler, Charles Dickens and Sarah Waters. I also love the books by my fellow 'New Romantics' authors: Kate Harrison, Milly Johnson, Veronica Henry, Jojo Moyes, Matt Dunn and Sarah Duncan.

As well as writing adult novels, you also write books for children and maintain your own blog (http://beinglucydiamond. blogspot.com). How do you find the time to do it all?
Working part-time whilst bringing up three children has actually made me very focused on my writing (as well as extremely tired, admittedly!). When I'm not at my desk working on a new book, I'm constantly thinking about my characters and mulling over what I'm going to write next, so by the time I switch on the PC, the words are ready to pour

out. My youngest child starts school this year though, so I'll have the luxury of a bit more time soon . . . and the house will probably look a *lot* tidier too!

Can you tell us anything about what you're working on next?
I'm working on a fourth novel, provisionally titled *Sweet Temptation*. It's about three women with very different lives who meet at a weight-watching club and go on to befriend and support one another. It's about friendship, love and chocolate cake, and is, I hope, funny, moving and uplifting.

Lucy Diamond's guide
to the perfect hen night

Hen Nights: A Survival Guide

So, what does a hen night mean to you? Is it your last wild night of freedom before settling down to sensible wifeyness? Or is it just a great excuse for a girls' night out to remember? Whatever your thoughts, if you've got a wedding on the horizon, it's never too soon to start planning the hen do. Whether you fancy blowing the budget with a girly holiday in the sun, or you'd prefer a spot of pampering in a swanky spa, or even if you're just a bit of a disco diva who wants to dance the night away, it's your call. However you choose to celebrate, the *Hens Reunited* girls can help you plan your biggest and best hen party. Katie, being the organised one, has tips on the practical stuff, Alice gets creative with themes and styles and as for Georgia, she's tackling the forfeits and booze (no surprises there). Over to you, ladies . . .

Katie: Who to invite

Choosing your hen party guests can be something of a minefield. Of course your best friends can go straight on the list – as long as they are all speaking to each other, of course – followed by sisters and any soon-to-be sisters-in-law. Work mates can by risky – although you might have a great laugh with them in the office every day, you need to weigh up carefully whether or not you can let them see you doing any of the following:

- wearing a flashing tiara/feather boa/L-plates
- doing karaoke and high-kicks to 'I Will Survive'
- snogging policemen/any other bloke in the vicinity

If you fear that your professional reputation may suffer as a consequence, leave the work-mates off the list. You don't want anyone cramping your style on the big night, after all!

Where to go

All right, I know I am efficient to the point of being a bit sad, but it is *really* important to book your accommodation early, if there's a big group of you. Make sure you check everyone's budget and find something you can all afford. There's no point falling in love with an amazing-looking hotel if all your mates are too skint to join you there.

The most popular hen night destinations in the UK are:

1. Brighton
2. Nottingham
3. Newcastle
4. Edinburgh
5. Bournemouth
6. London
7. Bristol
8. Newquay
9. Cardiff
10. Leeds

Alice: Types of hen night

It's your party, so anything goes! Here are just a few suggestions for activities which you and your fellow hens might enjoy:

- *Indulgence* – a pamper package in a spa will revive any weary bride-to-be, but there are other ways to relax too. How about a wine-tasting session, afternoon tea in a country house, a cocktail mixing tutorial, or enjoying a makeover and photo shoot?
- *Activity* – there are all sorts of ways a sporty hen can have fun. Have a go at quad biking, horse-riding, go-karting, paintballing, maybe even a surfing lesson if you're by the sea. Try not to break any bones though . . . hobbling up the aisle on crutches is such a bad look!
- *Fun* – a comedy club is a great place to start a hen night. Or maybe you could try something brand new – belly-

dancing or burlesque, anyone? You can even let out all that Bridezilla stress by booking a sumo-wrestling session for you and your hens. (I'm not joking – they exist!) Go on, you know you've always fancied wearing an inflatable fat suit.

Hen night themes and what to wear

If there's a whole bunch of you out on the town, it can be fun to have a theme so that everyone can dress similarly. It creates a fab group feeling – and also alerts nervous men to the fact that you're on the rampage. Popular themes include:

Angels – wings, halo and wand. Say no more.
Devils – if you're feeling a bit naughty.
Cheerleaders – for that inner High School Musical fan.
French maids – ooh la la!
Policewomen – any excuse for furry handcuffs . . .

Or, of course, you can choose a particular colour and all try to wear something in that shade. Don't forget the L-plates!

Georgia: Forfeits

Also known as ways to *completely* humiliate the poor bride-to-be . . . If she's up for a laugh, you can make a list of challenges or forfeits that she has to complete before dawn. Remember the hens' code, though: what happens on the hen night, stays on the hen night. In other words, don't tell the groom!

Here are just some of the forfeits I had to endure (and yes, I did complete them all, thank you very much). Feel free to borrow them – if you have the stamina, of course . . .

- Snog three random strangers
- Persuade someone to buy you a drink (make it a double)
- Kiss a policeman
- Swap underwear with the man of your choice
- Dance like MC Hammer on a crowded dancefloor. Then try some break-dancing. End with a bit of Riverdance – clears the floor every time!
- Corrupt the youngest, sweetest-looking barman you can find by whispering something filthy into his ear
- Ask the bouncer at the club door: 'Don't you know who I *am*?'

Cocktails

Ah, what would a hen night be without cocktails? A lot less rowdy, probably. Here are some of my favourite recipes:

Lucy Diamond

Dancing Queen

10ml white crème de cacao
10ml Cointreau
25ml blackcurrant vodka
10ml lemon juice

50ml apple juice
50ml grenadine
2 tsp sugar
6 ice cubes

Woo Woo

25ml peach schnapps
25ml vodka
50ml cranberry juice

Brazen Hussy

25ml vodka
25ml triple sec
10ml lemon juice

Party Animal

35ml tequila
10ml peppermint schnapps
1 tbsp grapefruit juice
1 tbsp powdered sugar

Naked Waiter

20ml Pernod
20ml Mandarine Napoléon
25ml pineapple juice
100ml bitter lemon

And for the morning after:

1 fried egg sandwich (ketchup optional)
1 pint of water
Go back to bed and sleep it off . . .

Enjoy!

Visit **www.panmacmillan.com** to read more about all our books and to buy them. You will also find features, author interviews and news of any author events, and you can sign up for e-newsletters so that you're always first to hear about our new releases.

www.panmacmillan.com

GIFT SELECTOR
YOUR ACCOUNT
WISH LIST
WAITING LIST

| HOME | ABOUT US | IMPRINTS | TRADE/MEDIA | CONTACT US | ADVANCED SEARCH | SEARCH | GO |

| BOOK CATEGORIES | WHAT'S NEW | AUTHORS/ILLUSTRATORS | BESTSELLERS | READING GROUPS |

Coming Soon...

Reading Groups

Competitions
Feeling Lucky?

Extracts
Sneak Previews

Interviews

Events
Meet Our Stars

Reviews
What The Critics Say

News & Awards

Editor's Choice
What We're Reading

© 2005 PAN MACMILLAN   ACCESSIBILITY   HELP   TERMS & CONDITIONS   PRIVACY POLICY   SEND PAGE TO A FRIEND